WRAITH

James R. Hannibal

TotalRecall Publications, Inc.

United States of America

Canada and United Kingdom

This is a work of fiction. The characters, events, views, and subject matter of this book are either the author's imagination or are used fictitiously. Any similarity or resemblance to any real people, real situations or actual events is purely coincidental and not intended to portray any person, place, or event in a false, disparaging or negative light.

ISBN: 978-1-59095-721-9

TotalRecallPress.com
1103 Middlecreek Friendswood, Texas 77546 281-992-3131 281-482-5390 Fax
6 Precedent Drive Rooksley, Milton Keynes MK13 8PR, UK
1385 Woodroffe Av Ottawa, ON K2G 1V8

Printed in the United States of America with
simultaneously printings in Canada, and
United Kingdom.

1 2 3 4 5 6 7 8 9 10

First Edition

WRAITH is dedicated to my loving and beautiful wife. Without her many words of sweet support, her unwavering love, and her patient spirit, this work never would have appeared on a publisher's desk. Thanks Love.*

*To the Reader:
While the dedication above is truly heartfelt, it also contains a hidden message about Wraith and its sequel. I hid a string of letters within the text using a set pattern. Decode this string using the Playfair cipher, invented by Charles Wheatstone in 1854. You will need two items to decode the message, a key word and the pattern of letters. You'll find clues to these hidden somewhere in the text of the book. Good luck, and thanks for reading.

Acknowledgments

There are a host of supporters that carry an author and his book from idea to publication. First there is the immediate family, the wife and children, who, without complaint, watch their husband and father come home from his day job and then disappear into his study night after night. Next there are the extended family and friends, who smile and nod (and sigh inwardly) every time a new manuscript is placed in their hands, still smelling of fresh ink and hope. Then there are the critiquers, that brave collection of souls who must walk the fine line between brutal honesty and maintaining a human relationship. The list goes on and on, and in my case some of these "author bearers" are characters so colorful that I could not have dreamed them in fiction. There is the friend who aspires to be the Benevolent Dictator of Texas and fashions himself my arch-nemesis, yet offers encouragement at just the right moments all along the way. There is the vibrant, mohawk bearing brother-in-law that inaugurated my fan site. There are the friends who suffered a myriad of trials of their own, including a garage that was knee deep in vegetable oil, yet still found time to read my work and offer their thoughts. There is the good friend who has the energy to spend all day orchestrating a television show, and yet still tap me out on the Jiu Jitsu mat that evening, all while looking so relaxed that he might actually be asleep. Finally, there are the Soldiers, Sailors, Marines, and Airmen, whose indomitable spirit and cornucopia of personalities are the inspirations for my stories. All of that being said, I must quickly thank a number of families that have carried me thus far. In alphabetical order, they are: the Byrds, the Carrolls, the Corbetts, the Edwards, the Huckabays, the Millers, and the Mitchams. Thank you to all of my supporters. I am so blessed to have all of you propelling me onward.

Prologue

A single F-117 Stealth Fighter lumbered down the runway at King Khalid Airfield – its angular black fuselage a glaring contrast to the bleached pavement under the merciless Arabian sun. The crew chief wiped the sweat from his brow and shook his head as he watched it lift precariously into the air. He'd never really thought a jet like that should fly – the thing looked like a fancy rock, and rocks should stay on the ground where they belong. Certainly it shouldn't fly in the daylight like this. Daytime flights were usually not part of the Nighthawk repertoire, especially when they were "in theater," but the Black Sheep had been doing it with regular frequency ever since they'd arrived in Saudi Arabia. A black jet in broad daylight didn't seem very stealthy at all. What's more, they were all training missions. There had been several minor strikes against Iraqi targets over the course of the last month, but the Nighthawks were left out of all of them.

"No matter," thought the crew chief as he began the long walk back to the hangar. "Worrying about the sense of it isn't my job. Ours is not to reason why…and so on and so on." Instead, he turned his thoughts toward the cold ice cream they'd be serving at the mess tent later. Lost in his musings, he failed to take note of the big AWACS aircraft sitting empty at its parking location across the ramp. In fact, the flight line was full of aircraft and none of them had their engines running. It was uncharacteristically quiet.

Half a mile away, in a small room beneath King Khalid's main command facility, General Robert Windsor hovered over a pair of sergeants. He paced back and forth and glared at the men as if the fate of the world rested solely upon the speed of their work. The three little black stars on each shoulder of his desert uniform seemed inadequate to their task. His eyes burned through the backs of the sergeants' necks and they quickened their pace, arranging laptop computers and cables atop a folding table.

The small room, known as The Room of Death, or ROD, to the

men and women associated with it, was the most secure American location in Saudi Arabia. With a primary purpose of storing secrets, it was buried two floors beneath the main facility, under several yards of concrete. The ROD's taupe walls were lined with shelves and locking file cabinets stocked with binders, tapes, hard-drives, and other forms of classified media. Most of the locking cabinets also held inventories and access lists for the two rows of tall safes that filled the room's interior. Next to the door sat a single desk with a computer, a printer, and a nameplate that read "Mr. Joseph Moore," but Mr. Moore was conspicuously absent. While many individuals from several different fields knew the combinations to one or another of the safes, only Mr. Moore knew them all, and it was a matter of great pride for him. Today he'd been unseated from his throne, exiled from his own empire.

Windsor smiled for just a moment, thinking of the diminutive bald man, sitting in the office across the hall, slowly coming to grips with the fact that there were still operations that he wasn't cleared for. Then the smile dropped from his lips. "Let's go gentlemen," he pushed, "Shadow Zero One is approaching the border and we need to get confirmation."

The general's men hooked the laptops up to a stack of appliances on a rolling cart. Once the computers booted up, the sergeants transformed from laborers to technicians, expertly typing commands, bending the machines to the general's will. On the left computer a map appeared with a little blue arrow near the border of Iraq; every ten seconds the little arrow inched forward. The right computer displayed two windows. In one there was a live video feed of a large house on the outskirts of Baghdad, a main residence with a north wing, a south wing, and a circular drive on the east side. The other window looked similar to an old DOS prompt. Above the flashing cursor two data lines read: LNK ESTBD and READY.

"Can't you get a better refresh rate on Shadow?" Windsor asked impatiently.

"I'm sorry sir, ten seconds is the best the software can do."

"Remind me to have Colonel Walker work on that."

"Yes, sir," the sergeant pulled out a small memo pad and made a note.

"There he is," said the general, turning his attention to the other laptop.

On the screen, a black Mercedes pulled into the driveway, followed by two more. A gaggle of uniformed men piled out of the trailing vehicles and fanned out. After a moment the driver of the lead Mercedes got out and opened the right rear door. A familiar figure stepped out sporting his signature beret and obnoxious black mustache.

"Get the snapshots."

The sergeant clicked his mouse a few times and a row of pictures appeared at the bottom of the window.

"That one," snapped Windsor. "Send it."

The sergeant grabbed the picture with his mouse and dropped it into a folder on the computer's desktop. Then he typed the file location into the DOS prompt along with the send command. There was a tense pause as the computer pondered its task and then XMTD flashed on the screen. A few moments later another message popped up: RCVD.

Suddenly the video in the other window disappeared, replaced with a flickering mix of purple and blue.

"What happened to the feed?"

"Fargo 21 is bingo sir; he's RTB," said one of the sergeants, indicating that the source of the video, a Predator Unmanned Aerial Vehicle, was low on fuel and its operator had turned the remote control airplane towards its recovery base.

"You've got to be kidding me."

"His loiter time is limited, sir. Don't worry, we have confirmation now and Shadow will be there within minutes. We'll get him."

"We'd better."

★ ★ ★ ★

Fifty miles south of Baghdad, Lieutenant Colonel Jason "Merlin" Boske pulled up the snapshot from the Predator feed on his right console display. He compared it to a hard copy photograph given to him by one of the same sergeants now operating a laptop in the Room of Death. The house on the screen matched the house in the photo, except the house in the photo had a little red triangle printed over the south wing; intelligence was certain that the bunker was under that section. Merlin checked his Tactical Situation Display – he'd be there in less then ten minutes.

The whole idea of this mission made the hair on the back of his neck stand up. They were putting him and his aircraft in a dangerous position; and for what...a practice run? No, it was...what had the Colonel called it...a validation? Merlin put it out of his mind – focusing instead on checking his systems one more time. Seven minutes later he called up his infrared targeting system, imaging the house in luminescent green. A chill went up his spine. He checked the snapshot again. It was the same house, the same as in the photograph and the same as in the video feed he'd seen just a few minutes before. "POTUS isn't gonna like this," he thought. The house was the same, but the vehicles were gone.

★ ★ ★ ★

General Windsor's eyes flared as a new message popped up on the right laptop. He balled up his fist and punched one of the aluminum filing cabinets, leaving a large dent. Despite his violent display the message from Shadow remained on the screen, blinking, taunting him, "SHADOW 01 RTB...REHRSL CNXD...TGT ESCAPED."

Windsor had been setting this up all year. In February POTUS, the President of the United States, requested that an option be quietly developed. A covert group in the Pentagon came up with the plan: clear a path for the Predator to get real-time coordinates for the target, and then pass the imagery and location to a pre-positioned Stealth Fighter. POTUS had liked the idea, but he needed proof. "I'll authorize whatever assets you need," he said. "Just show me that you can make it happen; everything but the final step."

By mid April the operation was under way, removing critical air defense nodes in southern Iraq. The Iraqis made it easy, taking potshots at US and British aircraft patrolling the No-Fly Zone, giving justification for "retaliation strikes" against certain enemy assets. The strikes slowly cleared a path through the radar net for the Predator. Then the Black Sheep of the 8th Fighter Squadron arrived in late July. At Windsor's direction, the Stealth Fighters flew training missions only, at all hours of the day, hugging the border but never crossing into Iraq. The idea was to lull the Iraqis into a false sense of security. Iraqi spies reported Nighthawk movements in and out of the airfield and AWACS made subtle references to the Stealth Fighters' flight paths over unsecure frequencies. Over time, the Iraqis became accustomed to the idea that the Black Sheep were just there to fly training missions and flex American muscle.

Things rose to a climax in August with a couple of F-16 strikes against early warning radars at a pair of Surface to Air Missile sites. With the objective radars taken out, Windsor moved forward by launching an unmanned surveillance plane on the 27th as a test case. Not only did the Iraqis see it, they shot it down. It was the first hint of a serious flaw in the plan. Maybe the Predator was just too easy to see on radar. Intelligence analysts determined which sites might have snagged the UAV and the strikers targeted those sites on the 28th. That was two weeks ago. Windsor thought it was enough. Apparently, it wasn't.

"He saw us coming...they must've picked up the Predator again," fumed the general. "POTUS wants an option that I can't give him with the assets we have. Clean up this mess, I've got to make a phone call."

The sergeants began packing up their temporary control center and General Windsor stepped out into the hallway, where a passing airman nearly mowed him down. He was in no mood for juvenile clumsiness. "What's your hurry mister?" he growled.

"Sorry 'bout that sir," mumbled the airman, and rushed on.

"What on earth?" He walked after the kid, ready to lay into him, but as his eyes followed the young man down the hallway he noticed several other people rushing into offices. The sound of tense voices emanated from every workspace.

Something was very wrong.

PART ONE: GENESIS

Chapter 1

Nineteen Stealth Bomber pilots sat at the two long tables in the flight kitchen at Whiteman Air Force Base. The rising Missouri sun burst through the wide glass entryway on the east side of the small facility, casting long shadows across the gray tile floor. Outside, the howl of a stiff wind hinted at colder temperatures than the bright sun promised.

At the end of the second table a short, stout man in his early forties stared reluctantly at his plate. Major Brit "Murph" Murphy ran his fingers through the disheveled mop of dark brown hair atop his head and sighed. Awkwardly he lifted a forkful of something akin to eggs and glanced at an older pilot that sat in the corner of the room. A yellow badge decorated the lieutenant colonel's flight jacket, its bold letters proclaiming his position as an Exercise Evaluator. Murph noticed the evaluator checking his watch and wondered if he would get the opportunity to finish his breakfast. "No real loss," he thought, tipping his fork to let the runny mixture fall back to his plate with a series of muted splats, "I just hope Tony has his receiver turned on."

Murph considered the high tech Motorola radio in the evaluator's hand and then eyed the ancient receivers that he and the other pilots wore strapped to their hips. "Cold war relics," he thought, "we fly a two billion dollar jet, yet we carry the very same radios that the B-52 pilots carried in the eighties. We'll be lucky if we hear the call at all." Murph and the other pilots were paired into two-man crews as part of a sortie generation exercise, or genex. There would have been twenty pilots at the tables, but Murph's partner had chosen to sleep through breakfast.

The genex was part of the 509th Bomb Wing's semi-annual Operational Readiness Inspection, a practice war. Just as in every ORI, it began on Saturday, when the Command Post called in the pilots and their support crews for the arduous task of readying their aircraft for combat. This was usually a fifteen hour job, but because of a leaky hydraulic reservoir, Murph and Tony's jet had taken more than forty sleepless hours to prepare. Since completing that task they'd been living in the alert shack.

Each day the crews listened to scripted intelligence briefings describing an ever-escalating and totally fictional political standoff, and in-between late night video game tournaments they studied the pre-planned missions that they would execute when that standoff reached its inevitable breaking point. In almost every exercise script, the breaking point occurred on Tuesday, and that was today.

Murph choked down his last piece of dehydrated bacon as he watched the evaluator stand up and walk toward the glass doors. The lieutenant colonel stepped out into the sun and lifted his collar to shield his face against the biting wind. After a brief glance up and down the flight line, he raised the Motorola to his lips.

"Here it comes," Murph warned the others.

The ancient receivers crackled to life. "ALERT FORCE, ALERT FORCE, SCRAMBLE, SCRAMBLE, SCRAMBLE! I SAY AGAIN, ALERT FORCE, ALERT FORCE, SCRAMBLE, SCRAMBLE, SCRAMBLE!"

For a split second the pilots sat frozen in time, staring at each other across the table like gunfighters about to draw. Then chairs flew and silverware clattered as they jumped from their seats and headed for the door. It was a mad dash for the alert vehicles and it was a matter of pride to be the first pair out of the parking lot.

Instead of racing with the other pilots, Murph calmly wiped a crumb of bacon from his lips, stood up, replaced his chair, and casually walked out of the facility. While the other pilots ran off in pairs, he jogged alone, shielding his eyes against the glare of the sun and scanning the flight line for the twentieth man. "Where the heck are you, Tony," he muttered, wondering if his partner's radio was loud enough to wake him up.

Fifty yards from the flight kitchen ten midnight blue sedans sat waiting for the sprint to the hangars, and fifty yards beyond the vehicles the alert shack tilted precariously with the wind, straining against its tie-down ropes. "The proud days of Strategic Air Command are gone," thought Murph, shaking his head. In the golden days breakfast would have been good, hot, and free, and the alert shack would have been a brick building with showers and a gym. This morning the food was nasty, cold, and four bucks a plate, and the alert facility amounted to nothing more than a big brown tent with a diesel generator.

Murph slowed to a walk, wondering if he should get the car running or go to the shack and retrieve Tony. Finally he made his decision and began a full sprint for the tent, assuming that he would have to drag his sleeping crewmate out of bed. His crewmate proved him wrong.

A tan, half naked figure shot through the tent flaps like a bullet from a gun. Anthony Merigold was new to the B-2, having finished mission qualification training just a week before. He stood six foot three inches tall with dark hair, broad shoulders, and strong Greek features. In a flight suit, Tony Merigold looked so much like a poster boy for the Air Force that the older pilots called him "Captain America" – a play on his official title, Captain Merigold.

As Murph looked on in horror, the younger officer sprinted across the pavement wearing nothing but a pair of white boxers and black boot-socks. His flight suit was slung over his right shoulder, whipping in the breeze, and his combat boots bounced along, dangling from his left hand by their strings. Murph stopped short, making an abrupt turn to join his streaking partner in the sprint to the car. "Oversleep did we?"

"How was I supposed to know it was gonna happen now?"

"It always happens on Tuesday morning!"

"Well maybe you could've told me that yesterday!"

Tony reached the car first and tossed his boots on the floorboard of the passenger side. Then Murph jumped in the driver's seat and cranked the engine. He punched the gas pedal to the floor as Tony desperately tried to get dressed.

"Crap!"

"What?"

"I forgot my shirt!"

"Well, zip it up to the neck and nobody'll notice."

Tony ripped the zipper to its upper limit. "Ow!"

"What now?"

"I caught some chest hair!"

Murph closed on the vehicle in front of them as both cars headed for the northern-most hangars, three quarters of a mile away. The alert crews were supposed to drive at a "safe but urgent speed," but Murph's speed was always a little more urgent than safe. As they passed the other car, they smiled and waved. The other driver shook his fist while his passenger pretended to write down their license plate number on his hand.

A few moments later Murph and Tony screeched to a halt in the white box painted on the pavement in front of Hangar Two. A deafening buzzer warned them to stay clear as the massive doors opened, slowly sliding across their tracks to reveal a beautiful charcoal colored aircraft. Both pilots hopped out of the car and paused, awed by the spectacle. The Spirit of Texas glared back at them over its slightly curved beak, looking mean and alien against the backdrop of a hundred halogen lights.

Inside the hangar, the crew chief punched a big red button on the B-2's nose gear. A contoured hatch appeared as if from nowhere, extending a short ladder to the floor, and a tremendous rushing sound filled the air as two huge generators fired up inside the aircraft. The sound of the generators startled the pilots back to reality and they ran into the hangar, where the crew chief high-fived Murph but stopped short and raised an eyebrow at Tony's socked feet.

"Hey, at least I'm not naked," Tony responded to the enlisted man's silent frown.

As Tony rushed up the ladder, Murph quickly examined the area surrounding the plane, checking for any tools or maintenance equipment that might obstruct the taxiing aircraft. Then he glanced at the munitions in the B-2's weapons bay. Even though the briefings were scripted and the enemy was fictitious, the bombers were loaded with real bombs – enough conventional firepower to turn a small country into a smoking crater. Murph's B-2 carried a thirty-six thousand pound mixture of GPS guided destruction, including four GBU-31V1 two thousand pound bombs, four GBU-31V3 two thousand pound penetrators, and four GBU-37 five thousand pound GAMs, better known as "Bunker Busters."

"The area's clear and the weapons are good!" shouted Murph as he climbed the stairs to join his partner. He jumped into his seat, put on his Bose headset, and waited for the lead aircraft to initiate a check-in.

"Fury, check."

"Two"

"Three…" Each crew counted off in sequence up to ten, and then there was silence.

"What now?" asked Tony.

"Now we wait," answered Murph. He checked his watch. It was 7:55 A.M. Central Time, September 11th, 2001.

Chapter 2

Pale rays of afternoon sunlight poured through the narrow windows of the fitness room at the 81st Fighter Squadron in Spangdahlem, Germany. The light formed two bright columns across the sectional rubber floor, yet it offered no heat at all. Captain Michael Baron, "Victor" to his squadron mates, attacked a 150 pound punching bag with fury. He moved his six foot tall frame around the bag with practiced ease, his steel blue eyes intently focused on the target, his blond hair matted to his forehead with sweat. He was not broad shouldered, but he was muscular, and the heavy bag shook violently under the power of his blows. As he shifted his weight for a roundhouse kick, Victor felt a presence enter the room. He paused for a fraction of a second, pulling the kick to avoid the new obstacle, and then continued to punish the bag. He would not be interrupted; he had sixty more seconds on the timer. Undaunted, the intruder moved to a more obvious position. The two columns of light fell into shadow.

"You're in my way and you're blocking my light," Victor warned the intruder.

"Sir, your presence is requested in the Vault."

The timer expired and Victor brushed the lieutenant aside as he punched off the alarm and grabbed a small towel to dab his face. "Tell Oso," he said between breaths, "that if he wants to interrupt my workout, he's going to have to drag my sweaty carcass out of the gym himself."

"Sir, we think the United States may be under attack."

Breaking news was always hit or miss at the 81st. Unlike their counterparts in the States, the American squadrons in Germany had no television news. It was a shame, too; the cable news networks were some of the best intelligence sources in the business. Instead, the pilots depended on their wives to call in with important news. The "Wives Network" funneled information on everything from current events to upcoming deployments, even if the information was classified. It was either a failure of Air Force Intelligence or a great testament to the wives that their information often outpaced the intelligence pipeline. A phone call from the commander's wife had alerted the squadron to the tragedy, but the lieutenant that interrupted Victor's workout was scant on details; all he knew was that an airplane had flown into the World Trade Center.

Victor walked quickly through the narrow hallways of the bunker-like structure that housed his squadron. The flat, drab building, built by the French near the beginning of the Cold War, looked more like a fall-out shelter than an office building. Several sections of the building had once boasted thick, steel blast doors to be sealed off in a nuclear attack, but most of the doors were long since removed and only the steel frames remained. They presented a series of annoying obstacles, rising eight inches off the floor and hanging twenty-four inches from the ceiling. Victor ducked through three of these hatches before arriving at the Vault which, because it was protected by the only blast door that was still on its hinges, housed most of the squadron's classified work. A giant map table, covered in charts detailing the squadron's "areas of interest," filled the center of the large room. The wall at the far end held three doors that led to small briefing rooms, while the other three walls were lined with computer workstations, one side for Intelligence, one for Weapons, and one for the Mission Planning Cell. A very agitated intelligence technician waited for Victor on that third side.

Young Staff Sergeant "Slick" McBride was the classic red-haired, freckle-faced kid. The sight of him made Victor think that Andy Griffith must be right around the corner, but he was one of the best intelligence analysts in the Air Force. "What's the story, Slick?" asked Victor.

"It's too early to get anything out of the system, sir, but at least the Wives Network has given us a start," answered McBride. "All we really know is that a commercial airliner crashed into the north tower of the World Trade Center and then, seventeen minutes later, another one hit the south tower. Is it possible this was an accident? How could two airline pilots get so low and off course that they would fly into a skyscraper?"

"I'm afraid they couldn't, Slick," replied Victor. "For one airline crew to be that bad at their jobs is extremely improbable – two on the same day is impossible." A short time later the report of a third crash tragically confirmed Victor's fears; this time they hit the Pentagon. "We're at war," he said quietly, placing his hand on Slick's shoulder. Then he bowed his head and silently uttered a prayer. He prayed for the souls lost in the attack. He prayed for comfort for their families. And he prayed that God would give all of them justice.

Chapter 3

"How long do you think it will take before we know who's responsible?" asked Slick.

"We don't have to wait," Victor replied with a grim look. "I know exactly who's responsible, and I even have a good idea where he's hiding."

Victor held a degree in Middle Eastern Studies from the US Air Force Academy. During his four years there he'd become an expert in Islamic Fundamentalism, Arabic, and Islamic Terrorism. Since his graduation in 1997, he had followed the activities of several terrorist masterminds, including Osama Bin Laden and Tariq Irhaab.

Victor's habit of keeping files of media reports about Islamic terrorists started as little more than an odd hobby, but as their activities escalated, it had become an obsession. Each heinous act struck him more deeply. The Hatshepsut Massacre in Egypt, the US Embassies in Kenya and Tanzania, the USS Cole in Yemen, with each event it became more personal.

Victor held a deep respect for life, and even though he tried to view killing on the battlefield as an impersonal consequence of war, he still questioned his own ability to pull the trigger against a nameless, faceless pawn on the wrong side of a political line. That was not an issue with the terrorists. Victor knew their names, he knew their faces, and because he knew their crimes he would gladly assassinate any of them if given the opportunity. That cold disregard for another life shamed him. He often wondered if the feeling could be labeled as hatred and, if he was willing to end a life for the sake of hate, then what distinguished him from the terrorists?

That shameful rage, that terrible need for blood retribution, welled up within Victor again. He needed to channel it, to put it to use before it consumed him. "Get the planning computers running, Slick," he ordered. "Let's try to nail down some targets."

"Yes sir." Slick immediately went to work flipping switches on the squadron's mission planning computers. The two big CPUs rumbled to life and Slick stepped back, smiling at the beautiful sound of raw computing power. "I love these babies," he said, patting the aluminum top of a CPU, "they may plug in to a standard outlet, but they sound like they're running on diesel."

Slick's "babies" contained a huge database of maps and satellite imagery covering every square inch of the globe. Their powerful software fed the images to three thirty-two inch LCD monitors that could display them in three dimensions from any angle or altitude. With his computers Slick could play through an entire strike plan, showing the pilots exactly what they would see during the real thing. He could also connect to a myriad of classified networks that were run by the nation's various intelligence services. "We're up and running, sir," he said, sitting down in front of the monitors. "Where would you like to go first?"

"Let's tap into the classified net and see if we can access the Congressional Task Force on Counter Terrorism," said Victor. "Oso's gonna want hard data."

Major Hector "Oso" Garcia was the 81st Fighter Squadron's Weapons Officer and Victor's boss. His tactical name had no great story behind it. The squadron commander had seen a big bear with a Latin American accent on his kid's favorite cartoon program. He thought it would be an entertaining contradiction to name the rather small Hector, a short, wiry man with angular features, after the oversized character.

Despite the cartoon nickname, Oso was well respected within the squadron. He was a graduate of the USAF Fighter Weapons School, the Air Force equivalent to the Navy's Top Gun. As the Weapons Officer he was the squadron's chief Instructor Pilot and the commander's trusted advisor on all issues of tactical importance. He was a gifted fighter pilot, a knowledgeable tactician, and an even match for Victor at the base Jiu Jitsu club despite Victor's twenty-pound weight advantage.

Less than two hours after Slick and Victor fired up the computers, Oso stood next to them, eyeing a map of the Taliban air defenses. "Are you sure about this?" he asked, looking at Victor.

"The attacks on the World Trade Center fit Bin Laden's MO," Victor replied. "Osama seeks a grander scale than most terrorists. He's never satisfied with the suicide bombing of a café, or the car bombing of a certain official. His attacks produce lots of bodies and they're very newsworthy – as in headlines, not just the ticker at the bottom of the screen. He also has a tendency to fixate on a location, and we know he's made an attempt to bring down the World Trade Center before. The FBI thinks he put Tariq Irhaab on the project sometime in '92. Mostly because Ramzi Yousef, one of Irhaab's known associates, blew up a van in the WTC parking garage in February of '93. The structure held then, but it looks like they came back with a new plan. There's no doubt that this was a Bin Laden sponsored event."

Oso still looked unconvinced so Victor changed his approach. "Hey, don't take my word for it; perhaps you'd like to read the latest report from the Congressional Task Force on Counter Terrorism," he said, thrusting a stack of papers the size of *War and Peace* in Oso's direction. He slammed the papers down on the desk next to his boss. "Everything out there and in here points to Bin Laden. He's the only terrorist big-wig that could have pulled this off and, according to the latest intelligence, Afghanistan is where he's hiding out these days."

"Take it easy Junior, I believe you," said Oso, staring reluctantly at the reams of paper. "I'll read it later. For now just tell me what you've got for potential targets."

"We can't be sure." Victor clicked an icon on the map and a series of symbols appeared. "These are the most likely initial targets, but the generals' decisions are always hard to predict. The brass won't come to us first anyway. They'll go to the heavy hitters." A hint of envy crept into Victor's voice. "I'll bet the B-2s are starting engines right now and just waiting for the right coordinates."

"I wish you'd let that pipe dream go," said Oso. "They already said you didn't have enough flight hours."

Victor shrugged. "Hey, you can't blame me for hoping." His "stealth envy" was no secret in the 81st. He'd submitted an application to the B-2 Wing several months before, despite the fact that he didn't meet the minimum experience requirements. To everyone's surprise the hiring board had flown him to Whiteman for an interview, but the reception was lukewarm. He'd returned in late August feeling defeated. Now he was just waiting for the rejection letter.

Chapter 4

Tony loved the nostalgic look of the historic B-29 that guarded the main gate of Whiteman Air Force Base; it served as a reminder of his squadron's long, distinguished, and somewhat controversial history. On 6 August, 1945 two 393rd B-29s departed the island of Tinian in the South Pacific. A few hours later the Enola Gay had dropped the atomic bomb on Hiroshima, with the Great Artiste flying in a chase position as a scientific observation platform. Since then the Tigers had flown B-47s, B-52s, F-111s, and finally B-2s, but the Great Artiste remained an honorary member of the fleet, preserved as a testament to the squadron's heritage.

Nearly every morning since his arrival at Whiteman six months before, Tony had slowed to admire the old bomber as he passed through the front gate, but not lately. For the last two weeks he'd hardly noticed it, hurrying past on his way to the squadron, anxious to find out if America had come any closer to striking back.

The squadron building, better known as Building 33, was a large brick-covered structure that the Tigers shared with 13th Squadron's Grim Reapers. It was more reminiscent of a maximum-security prison than a flying squadron. A ten-foot fence covered in motion sensors and topped with concertina wire surrounded the facility while unseen eyes packing unseen weaponry monitored the perimeter. Tony parked his car and approached the gate, instinctively looking up at the guard standing in the tower at the corner of the fenced area. The young man hefted his M-16 and gave him a disinterested nod. Another guard, seated behind bulletproof glass, buzzed Tony through one of three, cage-like turnstiles into a holding pen and carefully inspected the pilot's two ID cards. Satisfied, the guard buzzed him through to the other side, where he finally reached the front door.

Tony passed through thick glass doors and into an open stairwell filled with images of past glory. A packed trophy case bragged of the

509th Bomb Wing's prowess at bombing competitions and the walls were covered with pictures of the men and women who'd written the unit's storied past. Still he hurried on, not stopping to absorb the history.

It was not until he reached the top of the stairs that Tony finally paused. There he placed his hand on a great glass case containing a large preserved tiger, a majestic animal, fixed in mid-stride as if patiently stalking her prey. "Well girl," he said quietly, "we took a big hit. Do you think we'll finally go out and settle the score?" The tiger, whose name was Autumn, looked back with empathetic eyes but stoically held her tongue. Tony sighed. "I don't know either," he said, and continued down the hallway.

After a few strides Tony stopped in an alcove and turned to face a door protected by a digital key pad and a biometric scanner. It was the entrance to the "Tiger's Cave" where he and Murph worked together in the Weapons Office. He placed his thumb on the pad and entered his code. As the door closed behind him, he climbed a short flight of carpeted stairs and emerged at the back of a small auditorium. He walked quickly down the aisle between blue corduroy seating set in threadbare blue carpet, found a door behind the lectern, and hurried through.

As Tony entered the Weapons Office, Murph jumped up and raised his hand for a high-five. Tony hesitantly reciprocated, wondering what the celebration was for. "What's up? Are we finally going to war?"

"Not yet, but if we do, you and I are up for night one!" Murph held up his hand again.

This time Tony threw his high-five with more fervor. At least things were getting serious enough for the commanders to set down a crew schedule. Murph explained that the colonels had laid out the framework for the first few missions, and the two of them had not just made the list, they'd been hand picked to go in on the first night.

Tony found it difficult to focus on his work. He spent the rest of the morning picking at busywork and daydreaming about the fear and glory of real combat. That afternoon he ran into Slapshot in the hallway of Building 33. "Hey Captain America, we've been looking all over for you," said the large pilot, his lips spreading into a crooked grin. It wasn't malice; it was just that the three inch scar left by a hockey puck distorted his smile. "There's a meeting at the Officer's Club in ten minutes. Don't be late!"

Tony hadn't heard about any meeting but he hurried over to the O' Club, hoping the commander would announce that combat operations were finally starting. When he pulled into the parking lot, it was already full, and he had the same awkward feeling that he'd had as a cadet when he was late to class. Then he saw Slapshot.

"Hurry up, dude, you're late...this way."

Tony paused. Scar or not, that smile looked devious.

"Don't just stand there, come on." Slapshot led him inside and motioned toward a door at the end of the bar labeled "Crud Room."

It occurred to Tony that the back of a bar was an odd place to hold a combat briefing, but he didn't have much time to think as Slapshot shoved him through the door. He stumbled into the room and gaped in surprise at what he saw. The room was small, almost completely filled by the large pool table used by the pilots for a violent game known as Crud. Every pilot from the Tigers stood at attention along either side of the table, with Murph at the head; he wore an absurd, tiger-patterned robe and held a sledgehammer like a king holding his scepter. On the pool table, in front of the pilots, were mugs of beer and soda. Slapshot smacked Tony on the back, closed the door, and took his place among the others.

"Attention to orders!" commanded Murph. "Let it be known to all these present that Captain Tony C. Merigold has successfully demonstrated the dedication and skill required of a combat ready Tiger." Murph locked eyes with Tony. "Captain Merigold, you have been deemed worthy by the unruly mob before you..." There was an awkward pause. "Ahem...the *unruly mob before you*..." Murph repeated, looking disapprovingly at the others. The pilots took the second cue and let out a series of loud grunts and grumbles to imitate the "unruly mob" their leader had mentioned. "As I was saying," Murph continued, "we now deem you worthy of joining the Tiger Pride and therefore we must christen you with an appropriate tactical callsign. Come forward!"

Tony nearly jumped out of his flight suit as the pilots started shouting wildly and propelled him toward the front of the room. Someone handed him an oversized shot of brown liquid and, without thinking, Tony tossed it back. Immediately another was placed in his hand. He gave Murph a confused look but the older pilot offered no explanation. Instead, Murph picked up a very ancient looking box and walked ominously in his direction.

★   ★   ★   ★

Tony woke up on his couch to the sound and smell of bacon sizzling in his kitchen.

"I hope you don't mind," said Murph, "but I took the liberty of raiding your fridge. Are you hungry?"

"Most definitely not," Tony replied, struggling to sit up. "Did you stay here all night?"

"I had to. You were in such a bad state when I drove you home that I couldn't bring myself to leave you here alone. You've got to get yourself a wife."

"I'll get right on that," said Tony, trying to force a smile, "but seriously, thanks."

"Hey, that's what friends are for. So, do you remember much of the ceremony last night?"

Tony winced as he tried to overcome the pounding in his skull. "I remember that you named me Drake, citing something about my naked exit from the alert tent looking like a baby lizard emerging from a leathery egg."

"Well, at least you remember your name. You are the mythical drake, the baby dragon, born into the world with great promise for combat. I came up with that one and I'm particularly proud of it. It could have been much worse, you know. Some guys get named after fish."

"Thanks for saving me from that."

"Don't mention it. Do you remember anything else?"

"Just that there was way too much booze and some ritual involving a pair of sweat socks that have been with the squadron since Vietnam."

"Very good. Most guys block that out."

Both men became quiet, and for a while the sizzle and pop of the bacon was the only sound.

"Murph?" said Drake, finally breaking the silence.

"Yeah?"

"We're gonna get him, right?"

"Who?"

"Bin Laden…and the rest of those Tally-whatevers, we're gonna take 'em down, right?"

"Yeah Drake, we'll get them…you and me bud."

Chapter 5

Victor felt detached from history, watching his country move along the path to war and wondering whether he'd be permitted to take part.

In the first two days after the attacks Victor had compiled a report on Bin Laden and Afghanistan for the Wing Intelligence Office. In it he'd theorized that Tariq Irhaab was one of the primary planners, which made Iraq a secondary battleground. Irhaab was Bin Laden's emissary to Iraq and the head of Saddam's home-grown terror organization, *a' Nur*. His report initially received a lot of interest from the local brass, but it was shelved when the order to go to war hadn't come. That was two weeks ago.

Victor and Oso were preparing for a training flight when the commander, whose tactical name was Soda, called a meeting. All thirty-six pilots gathered excitedly in the squadron's auditorium-like Main Briefing Room and Victor was certain that Soda would finally announce they were headed for Afghanistan. Instead, like a doctor giving his patient the bad news, the commander informed the pilots that the Joint Chiefs had decided to leave the European squadrons out of the war. The air of anger and frustration in the room was palpable.

After the meeting the pilots returned to their duties with their heads hung low in disgust. "Now we'll have to watch the war on TV like everybody else," grumbled Victor. He felt impotent, emasculated. He didn't just *want* to go to war against the terrorists; he *needed* to go to war. He needed retribution, but it simply wasn't going to happen.

"Shake it off," said Oso. "We've got a flight to brief." He opened the door to a small briefing room and stood to one side as Victor and two other pilots filed in. The three sat down at a table that was far too short for its purpose, as if they'd been banished to the children's table at a Thanksgiving meal, while Oso walked to the front and stood beside a dry-erase board filled with a complicated series of outlines and sketches. "Welcome to Wizard flight," he said. "The date is three October. In ten seconds the time will be fourteen thirty local…five seconds…three…two…one…hack."

The small briefing room was stuffy and cramped, much too small for four grown men, but Oso seemed oblivious to the others' discomfort. He slowly detailed the contingencies of the training mission, covering all of the reasonable what-ifs that could occur, like radio failures, in-flight emergencies, and a downed flight member. "If anyone goes down we'll call a 'knock-it-off' and end the scenario. At that point our only focus will be getting the survivor home safe. I'll have on-scene command. We'll mark the survivor's last known position, set a new bingo fuel, and hold to coordinate the rescue. Expect the survivor to pipe up on Guard and then we'll switch over to the Search and Rescue frequency, SAR Alpha."

Oso pointed to a line on the map that snaked through the interlocking valleys of southwestern Germany "This is our route for ingress," he said, switching to the tactical portion of the briefing, "and this ridgeline marks The Forward Edge of the Battle Area; better known as 'the line of scrimmage.' We'll report in at Control Point Bravo and then split to hold at Initial Points Yankee and X-ray, north and south of the target area. Keep your Hogs five hundred feet off the deck, masking against the ridgeline, and climb only for radio relay; things are always easier if we can avoid being seen. Our contact is Snake One Five on UHF three one seven point two. His simulated platoon is penned in, two kilometers into enemy territory. Today, Snake One Five is played by our rent-a-lieutenant, Joe Forester. He drove out to the target area early this morning and I told him to be somewhere near the small town of Boechingen, so I'm sure we'll find him within a hundred yards of the pub on the east side of town. He'll spot targets for us, pass us the coordinates, and talk our eyes on for confirmation." Finally Oso turned to the youngest pilot in the room. "Collins, let's get it right today and knock this one out. You need to be qualified in case they let us into this fight."

Victor glanced up from the map in front of him and looked at the young wingman. The primary purpose of the mission was training for the kid, Brent Collins, who would fly as the "number two" wingman. Every new wingman that showed up from the schoolhouse had to fly several mission qualification sorties before they were considered ready for combat, and Oso was Brent's instructor for this one. No wingman ever wanted to screw up in front of the Weapons Officer, but Collins had greater cause to be nervous. He had already failed several mission qualification sorties.

Brent looked at the maps in front of him as if they were written in Chinese. "No questions, sir, I think I've got it."

On the way to the aircraft Bug pulled Victor aside. A look of concern clouded his face. Vernon "Bug" Wahler was a "cross-flow" pilot from the bomber side. He was a big blond Nebraskan, whose lowly status as a wingman in the A-10 masked an extra eleven hundred hours of flight experience in the B-52, including combat time over Kosovo. His first and last initials, VW, had guaranteed his tactical name, making Vernon the only six-foot three, two hundred and twenty pound guy named "Bug" in the entire Air Force. "Do you think Brent is ready for this?" he asked. "He didn't look very confident in there."

"He's just scared of Oso," Victor replied. "We're not doing anything today that he hasn't done twenty times already at the schoolhouse."

"What about the Irish Cross?"

The Irish Cross was arguably the most complex maneuver in the Warthog tactics manual. It involved four aircraft employing multiple weapon types on multiple targets and, most importantly, it involved a direct attack on a heavy threat, such as Anti Aircraft Artillery or a Surface to Air Missile system. The maneuver was named for the pattern it formed, a cross overlaid with a circle, which was similar to a symbol once adopted by Saint Patrick. It began with two pairs of A-10s heading toward the target from widely divergent directions. The lower ranking set of aircraft, called Three and Four, usually went in first. Four would fly directly toward the enemy, baiting the SAM or triple-A operator to turn his barrels toward the approaching aircraft. Just before the edge of the threat's range, Four would turn away, spoiling the enemy's shot. About that time Three would reach a point ninety degrees away and turn toward the threat, actually moving inside the enemy's range to fire a few rounds of thirty millimeter before turning and racing away. That was rarely enough to kill the enemy; the real purpose was to bait him into pointing his guns or missiles at the retreating A-10.

If all went according to plan, the enemy would take the bait, sealing his fate. One hundred and eighty degrees away from Three, on the opposite side of the circle, One would penetrate the enemy's lethal range, lock up the target with a maverick missile, and turn it into a pile of burning wreckage. Still, even with the primary threat destroyed, the danger was not over. Once the threat was destroyed, the other aircraft would turn inward from the points of the cross and bomb the other ground targets. Such a maneuver, flying from opposing headings to attack a small area, could easily result in a mid-air collision or fragmentation from another fighter's bombs. The Irish Cross required great timing and skill, even when the enemy was simulated.

Victor looked reassuringly at Bug, "I know for a fact that Oso has practiced it with him before. He'll be okay."

Chapter 6

A thin, brown-haired man wearing the crisp blue uniform of an Air Force officer slapped his briefcase down on a cluttered desk, flipped his computer on, and slumped bitterly into his chair. "Another exciting day of reading emails and shuffling paperwork," he muttered to himself, raising a hand to adjust the round, rimless glasses resting on his slightly crooked nose. This job was a complete disappointment; it was not at all what he'd hoped for.

Major Daniel "Crash" Warren sat in his cramped office at the Combat Plans division of the Pentagon. In the surrounding offices sat his Army, Navy, and Marine counterparts – all of whom were just as frustrated as he was. It amazed Dan how four guys could be so incredibly busy throughout the day, yet so undeniably bored with their jobs. It wasn't for a lack of work – they shuffled a rainforest of paperwork up and down the chain-of-command every day – it was just that none of it really accomplished anything worthwhile.

"How far I've fallen," thought Dan. He'd arrived in late September, motivated and excited, expecting to have a lot of important assignments; after all, there was a big hole in the side of the Pentagon and Operation Enduring Freedom was about to kick off. Unfortunately he'd soon found that command of the battle had already shifted to CENTCOM and most of the high level work was over. His division had moved on to other areas of the world, updating and maintaining dusty conventional war plans that had occupied the Pentagon's shelves for decades. What really irked him was that he'd left a combat unit in order to take this job. In fact, his former squadron was currently deployed to Kuwait, a prime location from which to springboard into Enduring Freedom.

Dan's last assignment was Holloman Air Force Base, New Mexico, and what a great assignment it was. Not only did he get to work in the exclusive stealth community, he also scored huge points at home because the base was close to his wife's family. At that time he was a mid-level captain, fresh out of the Intelligence Weapons School at Nellis – a prestigious, graduate level course offered to the best and the brightest of Air Force intelligence officers. At first the Operations Group Commander placed him in the Wing Intelligence section, where Dan's knowledge and experience would benefit the young airmen on his staff; but Dan was unhappy with being distanced from the action and soon finagled his way into one of the fighter squadrons.

For a captain in the intelligence world, the squadron level shop is where the action is, and Dan was on the front line with the operators of the Stealth Fighter. That was where he'd earned his tactical name. In his first week at the squadron he'd joined the intramural soccer team. Pre-season practices and scrimmages went well and Dan showed a particular talent on the forward field, but he'd always been a little clumsy. In the second tournament game he tripped over his own feet and careened into the side of the goal, damaging his knee. The doctor put him on crutches for two weeks, but he still showed up to every game to support his team. In his very first game back from the bench Dan collided with another player, resulting in his second injury. They were both knocked down, but Dan took the worst of the impact with two broken ribs, putting him out for the remainder of the season.

The humor in Dan's misfortune was not lost on the pilots. They requisitioned an old Kevlar helmet from supply and presented it to him as a war memorial. There were brass plates with black lettering tacked to both sides. On the front, the label simply read, "Captain Crash Warren," but the back plate was more detailed, reading:

> My name is Dan "Crash" Warren. I also answer to Dan, Danny, Daniel, Hey You, and Look Out! If I am unconscious don't worry, that is normal. Please revive me or return me to the 93rd Fighter Squadron, Holloman Air Force Base, New Mexico.

During his time at the fighter squadron, Crash could honestly say he looked forward to every day of work. Although he truly missed his family when he was deployed, he enjoyed the rush of working out of a Forward Operating Location. Whether at home or on deployments, Crash's enthusiasm and the quality of his work had a direct effect on the flyers, and nothing bolsters a soldier's spirit like seeing firsthand the positive effects of his work. Unfortunately, no good deal lasts forever – certainly not in the US Air Force.

After a couple of years in the flying squadron, Crash's supervisor told him that if he wanted to be competitive for promotion, he would need to "diversify his performance reports." That meant Crash needed a new job title. To accomplish this he moved to the Combat Plans section back in the OSS. During his stay there he was promoted to the rank of major and told to start thinking about his next assignment. It was around that time that the hiring message for his current job came down from the Pentagon. It was the natural thing to do: he had a great resume, experience in Combat Plans, and the Pentagon was always the right career move for a major; everybody said so. By the time September 11th hit, Crash already had orders to move. Now his former squadron was camped at the enemy's doorstep and he was stuck here, and the most exciting part of his day was lunch, when he could sit in the cafeteria and listen to the stories about moments of terror and acts of heroism on the day the airplane came through the wall.

A beep from his computer stirred Crash from his self-pity and Microsoft Outlook advised him that he had a new email from the Colonel. "Great," he thought. "That'll be more busywork to occupy my time."

> Maj Warren,
> Pay me a visit. I need your advice on something.
> v/r,
> Richard T. Walker, Col, US ARMY
> Director, JCS Combat Plans

"That's odd," thought Crash. Colonel-Richard-T-Walker-US-Army – that was probably what it said on his driver's license – never needed advice from anyone, let alone an Air Force major. Crash hardly ever spoke to the guy, particularly since most of his work had to go through the Assistant Director's office. If anything, however, it might be something different that he could talk to his wife about over dinner. Crash immediately withdrew the thought; ever since joining the Stealth community he'd learned that "something different" was usually not something you could discuss outside of a sterilized room. In any case, he decided, he'd better not keep the Colonel waiting.

"You wanted to see me sir?" asked Crash as he cautiously stepped into the Colonel's office.

Richard Walker was a broad-shouldered individual with a square jaw, a good tan, and a tight crew cut. "Sit down," he said as he shut the door. His voice carried so much "huah" that Crash would have obediently sat down whether the man was a colonel or not. When he sat in the low chair, the Colonel's desk practically came up to his shoulders; Crash felt tiny. It occurred to him that this was probably intentional.

"Read that paper in front of you and sign it. You've got a pen don't you?"

"Yes sir." Crash tensed, this was the point in his nightmares when he reached into his pocket and withdrew his daughter's pink Barbie pen. He relaxed a bit as a black pen labeled "Lockheed-Martin" emerged in his hand. The paper in front of him was a non-disclosure statement, a type of document he'd signed on several occasions before. The language was the same as always, "I will not reveal or release any information pertaining to...blah...blah...blah...a prison term of...blah...blah...blah...on pain of death...blah...blah...cross my heart and hope to die." Crash was intrigued, though, by the name of the program at the top of the paper: Cerberus, the name of the three-headed dog that guards the gates of Hades. Sometimes these names were randomly chosen and had no bearing on the project, but something told Crash that this project was different.

"Read faster Crash, I've got a meeting in half an hour."

"Yes sir." Crash signed the document and pocketed his pen.

Colonel Walker held up two fingers pressed together and waived them in front of Crash's face in a mock blessing. "You're now cleared into Cerberus, Major Warren; a project that, like the hound himself, is a real pain in the rear. All of your clearance work is already done." He scribbled a couple of lines on a piece of flash paper and handed it to Crash. "Here, take this. Memorize it and burn it."

Crash stared at the cryptic lines on the paper. "What are these?" he asked.

"The first item is a six letter key word, a combination that unlocks a safe in the Lockup. The second item is the safe's identification: whiskey one four echo. There you'll find a file with all the details you'll need to get started. In the meantime, here's the jist: We were handed this from the Joint Chiefs at the beginning of the year. It came down from POTUS right after he took office. He wants an option that allows us to take out certain undesirable opposition leadership with minimal collateral damage; and no, by 'undesirable opposition leader' I don't mean Dick Gephardt, if that's what you're thinking."

Dan wiped away a smirk; cursing his inability to maintain a poker face.

"Over the last year we've been pursuing an option that just isn't panning out. We decided that it was best to tailor the plan to the target on a case-by-case basis. At that time Target Three had the most priority, so we manipulated operations in Southern Watch to facilitate the requested time frame. After six months of prepping the battlefield, we made a couple of test runs but both of them were utter failures. The job isn't getting done and Cerberus is floundering. We need a fresh face and some new ideas."

Walker took a breath while he let Crash process the information. "I'm not going to pull any punches here, Crash" he continued. "Your record is nothing spectacular; there were ten other guys in line for the job that were just as qualified as you, some even more."

"You sure know how to make a guy feel good sir."

Walker was not amused. "Don't interrupt. Your stealth background is what got you here and I think somewhere in that oft-injured cranium of yours is the solution to my problem. That makes you the fresh face, so you'd better come up with some new ideas, and quick."

Chapter 7

Victor led Bug past rolling hills covered in the rusty hues of autumn, sticking to the valleys as much as possible as he picked his way south and east. Wizard Flight had just arrived in the training area and Oso had split the flight, sending Victor and Bug to their briefed holding point.

Finding the ridgeline that formed the line between the simulated friendly and enemy territories, Victor turned due south and followed it until he spotted the small microwave tower that marked their holding point. He checked the point against a satellite picture on his kneeboard. Just as the photograph showed, an access road ran north from the tower facility, and then made a gentle turn to the east and climbed through a saddle in the ridgeline. "Wizard Three is established at X-ray," he called.

"Wizard One is established as well." Oso's voice sounded distant over the UHF radio. "Snake One Five, Snake One Five, this is Wizard Zero One how do you copy?"

"Wizard Zero One, Snake One Five reads you loud and clear," Lieutenant Joe Forester replied. "Call ready for my position and your first target."

"Standby Snake," said Oso. "Wizard flight, move to Position One."

Victor led Bug through the saddle to the forward side of the ridgeline, where both pilots could get a clear view of the target area. Beyond the saddle the terrain rapidly fell away, exposing the flat expanse of the Rhein River Valley. The orange and red foliage gave way to tan and brown fields separating a few small Rheinland towns; among them the target area, Boechingen, several kilometers past the ridge. Both pilots made sure to stay low, well below the terrain behind them, so that a civilian in Boechingin might not see the Hogs even if he looked directly at them. "Wraith Three is in position,"

Victor transmitted.

"Wraith Flight is ready. Go ahead Snake," said Oso.

The lieutenant described his position to the A-10 drivers and Oso confirmed that they all had visual contact. From that point forward Joe described the targets in relation to his own location. "Do you see the soccer field west of my position?" he asked, using the field as a reference that would give the pilots an easy way to visualize distances on the ground.

"Affirmative," Oso responded.

"Using the length of the soccer field as one unit, look two units northwest and describe what you see."

"Looks like a grouping of twenty vehicles or so, mostly gray and white, on the southeast side of an 'L' shaped building."

"That's correct. That parking lot is an enemy staging area; the vehicles are your targets. We are taking mortar fire from that position. Destroy it immediately."

"Wizard Flight, we'll use Strike Pattern One with mavericks. Wizard One Element has the north side of the target, Wizard Three your element has the south side. Return to your hold point when complete. Start your ingress at one minute from the hack. Three, sound off when you're ready."

Victor looked at Bug who gave a rock of his wings to signal that he was ready for the attack. "Three's ready," he reported.

"Wizard Flight execute in three…two…one…hack!"

Victor looked north and strained to see Oso turning his Hog toward the target. He mentally reviewed the strike pattern, remembering that he had to wait an additional sixty seconds past Oso's start time before he could lead Bug in. The timing would keep him out of the first element's imaginary fragmentation patterns, but that was only part of the equation. In his mind's eye he could see Oso, standing in the briefing room, drawing a line on the map along an east/west running road through the target. To separate their flight paths, Victor had to keep his element south of that road. Looking to the north, he could see Oso's aircraft pressing toward the target. He knew his flight lead would climb, point at the target, and eventually fire two simulated mavericks. Brent would follow shortly thereafter and do the same, but Victor couldn't see him. Where was he? "Shoot, the kid's lagging the fight," Victor muttered to himself. He hit the record switch on his Heads Up Display video and made a vocal note, "Three October, Wizard Zero Three, first attack, this is Victor. Briefed attack is Pattern One with mavericks, Wizard Two is at least a mile late; I'll have to delay my attack to avoid his frag."

Victor maneuvered his element to account for the extra time. When he was ready to attack he gave Bug a wing flash and turned toward the target area. Bug followed suit and the two A-10s swept low across the rural German landscape. A patchwork of fields passed beneath them in a blur of brown and green. Eight miles from the target Victor angled his aircraft slightly away, making the space that would allow him to "pop up" and roll in for the strike.

"Wizard One, off hot." Oso launched his imaginary missiles.

Victor checked his distance from the target. It looked like his adjustment for Brent's delay had worked.

"Wizard Two, off hot."

Victor counted a few more seconds, giving Brent's missiles time to find their targets, and then pulled the nose of his Hog toward heaven, knowing that – in a real fight – this was the most exposed he'd be to enemy fire. While still climbing he banked hard to the left and pulled toward the target, cutting an arc through the horizon to point back at the earth. Then, after he settled on the attack axis, he commanded his missile to open its infrared eye. The green tinted screen showed the target parking lot as a jumble of muddled shapes and shadows. He placed his cross hairs on the southwest side of the lot and zoomed in, picking out a vehicle that was glowing nicely on the display. "Someone must have just arrived," he thought, "the engine's still warm." He commanded the missile seeker to lock, crosschecked his Heads Up Display, and pressed hard on the "pickle" button. The maverick screen went blank, simulating a successful launch and Victor held the aircraft steady, patiently waiting for the system to reset. When the image of the parking lot returned he locked up another target and fired his second weapon. The entire process, from settling his jet on the attack axis to launching his second maverick took Victor less than seven seconds. "Wizard Three, off hot," he called into the radio. He rolled the Hog on its side and pulled hard, turning it to avoid being fragged by his own weapons. Once clear of the fragmentation pattern, he turned his attention to Bug. He stayed low and arced around the target, ready to provide covering fire.

"Wizard Four, off, hot."

Victor watched his wingman turn away from the target. When Bug's nose was pointed his way he flashed his wings to make himself more visible. "Four, Three's at your twelve. Follow me back to X-ray."

"Wizard Four is visual Three. WILCO," Bug replied, letting Victor know that he saw him and would follow him across the ridge to the hold point.

"Wizard call ready for next target," Joe prompted again.

"Wizard Zero One, ready."

Victor listened intently to the next description. On this attack they were to practice finding the target on the fly, meaning that Victor was not permitted to take his element to the other side of the ridge and watch while Joe described the target, as he'd done the first time. They'd have to stay low and out of sight, memorize the description of the target, and then locate it once they began pressing in for the attack. This also gave them less time to gain visual contact with the each other. Each member of the formation depended on the rest to get the timing right.

"Your new target is an enemy command post consisting of three adjacent buildings running east to west," said Joe. "Using the same soccer field as one unit, look half a unit southeast of your previous target. The group of target buildings is separated from all the other buildings by at least fifty yards on each side. They are wooden structures with white paint and they're the only buildings in the area with blue shingled roofs."

Victor pictured the target in his mind, trying to remember what the area surrounding the parking lot looked like. The blue roofs and the orientation of the buildings were the keys to locating his target. He remembered that the previous target had been the length of two soccer fields northwest of the "friendly ground forces" represented by Lieutenant Forester. If the new target was half a soccer field southeast of the old one, then it was that much closer to the good guys. He'd have to avoid flying over the friendly forces during the attack. If an imaginary bomb fell well short of the imaginary target it could really hurt the imaginary good guys, and Victor would feel really bad about that; at least he imagined he would.

Then Oso threw a wrench in the works. "Wizards," he commanded, "this will be Strike Pattern Three, with guns, mavericks, and bombs. On this attack we'll simulate a twenty-three millimeter gun protecting the target area. Wizard Three, your element has the western two buildings. My element will take out the threat and the eastern building. Call ready for the hack."

Victor paused to absorb the new information, looked to Bug for a ready signal, and then responded, "Three's ready."

"Wizards, three…two…one…hack!"

"What're you doing Oso?" thought Victor as he started his clock. For this mission, Strike Pattern Three was the Irish Cross, and Oso had just combined it with a blind attack. That was pushing the envelope for a fully qualified Hog driver, let alone a new guy like Brent. At the schoolhouse Brent had likely practiced both maneuvers, but probably not at the same time. Victor was less concerned about Brent's capability to handle the first portion of the attack as the second. The first half focused on neutralizing the triple-A, and Brent's role in that was merely to provide cover for Oso. Once the threat was neutralized, though, he had a whole new issue to overcome. On the previous target they'd used "stand-off" weapons, fired from a distance, but this time they'd be using dumb bombs. Three of the four Hogs had to fly almost directly over the targets for their bombs to reach them from only five hundred feet in the air. That meant that all three aircraft had to occupy the same piece of sky at some point during the attack, so timing was everything, and Brent hadn't done that well with the timing on his first attack.

Victor waited for his clock to count down and then flashed his wings at Bug, driving low toward the saddle as if he intended to scrape his jet along the road at its center. As the trees flashed by on either side, Victor's radar altimeter read ninety feet off the ground. Then the rushing terrain once again became blue sky and he rolled his aircraft on its back, pulling it down the east side of the ridge. When he leveled out over the plain he searched for his target, as well as the other element. He checked his six and saw Bug sliding into perfect position. "Wizard Three, execute," said Victor. With that command he turned slightly away from Bug and headed east, searching the ground for references that would help him approximate the circle of the anti-aircraft gun's range. By this time the imaginary enemy would have picked up Bug on his radar, and hopefully pointed their gun barrels at him.

Right on schedule, Bug turned away from the threat, staying outside of its envelope. Then Victor achieved his ninety-degree offset and turned in to become the decoy himself. He pulled the nose of his A-10 up and rolled in to point his gun at the threat. At a distance that promised very little damage but enough fireworks to get the enemy's attention, he squeezed the trigger, lobbing a volley of simulated thirty millimeter at the enemy gun.

"Wizard Three, guns, guns, guns," Victor said into the radio, alerting the others that he'd fired his imaginary rounds. He looked up from the target and searched for the other Hogs as he turned his own jet to get out of the gun's range. He found Oso right where he should be, directly across the circle, about to fire a maverick and put the simulated anti-aircraft gun out of its misery, but he couldn't find

Brent. There was no time. Victor refocused his attention on getting into position for the follow-on attacks; he'd have to locate Brent later.

"Wizard One, off hot," Oso said as he released his weapon; the threat would soon be a twisted mass of molten metal.

By the time he was ready for the second half of the strike, Victor still hadn't found Brent. He shook his head in frustration; he had to base his timing on the fragmentation pattern of Brent's bombs, but he couldn't do that unless he got a visual. Then, finally, Victor found him, well north of where he should be. Brent was late again, way late. If the kid continued in to strike, his frag would force Victor to turn away, spoiling the attack.

Oso saw it too. "Wizard Two, withhold, withhold, withhold!" he shouted, ordering Brent not to drop his bombs. "Turn west immediately and follow me to the hold point."

Brent was obviously flustered by the call, "Wizard T-Two...off dry," he stammered back at his instructor.

Victor watched as the kid rolled his wings and pulled the Hog away from its attack run, but he turned the wrong way. "He's going east," Victor called over the radio. It wasn't a very professional call, but he was fed up with the younger pilot's mistakes. Oso didn't respond, but that wasn't unusual and Victor assumed he'd heard the call. "It's not important," he thought, "as long as he's out of my way."

Victor banked his Hog toward the target and checked his systems one more time. On his HUD the green symbols showed the aircraft's airspeed, altitude, and attitude along with navigation and targeting information. In the center of the display was the bombsight, which looked like an upside-down lollypop with a little dot in the middle of the circle. The lollypop was the targeting solution and the little dot showed exactly where Victor's bombs would fall if he hit the pickle button at that moment. He rolled out on his final attack heading and made a minor adjustment so that the blue-roofed building was centered at the top of the lollypop's stick. As he closed the distance to the target, the building appeared to track down the stick until finally it fell beneath the dot at the center of the circle. "Gotcha." He pressed the pickle button and released his imaginary bombs. "Wizard Three, off hot." He looked over his shoulder to check Bug's position. It looked good, Bug was all over it.

"Wizard Four, off hot," Bug reported less than a minute later.

Victor smiled, despite Brent's mistakes the attack had come off well. Then he heard an unexpected radio call, "Wizard Two, say posit." It was Oso's voice. He was trying to locate his wingman.

In a split second Victor processed the unexpected information and chose to ignore it. Oso was dealing with a lost wingman, but that was not his problem; his job was to get his element safely back to the hold point. Once that was accomplished, he could help his flight lead sort out Brent. "Four, turn back to the hold now, I'll follow you," he commanded. Then something in his subconscious prompted him to force Oso's situation back to the forefront of his mind. "Wizard Four, keep a look out for Two," he said, scanning the horizon. He looked past Bug's A-10, now less than a mile in front of him, and scanned the ridge for signs of Brent's Hog. Then the radio crackled again.

"Lead, Wizard Two is visual. I'm at your six o'clock," Brent said, and this time he sounded confident.

Victor let himself relax a little. Brent must have found Oso and fallen into trail, well to their north. With the potential conflict averted he let his eyes focus on Bug, who was just crossing through the saddle. Then suddenly he caught a flash of gray in his peripheral vision. Instinctively he turned his head to see what it was and gasped in disbelief. Another A-10 nearly filled the left side of his canopy, and it was getting bigger...fast.

Chapter 8

"Wizards, climb! Climb!" Victor shouted into the radio, violently pushing forward on the stick to force his jet earthward. As he buried the stick in the forward control panel Victor watched his G-meter peg at the negative limit, sending loose charts flying to the top of his canopy. Then he pulled hard left to dodge a radio tower and the charts slammed back down as the G-meter swung back up to positive six. Finally he leveled out at a hundred feet, still trying to find the other A-10 and still trying to figure out what had just happened. Through the rush of blood in his ears he heard Bug's voice.

"Wizards, knock it off!"

"Wizard One, knock it off."

There was a moment of tense silence…

"Wizard Three, knock it off," Victor called, getting his nerves and pulse under control. He cautiously began a climb back up to five hundred feet.

"Wizard Four, knock it off," Bug finished. The fear in his voice was unmistakable.

Like any good flight lead, Oso immediately followed the first sequence with another. "Wizards, knock it off, Wizard One, knock it off."

Silence…

"Wizard Three, knock it off"

"Wizard Four, knock it off."

"I need an explanation Four," Oso prompted, the impatience in his voice barely overshadowing the fear.

"There's a large fire with black smoke about a mile southwest of Boechingen," Bug explained. "I think it might be Wizard Two."

Oso did not directly respond to Bug's revelation; instead, he barked out another order. "Wizard Three and Four, climb to five thousand and rejoin at Yankee. I'm already established at Yankee and climbing to six thousand."

"Four say posit," prompted Victor, unwilling to climb until he had visual contact with his wingman again.

"One mile at your six, Three," answered Bug.

Victor brought his Hog around to look for Bug. As he looked east he saw the pillar of black smoke rising out of a green field outside of the town. He looked away, refusing to speculate on what it might mean, and found Bug following him right where he should be. He began a slow climb, continuing his turn to allow Bug to close the distance to a tight formation.

On the second turn Victor looked at the wreckage again. From the higher altitude his view was better and through the black smoke and the flames he saw the distinct nose section of an A-10. It looked like part of the canopy was still with the aircraft, but he wasn't ready to accept the implications of that information. He logged it in his brain and suppressed the consequences, focusing on getting his element back together with Oso. Looking to the north he picked up Oso's A-10, orbiting six thousand feet over Yankee. "Wizard One, this is Three, I'm at your four o'clock and level at five thousand."

"I see you Wizard Three. Hold over Yankee with your element and come up on SAR Alpha. I'm pressing south to get a look at the wreckage."

"WILCO. Break, break...Wizard Four push SAR Alpha now," Victor said. Then he switched to the other frequency and waited for Oso to check them in.

"Wizard Flight, check."

Victor gave the required pause to allow Brent to join the sequence, but there was only static. "Three," he said, trying to keep his voice level.

"Four," Bug finished the sequence.

"Wizard Two, this is Wizard One on SAR Alpha, respond."

Silence...

Victor let the image of the burning cockpit resurface in his mind.

"One, this is Three,"

"Go ahead Three." Oso sounded tired.

"I saw the canopy in the wreckage. It was still with the fuselage." Victor paused to steady his voice before continuing, "I think he stayed with the plane."

Oso ignored the information and tried again, "Wizard Two, this is Wizard One on SAR Alpha, respond."

Silence…

"Wizard One, this is Wizard Three. I think he stayed with the plane."

"I heard you Three," Oso snapped, but he repeated his call again. "Wizard Two, this is Wizard One on SAR Alpha, respond."

With only the ghostly whisper of static to answer his calls, Oso finally gave in. He coordinated for fire fighters from a nearby Army base to respond to the accident, knowing that Boechingen's *Freiwillige Feuerwehr* wouldn't have the tools to deal with burning jet fuel.

At Oso's request, Victor returned to the lieutenant's frequency and gave him the coordinates of the site, but Joe was already half way there, guided by the thick black smoke. "Be careful, there's still a lot of fuel burning out there," Victor cautioned. "Two's gun was cold but he was carrying rounds for ballast, and they could cook off at any time. Just get close enough to survey the site with your binoculars and look for a survivor." He knew it was dangerous to send such a young officer into a mess like that, but Joe was the closest squadron member on the ground.

Orbiting high above the crash site, Oso directed Army helicopters to the wreckage and used Victor as a radio relay to coordinate with Ramstein Air Base, the closest Air Force facility with an Emergency Response Team, until all three of the Hogs reached bingo fuel and had to return to Spangdahlem. Victor ordered Joe to stay near the wreckage, hand off to the incoming ERT, and then drive home as soon as possible.

As the A-10s turned northwest for the flight home, Victor led Bug back into formation with Oso. They flew in a loose "fingertip" configuration with Victor at Oso's left and Bug at his right. The Moselle River wound lazily along beneath them, snaking its way toward the base. Although the pilots were accustomed to following the river at very low altitudes, there was no more room for risk on this mission; Oso had them at a safe and comfortable five thousand feet. Victor understood, his flight lead wasn't taking any chances – right now he just wanted to get the remaining wingmen safely on the deck.

It occurred to Victor that he'd never taken the time to observe the Moselle Valley from such a mid-level altitude. Even on the rare occasions that he took his Hog through five thousand feet, it would be on the way to twenty-five thousand, and a mid-level cloud deck usually obscured the ground. At the moment, though, there were no clouds and the view was breathtaking. The fading light of the setting sun refracted through the mist that rose from the vineyards, covering the hillsides in a translucent film of gold and auburn. It seemed like an old photograph, once rich in color and detail, now faded and subdued by age, and for a moment Victor thought, "This is what a memory looks like."

During their return, Victor tried to focus on flying his aircraft; but he couldn't help thinking about the painful hours ahead. There would be immediate calls home to reassure their wives, yet they could not share details or devote much time to the task. The base leadership would give them time, if only a little, to stow their equipment and recover from the flight, but they would have to use the spare lockers because theirs would be locked off, the contents preserved for the accident investigation. Then the questioning would begin. First they'd be separated and interviewed one on one to get their individual perspectives before the other perspectives could taint them. The safety investigators would assure each man that nothing he said would be used against the other flight members, but each would carefully choose his words because none of them would believe it. Then they would be debriefed as a group, to bring out events that might not surface without cues from the others' memories. Most likely there would also be blood and urine tests, to ensure no alcohol or drugs were involved in the accident. Once released they would want nothing but to get in their cars and go home; instead, they'd have to fight through the questions of their squadron mates, answering what they could and avoiding what had to be guarded for the sanctity of the investigation.

Victor replayed the last attack in his mind over and again, trying to cope with what had just happened. He remembered that the last time he saw Brent was just before striking the target. He'd seen the kid turning east, away from Oso and away from the direction Oso commanded him to go. Then, after the attack, Brent had reported that he was following his flight lead back to the hold. That meant he should have been well to the north. Even with the erroneous turn, Brent should never have gotten to the south side of the target where Victor was because Oso had called him off the attack early. Then, during the near mid-air collision, Victor had ordered all of the others to climb. Why had Brent descended instead? He struggled to determine where he'd made a mistake that could have caused the accident, but he couldn't find one. It shamed him that a comrade was dead and his biggest concern was whether or not he would be blamed, but the thought remained: this was not his fault.

Oso took the three-ship down to fifteen hundred feet for their entry into the traffic pattern. There were usually greetings or glib comments from the tower controllers when a formation returned from training, but today there was nothing but somber professionalism.

"Tower, Wizard Zero One, flight of three, entry at Bravo for Initial, full stop."

"Wizard Zero One, Tower copies. Report Initial."

The tower pattern was uncharacteristically quiet. At a base with three fighter squadrons the radio would normally buzz with a cacophony of calls as numerous aircraft reported their positions or requested permission for landing patterns, but now the radios were silent. The three Warthogs were the only airplanes in the sky. Victor glanced away from Oso's jet and eyed the airfield. He noted that there was not much activity on the ground either. Flight operations had ceased and the other jets were bedded down, perhaps for a long time. The only ground activities were scattered clean-up operations.

Oso signaled the formation into "echelon right" and Bug shifted his aircraft fifty feet away from Oso, making space for Victor. Then Victor reduced power, crossed behind Oso, and slid into the gap.

"Tower, Wizard Zero One, Initial, full stop for three." The A-10's rolled out for their pass over the runway. Without a word from Oso, Victor and Bug moved over, opening a space for the wingman that hadn't returned. On the ground the few people still active on the flight line stopped what they were doing to gaze in silence at the "Missing Man" formation. One young airman continued his work, stowing a fuel hose, until a sergeant smacked him across the top of the head with the palm of his hand. "Show some respect kid," the older man ordered, pointing up at the aircraft.

One by one the A-10's pitched out of the formation, separating into the final landing pattern. After touching down Victor bedded down his aircraft with hardly a word to the crew chief, and made his way back to the squadron. The commander met the pilots at the door and directed all three into his office. Oso tried to speak but the senior officer cut him off. "Shut up, nobody say a word," he said. "The regulations say you have to talk to Flight Safety before you can talk to me, but there's nothing that says I can't talk to you." Soda folded his arms and sat down on the edge of his desk. "You're about to go through a process that we all prefer to forget about until it rears its ugly head. I don't know exactly what happened out there, but I know the men that stand before me now. I know your skill, I know your professionalism, and I know your character, so I'm confident that you'll all come out okay on the other side. Gentlemen, the measure of a combat pilot is taken in the dogfight and on the bombing range...but the measure of an officer is taken at moments like this."

After an ordeal that seemed like it would never end, the senior investigating officer released Victor to go home, where he faced another barrage of worried questions. Despite her worried tirade, his wife Katy smothered him in affection, grateful that he had come home unscathed.

Several hours later, far from Katy's grateful tears in Germany, a blue sedan pulled into the driveway of Gregory and Barbara Collins' house in a quiet suburb of Atlanta, Georgia. Two men stepped out with their hats in hand, one bearing stars, the other bearing a cross.

Chapter 9

Crash drove his family through the labyrinth of central DC on the way to the National Museum of the American Indian, a division of the Smithsonian. He'd never been fond of meandering around a cavernous building to look at other people's stuff, but Carol had a heavy dose of Mogollon Indian in her blood and she wanted the kids to learn about the Native American role in history. She was talking about something that was obviously important to her, but Crash could not get Cerberus off his mind.

Crash had always struggled with leaving his work at the office. The official term was "compartmentalization." Academically he knew how it worked, mentally separating an emotion or a piece of information and locking it away in a subconscious filing cabinet, but he was never very successful in its application. Pilots use compartmentalization to help them shut out all other concerns and focus on flying, while intelligence operatives use it to help them bury a secret so deep that even a drunken stupor cannot bring it to the surface.

Unfortunately compartmentalization is a developed skill that some people have a knack for and some don't, and Crash had discovered long ago that it was a good thing he wasn't a drinker. He'd never developed a knack for compartmentalizing his work, particularly when he found it as interesting as Cerberus. He knew that he should let it go, that he should focus on his family on his day off, but he was obsessed with solving the problem Walker had entrusted to him. Cerberus was dead in the water until he found a solution and he simply couldn't let it go until the task was complete.

"We can do that. Right, Dan?" Carol's voice snapped him back to the moment.

"Uh, right," Crash answered, confidently supporting whatever statement she'd just made and wondering what he'd just agreed to.

He let it go, he was sure to find out eventually; probably during an argument two or three weeks down the road.

They left the car in a nearby parking garage and walked over to the rust-colored building. As they entered, Crash tried to purge his work-related demons and let the atmosphere absorb him. Before him lay a series of landscapes from Native American life, accented with several fountains and a myriad of pleasant scents. He followed his nose and saw the Mitsitam Café, where museum employees were showing other patrons how to prepare some Native American dishes. He took a deep breath and let his body relax; maybe he would finally be able to put his work aside and enjoy just one afternoon with his family.

After a walk through several exhibits and a quick break at the cafe, Carol suggested they find the display of Mogollan art. Laughing with his kids and flirting with his wife, Crash followed the signs to the back of the museum, but as they rounded the last corner something stopped him dead in his tracks. Before him, hanging in a large case next to the entrance of the exhibit, was a stunning piece of art. A beautiful assortment of earth-toned feathers and colorful beads hung from a two foot diameter wicker ring that encircled a web of chords. With the length of the hanging feathers the whole thing must have been five feet tall, but it wasn't the size or the beauty of the artwork that made Crash stop short.

"Dreamcatcher," he let the word audibly slip from his mind.

"Du-uh," teased Carol. "You act like you've never seen one before."

He didn't respond.

Dreamcatcher. Crash couldn't focus on anything else for the rest of the trip. No amount of stunning art or sweet scents could snap him out of it. The solution worked itself out in his mind naturally, as if it were a process that he simply observed rather than propelled. It all made sense, assuming they could get the funds. The boss might not like the idea of a new piece of hardware, but it was the only solution

Crash could see. Scott would help him. Scott would argue the viability of his creation with enough diagrams and formulas to make any man's head spin, let alone Colonel Dick Walker. "It'll work," Crash said to himself, "I know it will."

"What, honey?"

"Nothing."

At home Crash picked at his dinner and continued to work out the details. He'd have to convince the Colonel to clear Scott into the program before he could even contact him. Then he'd have to get Scott to forward a paper summarizing the Dreamcatcher concept. No, that wouldn't be enough. He needed to get to Ohio, to see the project at its birthplace, before he could make a solid plan.

Crash's mind was still racing through the options as he lay in his room waiting for Carol to put the kids to bed. Maybe he should call the Colonel and go into work tonight. After all, this thing was a national priority, a tasker from POTUS himself. If this solution was really viable, then maybe he should get cracking. Of course, it was the weekend. There were a lot of wickets to pass through to get this thing moving, many of which would be unavailable until Monday. He paused in his reverie as Carol smiled and quietly shut the door. There was something pleasantly odd in her expression.

"The kids are asleep," she whispered, giving him a little wink. She made a show of pulling something very small and silky out of the dresser, lit a candle, doused the lights, and slinked into the bathroom.

Suddenly compartmentalizing Cerberus didn't seem so difficult. "Yeah, it can definitely wait until Monday," thought Crash.

Chapter 10

Bright and early Monday morning, Crash stood in front of Colonel Walker's desk, trying to summon his courage while waiting for his boss to finish a phone call.

"Look Tarpin," Walker growled into the receiver, "I don't like the sound of blackmail I hear in your voice. I have no intention of giving you those clearances. You'll get me the information I need out of the pure goodness of your heart or I'll go to the VP and identify you *by name* as an interagency road block!" He slammed the receiver down in its cradle, scowled at it for a moment, and then turned his attention to Crash. "Alright, tell me what you've got, and make it quick," he snarled.

"Sir, I have that new idea you're looking for in regards to Cerberus," said Crash. He had hoped the news would lighten the Colonel's mood, but all he got was a grunted "Mmhmm, spit it out." He regrouped and tried to continue. "Uh, I saw something in the post-action report from the last operation. The supervising general noted with emphasis that he couldn't 'accomplish the goal with the tools at hand.' I think he's right, I think what we need is a new tool." He stopped and took a breath.

"Go on Warren, you have my interest," pressed the Colonel, his mood beginning to turn.

"Sir, I think our problem is not in the striker, but in the reconnaissance aircraft. The Predator just doesn't fit the bill. To use it we have to knock down portions of any radar net and, in the Iraqi's case, so many of their radars are mobile that they quickly fill any gaps we create."

"I'd have to agree with that. Okay, what do you have in mind?"

Colonel Walker's sudden openness boosted Crash's resolve. Confidence filled his voice. "Sir, what we need is a new piece of hardware – one that will enable us to determine a human target's position without being detected, even in a robust air defense environment." Crash took another breath and prepared for the final pitch. "When I was at Holloman we had a civilian that worked on our stealth materials, a 'stealth engineer' if you will, he also spent a lot of time at Whiteman Air Force Base, working with the Stealth Bombers; his name was Dr. Scott Stone. Dr. Stone once told me about an idea for an unmanned reconnaissance jet that could be launched from a B-2's bomb bay, completely integrating the reconnaissance and attack pieces of the puzzle. I think he's still working on that concept at Wright Patterson, but I don't know how far he's taken it."

"Did he have a name for this aircraft?"

"Yes sir, he called it Dreamcatcher."

That evening Crash stood in his living room, trying to placate his fuming spouse without really answering her questions. "Yeah honey, I know that I said this job would mean less travel," he said with a conciliatory tone, "and it does, but I never said it meant no travel at all."

Carol did not respond, she just folded her arms and scowled.

"Look, it's not like I have a choice here; TDYs are part and parcel with the whole military gig, you know. When Uncle Sam says go to Ohio, you go to Ohio."

"Fine," came the terse reply, "but I don't understand what this thing is, and why you didn't know about it until today. You'd think you would have remembered to give me a few days' warning that you were going to miss your daughter's birthday."

Colonel Walker had been surprisingly accommodating, at least where the Dreamcatcher idea was concerned. Crash even thought he'd seen a hint of excitement in that stone-wall face. Unfortunately his proposal was so successful that it shot him directly in the foot. He'd thought it would take at least a couple of days to coordinate all of the details, but his boss smelled progress, and Colonel-Richard-T-Walker-US-Army was never one to put off progress. He immediately started making phone calls and pulling strings. Tomorrow, instead of having birthday cake with his daughter, Crash would fly out to Wright Patterson and indoctrinate Dr. Stone into Cerberus. Then he would spend a week getting to know the details of Dreamcatcher and help Scott develop a timeline to bring the concept to reality. "Air Force Materials Command has a new concept," he explained to Carol, "and they want somebody from Plans Division to take a look at it." It was the best explanation he could offer without getting her a Top Secret clearance.

"Well, why can't Frank go?" Carol persisted.

"Frank is in the Navy."

"So, what happened to 'One Team, One Fight'?"

"That's just something we say around the foreigners, Honey…nobody really believes it."

Crash packed as lightly as possible and gently explained to his daughter why Daddy wouldn't be there for her party. He hated missing any family event, particularly his kids' birthdays, but this wasn't the first one he'd miss, and he knew that, as long as he was a soldier, it wouldn't be the last.

Chapter 11

"We're twelve hours from the target and thirty minutes from feet wet. The weapons are looking good, the system altitude is stable, and the fuel curve is right on track." Drake rattled off the liturgy like he was calling a horse race. He was more than a bit nervous. He and Murph were flying the Spirit of Texas under the callsign Ghost One One and they would soon depart the US Coastal Defense Zone for international waters, well on their way to 'night one' of Enduring Freedom.

"Relax man," said Murph. "It works, I promise you."

Like all B-2 pilots Drake was trained to optimize stealth. He knew the basic science and he'd practiced the mechanics but somehow, in the back of his mind, stealth still required a bit of ethereal magic.

Murph leaned back and stretched. "Let me share a story that might help settle your nerves. I flew on the first night of Allied Force. It was the first time the B-2 had ever been to combat and we were all afraid that we were betting our lives on a lot of smoke and mirrors. When we entered the strike zone there were triple-A flashes all around us, not to mention the occasional fiery plume of a surface to air missile streaking skyward. We could never be sure whether the bullets and missiles were meant for the aluminum jets or for us, but we kept our heads low and pressed forward anyway. A few minutes before we reached our target I heard AWACS call out the position of a MiG-29 Fulcrum. He was getting way too close. We debated whether or not we should call for help, potentially betraying our position, but before we could do anything the MiG was engaged by an F-15 Eagle. They tangled for a bit and then the Eagle shot him down. That dogfight took place almost directly below our jet, so close that we saw the fireball when the Eagle's sidewinder hit its mark. With the threat removed we continued to the target and dropped our bombs, and the next day I got up and mowed my lawn back at home as if I'd never left. A few weeks later we found out that the MiG wasn't after us at all; he was going after a pair of F-16's on a strike mission. After the war we flew the F-15 pilot and both F-16 drivers in for a joint intelligence debriefing. All three pilots confessed that they had no clue that we'd been there, right above them all. Like I said man, it works, I promise." Murph sat back in his seat; he was the picture of serenity. "You've got the jet, Drake," he said with a yawn. "I'm going to take a nap."

Several hours later Drake cringed as Murph slammed his fist on the forward console; the previous picture of serenity had long since been shattered. "Where the heck is he?" the older pilot shouted at the darkness beyond the windshield.

"I don't know," Drake answered, "but if he doesn't show up soon, we'll have to turn back." They were halfway to the target. They'd reached the rendezvous point for their final refueling twenty minutes ago, but there was no tanker in sight. Soon they would have to turn around. There was barely enough fuel to get home, let alone to the target and back.

"We'll give it another five minutes," said Murph, "these fuel calculations are conservative so we can afford to push the envelope a bit."

Suddenly the secure radio crackled to life. "Ghost One One, this is Exxon Seven One, how copy?"

"Loud and clear, Exxon," responded Murph coldly. Drake was sure the tanker commander could hear the edge in Murph's voice as clear as a bell, despite the transmission being scrambled, transmitted, received, and de-scrambled, before it was broadcast at the other end.

"Sorry we're late," replied the refueler, "we had some engine trouble on the ground. We made up as much time as we could but the winds were killing us."

"Copy all," replied Murph, the edge in his voice lessening, "we're ten miles east of the IP, heading west."

"Roger, Ghost, we've got your beacon. Start your turn back to the east now and you should roll out right underneath us."

Drake looked at the glowing blue fuel readout on the panel in front of him. "We've burned both time and gas in the hold," he said over the radio. "We're gonna need all the gas you can give us to make up the difference."

"Roger that, Ghost, you're our only customer. Take as much as you need."

Drake looked across the cockpit at Murph and tapped his watch, letting his face show his concern.

"Yeah, I know bud, we're gonna be late," Murph replied.

Chapter 12

"Range to Target One is sixty five miles, bearing zero three five. Weapons are active and aligned, this will be four 'version one' J-DAMs."

"Copy," Murph replied, "the radar is armed and ready for map one."

Ghost One One had three targets. The second two were bunkers with minimal defenses, but the first was a Surface to Air Missile site. It was their job to take down the SAM, clearing a path for conventional forces to follow, but the late re-fueling had put them nearly half an hour behind schedule. They'd made up all but five minutes by burning extra fuel, but five minutes could mean everything; a late arrival over the target would cost Ghost the element of surprise. Their expected Time on Target, or TOT, was set to coincide with a cruise missile strike against strategic targets all over Afghanistan, and once those missiles began to hit, the jig was up; triple-A and SAMs would start flying up all over the country. Murph had tried to convince Command and Control to "slip" the whole attack by a few minutes, but they wouldn't budge. Now the cruise missiles would hit nearly five minutes before the B-2 reached the target; the strike zone would be stirred up like a hornet's nest. Control gave them the opportunity to opt out, but leaving that SAM untouched would force many aircraft to abort their missions, so they decided to press on.

"Target range is now fifty miles, bearing zero five zero, all four impact points are showing achievable."

Drake pressed a button to take his first radar picture. A thin beam of radar shot out from the B-2's antenna, holding steady on the target as the aircraft tracked across the night sky. The computer constantly calculated the aircraft's position and movement to keep the radar steady. The Synthetic Aperture Radar, or SAR, enabled the small antenna to behave like it was several miles wide, and the bigger the radar antenna, the better the resolution. The picture it generated on Murph's display was photo quality. Murph examined the target while the computer placed small crosses on the screen to predict the weapons' impact points, known as Desired Points of Impact or DPIs. If everything was as it should be, the DPIs on the screen would match the picture in his strike folder and they could press with the strike. If something had moved they would have to find it on the radar map, mark it, and then fire the radar again, enabling the computer to calculate the new coordinates. The whole process was known as GPS Aided Targeting, what the pilots liked to call GAT.

"The control van has moved," Murph said, frowning at the screen. "It couldn't have gone far...wait, there it is...I'm marking it...OK, standby for GAT two."

"Thirty-five miles to target, bearing zero six zero, you're..." Drake's voice broke in mid sentence. He stared in awe as the ground suddenly erupted in a series of explosions. "There go the cruise missiles, now we're in for it." As if to affirm his prediction, the sky lit up with tracer rounds and flack, reminding Drake of the images he'd seen on TV during Desert Storm.

"Firing GAT two," said Murph. Drake knew his partner was trying to pull his attention back to the targeting procedure, but his eyes were still fixed on the fireworks outside. Then there was a bright flash where their target was supposed to be. For a moment Drake wondered if they were pulling double duty with a cruise missile, but the explosion didn't fade away like all the others; the flame was constant, and it was moving.

"SAM launch!" Drake shouted. "It's coming straight out of our target site."

"Steady..." cautioned Murph with a calm voice, "he can't see us, he's shooting blind because of the cruise missiles. Just focus on the task at hand and pray they don't get lucky. The second map is good; the computer is feeding the new coordinates to the J-DAM."

Drake focused on the targeting display and resumed his duties. "OK, um, all DPIs are showing achievable; we are three minutes from weapons release."

The three minutes felt like three hours as they inched closer to the target, wading through a sky that was thick with lead and fire. Fortunately, none of the tracers or missiles seemed to be aimed at anything but sky. Drake comforted himself with the knowledge that, to those on the ground, the B-2 was nothing more than a wisp, a spirit of death passing in the night. At high altitude the four embedded engines would make no sound for the enemy to hear, and against the night sky, the charcoal gray jet would barely seem a shadow, a black void sweeping over the stars of a moonless sky. It was only the volume of lead in the air that worried him. What if one of those unguided projectiles was lucky enough to find its mark? It was a phenomenon the older pilot's liked to call the Golden BB, and the Golden BB was something to be feared.

The Golden BB wasn't the only fear on Drake's mind. Before the cruise missile impacts, the enemy SAM operators would have been passively watching their radars, maybe even eating a snack or dozing off, but now they would search in earnest. They had no way to tell that they were being attacked with missiles fired from outside their borders and they would search for aircraft dropping bombs. They wouldn't be able to find the B-2 before its target run, but close to the SAM site Ghost One One would have to open their doors and release their bombs. That would be just like unzipping their fly in Time Square; for a fleeting moment they would be exposed. Everything he'd been taught told Drake that it wasn't enough exposure to allow a SAM operator to shoot him down, but it was still exposure.

"Three...two...one...weapons away," Drake said, unconsciously holding his breath when the doors swung open. He watched his weapons screen as the rotary launchers moved each weapon into position and dropped them into the night. Then Murph began the turn toward the next target. "All four bombs show a good release,"

Drake advised. In a few seconds the SAM site would be no more, and a new hole in the Taliban's defenses would open for other strikers to follow. There was no way to distinguish the flash of their own weapons from the rest of the fireworks below; they'd just have to go on faith that all of their bombs detonated on impact. Even if a weapon failed to explode, a two thousand pound bomb passing through its target at a thousand feet per second would put that target out of commission for a while. Satisfied that he would survive, at least for another few minutes, Drake let go of his breath and inhaled deeply.

"Get on the SATCOM. Tell them that Dallas Three is down, I-45 is clear," said Murph, referring to the codes that would inform Command and Control that their SAM target was destroyed and the path was clear for the aluminum jets.

Drake did as he was commanded and then returned to his targeting display. "The five thousand pound GAMs are in position and aligned, we are forty-three miles from the target, and both DPIs are achievable," he reported. "The two bunker targets should be fairly easy. Do you think we'll catch 'you know who' sleeping?"

"I hope so," replied Murph, "but it just seems too easy. I think we'll pick off a few of their generals tonight, but something tells me it's gonna be a little more difficult to catch Bin Laden off his guard."

Drake checked the position of the bombs on his rotary launcher; picturing the big five thousand pounders suspended above the weapons bay doors. He'd walked under the bay during his pre-flight inspection, admiring the big weapons despite their odd appearance. The five thousand pound GAMs, or GPS Aided Munitions, had a unique look. The bombs had been rapidly produced by filling old M-201 Howitzer barrels with explosives, but Howitzer barrels were not designed with aerodynamic stability in mind. To compensate for this Northrop Grumman had fit the bombs with leather bras, like those found on sports cars in the eighties. The bras wrapped around the weapons and fastened in place with tension clips, making each GAM look like a Great Dane wearing a poodle's sweater.

Drake smiled, knowing that the Taliban would not find his bombs nearly as entertaining as he did. "We'll use station eight on both launchers, and then rotate to six for the next target," he told Murph.

"I hope the coordinates are as good as we think they are."

"Why can't we just use GAT to make sure?"

"First of all, bunkers aren't terribly mobile," answered Murph. "It's unlikely that the Taliban dug them up and moved them after Intelligence got their locations. Secondly, attempting to map them with the radar will only get us pictures of dirt and hills – not much use in correcting the coordinates."

"I guess you're right. Sixty seconds to the target, showing both DPIs achievable, watch the corridor," Drake cautioned.

"Don't worry," replied Murph, "in twenty seconds I'll have it lined up nice and sweet. We'll put 'em right in the basket." Murph expertly guided the big bomber into the weapons delivery corridor depicted on his screen. Even though the GAMs were GPS guided, he still had to align the jet with the target and release the weapons at the right moment. Guided or not, the GAMs were still freefall bombs; they didn't have rocket engines like missiles. If Murph didn't release them at the right angle and close enough to the target, all the GPS guidance in the world couldn't get them to the bunkers. The "basket" was the small volume of airspace into which the GAMs had to be tossed and, with their large mass and tiny flight controls, the GAMs had a really small basket.

"Ten seconds, safe and in range," said Drake, watching Murph ease the jet into the north side of the corridor, compensating for the winds. "Both DPIs are achievable...standby for release in three...two...one..." The aircraft shook as two massive bombs dropped from the launchers, changing the bomber's weight by over ten thousand pounds. "Weapon's away," continued Drake. "You're cleared for the turn; the next target is thirty seconds out."

The next target came up fast and the last two weapons were on their way to the second bunker before the first two were even halfway to the surface. Even as the last weapon fell from the bay, there were still thirty seconds to wait before the first impacts. Murph and Drake had left the aluminum jets well behind, leaving no one else to invite another eruption of triple-A. The air was silent, at least for another few seconds.

The big bombs buried themselves deep in the earth, but still the flashes were evident. With two great explosions, the darkness beneath them erupted in light. Then, thirty seconds later, two more flashes lit the sky as the second set of GAMs found their bunker. For a moment there was peace, and darkness reclaimed northern Afghanistan. Then the night opened into the same fireworks display they'd seen at the SAM target – the hornet's nest was stirred up again. They knew the enemy had no idea what they were shooting at, or where, but that didn't change the fact that the air beneath them was filling with lead.

"The twenty minutes to the border are gonna be a little stressful," remarked Murph.

Drake gripped the dashboard with white knuckles and peered into the night. "That's an understatement."

Chapter 13

Crash stepped off the stairs of a C-21 Learjet onto the tarmac in front of the Base Operations building at Wright Patterson Air Force Base. He wore his standard blue uniform and carried with him a thick, blue canvas satchel. A short, dark haired man met him halfway between the building and the jet and offered a hand in welcome. "Daniel, it's good to see you again," he said. Scott had never been good with using nicknames. He wasn't much older than Crash, but his academic nature led him to use formal language in any setting.

"Only my mother calls me Daniel, Scott," Crash replied, "and even then she only uses it when I'm in trouble. Call me Crash, or at least Dan."

Scott shrugged and rolled his eyes; they nearly disappeared in the sunken sockets on his pale, gaunt face. "OK...Dan...what's going on?"

"I'll have to explain when we get to your office."

Scott shrugged again and turned toward the Base Operations building without another word. He was a not a large man in any physical sense, but he was a genius, pure and simple.

As a young man, Scott had not done well in high school, mostly because he found the curriculum very boring but partly because he was incredibly absent minded and never turned in his homework. With no money and no scholarship offers, he'd enlisted in the United States Air Force after graduation. There he struggled through the physical challenges of boot camp, but he excelled at everything else. His testing scores were well above those of his peers and before he knew it, Scott was spirited back to Ohio for a bachelor's program in Aerodynamic Engineering with the Air Force Institute of Technology. Upon graduation he was commissioned as an officer and placed as an engineer in the budding field known as Low Observable Technology, the technical name for stealth.

The next few years included short excursions into the operational Air Force that always ended in a return to AFIT for another degree. In the end, Scott earned two Master's Degrees, one in Aerodynamics and the other in Electrical Engineering, and a Special Doctorate in Low Observable Engineering and Design. By the time he finished the doctorate program, at the rank of major, the Air Force had no real position that suited him. Instead, they offered him an early retirement, contingent upon an additional seven years of work as a DoD civilian in the stealth field. He spent a couple of years at Holloman, dividing his time between the Stealth Fighters and the B-2 at Whiteman, and finally returned to Wright Patterson, where he led a covert think tank. Scott had never been married; in fact he'd hardly even dated. To him women defied all logic and were therefore not worth the pain and effort.

After a long walk with very little small talk, Crash and Scott stood at the end of a hallway in front of a thick steel door protected by a biometric lock and a numeric keypad.

"You'll have to wait outside while I clear the office and sign you in," said Scott.

"No, I won't," smiled Crash as he placed his thumb on the scanner and typed in a code. The door clicked open without complaint and Scott gaped at Crash in shock. Crash brushed the look aside and entered the office. "You'll find that you too have more access than you did yesterday. Colonel Walker's phone calls can literally open doors."

In light of the drama of gaining entrance, Scott's office was disappointingly small. Crash half expected the door to open into a massive hangar filled with super-secret aircraft and weaponry, guarded by black masked ninjas. Instead, they entered a very short hallway with only seven small rooms, three on each side and one at the end. The walls, the carpet, the desks, and the chairs were varying shades of gray. The only other color in the office was beige – beige shelves, beige computers, beige printers, and so on. "This is an interior designer's worst nightmare," said Crash. "Then again, I doubt if there are any interior designers with clearance enough to set foot in this place."

Scott simply shook his head.

As Crash chuckled, he stepped backward and nearly knocked over a coffee maker that was sitting on top of a short beige filing cabinet.

"Don't tell anybody about that," said Scott, as Crash steadied the coffee maker. "It's a fire hazard and they'll take it away from us if the ground safety guys find out."

"Why Scotty old boy," said Crash with a sly grin, "as I recall, it's not like you to flagrantly violate a regulation."

Scott's eyes narrowed, "The other guys won't let me get rid of it," he replied, "and please don't call me Scotty." He motioned Crash into one of the small rooms. "In here."

"I've never seen a door like that," said Crash, "It looks like it's made of composites."

"It is," said Scott, shutting the door behind them. "Each room in this office is sound proof; the doors are filled with special foam. No one outside this room can hear us, even if they're standing right next to the door. Now, what is this great secret that brings you into my domain?"

"First there's some paperwork I need you to sign." With that formality, out of the way Crash tucked the papers into his blue canvas satchel and smiled at Scott. "Welcome to Cerberus," he began, and then he explained everything – the objective of the program, the failed missions, and the reason he'd come to Wright Patterson. "We need Dreamcatcher. The circle of stealth isn't complete without reconnaissance."

Scott took a moment to absorb it all and then, without a word, he opened a small safe, pulled out a CD, and inserted it into his computer.

Twenty minutes later Crash had yet to utter another word.

Dreamcatcher wasn't just a concept; it was a completed design. There were scaled schematics surrounded by equations that he couldn't hope to understand. There were pages of detailed explanations of each system, including avionics, propulsion, structures, skin, and more. There was even a diagram of what appeared to be the weapons bay of a B-2, containing some sort of rack instead of bombs. Scott broke the silence but Crash was too busy staring in wonderment at the screen to process the words. "I'm sorry, what did you say?" he asked, regaining his sense of speech.

"Help," repeated Scott. "I'm going to need some help. As much as I'd like to take the credit, I didn't do all of this myself. Dreamcatcher falls under a generic stealth reconnaissance program known as Specter Blue. While it is certainly the most mature project we have, it's not the only one. There are twelve of us working on different aspects of the Dreamcatcher concept alone, and that's only the 'paper airplane'; we'll need a real live manufacturer to put this thing together."

"I know Scott," Crash reassured him, "and I'm told we'll get all the support we need. You're going to be the project director because it's your brainchild. We need to determine the initial core group of experts, indoctrinate them, and develop a timeline that I can take back to the Pentagon. This is going to move fast; Dreamcatcher won't remain a paper airplane for long."

Crash and Scott wasted no time in getting to work. First they put together a list of names for the project's core team and then funneled those names through Colonel Walker to the NSA, where they'd be processed for access to Cerberus. After submitting the names, they spent the rest of the day trying to determine a schedule for the week. The group needed to determine the phases for the project from initial coordination to final flight-testing, including some milestones to monitor the project's progress. That would enable them to generate a rough timeline and give the Pentagon an idea of the time and money constraints. Then there was the problem of contracting a manufacturer. Neither Crash nor Scott had any clue as to how they would do that, but Crash was sure there would have to be a covert bidding process. They finally decided that they would have to bring in someone from acquisitions to figure it out, and they could leave that up to Colonel Walker.

By early afternoon the core group sat around a table in Specter Blue's tiny conference room, already deep into their first planning session. Crash was getting claustrophobic; the conference table took up the whole room and there were thirteen people packed around it like sardines. Scott sat at the head, typing away at a keyboard and watching a computer monitor embedded in the table underneath a glass panel. A ceiling mounted projector replicated everything that he typed onto a big white screen.

"No, no, that's not right," said a blond woman halfway down the table. She was in her early thirties but the men would have guessed that she was younger. "It's going to take at least three more weeks to get the kinks out of that engine design, and that doesn't even account for testing the fire proof foam between it and the long range transmitters." The woman was sitting directly across from Crash. He noted that she was attractive in her own right and might even be striking if she made an attempt to fix her hair and put on some make-up, but clearly such things did not concern her.

"Look Amanda, I understand your concerns," pressed Scott, "but we're going to have to stretch our limits on this one. POTUS wants it done yesterday, not in three years."

A two-time graduate from MIT, with Master's degrees in Mechanical Engineering and Thermodynamics, Amanda Navistrova was the lead engineer for Dreamcatcher's propulsion systems. She'd never bothered to get a doctorate in her field, but her breadth of experience more than covered for any lack in paper credibility. Like Scott, Amanda was a civilian working directly for the Air Force in a GS position. Two light-haired men sat on either side of her, both dressed in khakis and short sleeved plaid shirts. Their names were

Jeremy and Ethan and they comprised Amanda's core propulsion team. Earlier, Scott had confided to Crash that he could never remember which of them was which, but he'd long since decided that they were mutes anyway; Amanda always did the talking while they feverishly took notes.

Suddenly one of them broke the mold. "What if we scrapped the long range transmitters altogether?" he asked, looking up from his notes.

"I'm sorry Jeremy, what was that?" Scott asked, looking surprised to hear one of the "propulsion twins" speak.

"I'm Ethan. We've been working together for a year now."

"Right...of course. Sorry Ethan. What was that you said?"

"We could run Dreamcatcher from the host bird," Ethan rephrased his idea. "As long as we're suddenly getting serious about making this thing real, we might as well explore some shortcuts. If we flew the thing from a localized station we could get rid of a lot of the bulky long range gear. We could also drop the entire satellite network plan, eliminating the need for all that coordination."

"What about the time and cost of putting the station in the B-2?" Crash asked.

"The B-2 was originally designed for three people anyway; it was supposed to have a navigator behind the two pilots. All of the third station wiring is still there; it's just covered by panels. Terry worked for Northrup Grumman in those days. It could be done, right Terry?"

The man to Crash's left slowly nodded his head. "Yeah, it could be done. The foundation is already there, and Ethan's right, a localized control station would save us time and cash."

Scott looked at the faces at the table. There seemed to be no disagreement. "Alright everybody, I want the preliminary redesigns in to me by Thursday."

Chapter 14

"Devil Zero One your next target is one and a half units north of the long rectangular orchard. It's a pair of tanks."

"Copy Grunge, Devil One is tally," said Victor, responding to the Ground Forward Air Controller. He kept his Hog just high enough to see over a short rise with his binoculars. "I have two tanks moving north across a brown field."

"Correct, Devil, that's your target."

"Two, how're we doing?"

"Two's tally," replied Bug. "They're easy pickins for some mavericks."

"We've got the target Grunge," said Victor, "We can have weapons on it in two mikes."

"Continue," called Grunge, "and call when you're on final with weapons hot."

"Devil Two take the western tank, I've got the other one," commanded Victor. "Attack will be Strike Pattern Two, mavericks."

Victor pointed his A-10 in the direction of the tanks. He would keep this heading to within a half mile, then vector away so that he could pop up and roll in on the eastern tank. Bug would follow with enough spacing to cover his back, ready to volley bullets at any surprise threats. Then, when Victor was clear, he would roll in to take out the other tank.

It took no time at all for Victor's A-10 to cover the distance to his roll-in point. He pulled the nose of the aircraft up, looking left to find his target, and then rolled to point directly at the tank.

"Devil Zero One, final, hot," he called over the radio.

"Grunge is visual, cleared hot."

Victor fired off his maverick and Bug rolled in behind. "Devil Zero Two, final, hot."

"Devil Two cleared hot."

Bug finished off the other tank, and the two A-10s turned back to their hold point.

"Two, say status," queried Victor.

"Devil Two, good release, solid lock."

Victor switched his radio transmitter to the other frequency. "Spiderman, this is Devil. We confirm two good releases against two tanks rolling north from bullseye two six zero at fifty-four."

"Devil, Spidy copies," replied the German ground controller. He was simulcasting on both the Red Force and Blue Force strike frequencies. "Red Tanks Three and Four, Devil Flight confirms good releases on your position...you're dead."

Victor pulled his Hog up just enough to watch the two British Challenger tanks make their one hundred and eighty degree turn and head back the way they came.

"Devil, this is Spidy..."

"Go for Devil."

"Red Three says you'd better be right or you're going to owe him some Guinness."

"Copy Spiderman," Victor took the challenge, "you can tell him I'll have the tapes waiting so he can see what his tank looked like just before I blew it up." He let down his oxygen mask, revealing a broad smile. He and Bug had just completed their first successful mission of Clean Hunter 2001, a massive NATO exercise.

For the first time in several weeks, Victor felt free of the accident. The investigation into Collins' death seemed deep in his past. It had taken more than two weeks, but just as Soda had predicted, the board had found no fault in the surviving pilots' actions. They attributed the accident to Collins' loss of situational awareness and left it at that, restoring the others to flight status with the cleansing strike of a gavel.

Slowly Victor had put the episode behind him, knowing that dwelling on it would only keep the pain at the surface, but Oso was having trouble moving on. In their first couple of training missions back on the flight line Victor had noticed his boss hesitating to make decisions; he was slow to commit his flight to any strikes more complex than a basic straight-in attack. Victor was relieved when Soda had separated him from Oso's four-ship, allowing him to lead his own two-ship as Devil Zero One in this historic exercise.

A year before, Clean Hunter 2000 had been the largest NATO air combat exercise in history. There were more sorties flown over Europe on each day than any day of Allied Force; in fact, not since World War II had the skies over Europe been so crowded with military aircraft. Despite initial misgivings about the dangers of such crowded skies, the exercise turned out to be a valuable training tool. What's more, it was a raging political success, so the NATO commanders made it an annual event. After September 11th 2001, the European generals weren't about to let some two-bit terrorists rain on their new parade and Clean Hunter continued as planned. While CENTCOM aircraft bombarded Afghanistan in real conflict, USAFE aircraft played war over Europe.

Victor and Bug launched earlier that day on a two-ship Close Air Support mission as part of the exercise. They'd been tasked, along with a flight of F-16's, to stop a column of Red Force tanks advancing across southern Germany. The F-16's did their part, dropping simulated cluster bombs on a few of the tanks, but they'd quickly reached bingo fuel and left for home. Devil Flight had cleaned up the rest with ease, and still had weapons and fuel to spare.

Victor needed this victory. He and Bug were paired for the duration of the exercise as Devil Flight, and Devil Flight had suffered a major setback earlier in the week. They were supposed to strike a railway target south of Frankfurt, but they were counting on a flight of Turkish F-18's to "sweep" for enemy fighters in their path. The sweepers were supposed to kill any Red Air that could oppose the Hogs, and that should have made Devil's route to the railway depot a cakewalk. Unfortunately, the Turks were late to the fight, and they neglected to inform anyone of their tardiness. Victor, hearing no report of enemy fighters from AWACS, pressed towards the target right on time, assuming that the Turks were a no show and that Red Air was busy somewhere else. Instead, the F-18's showed up at his six o'clock. Finding targets on their radar screens, and knowing that they were behind schedule, the Turks fired their simulated missiles without waiting for confirmation that the targets were hostile. Victor and Bug were caught unaware and were shot in the back by their would-be defenders. Shortly after that, Red Air showed up in the form of four French Mirages and shot the Turks down; at least there was a little justice in the world. Today's victory would cancel out Devil's previous misfortune and they could now return to the squadron with their self-respect intact.

"Devil this is Grunge Three One, I have something else for you," the FAC reported.

"Copy Grunge, go ahead for Devil."

"If you have the fuel and weapons, there is another target that requires your attention."

Victor looked at a grease pencil diagram he'd drawn on his canopy. Bug still had three Mark 82s, two mavericks, and a full load of 30 mm bullets, and he had the same. Then he signaled Bug in close and gave him a visual sign to check his fuel. Bug confirmed what Victor suspected – they had plenty of gas for a little more fun.

"Grunge, Devil Zero One, we have forty minutes of playtime remaining with a variety of weapons. What'd you have in mind?"

"I've been told to send you to an airfield at bullseye two three zero for sixty miles. It's protected by a SAM system, but there will be a flight of Wild Weasels and another pair of Hogs there to help. Switch to frequency four and talk to Raven. They'll put you in touch with Blade and Wizard.

"WILCO," responded Victor. He checked his map. The new target was thirty miles to his south, across the French border. He gave Bug a wing flash and they turned for the designated border crossing. The crossing was twenty miles out of his way, but he couldn't just take a pair of war planes willy-nilly across an international border. Victor chuckled to himself. "We could always try it," he thought, "maybe if we pretend to be Germans they'll just surrender."

"Devil Flight, push TAD four." Victor said, switching his radio frequency. "Devil check."

"Two."

"Raven, this is Devil checking in for target coordinates and picture south."

"Devil, this is Raven. The target coordinates are north four nine…zero three…decimal three six one, east zero zero seven…two five…decimal four one three. Red Air in this area has been neutralized. There is an active SAM located in the northwest corner of the target area. Its callsign for kill-removal is Red SAM Eight. Take out the SAM and then destroy any aircraft and ordinance you find on the airfield. Contact Wizard on this frequency."

Victor frowned; something was missing. "Raven, this is Devil. What about Blade? Is he on freq as well?"

"Negative. Blade never launched, due to a maintenance malfunction. Sorry Devil, no Wild Weasels today."

Victor's grip on the control stick tightened so much that his knuckles whitened beneath his green Nomex gloves. He did not relish confronting the SAM without Blade; the Wild Weasels would have made this attack a whole lot easier. They were special F-16 "CJs", whose express purpose was taking out SAM sites. They could hover near the limits of the SAM system and target it with radar homing missiles called HARMs. The A-10s had tactics like the Irish Cross that they could use to confront the SAM, but the Hogs weren't really designed for that kind of work. His chances of walking into the squadron bar later with his head held high had just taken a major hit.

"Devil Zero One, Wizard, how copy?" Oso's familiar voice came over the radio.

"Devil has you loud and clear," Victor replied, and then remained silent. He waited out of deference for Oso's position, allowing him the opportunity to take command of the four Hogs that were now on the scene.

"Wizard has on scene command," Oso took the cue. "Devil, assume a holding pattern six miles south of the target. I'll take the north."

"Devil, WILCO." Victor signaled Bug to follow him into a holding pattern. He reported his flight's weapons and fuel to Oso so that his boss would know what resources were at his disposal. Then he pulled out his map and drew a circle around the target airfield. He studied the area; there was not much terrain cover here. They'd have to contend with that SAM first, or they'd get picked off trying to attack the rest of the target. Victor knew there was only one attack that would work, but he had to wait and see what Oso would suggest. Unfortunately Oso wasn't suggesting much.

The four Hogs continued to orbit for another few minutes, burning holes in the sky and burning precious fuel. Victor started to worry. If Oso didn't get things moving, they'd run out of gas and have to go home, abandoning the target...a French target...and that would be a serious *faux pas*. Finally he couldn't take it anymore. "Wizard, Devil One."

"Go ahead, Devil."

"I suggest we use an Irish Cross with mavericks and bombs. I think it's the only way."

"Negative, Devil," Oso replied. "Save your weapons, I'll take care of this myself. After that we'll split up the airfield."

Victor couldn't believe it. "Are you insane?!" he wanted to ask. Going *mono e mono* with a SAM was suicide for an A-10.

"Devil flight, continue to hold. Wizard flight, Strike Pattern One, decoy, maverick. Sound off when you're ready," Oso commanded his wingman, whose tactical name was Shooter.

"Wizard Two's ready," responded Shooter. It was obvious from his tone of voice that Shooter did not like his flight lead's plan, and he certainly did not like being assigned the task of "decoy" within range of an active SAM.

"Wizards execute...now." Oso turned his A-10 toward the target area and Shooter followed. When they were on the edge of the SAM's range he split north, allowing Shooter to press in a little farther and then turn away. Victor watched from miles away with his binoculars, straining to see what was happening. At first it appeared as though it might work, with the SAM turning toward the decoy, but Shooter could only get so close before he had to turn away. Oso didn't have the time to build up his angle and when he pulled up and tried to point his maverick at the target, the SAM was already turning back. A white trail of smoke shot straight up from the SAM site. Victor shook his head; the Frenchmen on the ground had fired off a rocket called a Smoky SAM, a visual cue that the SAM was simulating a launch. Shooter saw the Smoky SAM as well and rolled back in to attack the system with his gun, hoping to deny a second shot.

A French voice calmly invaded their radio frequency, "In range kill on northern A-10...Confirmed." The SAM operator hadn't needed a second shot.

Victor then gaped at the other A-10 as Shooter continued toward the SAM. Apparently he'd decided it was too late to retreat and thrown caution to the wind. Before Victor could warn him off, the young wingman was well within the SAM's range, "Wizard Two, guns, guns, guns, on Red SAM Eight."

The SAM operator was ready for him. He'd already turned his missiles to greet the second attacker and, as he made his radio call, another Smoky SAM shot skyward. "In range kill on eastern A-10...Confirmed," the French voice practically taunted them over the radio.

"Wizard Flight, this is Spiderman, you're both dead. Return to base."

"Holy mackerel, that was fast," Victor said out loud. Oso's two Hogs were eliminated in a matter of seconds. It was like watching someone throw a hundred bucks down on the roulette table in Vegas – in a flash the money was gone and so was their self-respect. "Devil Two, I guess it's up to us," he reluctantly told Bug. "This attack will be a Two Ship Pincer, your gun, my maverick. Try to build all the angles you can. Drive seven miles to the south and call ready."

Bug reluctantly did as he was commanded. "We're both going to die you know."

"I know, but so will he."

"Roger that, Devil Two is ready."

"Devil Flight, turn inbound on my mark. Three...two...one...mark!"

Bug turned toward the SAM, angling his jet slightly away before rolling in. "Guns, guns, guns on Red SAM Eight," he said without enthusiasm.

Victor could see the missiles turning on their pivots to point in his wingman's direction. "Just a little further, Bug" he said under his breath. When the SAM appeared committed toward Bug, Victor rolled in. He felt a flicker of hope as he watched Bug pull hard right in an effort to get out of range, but then he saw the familiar white smoke trail.

"In range kill on the southern A-10...Confirmed," the French voice was cool and calm. The SAM swung back the other way, searching for Victor's A-10.

"Maverick away on Red SAM Eight, in range, solid lock," Victor spat into the radio.

Another Smoky SAM shot up. "In range launch on northeastern A-10," the Frenchman spat back. The imaginary projectiles passed each other in the air. "Kill...Confirmed."

Spiderman released his final verdicts, "Devil One and Two, this is Spidy, you're both dead...break, break, Red SAM Eight you're dead too."

"Devil Two, this is One, I'm five miles to your south, turn toward the exit, let's return to base," Victor tried to keep his radio calls cold and emotionless. He didn't want to sound unprofessional in front of the French. The Frogs had clearly won this battle with a score of four to one and that was more than a little embarrassing for the American

A-10 pilots. There'd be a severe brow beating waiting for them when they got back. As he crossed the border into Germany, Victor's suppressed anger simmered to the surface and he hammered the canopy with his fist. This was all Oso's fault.

Chapter 15

Crash and Scott arrived at the Pentagon in the mid-morning and headed straight for Walker's office. The two walked side by side with a brisk, nervous gait.

"I hope he's at his desk," said Scott, "I'd like to get this over with."

"He'll be there. If Colonel Walker is anything, he's predictable. He arrives at the fitness center every morning at precisely zero five hundred hours. After an hour of sculpting his girlish figure, he hits the showers and then eats breakfast at the cafeteria. By zero seven thirty he's riveted to his desk. He'll stay there, barking orders via email, until eleven thirty when he heads back to the cafeteria for lunch. We've got at least an hour and a haahgg…" Crash stumbled forward, having caught his toe on what he would later claim was the only piece of loose carpeting in the entire Pentagon. He fell to the floor face first, his head just missing a white painted windowpane on the right side of the hallway. The black hardened case he carried slipped from his sweaty palm and bounced down the hallway, sliding to a stop several feet away.

Scott ran forward and picked up the case, turning it over to inspect it. "That was close."

"Yeah, I nearly knocked myself unconscious there."

"Hmm? Oh, yeah, but I mean the case," Scott held it out for Crash to see, "look, it's still sealed."

"Right, great, good for the case," replied Crash, picking himself up and straightening his uniform.

"Hey, you don't want these papers spilling out all over the hallway do you?" Scott held the case close, as if he felt it was much safer in his hands than in Crash's. "This timeline is probably the most classified thing you've ever carried."

"You know," said Crash, ignoring Scott's subtle verbal jab,

"having concern, or even feigning concern, for your fellow man might make you seem more human."

"Say again?"

"Nothing." Despite the crack about Scott being inhuman, Crash knew he was right. If that case had popped open in the hallway, in front of all those windows, there'd be a huge pile of paperwork to fill out.

A few minutes later they were standing in the Colonel's office. Walker was not pleased. "One year?! Are you out of your mind?! I can't send these numbers up the chain. They'll laugh me back to Fort Benning." He was clutching their proposal for the Dreamcatcher timeline and several veins were popping out of his forehead.

"Sir, you have to understand, we're talking about building a completely new piece of hardware, in addition to making a major modification to the B-2 weapons bay. We haven't even bid out the contract for manufacture yet." Crash had the urge to press one particular vein back into the Army officer's forehead, but he resisted.

"Contract?! Bid?! Did you two fall off the tomato truck yesterday? This is a matter of national security, a program created under the umbrella of Executive Authority. Did you really think we always follow those ridiculous acquisitions regs? Northrop Grumman will build Dreamcatcher; I've already set the wheels in motion. What Boeing and Lockheed don't know won't kill them."

Crash and Scott exchanged a wary look. "Sir the contractors on my team work for several different companies," cautioned Scott. "We're talking Raytheon and BAE in addition to Boeing and Lockheed."

"Look," the Colonel changed his tone to that of a father teaching his son the family business. "I'll chalk up your mistakes to inexperience. Every one of your people signed their life away to me on keeping this secret, so not one of them is going to go crying home to their parent company. They'll do the job, their companies will get paid for their time under non-descript headings, and if they ever spill the beans we'll string 'em up by their thumbs."

Scott shrugged in submission. "Alright sir, that cuts a month off the list right there."

"Not enough. I need this thing ready for testing no later than next September, preferably August. Find me some more time to cut."

"Sir, Scott and I will have to return to Wright Patterson and confer with the team. We'll try to cut back the schedule, but it may take a couple of days."

"Denied."

Crash and Scott exchanged a look of shock and helplessness.

"It's not a matter of *try*, Major Warren. You *will* make the cuts and you *will* get the revised schedule to me by eleven hundred hours tomorrow, because at noon you're meeting with Martin Baker from Northrop Grumman to discuss the integration of his team."

Both men knew there was only one response to this totally unreasonable command. "Yes sir," they said in unison.

Very early the next morning Crash and Scott sat in a secure room and stared at each other over a pile of papers. They'd been there through the night and still hadn't trimmed the timeline enough. "Look *Scotty*," Crash had run out of patience, "I'm telling you that we have to kill this 'X-Factor' padding or we'll never be able to meet Colonel Walker's requirements."

"And I'm telling you, *Daniel*, that if you eliminate the pads, something unexpected will crop up and we'll just end up delivering behind schedule anyway!"

"Do you really need an extra two weeks for the propulsion integration phase?"

"No, I might need an extra four days for that, but I'll need the other ten to cover delays in other areas. A few big pads mean I don't have to add days to every phase. I can't predict where I'm going to be ahead of schedule and where I'm going to be behind. You can't build an advanced technology aircraft from scratch in this short of a time period."

Crash felt the tension ramping up to the point that nothing would be accomplished. He had to do something to bring peace back to the negotiations. "Look," he said, "we both obviously need some coffee. Let's take a break and get out of here."

Crash led Scott through the labyrinth of hallways and stairwells until they emerged on Rotary Road, on the south side of the Pentagon. He headed for the only place where he knew they could find good coffee at four o'clock in the morning. At 12th and Hayes he found his target. The lights at Charla's were just flickering on as they approached the storefront, backlighting the large image on the window glass of a Franciscan monk holding a steaming mug of coffee. A short woman with salt and pepper hair, a kind face, and striking blue eyes opened the door for them. "You boys are up pretty early," she observed with the tone of a soccer mom about to offer her team some Gatorade.

"We never went to bed," Crash admitted.

"I see. We'd better make it two double espressos then," she said. She turned and signaled to a teenager behind the counter who looked like he could use some coffee of his own.

"You read my mind," replied Crash.

The two bleary eyed men sat on stools at a small round table and sipped at their coffee, unable to discuss their classified work and unwilling to engage in small talk.

After a few sips the cobwebs began to fade and Scott started looking back and forth between the Franciscan monk and the cup in his hand. "What's up with 'GC'?" he asked, pointing at the logo on his cup. "It doesn't match the monk or Charla."

Crash shrugged. "This place used to be Gourmet Creations, but Charla bought it when they went out of business. She must be using the stuff that was left on the shelf until her own cups come in. It probably saves her some cash."

Scott accepted Crash's explanation and raised his cup for another sip, but he stopped before it reached his lips. He looked at Crash with a face full of renewed vigor, like a runner who's just gotten his second wind. "Hurry up and finish your coffee," he said, "I've got an idea."

By the time they got back to their planning room Crash was in a foul mood. He hated being rushed, especially when he was already tired and irritable, and Scott had pushed and prodded him all the way through his cup of coffee. After that, Scott had walked at such a brisk pace back to the office that Crash practically had to jog to keep up. Now he was sweaty on top of being tired and cranky, and no one should be sweaty in Washington DC in winter at a quarter to five in the morning, it just wasn't right.

"Fine, we're back, what's your big idea?"

"What did you say about the GC cups?"

Crash wasn't in the mood for games. "I said she was using cups that were already there when she bought the store," he replied, wondering if this room was sound proof enough to mask Scott's screams when he killed him.

"No, you said she was using stuff that was *left on the shelf.*"

Crash was unimpressed. Obviously Scott wanted him to make some sort of connection, but he was too tired and annoyed to even try.

"*Off the shelf,*" said Scott. "It's an acquisitions concept that speeds the development of new systems. Do you think the B-2 is all new technology? No, we stole the fly-by-wire system out of an F-16 and the navigation system out of a B-1. We even used modified F-16 engines. A very large percentage of that aircraft is off the shelf technology. We can do the same thing with Dreamcatcher."

Crash let the annoyed expression fall from his face; he was beginning to catch on. "You mean we could cut back development time by integrating old technology with new parts? It would be like building Frankenstein's stealth jet."

"Exactly! For example, we don't have to completely build a new engine; we just have to find one that's already in use somewhere in the Department of Defense that meets our specs, say...the engine used in the Global Hawk. Then we purchase a couple of extras for that program, only they don't go to the Hawk, they go to Wright Patterson for 'developmental use.' Each system in the aircraft has a myriad of subsystems, all of which will take loads of time to develop and prove, but if we can integrate existing technology that already has the kinks worked out; we can save a boatload of time and money."

Crash considered the plan. It might actually be the solution they needed. Of course, they'd have to negotiate with Walker for another week to sort out the details before they could produce a new timeline, but he should acquiesce, given the potential savings in dollars and time. "I like it," Crash said finally. "And the best thing is: now we can go home and get some sleep!"

Chapter 16

Victor had always hated the gym in winter. Everything was colder, and because of that, it all seemed harder – the heavy bag, the mat, even the other guys' knuckles. He rubbed his hands together and tried to make his way from the locker room to the auxiliary gym without letting his feet make contact with the tile floor. He was glad when he finally made the transition from tile to mat, where the surface seemed at least ten degrees warmer. Following tradition, Victor made a short bow while standing in the doorway and then quickly made his way to the other side of the room, where he found Oso warming up. For a while the two of them stood quietly against the back wall of the auxiliary gymnasium, working through their pre-class stretches.

After the mission Oso's Wizard flight had returned to the base several minutes ahead of Devil, and by the time Victor landed they were gone. Oso's rapid departure from the squadron made him uncomfortable. Even though Wizard and Devil were separate flights with separate missions, they'd ended the day working together at the same target, and that was normally cause for a joint debrief. It wasn't like Oso to blow off procedure.

"I guess you had a pretty short debrief with Shooter," said Victor, trying to open the conversation with the indirect approach. "By the time I got back you were already gone."

"Yeah," Oso barely acknowledged the statement and continued his stretching. His mind was somewhere else.

Victor noted Oso's detached look and decided to cease his interrogation for a while. He slipped back into a habitual rhythm of silent stretches, attempting to limber up in the cold air. Soon, however, the lack of conversation became awkward, and Victor was never good at awkward silences. "Are you okay?" he asked, knowing that nothing good could come from this conversation.

Oso was stretching his neck muscles and had turned his face away. When he turned back, his face held a calm but melancholy look of resignation. He locked eyes with Victor. "We're screwed," he said.

"Whaddaya mean we're screwed?" Victor felt a surge of anger rising to the surface.

"I mean the commander's really ticked about what happened today, didn't you get the message?"

"No, I didn't check my email after the flight. I was too busy looking for my Weapons Officer, but he bugged out without a debrief." A subconscious flag told Victor he was letting the conversation get out of control, but he chose to ignore it.

"We're to report in at the commander's office at zero seven hundred tomorrow morning."

"Great," said Victor dryly, "thanks for telling me now. You could've at least let me get a decent night's sleep and told me in the morning."

"Nah, I wanted you to suffer with me. Misery loves company, you know."

"I don't need any misery. You're miserable enough for all of us."

"Whatever, man," Oso turned immediately cold.

At the front of the room, the coach stood up and clapped his hands a few times. "Alright everybody, let's line up and get ready for the first drill."

The other students paired up and Victor and Oso became unwilling training partners for the rest of the evening, making Victor's final comment an even bigger mistake. The very first drill was torso conditioning, something Victor despised. Two fighters would stand side by side with their hands placed on the back of their heads and then trade round-house kicks to the gut in an attempt to strengthen their physiological core. As if that wasn't enough abuse, the coach always followed with leg conditioning, for which the fighters stood face to face and traded kicks to each other's thighs.

Most of the time Victor could depend on Oso to use about half his power; not wanting to cause real damage or accidentally break a rib; but today the first kick to his gut confirmed that Oso was carrying a lot of pent up aggression. Victor responded in kind and received an even stronger kick in return. "I'm really gonna feel this in the morning," he thought.

After the conditioning drills, the coach spent a little time on some new techniques, and then dedicated the rest of the evening to sparring. Victor and Oso remained paired, both trying to mask the pain from the conditioning drills. They were used to sparring each other, but never in the midst of an argument.

The two pilots limped to a corner of the room and squared off. The only protective gear they wore were cups and mouth guards; other pads might get in the way of a takedown or grappling on the mat.

"So, what made you wuss out today?" Victor asked. He had decided that as long as they were going to have an argument, he might as well go all out.

"What's that supposed to mean?" Oso landed a punishing kick on Victor's thigh and then threw a jab at his chest that sent him retreating backward.

"I mean the Irish Cross. We could've taken out that SAM without losing anybody," Victor feigned a straight kick then stepped in with a hooking punch, lightly popping Oso across the jaw. "Don't forget to keep your hands up, boss," he said with a taunting smile. The distraction of the conversation was working to his favor.

"Very funny, *Junior*," Oso replied, throwing a jab at Victor's nose. "It just didn't look good. Bug and Shooter weren't ready."

"The wingmen?" Victor circled left, looking for an opening. "Those two are plenty capable of handling that attack. Besides," he blocked Oso's right cross, "all they had to do was fly around and not get shot. Your two-ship attack was doomed from the beginning, and you left me holding the bag." The last word came out as a grunt as Victor shot in with another right hook. This time Oso deflected the punch, but it was all the distraction that Victor needed. With his deflected right hand he grabbed the cloth of Oso's gi. He stepped in, placing his left foot just past Oso's right, and grabbed Oso's upper sleeve with his other hand. Then he shot his right foot past Oso's right leg and came back under him with tremendous force. The sweep caught both of Oso's legs and the older pilot sailed toward the mat, landing hard on his back. Victor took a step back to admire his work, motioning to Oso. "Get up. Let's try that one again. Or maybe you've lost your nerve on the mat too."

His last statement hung in the cold air and Victor suddenly realized that he'd gone too far. The other students sensed the tension and stopped sparring to watch, gathering in a circle around the two pilots. All pretense of civility was gone. Oso pressed forward and began landing punches and kicks with heavy force. The blows came so fast that it took every ounce of Victor's knowledge to fend them off. He made several attempts to return fire, slowing the onslaught with a couple of well-placed shots of his own, but it only delayed the inevitable. Before he knew it, Oso was inside his defenses and had a solid hold of his gi. Victor knew what was coming but Oso was moving too fast; he couldn't do anything but brace for the impact. Oso simultaneously twisted around and bent his knees, shifting his center of gravity below Victor's hipline. Then he pulled the younger man's chest close to his shoulder and exploded upward, taking all of Victor with him.

Victor felt his feet leave terra firma and watched the gym spin in front of him. It was a full shoulder throw, the one that puts as much air between the victim and the ground as any throw in Jiu Jitsu. The impact felt like someone had taken a sledgehammer to his body, knocking every bit of wind from his lungs. When he could finally speak again, the words trickled from his throat, his voice like that of a dying man. "It wasn't your fault."

Oso bent over Victor and grabbed the lapels of his gi. He pulled the younger pilot's shoulders off the mat so that their noses were just inches apart. "Tell that to Brent," he spat. Their eyes locked for another moment and then Oso shoved Victor back onto the mat and walked out of the gym.

Chapter 17

At seven o'clock sharp Oso and Victor stood in front of Soda's desk, expecting the worst. They felt like school children waiting to talk to the principal and the commander knew it; he let them stand there at attention for a full two minutes before he even acknowledged their presence. Finally he looked up from the papers on his desk.

"Do you know what this is?" asked Soda, holding up one of the papers.

"No sir," Oso answered for both of them.

The commander interrupted his own train of thought, standing and leaning across his desk to get a closer look at the two pilots. "What happened to you two? Did you get in a bar fight or something?"

Oso and Victor looked at each other, noticing for the first time the marks from the previous night's brawl. The left side of Victor's face had a wide red blotch and Oso had a nice purple shiner under his right eye. Victor couldn't even remember connecting a punch there. They looked back at the commander.

"I slipped in the shower."

"I ran into a door."

"Uh, huh...Anyway...this is the first draft of the memo I've been asked to submit to the Wing Commander, explaining how I could loose four Hogs to a single French missile system. Would you like to help me with it?"

Oso remained silent, able to recognize a rhetorical question when he saw one, but Victor wasn't quite as savvy. "Blade, our Wild Weasel support, never showed. We had to deal with SAM alone," he said.

The commander glared at Victor, obviously annoyed at the younger pilot's inability to read the situation. "There never was a Blade Flight, Victor."

Both pilots looked surprised and Soda raised his eyebrows. "Oh, you guys really hadn't figured that out? I thought you two were smarter. The re-tasking of your two flights was a planned portion of the exercise. I earmarked you two to face that SAM three days ago, in response to a directive from the planning committee. The whole thing was a test of this squadron's ability to handle that type of mission with minimal support. They were watching this one at the NATO staff level. I put your flights against it because I thought you two could handle the challenge. You proved me wrong."

The color drained from Oso's face as the commander explained the gravity of their failure. They hadn't just lost a few points in the exercise; they'd embarrassed their whole squadron, perhaps even their whole country. In contrast, Victor's color went red with rage, the rest of his face blending with last night's welt. He wanted to point a finger at Oso and shout, "I told you so!" Instead, he held his tongue and waited to hear the consequences.

"We've been given another shot at a similar situation tomorrow, but I'm putting Trash and Psych against it," continued the commander. "Hopefully they won't pork it like you two did." He sat back in his chair as if trying to regain his calm. "I reviewed the GPS tracks and the cockpit tapes. I know everything that happened out there; so both of you can save your excuses. Oso, trying to take on that SAM with only two aircraft was just plain stupid, especially when you had another formation out there to help. Victor, I know you tried to get him to use the Irish Cross, and by the book that was the correct answer, but you gave up too easily, costing us two pilots and two jets."

Victor's anger faded and he cast his eyes at the carpet.

"And then what did you do?" Soda continued. "Knowing that Oso couldn't pull it off, you tried the same thing. You should have called it a day and gone home; instead, you cost us two more pilots and another twenty-six million dollars in assets. What on earth made you think that you could do better against that thing than a Weapons School Grad with three times the experience?"

Victor's eyes flashed up again and locked with the commander's, but this time he recognized the rhetorical question and kept his mouth shut, even though the competitor in him wanted to point out that he'd at least killed the SAM where Oso had failed.

"Sure," the commander read his mind, "you neutralized the SAM before it was over, but that was just the first step." Soda's voice rose in a crescendo. "The real objective was to take out the airfield targets and you couldn't do that because you were dead!" The commander practically shouted the last word, but then he stopped and leaned back in his chair, taking a moment to bring his voice back to a conversational tone. "The bottom line is you demonstrated poor decision making and cowboy tactics, and in a real war it would have cost lives." Soda paused, letting his words sink in. "Well, Victor, any last words?"

Victor's eyes were downcast again. "No sir," was his barely audible response.

"I'm done with you then. That was your last flight in this squadron."

Victor looked up in shock. "What?"

The commander opened a drawer in his desk and pulled out a manila envelope. He held it up for Victor to take. "In an odd twist of fortune you just became someone else's problem. These are your orders to Whiteman Air Force Base. Congratulations, you've been selected to fly the Stealth Bomber. You'll get no final flight in the A-10 though, today was it for you."

Victor was speechless. It was such an inglorious way to receive news that he thought he'd never hear. He slowly reached up and took the envelope from Soda's hand.

Soda let go and turned to look at Oso. "And you, Major. You've got a real problem son. I tried to let you fix it on your own but now I'm gonna fix it for you. I realize that you're still beating yourself up over Brent. I'd hoped that time would heal you, that a couple of weeks back in the saddle would snap you out of it, but obviously that didn't work. You backed away from the Irish Cross because somehow you thought Shooter was going to end up like Brent."

The commander sighed. "I don't know Oso, maybe you just need a few more flights and a little more time, but that's gas and time that I don't have. Nine-Eleven changed things. The world's going to hell in a hand basket and any moment we could get the call. Whether it's Afghanistan or Iran or our old friend Saddam, I need a Weapons Officer with his head on straight that can get the job done, and right now you're not him. I'm going to make some phone calls and cash in a couple of favors. Barring any surprises I'll have you shipped out of here in a month."

"Shipped where, sir?" Oso asked slowly, his face ashen with disbelief.

"If you want to mother hen the younger wingmen, I'm gonna put you somewhere that it'll do some good. I'm sending you to the Dragons, the A-10 schoolhouse in Tucson. I'm not sending you there because I think you'll be the best instructor they've ever seen, I'm sending you there to keep you out of combat until you get your head on straight. Here's my last bit of advice: you didn't kill Brent; he killed himself by letting his own incompetence get the better of him. I'm certainly not going to say that to his mom, but that's the painful truth. Brent is gone, and if you don't let him go, you'll be just one more pilot that we've lost."

The commander returned his gaze to the papers on his desk. "That's all I've got. You're both dismissed."

Victor left the commander's office and headed straight for the small squadron fitness room. He couldn't believe that he'd been grounded. Even though he'd only miss one flight, it was an important one. A pilot's last flight in an attack squadron was a big deal, a way to honor his contributions to the squadron, and being denied that flight was slap in the face. He rounded the last corner of the hallway and unzipped his flight suit down to the waist, pulling his arms from the sleeves. By the time he burst through the door of the fitness room

Victor had the sleeves of his flight suit tied securely around his midsection. He headed straight for the heavy bag. He didn't bother wrapping his knuckles. He just started pummeling the canvas bag with his fists.

As Victor let the punches fly, form and technique gave way to heat and anger. The old canvas worked like sandpaper on his unprotected knuckles and it wasn't long before small spots of blood appeared after each punch, but he ignored the pain. Victor punished the bag for his lost chance at retribution for September 11th, for his loss of face in front of the French, and for the loss of his final flight; but mostly he punished the bag because something inside him needed to bloody something up, even if it was his own hands.

When finally his arms ached, so heavy that he could no longer raise them to strike, Victor ceased his onslaught. He looked at the mess he'd made of his knuckles and wondered where this had come from. Was this his way of mourning? It shamed him to see that Oso took Brent's loss so hard while he just continued life as if nothing happened. It shamed him to realize that even now he wasn't so much mourning Brent as he was mourning his own inability to prevent a comrade's death. Part of him had been lost along with Brent in that wreckage near Boechingen. That part of him that was invincible and infallible, that part that could walk through fire unsigned, was now gone and he could feel the empty space where it had been. That part of him should have seen the accident coming a mile away, but it didn't, it evaporated when he'd needed it most and then refused to return.

Victor grabbed a towel and made a feeble attempt to wipe the blood from the canvas, but it had soaked too deep; the stain would be there forever. He gave up and walked to the restroom to clean himself up. He had been numb in his fury, but now he winced as the force of the water that rinsed the blood away also opened the wounds. Victor resisted the urge to pull his hands back, allowing himself to feel the pain, because he knew that without that pain, there would be no healing.

PART TWO

REFINEMENT

Chapter 18

Eight months after the epiphany at the coffee shop, Crash sat with Scott and the core Dreamcatcher team at the small table in the cramped conference room at Wright Patterson Air Force Base, trying not to wither under Colonel Richard Walker's dark scowl.

"General Windsor sends his apologies for being unable to attend," Walker began. "He'd love to be here, but he feels that the presence of a flag officer might draw undue attention to these proceedings. Since that leaves me to be the judge of your work, you'd better impress me. If I'm not impressed, then the general certainly won't be, got it?"

Crash turned to Scott and raised an eyebrow. "Here we go," he whispered, and then he stood and walked to the end of the table. "Right through here, Colonel," he said, indicating an open door that led into a large dark hangar. The group followed Crash through the door and onto the polished concrete floor, their footsteps echoing through the massive room. "It's over there, sir," said Crash, pointing into the darkness, his words reverberating uncomfortably off of the corrugated steel walls.

A small makeshift enclosure stood in the far corner of the hangar, constructed of steel frame walls covered with burgundy curtains. There were four large work lights attached to the upper frame of each wall, but they were not in use; instead, a pair of spotlights hanging from the hangar ceiling bathed the interior in a soft white light. A single guard, armed with the obligatory M-16 rifle, stood at the entrance. After reviewing the Colonel's ID, the young man snapped to attention, bringing his rifle to rest at his side and his right hand up in salute. "Enter at your leisure sir," he said crisply.

"Thank you sergeant," said Walker, returning the salute.

Crash wasn't sure of the ceremony necessary at a time like this, but he knew that Richard Walker was not a patient man. He chose to keep it simple. "Colonel Walker, may I present Dreamcatcher," he said, and pulled back the curtain to reveal the Colonel's prize.

An alien object, scarcely bigger than a speed boat, rested on a low pedestal at the center of the space. Its dark skin seemed to absorb light, giving no reflection from the spotlights above. The craft's profile reminded Crash of an elongated teardrop, sloping quickly upward to its thickest height and then gradually thinning until it terminated in a point at the rear. From above it looked like a traditional teardrop, with the bulb serving as the forward section of the aircraft. There was no vertical stabilizer; in fact there were no right angles at all. Graceful slopes and gentle curves shaped the entire vessel. Even the intake scoop and exhaust port conformed to the contour of the airframe, rather than rise above the profile like a traditional engine nacelle.

"So this is Dreamcatcher," said Walker.

"Actually sir," answered Scott, "the technical name for this vessel is the Low Observable Reconnaissance Aircraft, or LORA. Dreamcatcher is the name of the underlying concept, referring to the mission of capturing signals from above a target."

Colonel Walker fixed his gaze upon Scott. "LORA is boring and academic Doctor. I think General Windsor will prefer the name Dreamcatcher. In covert operations we still maintain the late Strategic Air Command's flair for the dramatic; it keeps the money flowing." He turned to the rest of the group. "What impact does the engine cavity have on signature?"

"Nil, sir," responded Amanda confidently, "we accounted for it in the original design; believe me when I say we've thought of everything."

The Colonel frowned, "Only fools believe they've thought of everything, Miss Navistrova." He continued his examination of the craft. "Now tell me why I can't see any flight control structures."

Amanda opened her mouth but no words came out. "The flight controls are under the skin, sir," answered one of the engineers, covering her stunned silence. "They cover the entire circumference of the aircraft, with twenty-one surfaces in all. The skin at the extremities is flexible and movement of the flight control structures underneath will cause the edges of the craft to ripple, much like you might see when observing a stingray at the aquarium."

"That's quite unique. What spawned that idea?"

"Actually sir," Scott replied, "the wing warping concept comes from the Wright Brothers, who used a wire and pulley system to change the shape of the wings and turn their aircraft. They stole their idea from the birds; we've simply improved on the concept. In flight, the control surfaces will ripple in a constant motion, continuously making minute corrections to improve the stability of the craft."

"Mmhmm," Walker moved toward the rear of Dreamcatcher. "Still," he said warily, "I don't trust any aircraft that has the pointy end at the rear instead of in front." He walked forward again, looking closely at the skin. "Where are the sensor windows?"

"Bob, get the lights," Crash said with a grin. A member of the group broke off and walked to the opposite side of the enclosure, flicking a switch mounted on the metal frame of the wall. The hangar went completely dark. Then Bob flicked another switch and the hum of electricity filled the air. The work lights mounted at the top of the walls blinked on and flooded the whole enclosure with a faint purple light, like black lights in a carnival fun house. The drone's skin changed from uniform black to a purple patchwork of diamonds and trapezoids.

Crash smiled, "I would have said 'abracadabra' but I thought that might be a bit much." He paused for the expected laughter, but the Colonel just looked at him impatiently.

Scott cleared his throat. "Ahem…Yes, um, as you can see, the skin appears to have a uniform texture and color to the naked eye, but it is actually a composite of several different materials that each have properties unique to their position and purpose. For instance, each individual sensor window is slightly different, engineered to allow the necessary signals, such as infrared images or radio signals, to pass through to the sensor packages inside. In addition, LORA has maintenance access panels for her more mundane systems, such as hydraulics and propulsion. These doors are made of the same material as the basic structure, but their frames – the seals if you will – are covered in a special substance that responds differently to certain wavelengths of light. Using this lighting we can easily see the panel outlines."

"That's great," said the Colonel without enthusiasm. "How do you get them open?"

Bob switched back to the spotlights. Then he walked over to a laptop sitting on a folding table and pressed a few keys. A miniature parabolic antenna, mounted on a small stand, swiveled to point at the aircraft. There was a sharp hiss and a trapezoidal panel popped open just in front of Walker, who instinctively stepped back. A fog of vapor slowly spread from the interior of the craft, revealing a tangle of wires and a panel of circuit breakers.

"Sir, Bob has just remotely activated the left forward avionics panel," said Scott. "The edges of the door and its frame are covered in similar putties. They bond when the panel is closed, forming a seamless skin and an air-tight seal. A small bottle of Freon is attached to the underside of the door. We use it to freeze the putties, causing them to separate."

"Incredible," said Walker, eliciting a smile from Crash, who realized that his team had finally been able to impress the old jerk.

The Colonel looked the craft over for a few moments, taking it all in. "When will it be ready for testing?" he asked finally.

Crash smiled again. "Dreamcatcher is ready for the proving ground now, sir."

Chapter 19

Oso banked his A-10 and looked out over the dull, cratered landscape of the East Tactical Range in Arizona. He squinted, attempting to break out the dilapidated military hardware that served as their targets. The late-morning sun afforded only scant shadows, making the half-buried vehicles even more difficult to find. "Well," he said over the radio, turning his gaze to the other A-10, circling a thousand feet below him, "you have your target, what are you waiting for?"

Without responding, the other pilot broke from his circle and dove toward the desert floor. He drew a line of white smoke across the bright blue sky as a hail of bullets exploded from his gun. A moment later the lifeless desert floor erupted in a flurry of sparks and a shower of dirt as more than a hundred steel slugs punished one of the ancient military vehicles.

Oso tried to control his frustration. "Triton, knock it off."

"Triton Two, knock it off."

"Triton Two, reform to combat trail." With the engagement suspended and the student returning to formation, Oso took a deep breath and carefully chose his rebuke. "Do you know what you did wrong?" he asked through the static of the radio.

"Negative, sir. I hit the correct target. I know I did."

"That's not all that's required, kid." Oso sighed. "State the situation," he prompted.

"Troops in Contact, no radar SAMs, the line of battle runs east to west."

"Where are the players?"

"Good guys to the north, bad guys to the south."

"Okay then, what did you do wrong?"

Silence...

"What was your attack heading?"

More silence.

Oso took another deep breath and counted to ten. "You attacked directly north to south, perpendicular to the line of scrimmage and right over the top of our imaginary good guys. If any of your bullets had fallen short you would have killed your own guys, and guess what...the high-explosive rounds mixed in with our combat loads *always* fall short. You've got to keep your attack heading parallel to the battle line. Got it?"

"Got it."

"Yeah right," thought Oso. It was late in the program for Sidearm; he shouldn't be making these kinds of errors. Oso didn't know what was worse – that the kid made such a basic mistake, or that he hadn't even known that he'd made it.

An hour later they landed back in Tucson. Oso shut his jet down, gave it a cursory post-flight, and headed for the crew bus, all the time working out the debriefing in his mind. He stepped onto the bus, ready to begin violently imparting wisdom to his student, when he was greeted by the colossal frame of Ronald Tesler, with whom he shared an office.

"Hey there, Oso."

"What's up Tank?"

"I just landed from a basic qual flight – an hour and a half of boredom followed by twenty minutes of sheer terror when goober over here entered the traffic pattern," he said, pointing with his thumb to the student next to him.

"It's early, I'm sure he'll get better," said Oso, suppressing his frustrations and smiling at the lieutenant, who was doing his best to disappear into the bench.

"Uh huh," replied Tank. "Don't let him fool ya, kid. When you reach the Surface Attack phase you'd better pray you don't draw the short straw and fly with this guy. He's flunked more students than any IP in the history of the schoolhouse. They call him the Terminator."

Oso laughed a little too loud. The joke hit close to home. It was true; some of the students actually called him the Terminator. Perhaps he didn't hold the record for handing out more "Unsafe" grades than any instructor in A-10 history, but he was probably close.

In the de-briefing room Oso brought Sidearm's mistakes to light with alarming clarity, but remembering Tank's words, he was a little more merciful on the grade-sheet. "These marks may be better than you deserve," he said, "so you'd better thank Major Tesler for putting me in an amenable mood."

Sidearm thanked Oso and left the room at the earliest possible moment. Instead of following him out and returning to his office, Oso sat back down, wondering if he should have been harder on the kid. The young pilot had struggled in the basic attack phase as well, slinging a rocket so wide that it almost flew off the range; that's why they called him Sidearm. What if he never fixed his mistakes? What if he slipped through the system and ended up like Brent? Oso shook it off and stood to leave, but Tank's broad shoulders blocked the door.

"Torch stopped by the office," said the big pilot, "he wants to talk to you."

A few minutes later Oso knocked on the door of the commander's office, steeling himself for whatever lay ahead.

"Enter." The reply was sharp and foreboding.

James "Torch" Woodruff sat at a desk cluttered with paper. He was a short man with thinning brown hair and the light structure of a marathon runner. He wore the weather worn features of a man who'd seen a little too much war already and still had a long way to go.

Oso stepped into the office and closed the door. He'd been in the squadron for several months, but he'd had little contact with Torch. This soft spoken man who always wore a kind expression remained a mystery to him. Torch rarely took part in the after-hours story swapping at the squadron bar, and when he did, he never drank anything stronger than a soda; yet the stories circulating about his past exploits were the stuff of legends. Oso put his awe aside, trying to look like a fighter pilot rather than a child before his father's desk. "You wanted to see me sir?"

"Yeah, take a seat."

Oso grabbed one of the two chairs in front of the commander's desk. Instinctively he sat at attention, his back straight, not touching the cushion behind him.

"Relax Oso, I didn't call you in here to yell at you."

"Yes sir," Oso tried to sit back and relax but found the position uncomfortable and awkward. After a moment's fidgeting, he sat forward again.

"Did you know that the senior students call you 'the Terminator'?"

"Yes sir."

"How do you feel about that?"

Oso wasn't sure how to respond. Was this guy a commander or a shrink? "I really hadn't thought about it sir," he said.

Torch frowned. "C'mon, don't lie to me son, I've been around the block a few times more than you. Every training squadron has their 'bad cop,' some jerk who feels that it's his job to filter the young pilots, to protect the high standard of his weapon system. Guys like that relish being called 'Captain Hook' or 'Terminator,' but somehow you don't fit the profile."

"You're right sir, I hate that name, but I'm afraid that if I don't come down hard on their mistakes now, they may never get fixed."

"Ah…I see. I figured it was something like that. Listen, Soda and I are old buddies. The fact is that I owed Soda a favor and he cashed in; otherwise you wouldn't be here. You're a talented pilot, but I really didn't want your baggage."

Oso sat in stunned silence.

"Yeah, I know your history. I wouldn't be fit to lead this squadron if I didn't know every victory and failure of the pilots under my command. You want someone to tell you that Collins' accident was your fault? Fine, it was your fault."

Oso cast his eyes at the floor. He'd always blamed himself, but this was the first time anyone else had supported the opinion. "I..." he began, but words failed him.

"Just be quiet and let me finish. It was your fault...but it was mine as well. That kid graduated from this training squadron. I flew with him and so did several other instructors in this building. The blame lies with every one of us."

Oso looked up. The commander's expression was as gentle as always.

"When you let Brent step into that jet on his last mission, you made a judgment call. You knew he had problems but you considered him trainable, right?"

"Yes sir."

"You were right, he was trainable. The rest of us made the same call. Unfortunately a set of circumstances that none of us foresaw overcame Brent's abilities that day. It stings, I know, but that's the nature of our business. We can all look back and ask 'what if.' What if Tank made him repeat a few more rides? What if I'd given him a failing grade on his checkride? What if you'd ended his flying career by refusing to let him fly that day? Maybe it would have saved his life...maybe not. The point is that you're part of a team here, and just like you can't take sole responsibility for Brent's death, you can't fail every kid who tries to get through this program."

Oso looked the commander in the eye, "I get it sir," he said passively.

The soft face suddenly turned hard. "I'm not sure you do. Listen, I'm not telling you not to fail a student if he deserves it; but I am telling you that you're failing an abnormal amount of kids and all the repeat flights are gumming up my schedule. I don't want to bench you, but I'll sit you at a desk for the next two years if you don't loosen up and loosen up quick."

Oso already considered this assignment a form of being benched. Now he was about to be benched from the bench. "How ironic," he thought. He straightened up and looked the commander in the eye again. "Yes sir, I get it now," he said, more firmly than before.

The commander cocked his head and looked across the desk at Oso with narrowed eyes. "Just remember this. The responsibility lies with the individual pilot. This is an all-volunteer force and every kid that steps through the front door knows exactly what the risks are. Every time a young man or woman lights their engines and takes that runway, whether in training or in combat, they do it knowing that they're putting the good of the nation ahead of their own lives. In the end it's their choice, not yours." Torch let his countenance relax and waved a hand toward the door, "Alright I'm off my soap box, but I'm watching you. You're dismissed."

Oso stood to attention, replaced his chair, and wheeled around to leave. He took three steps, grabbed the doorknob and then paused, as if to say one more thing.

"You're a great pilot, Oso," the commander spoke first, "but you'll never be a great instructor until you learn to share the burdens of the position with the rest of us."

"Yes sir," Oso said over his shoulder. There was nothing else to say.

Chapter 20

"We're three minutes from the target and the weapons are green," said Murph.

"Roger," Drake acknowledged, but it was little more than a grunt. He was focused on the screen in front of him, calculating the moment that he would take the radar shot. He gently took hold of the controls and punched off the autopilot; he would have to hand-fly the attack. As impressive as the bomber's autopilot was, it couldn't keep up with these angles, not when they were flying this low. Dark terrain whipped past the windshield. Drake's radar altimeter indicated a mere three hundred feet above the ground.

"Two minutes, both weapons are in position. The DPIs are the two square buildings at the center of the complex," Murph advised.

Drake glanced down at his satellite imagery. He memorized the position of the crosshairs, hoping they would match the radar generated image that would soon appear on his screen.

"Thirty seconds, two targeted, two achievable, you're in range."

Drake gingerly banked the aircraft away from the target and pulled the nose into a climb before activating the bomber's powerful radar. Within a few seconds the image appeared on his screen. The crosshairs fell right where they were supposed to be. "Target confirmed," he said, turning the jet back to its original course but continuing to climb.

Murph initiated the automatic release sequence. A few seconds later the computer opened the weapons bay doors and kicked out the bombs. "Weapons away and clear," he said.

Drake rolled the aircraft on its edge, allowing the nose to slice through the horizon into a steep descent. When the wings were level again, he reactivated the autopilot and prayed that it would do its job. The numbers on his altimeter rapidly counted down until a serene female voice said, "Terrain following...activated." The bomber pulled itself out of the dive and leveled back at exactly three hundred feet. Drake pushed up his throttles to compensate for the loss in speed and looked at Murph. "Looks like another job well done. They never saw that one coming."

"Yeah," Murph replied, "and that's a lot more fun than all of the straight and level flying we do at high altitude. Say...do you want to see something cool?"

"That," said Drake, "along with 'What could possibly go wrong?' and 'Here, hold my beer,' is something you never want to hear your pilot say." Then he shrugged, "Hey, the mission's complete, so why not?"

"Watch this." Murph cancelled the autopilot and took the controls, pushing the throttles to their limit and diving to fifty feet off the deck. At the Stealth's maximum speed he pulled the nose into a steep climb, causing the altimeter needle to spin wildly. Then, at ten thousand feet, he shoved the control stick all the way to the left.

"Whoa!" exclaimed Drake, instinctively gripping the dashboard. "Are you crazy?"

"Trust me," Murph said calmly, yanking the throttles to idle as his wings banked past the vertical position. By the time the bomber became completely inverted, the nose was well below the horizon and they were accelerating back toward the dark earth. Murph gave the aircraft a negative-G push to control the dive and then continued the roll.

Before Drake could recover his composure, the wings were once again level and Murph was aggressively pulling out of the dive, pushing the aircraft's G limits to make it level by three hundred feet. "That's how it's done sonny-boy," he said with a wry smile.

Suddenly the aircraft stopped in mid air. The world beyond the windscreens froze and the cockpit flooded with light. Both pilots turned and looked over their shoulders to see a thin figure silhouetted against a very ordinary looking doorframe. The intruder angrily stepped into the cockpit and slammed the door.

"Which one of you two chuckleheads wants to explain what you're doing with my simulator?" asked Lieutenant Colonel Steven "Drag" Jansen. Drag was scary enough when he was happy, but at the moment he looked downright angry. A thin man with red hair and sharp features, Drag was not physically imposing, but he had a very abrasive personality and a reputation as one of the best pilots ever to fly the B-2.

"Uh, sir, we...uh..." Drake could not come up with a response.

Murph broke in, "Sir, we completed the training mission and I was just experimenting with the capabilities of the aircraft."

"Baloney, you were screwing around. Do you have any idea how much it costs per hour to run this simulator?"

Drake and Murph sheepishly shrugged their shoulders.

"A lot more than you two minions make in a day," Drag assured them. "I saw your fancy aileron roll. Number one: I shouldn't have to remind you how a simulator works. It only knows what's been programmed into it. When you take it into a flight regime that it doesn't recognize, you're flying in uncharted skies. If a maneuver hasn't been tested in the real aircraft, then the simulator's reaction is no guarantee that it will work in the real jet; besides, the bank angle limiter in the real bomber would never let you roll it over like that. Number Two: you two are supposed to be above that sort of behavior. You both won the Distinguished Flying Cross for your mission over Afghanistan last year, and with good reason, but that honor carries with it certain responsibilities. What if one of the new pilots saw that foolishness? You no longer have the leeway for childish games. You're leaders in this community whether you like it or not. Have I made myself clear?"

The abashed pilots both nodded. "Yes sir," they said in unison.

"Good, then let's go. I have some papers for you to sign."

As they followed Drag out of the simulator, Drake wondered if the "papers" would be forms authorizing Drag to dock their pay for wasting simulator time. To his relief the DO led them into a secure room and handed them clearance paperwork instead.

"Sign these," said Drag. When they set the pens down, he took the papers and shook their hands. "Congratulations gentlemen, you've been selected to join a covert program known as Cerberus." He explained the details of the operation and then briefed them on their specific role. "You two will fly the modified B-2 that carries the Dreamcatcher drone," he said. "Officially you'll be attending a two-week conference at Nellis Air Force Base in Las Vegas, Nevada. It's a huge gathering including officers from all over the Combat Air Force, so you won't be missed when you sneak away and return to Whiteman. Back here you'll take command of the modified B-2 and fly it to the test site."

Noting the pilots' enthusiastic expressions, Drag held up his hands, palms out. "Easy boys, you two are just the bus drivers for the new reconnaissance aircraft. You'll fly circles in the sky while the engineers run tests on the sensors and prove that the drone can be launched and recovered from your weapons bay." Then he turned deadly serious. "I don't have to remind you of the highly classified nature of this mission. Before you leave, stick to your cover, but say as little as possible. It's just a conference at Nellis – there will be no adlibbing about what casinos or other unsavory institutions you plan to visit in your fictitious spare time."

"No problem, sir. We've got it," said Murph. He turned to Drake and held out his fist, "What happens in Vegas…"

"Stays in Vegas," Drake responded, bumping Murph's knuckles with his own, "even when you're not really there."

Chapter 21

"It's dead ahead sir!" the pilot of the C-130 Hercules shouted to Crash over the engine noise. His smile was painted an eerie green by the faint glow of his Night Vision Goggles.

The team had been riding in the loud, poorly air conditioned aircraft for hours. Bored to tears and a little sore in the backside, Crash had taken a walk up to the cockpit, where he'd been pleasantly surprised to learn that they'd almost arrived at the test site. "I don't see anything but darkness," he said, standing behind the left pilot seat and peering out through the windscreen.

"Oh, sorry about that...here, use this," the pilot handed him a night vision monocle. "And you're gonna want to sit down in that engineer's seat and strap in. This runway's a little rough."

Crash sat in the seat centered behind the pilots and clipped on the restraints. The seat wasn't exactly comfortable, but at least it had a cushion, a welcome relief from the nylon web seating in the back of the plane. He flipped on the monocle and peered over the pilots' shoulders at the scene before them. Ahead lay an all but forgotten airstrip, forty-five miles northwest of Alamogordo, New Mexico. Large yellow X's that appeared light green in Crash's monocle marked the full length of the runway. They warned civilian pilots that the field was abandoned and unusable, but the warning was hardly necessary. The field was well protected beneath the several hundred square miles of restricted airspace belonging to Holloman Air Force Base.

During the journey, Scott had filled Crash in on the testing facility's history. In its heyday it was known as Biggs North One, serving as a practice deployment facility for the men preparing to take F-86 Saberjets into combat over Korea. Later, during the Vietnam conflict, it was used as a target field for B-52 crews to practice runway bombing, which explained the tall chain-link fence with rusty signs proclaiming the dangers of unexploded ordinance.

Most of those who remembered the service of Biggs North One had disappeared, fading into retirement. The little field appeared to have taken its place in history, soon to be consumed by the dust and the desert wind, but appearances are often deceiving. Biggs North One continued to serve; it just had a new name.

"Welcome to Romeo Seven!" shouted the C-130 pilot.

They were just crossing the fence-line and Crash could see the small apron with its rundown barracks and two crumbling hangars. There was no light coming from them at all. "Where's the real facility?" he asked, but the pilots were too busy to answer. The left seat pilot focused on the runway and expertly manipulated the controls while the right seat pilot peered under his goggles and counted off the altitude from the radar altimeter.

"Two hundred...one hundred...fifty...thirty...ten..."

In one slow, deft movement the pilot brought the control wheel back and reduced the throttles to idle. Crash felt the thump of the wheels touching down and then the second impact of the nose-gear as it found the pavement. The pilot wasn't kidding about the rough runway; the big prop plane bounced along like a four-by-four on a jeep trail until it eased to a slow crawl. Still using his NVGs, the pilot coaxed his craft to one side of the runway and then reversed direction to head back toward the buildings. Finally he stopped on the apron in front of one of the old hangars.

"Aren't you going to shut her down?" shouted Crash.

"Nope. You guys get off and then we're outta here. Watch out for the props; we can't risk shutting 'em down in case one of 'em doesn't start back up. Our tail won't clear the hangar doors and we can't be sitting here when the sun comes up."

Crash unbuckled his harness and went back to supervise the off-loading process. The crew walked Dreamcatcher down the ramp of the C-130 like pallbearers carrying a fallen soldier off of his last flight. They moved with care and precision; white gloves protected the drone's skin from contaminants on their hands. It seemed ludicrous that they were working so hard to keep Dreamcatcher pristine. Soon they would strap the drone into the bomber's bay and then drop it into the troposphere from twenty thousand feet. If it survived that, they would still have to get it back into the bay in mid-flight, and that would be the real trick. Crash shook his head. "Remind me again how the docking system works," he said to Scott.

"It's fairly simple. LORA will fly on her programmed profile up to the bomber's open bay. On the spine of the craft there is a rotating panel where the docking latch is housed. LORA will use laser spotting to center herself and then flip the panel, exposing the docking latch. After that she'll fine tune her position until the two are connected."

"You make it sound so easy, but it seems like there's a lot that could go wrong."

Scott took on an offended look. "Trust me Daniel. The computer simulations went off without a hitch. It's going to work."

"Maybe, but I'll be a lot happier when we've completed a few successful flight tests." Crash turned from Scott and looked around for the first time. He was struck by the dark, barren wasteland surrounding them; there was nothing here but dilapidated buildings and dry dusty landscape. He sighed, muttering under his breath, "Join the Air Force, see the world."

Chapter 22

Crash stood in the dark for what seemed an eternity, until the sound of the C-130's engines faded away. The test team and the security troops looked to him for what to do next, but he was at a loss. He looked to Scott, but the engineer just raised his eyebrows and grinned, obviously relishing the fact that he knew much more about the facility than Crash.

Suddenly the sound of an electric motor and gears grinding broke the silence. The doors in front of them slowly slid open, revealing an interior that was just as dark as the night outside. Crash could make out very little of the scene before him, but when the sound of the doors stopped, he heard the distinctive clop of combat boots on concrete. Presently an imposing silhouette came into view, like a shadow stepping out of the fog. A familiar voice boomed from the darkness, "Well, don't just stand there like idiots. Get that junk in here before you blow the whole thing!"

Crash smiled. "Good evening Colonel Walker, I thought I left you at the Pentagon less than twenty four hours ago."

"Yes...well...I have an excellent travel agent," answered the Colonel. "The illusion of being in two places at once adds to my personal mystique. Okay, let's step it up people, we still have a long night ahead of us."

Another soldier joined the Colonel and directed the loaders as they brought Dreamcatcher into the hangar. The others grabbed the luggage and the crates of equipment and made a pile just inside the doors. Once that operation was complete, an unseen hand re-activated the door motor and the hangar doors slid slowly closed, enveloping the group in total darkness.

"All secure?" the Colonel asked the darkness.

"Locked and ready sir," a voice replied.

"Lights!"

Crash heard the metallic percussion of a large electric switch being thrown and a series of powerful florescent lights flickered on, flooding the interior of the structure with bluish-white light. It took a few moments for his eyes to adjust to the change, but what came into focus was the polar opposite to the view outside. There was no hint of abandonment here, everything was clean and new. In the bright lighting of the interior, the hangar looked big enough to hold two Stealth Bombers.

"Gentlemen and Miss Navistrova, welcome to Romeo Seven," said Colonel Walker with a grandiose wave of his hand. "I needn't remind you of the sensitive nature of this facility, people, but I will anyway. This testing ground does not exist. You will all carry the knowledge of it and its uses to your graves. In fact, if Saint Peter asks you about it at the Pearly Gates, you will deny everything. Is that clear?"

There were yes-sir's all around.

The Colonel smiled. "Good, then let's get started with the tour. Leave your junk here, we'll come back and get it later." He led them towards a large box painted on the floor of the hangar, a black outline with yellow hash marks. As they drew closer, Crash could make out a thin space cut in the floor along the edges and the words "LIFT THREE" painted in the center.

"Everyone stand towards the center of the lift please," Colonel Walker said. "You don't want to touch the sides as we go down; they're covered in black grease that'll never wash out of your clothes." He pressed a button on a small pedestal and the lift jerked into motion.

Crash estimated that they'd traveled downward thirty feet before a small, underground world finally opened around them. No one spoke; there is a silent reverence that is honored when something secret is revealed.

"The original builders did not intend this place to be a top-secret testing facility," Walker explained, playing tour guide. "Back when the base was still called Biggs North One, Strategic Air Command built a large nuclear fallout shelter down here. It contained everything that a small force would need to survive for several years underground. There is a galley and dining facility with food and water storage. There also used to be living quarters and medical facilities, even a jail and a morgue. When the base was closed, some far-sighted individual decided to capitalize on this cold war relic and converted it into a state-of-the-art testing facility."

The group followed Colonel Walker off of the elevator and Crash could see recognition in the faces of his engineers as they identified their individual workstations simply by familiarity with the equipment. The dominating feature of the room was a huge black screen on one wall. Large white polygons covered the display and yellow and green symbols moved in and out of them at random. Crash watched the moving symbols, mesmerized, until the weight of a hand on his shoulder broke his awed stupor. He looked to his left and was surprised to see that the hand belonged to Amanda. She looked pale. "Are you alright?" he asked.

"Fine," she replied, "I just stumbled a bit. It's these new shoes."

Crash looked down. The flats she wore looked well worn.

"As you can see," Colonel Walker continued, "there are several workstations in this room, many of which you'll be using in the next couple of weeks. To our right is the TSD or Test Situation Display. The polygons represent the restricted airspace above us and you can see several Holloman aircraft operating there. On the outskirts of the area, the red symbols represent airliners passing close to the airspace. We receive radar feeds from Holloman and indirect feeds from local Air Traffic Control facilities. We can also track our test aircraft here using GPS feeds."

"Where do we sleep?" asked Crash.

Walker led them past the screen and down a hallway. "There are no longer living quarters down here. For that you can walk under the flight line and take Lift One up to the barracks building. It holds thirty people, each with their own room. There are only two bathrooms though, and Miss Navistrova gets one to herself."

Cued by the comment, Crash and several others glanced at Amanda. "Hmm?" she said, as if recovering from a daydream. A hint of perspiration glistened on her forehead.

"The other hangar is also useable and accessed by Lift Two," continued Walker. "It houses our chase planes and the small transport that brought me here. Both hangars can be accessed from the outside just as you saw this evening, by ensuring that no light is burning when the doors open. The barracks also have an emergency escape hatch on the flight line side, but are normally accessed through the tunnel system and the lifts. Remember, this is an abandoned airfield. The outside must appear dead at all times. No one goes in or out unless an active test is in progress."

When the tour was over, Walker led them back to Lift Three. "Alright folks, lets get moving. Get your gear and settle in to your stations, but don't take too long to turn in for the night – or rather for the day; we've got a lot of work ahead of us. The galley opens at noon for breakfast. Dismissed."

With that the group surrounding Crash broke into fragments, a few went over to the analysis cart and rolled it onto the lift and the rest followed in order to get topside and grab their gear. Only one individual stood motionless. Amanda Navistrova stared straight ahead, her gaze lost in an endless void. She looked as though she was going to pass out.

Crash touched her arm to stir her back to consciousness. "Hey, you don't look so good. Tell me what's going on...and don't give me the shoe line again, I'm not buying it."

Amanda took on the sheepish look of a child who's been caught in a lie. "Sorry, I didn't want anyone to think I was the weak girl of the group."

"We all know you too well to think of you as weak, or as a girl for that matter."

Amanda managed a smile. "Very funny," she said. "The truth is I have a problem with small places."

"Don't be ridiculous, I've seen you work in much more cramped environments than this."

"But none of those were thirty feet under ground. The thought of tons of dirt and concrete ready to collapse and bury me alive is almost unbearable. I don't know if I can do this. What if I miss something and cost us a test? The Colonel will have my job."

"Nobody's going to fire you, Amanda. If you can overcome the tight, closed offices of Wright Patterson, you can work in here. Listen, I know enough to get your equipment set up at the propulsion station. Go and get your gear and then get topside and call it a night...or day...whatever. I'll cover for you tonight so that you can get some rest."

Amanda took his offer and headed for the hangar to get her luggage. Watching her go, Crash wondered if she'd be okay, or if he'd have to bring out one of the "propulsion twins" to take her place.

Chapter 23

Victor roared down Missouri's Highway 50 in his midnight blue '67 Shelby GT. He loved driving the classic Mustang. Somehow he felt as though he was genetically bonded to its design, like it was part of his DNA. His dad had given him the car when he graduated from the Academy; back then it was mostly the color of rust and Bondo. During pilot training he'd spent more time restoring the Mustang's muscular lines than studying for his tests, but the car was worth it. When he'd finished putting on the last coat of polish, he'd named her Betsy.

When the Air Force sent Victor to Germany he didn't have the heart to put Betsy in the clumsy hands of the shipping company, so he'd left her in a rented garage near his parent's home in Colorado Springs. Now he'd been back in the States for more than eight months and still the honeymoon with Betsy hadn't ended. Today, however, even the throaty roar of her two hundred and eighty-nine cubic inch V-8 could not get Victor's mind off his troubles.

Victor's move to the Stealth Wing had proved to be a mixed blessing. He didn't regret his choice to join the B-2; piloting one of the world's most advanced aircraft was the opportunity of a lifetime. The problem was that he still hadn't actually piloted one.

Even though he'd been accepted into the Stealth Wing, Victor's flight experience was short of the B-2's normal requirements. Consequently, the Wing Commander had given him a one year assignment as an instructor in the wing's Companion Trainer Program to beef up his log book. The B-2 was expensive to fly and the CTP allowed B-2 pilots to fly the Northrop T-38 Talon as a supplement. Victor's job was to train new arrivals to fly the T-38.

The assignment wasn't a bad deal from a flying standpoint. The T-38 was a supersonic fighter trainer with a sleek design and a fond favorite of every Air Force jet jockey. Unfortunately, the one-year delay had benched Victor from the Combat Air Force. With things heating up in Iraq, it looked like he might miss out on another war.

Victor walked dejectedly into his office on the second floor of the Combat Training Squadron. Without speaking to the other pilot in the room, he walked over to a safe, pulled out a file with "SECRET" hand-written on the cover, and sat down at his desk to study it. The other flyer looked up from his computer and opened his mouth to speak, but he took the cue from Victor's expression that conversation was not an option.

The room was sparsely furnished and cavernously oversized for its purpose, making it feel more like a blue-carpeted basketball court than an office. In the last week Victor and his officemate, Bill "Putty" Holley, had embarked on a campaign to fill the space with old furniture from other squadrons, but all they'd succeeded in requisitioning so far was a dented aluminum coffee table, a lava lamp from Putty's personal collection, and an old blue couch. Putty looked up at the latter's ragged but inviting blue cushions and pushed back from his computer. "Time to break in the new addition," he said.

Victor merely grunted in reply.

Putty hefted his short, round body up from the desk chair, crossed over to the couch, and dropped heavily onto the worn cushions. He kicked his feet up on the coffee table and stared at Victor, no longer willing to let him stew in silence. "Still obsessing over that file?" he asked.

Victor reluctantly looked up from his work. He didn't feel like chatting, but there was nowhere to hide. "I'm not obsessing," he replied. "It's a hobby. It's therapeutic."

"Some therapy," scoffed Putty. "I've looked at that thing. News clippings, intelligence reports, maps...red lines running everywhere with dates and times...sometimes I worry about how you're getting all that information."

"I have a friend over at Wing Intelligence who helps me out. We share information about Bin Laden and Irhaab."

"It's unhealthy. You're a pilot for crying out loud. Leave that stuff to the Intel guys."

"I can't. I sat out Enduring Freedom because CENTCOM didn't want to share the glory with USAFE. Now it looks like we're finally going to take care of business in Iraq and I'm going to miss that too. I have to do something to feel like I'm involved in the process. Who knows, maybe somebody will be able to use this stuff, even if I'm stuck on the sidelines."

"Have it your way," said Putty, turning his attention to the lava lamp. With a philosophic gaze he pondered the lazy movement of the blobs until Victor finally closed his file and stood up.

"Where're you going?"

"I'll give you a hint. In case you need it later, my Last Will and Testament is filed in my left desk drawer."

"Flying with another new guy, are we? So what's the background, bomber or cargo?"

Victor sighed and walked to the door. "B-52."

Putty let out a low whistle. "Nose diver, eh; you're a marked man indeed."

Victor was sure he'd lost years of his life from the trauma of yelling "Pull up!" at the former B-52 pilots that he trained in the T-38. On takeoff B-52s climbed away from the runway in a unique, nose-down attitude, and pilots from the old bomber often attempted to fly the T-38 the same way. Unfortunately, their actions would drive the Talon straight for the pavement.

Still lounging on the couch, Putty lifted a thick hand in mock salute. "Good luck, we're all counting on you. If you're not back in two hours I'll tell Katy that, with your last words, you spoke of your undying love...for Betsy."

"Thanks, you're a true friend." Victor smartly returned the salute, wheeled around in an about face, and left the office.

Two hours later Victor and his student, Nick "Motor" Palaski, pulled their T-38 up to the hold short line at Whiteman's Runway One

Seven. Victor had flown with Palaski twice before and he'd never had to ask where the B-52 pilot had gotten his nickname. Motor was a short, dark, and powerful man who greatly appreciated the spoken word. He also greatly appreciated cappuccinos. If something could be said with 10 words, Motor would use 20 in half the time.

"Tower, Fast Two One is holding short," said Motor before taking a final swig of coffee from a metallic thermos that seemed to follow him like a security blanket follows a toddler.

"Fast Two One, you are cleared for takeoff," the tower controller replied.

Victor took a deep breath, remembering Motor's B-52 heritage. "I hope I don't have to remind you to keep the nose pointed *up* after we take off," he cautioned as they took the runway.

"You just *did* remind me."

"I know."

Motor lit the afterburners and the jet lurched forward, spouting blue fire. The T-38 rapidly accelerated to rotation speed and Motor pulled it into the air.

"Keep the nose up."

"Yeah, yeah, I got it."

Despite Victor's misgivings, Motor took the jet through the planned series of aerobatic maneuvers with very few errors. Since his student was doing so well, Victor allowed himself a moment to enjoy the picture outside. The view had always been one of the best parts of his job. It was as if an artist painted a new canvas for every flight, each work unique and stunning. The depth and texture of the clouds, the infinite shades of blue in the sky, all of them were breathtaking if only he remembered to pause and absorb the beauty.

Finally Motor turned the jet toward home and Victor smiled with pride as the B-52 pilot flew a nice symmetrical landing pattern. He was about to offer a compliment when the landing gear hit the runway hard. "*Easy*," he cautioned.

"Sorry," said Motor, pulling the jet back into the air, "that was an incomplete flare."

"No kidding," said Victor, "I think you left a big dent in the landing zone." They leveled off for another pattern and Victor decided to give Motor a break. "Why don't you let me take this next one so I can refresh your picture of the final flare?" he asked.

Motor consented and Victor took control of the aircraft. As they approached the last turn for the runway, Motor took the opportunity to pull out his thermos and take a few gulps of coffee.

"I think you should take it easy on that stuff," Victor started to say, but he stopped in mid sentence. A red light flashed on, glaring from his dashboard.

"Left fire light! We've got a left fire light!" shouted Motor, slamming the cap back onto the thermos.

Victor pushed the right engine into afterburner and reduced the left engine to idle, praying that it was just overheated. He hoped the engine would cool and the warning light would go out, but when he glanced at the gauges they did not look good. The tachometer jumped around wildly and the temperature needle was pegged. There was a no-kidding fire back there. "Tower, Fast Two One Emergency, we have an engine fire. We're making this a full-stop, roll the trucks...I repeat, roll the trucks," said Victor as he lowered the gear and flaps.

"It's not going out," said Motor.

"I know. Disengage the throttle gate for me."

"Done."

"Good. Okay, I've got the right engine. Go ahead and shut down the left one."

Motor complied and Victor felt the change in thrust as the engine spooled down. Then he checked his speed and position and cursed himself. He'd overcompensated with the afterburner; he was way too fast. He cautiously brought the good engine to idle, an uncomfortable place to put it considering that the other engine was dead. Then, as he fought to bring his speed under control, the red light extinguished.

"Whaddaya know, the fire's out," said Motor with renewed optimism.

"Standby," said Victor, "I'm not so sure." He checked the gauges again. The temperature needle was still pegged. That didn't make sense. He strained to look over his left shoulder and saw black smoke still trailing from the engine. A quick test of the fire sensors confirmed his fears. "Bad news, Motor," he said, "the fire is still burning back there."

"What's the good news?"

"It burned through the sensors. That means it's working its way forward."

"I asked for *good* news."

"Sorry, I'm fresh out. We need to get this thing on the ground and get out before the flames get to the fuel tanks. After touchdown I want you to shut down number two."

"Don't we need that engine to power the brakes?"

"I'll use the emergency brakes...trust me, it'll work. Pop the canopies when the speed gets below thirty-five and we'll jump as soon as we stop."

"Fast Two One Emergency, this is Whiteman Tower. You're cleared to land. We can see smoke trailing from your aircraft. The fire trucks are on the way," said the tower controller.

"Copy, cleared to land," responded Victor, unwilling to offer a more detailed response; the runway was coming up too quickly. "Hold on, I'm gonna land her hard to kill some knots," he said to Motor. A moment later he slammed the jet onto the pavement, instantly knocking fifteen knots off the speed. As soon as the nose was down he pressed hard on the brakes. "Now Motor!"

Motor shut down the good engine and Victor was left with just the emergency brakes. His legs burned as he struggled with the steering pedals but he couldn't let up on the pressure. The emergency brakes were only good for one push; if he let off the pedals now the brake pressure might never come back.

Halfway down the runway, Victor finally brought the jet to a halt. He threw off his helmet and harness, climbed over the right side, and dropped to the ground. Then he stopped, sensing that Motor was not with him. Looking back, he was shocked to see Motor still bent over his seat, struggling with something. A pillar of black smoke rose from the fire behind him.

"What are you doing!?" Victor shouted.

"My thermos is stuck!"

"Nick! The *plane* is on *fire!*"

Motor stood up and looked over his shoulder. "Good point." He clambered over the side and dropped to the ground to follow Victor. They ran away from the burning jet at a full sprint, not stopping until they were well over a hundred feet away. Just as they turned to survey the damage, the fire reached the fuel tanks and the jet exploded in a mushroom of fire and debris. Instinctively they turned away, shielding their faces against the intense heat of the blast. A few seconds later the fire trucks sped in and the fire fighters unleashed their hoses on the burning wreckage, turning the runway into a sea of blackened debris and dirty white foam.

The two pilots stood for a while and gaped at the mess, their mouths hanging open in stunned silence. Finally Motor, his eyes still fixed on the wreckage, reached up and placed an arm across Victor's shoulders. "Boy do you have a lot of paperwork to do."

Chapter 24

Victor wiggled his fingers as he walked down the hallway, trying to recover some feeling in his writing hand. He'd spent the better portion of two hours in the crew room filling out paperwork on the engine fire. There were forms for the Squadron Commander, forms for the Safety Office, forms for the Tower, in fact there were forms for just about everyone. He was shaken, he was tired, and all he wanted to do now was disappear into his office and hide behind his computer; but as soon as he reached the solace of his desk, the phone rang.

"I should unplug that thing," thought Victor, but he picked up the receiver. "T-38 desk...Unsecure," he said wearily.

"Victor?" queried the caller. Drag's raspy voice was unmistakable, his tone ominous.

"Yes sir, how can I help you?"

"I need to see you in my office right now."

"Can't it wait?" Victor wanted to ask, but he knew better than that. It was never wise to argue with Drag. Instead, he turned and began the long trek to the DO's office. "Great," he thought. "You can't even blow up a jet around here without getting second guessed." The problem with being in a community full of aviators at the top of their game was that everybody had their own theory or opinion about everything. It fostered a constant clash of type-A personalities, and rank usually won. A common joke in the wing said that if you locked two B-2 pilots in a room with a single tactical problem, you'd wind up with four solutions and a big argument. Unless, of course, one of the pilots was a colonel, in which case you'd get no argument and one solution that would never work.

Victor was sure that the DO had found something wrong with the way he'd handled the engine fire and he knew Drag's reputation for painfully and publicly reprimanding those who'd screwed up. The man's unfortunate cigarette habit compounded his intimidation. Drag would undoubtedly deliver a barrage of verbal abuse in close proximity to Victor's nose and his smoker's breath would make it nearly impossible to breathe. Victor stopped in front of Drag's office, took a last breath of fresh air, and hesitantly knocked on the door.

Instead of shouting, "Get in here!" as expected, Drag opened the door and barreled out, nearly knocking Victor over. "Follow me," he said.

Victor followed Drag down the hallway to a set of big steel double doors. He knew that the B-2 mission planning rooms were behind them, but he'd never been back there. He had the clearances but he'd never had a purpose, and it was an unwritten rule at the Stealth Wing that you didn't go wandering into secure rooms unless you had a purpose.

"You ever use this one before?" Drag asked, indicating the entry system next to the door.

"No sir," Victor replied.

"You'd better do the honors then. Just because you're supposed to be in the system doesn't necessarily mean you are. We'd better make sure your code works."

Victor pressed his thumb against the small red touch-screen and entered his personal code into the keypad. The big vault door cracked open an inch and Drag pushed it wide and ushered Victor inside. They stood at the beginning of a long hallway lined with rooms. At the opposite end another steel door held a large red and white sign. Big block letters warned, EMERGENCY EXIT ONLY - ALARM WILL SOUND - LETHAL FORCE IS AUTHORIZED.

"Great," thought Victor, "If the building catches on fire you get to choose between burning to death and getting shot."

"This is us," said Drag, indicating a third steel door to their right. "I'm pretty sure you don't have access to this one; not many people do." He opened the door and Victor obediently followed him into the room. It was little more than a broom closet. There was nothing but a heavy safe, two stools, a desk with a pen on it, and an industrial sized shredder.

"That's disappointing," said Victor.

Drag just frowned at the comment and turned on the shredder, filling the room with the whir of gears ready to grind secrets into mulch. Next, the DO stepped behind the desk and sat down on a stool. He spun the combination lock on the safe, opened the door and removed a small stack of papers, placing them on the desk. Finally he folded his hands and looked up at Victor.

"Great, more paperwork," said Victor, immediately wishing he could learn to keep his mouth shut.

"Did you ever hear the phrase 'seen but not heard'?"

"Yes sir."

"Let's try it. Listen, I think you did a great job today, saving Motor's life as well as your own. Your flying skills are part of the reason you're here, but these papers have nothing to do with the fire." Drag's eyes narrowed. "What I'm about to tell you is above your clearance level, but I've arranged for you to get that clearance. All that's required is your signature on a few of these papers."

Victor reached for the pen but Drag snatched it away.

"Not so fast, this is not a decision to be made lightly. You don't even know what the clearance is for. You've been selected for an assignment, but you won't be able to tell anybody what you're doing or where you're going, not even your wife. In fact, you may be separated from her for a long period of time and you won't be allowed to tell her why. Until you make your choice, I can't tell you what the assignment is, where it is, or how long it will take; all I can tell you at this moment is that you must make that choice right here, right now."

Drag handed Victor a single piece of paper off the top of the stack and placed the pen back on the desk. "Option One: you can pick up that pen and sign the paper in your hand. If you do that, this conversation never happened; we never speak of it again. Option Two: you can shred that piece of trash you're holding, sit down at this stool, and sign every form in this pile. Take Option Two and I've got lots more to tell you. What'll it be?"

Victor stepped up to the desk, paused to whisper a prayer, and shoved his piece of paper into the shredder.

"Good choice," said Drag.

As Victor set about signing all of the papers in the large stack on the desk, Drag pulled a binder out of the safe. "First things first, I need you to stop keeping that file of yours," he said as he set the binder on the desk.

Victor set down his pen and looked up in surprise.

"Yeah, I know about your little file," said Drag. "If you're going to do this you'll have to let it go."

"But sir," Victor started to protest.

"No buts, kid," said Drag, shaking his head, "it'll draw attention that we don't need." Then he opened the binder to a tab marked "Targets" and tapped it with his finger, his thin lips stretching into a broad smile. "Besides, now you've got people to do that sort of thing for you."

Drag fell silent as Victor continued with his paperwork. When the younger pilot finally set down his pen and looked up, the DO smiled again. "Very good. So tell me, how's your Arabic these days?"

Chapter 25

An unmarked C-21 Learjet rolled quietly to a stop at the north end of Whiteman's twelve thousand foot runway. The pilot shut down the left engine as soon as the wheels stopped and looked back at Murph and Drake. "This is where you get off boys."

Without a response the two B-2 pilots stepped out through the cabin door. Drag was waiting for them on the runway. "How's the conference going?" he asked.

"Better than most, sir," replied Drake, "I usually sleep through these thi…" He was cutoff by the noise of the Lear's engines running up. The three Stealth pilots made a dash for the grass as the jet shot past them, rapidly climbing into the night.

"In a bit of a hurry, isn't he?" asked Drake, a little annoyed at being interrupted.

"He's gotta keep his ground time minimal, seeing as how he was never here," answered Drag. He handed Drake an olive drab satchel secured with a brittle wire seal. "In there you'll find all of your navigational plots, your data disk, and a copy of the procedures I showed you last week. Fly this one lights-out and let the autopilot do the work. Your NVGs are on the jet along with the rest of your flight gear. Your ride-along is up there as well."

Drag turned toward the truck and Murph and Drake trailed behind, exchanging a wary look. They'd almost forgotten about the extra baggage. "Great," muttered Drake, "nothing ruins the fun of a long, clandestine flight like some test geek who wants to talk your ears off."

"Hurry up gentlemen, wasted time is unnecessary exposure," said Drag, hustling them into the back of the pickup. He drove them over to the alert ramp where the B-2 waited, running on auxiliary power to keep the noise down. When Drag stopped the truck, Murph and Drake vaulted over the side and ran to the jet. Drake knew it had been modified, but he was still surprised by what he saw when he climbed up to the flight deck. Instead of the usual empty space behind the pilots' seats, the modified B-2 had a third crew station with a standard Aces-II ejection seat mounted on a swivel. To the right of the seat was a workstation with a joystick, a communications panel, and a complicated set of controls. Even more surprising than the workstation was the person seated there.

"Hey guys, fancy meeting you here," said Victor with a slight wave.

"You're not an engineer," said Drake, climbing into his seat.

"No kidding. Do you like my nifty setup here?"

Murph reached down and sealed the hatch beneath his feet. "Listen kid," he grunted as he secured the lock, "you may not be an engineer, but you're certainly going to be labeled as a geek if you keep using words like 'nifty.' In fact, I'm putting a moratorium on the use of 'nifty,' 'neat-oh,' and 'swell' for the rest of this trip."

"Okey-dokey," replied Victor, saluting smartly.

"Hilarious," Murph rolled his eyes and climbed into his seat.

Victor already knew the two B-2 pilots.; they'd often crossed paths in the T-38 planning room and Victor had even flown one or two Talon sorties with Drake. For now, though, he kept silent as the Stealth pilots dove into their checklists. They worked quickly, loading their navigation data and firing up the engines, and less than ten minutes later they were accelerating down the runway for takeoff. Halfway down the runway the black bomber lifted into the sky and quickly disappeared into the dark Midwestern night. Finally, at ten thousand feet and with clear weather ahead, Murph relinquished control to the autopilot. "Is the Climb Check complete?" he asked.

"Complete," Drake responded.

"Good." Murph turned to face Victor. "Okay, now that we're well on our way, maybe you can tell me what the heck you're doing here?"

"I was hoping you could tell me."

"Very funny."

"Honestly, I'm not sure. All I really know is that I've got a job to do during the test and it won't be to occupy this seat; I'm told that a real engineer will be doing that. However, I have a hunch that in the future, this *will* be my seat."

"What gave you that idea?" asked Murph.

"Earlier this evening, when I first crawled up here, Drag said, 'Get used to it, in the future that's going to be your seat.'"

"That's a good solid hunch you got there," said Drake.

"So what's your cover?" asked Murph.

"Not too different from yours. I'm supposed to be going to Squadron Officer School at the Air University in Montgomery Alabama for six weeks. Just like the throng at your conference helped you disappear, the four hundred captains attending SOS will mask my absence. The only difference is that I signed in to SOS online, so I never even had to set foot in Alabama."

"What did your wife think about a short notice TDY for six weeks?" asked Drake.

"She wasn't happy. Despite the initials, SOS isn't any kind of emergency, so Katy didn't understand why it had to be me and why I had to go right now. Drag even called our house. He explained the Wing had to send someone on short notice and I drew the short straw. That didn't really help. She cried, she got mad, she threw things, but at least she didn't throw anything at the Mustang. Eventually she rolled with it like she always does. The worst part was lying to her. I've never had to do that before."

"Get used to it, kid," said Murph. "You'll have to do that a lot around here."

Small talk ensued as Victor got better acquainted with the B-2 pilots, and he and Drake figured out that they'd crossed paths at the Academy, though they were a few years apart. They talked mostly of family and flying, until a few hours later when Murph took on a faraway look.

"What's with you?" Drake tapped him on the shoulder.

"I think I've figured out why Victor is here," Murph said slowly.

"Really?" asked Victor, his interest piqued.

"Yeah, it's really just a process of elimination. Victor is only qualified in the T-38 right now, so that leaves him out of flying the B-2. He doesn't hold an engineering degree, so they're probably not relying on him for any brilliant technical analysis either. No offense, Victor."

"None taken."

"There's really only one role left." Murph ceremoniously waved an open palm toward Victor. "Drake, meet Dreamcatcher's chase pilot."

Chapter 26

"Well this is creepy," said Victor as he stepped off the crew ladder. The crew chief who'd guided them into the hangar had disappeared and then the doors had inexplicably closed behind them, leaving them in total darkness.

"Hello!" called Drake, smiling as his voice reverberated off the unseen walls. "At least it's got a nice echo," he said.

All three pilots jumped as the lights flashed on with an electric bang. Walker stepped out of the shadows. "Gentlemen," he said grandly, "welcome to Romeo Seven."

Murph began to introduce his small crew, but the Colonel cut him off. "No need for introductions, Major Murphy, I've read your file, along with those of your two comrades here. Get your gear on that elevator over there and I'll show you the rest of the facility." While Murph and Drake gathered up their flight harnesses and checklists, the Colonel walked over to Victor. "So you're the chase pilot, eh?" he asked.

Victor eyed the Colonel warily, unsure whether he should reveal his complete ignorance of the road ahead. "Actually sir," he said, "I don't have the first clue as to why I'm here."

Walker nodded. "I know that. I just wanted to see if you were the standard cocky young pilot, or if you were smart enough to admit that you're out of your element."

"I'm a fish out of water, sir," Victor said with a shrug.

"Perfect, I like starting with a blank page."

Victor turned to lug his bag over to the elevator, not certain if he liked being referred to as a blank page.

Down in the bunker, Walker led the pilots to the Life Support room where they could unload their flight gear. There he left Victor alone and led Murph and Drake off to a safe to store their classified materials. Unsure of what to do next, Victor absentmindedly milled about the room until he noticed a felt board covered in unit patches hanging on the back wall. He walked over to get a closer look and gazed in awe at the display.

The patch board formed a pictorial legacy of the individuals who had stood there before. There were a few patches from units Victor recognized, units that flew F-16 Fighting Falcons or F-15 Eagles, but there were also several patches that contained the silhouettes of aircraft that he did not recognize, odd shaped jets that looked like only a miracle would make them fly. There were no A-10 patches and Victor surmised that there had never been a cause to bring the technologically deficient Hog to the secret test base. Feeling a bit slighted, he pulled an old 81st patch from his flight suit pocket and added it to the display. "There you go guys," he said quietly, "now we're spoken for."

The patch at the center of the display seemed set apart, as if there was a deliberate effort to leave a few inches of empty space around its place, making it a place of honor. It was a triangle with long sides and a short base. A T-38 climbed heavenward, woven from gray thread so dark that it nearly disappeared into the black background. At the bottom of the patch the number "777" was emblazoned in blood red. Gray, ribbon-shaped banners, like those found on so many military patches, rose vertically from the base of the triangle. They curled around the wingtips of the T-38 as if it had flown through them and was dragging them skyward, with both ends streaming in the wind behind. The two tails of the ribbon hanging from the left wing bore mottos that read: "Triple Seven Chase" and "Third Time Lucky." The tails of the ribbon hanging from the right wing each held a name: "Frank 'Sideshow' Eubanks" and "Mike 'Rat' Shaw."

Victor jumped as a heavy hand clapped him on the arm. He turned to see Colonel Walker smiling at him and was about to make a smart remark about the senior officer sneaking up on him, when he noticed that the pat was not just a friendly gesture. Walker had stuck a patch to the Velcro on Victor's right arm, and it was the same triangular patch that he'd just been admiring.

Walker extended a hand, "Congratulations Victor, you've just been inducted into the Triple Seven Chase Squadron."

Victor looked at his new boss in bewilderment, "Thank you, sir," he said, taking the hand, "but could you please explain what that means?"

"Sorry. No time." Walker stepped back and addressed all three pilots, "Come on gentlemen, it's time to meet the rest of the team."

Walker led them through the main operations center, introducing them to the engineers as they went. Each said something to the effect of "Nice to meet you," or "Welcome to the Cave," but really they seemed bothered by the interruption of their work. In one corner of the room, Amanda sat hunched over a computer, clicking away with the mouse in her left hand and writing furiously on a yellow pad with the mechanical pencil in her right. Her hair was pulled back and held in place with a small clip, but the clip was insufficient and frazzled tufts of hair shot out from her skull at random angles. Walker strode up and lightly tapped her on the shoulder.

"What now?!" she asked testily, not bothering to look up. The Colonel loudly cleared his throat and Amanda stiffened. "I'm sorry sir, I didn't realize it was you," she said, slowly swiveling her chair around, her head bowed in embarrassment. As she stood up she lifted her head and noticed for the first time that Walker was not alone. "Oh," was all she could manage.

"Amanda Navistrova, meet Brit Murphy, Michael Baron, and Tony Merigold – better known as Murph, Victor, and Drake. Boys, this is Amanda, our lead propulsion engineer."

All three men reached out their hands to shake hers. Amanda started to extend her own and then realized she was still holding her pencil. She smiled at the new acquaintances and tried to place the pencil behind her ear, but as she did, her eyes met squarely with Drake's and she missed her ear entirely. The pencil fell to the floor with a light clatter and Amanda giggled at her own clumsiness and knelt to pick it up. She made a small show of gingerly placing it on the table and then once again extended her hand to shake the pilots'. The clip that so poorly held her hair had been loosened by all of the commotion and loosened even more with each handshake. When Amanda finally grasped Drake's hand, it lost its grip entirely, allowing the mess of blond hair to fall in front of her face. As the clip fell, it managed to make a stop at the table and take the pencil with it. They both clattered obnoxiously to the floor at Amanda's feet.

"Are you all right?" asked Drake, bending to pick up the wayward accessories and offer them to their owner.

"Fine, really." Amanda managed a smile as she took the pencil and once again placed it on the table, followed by its new friend. "It's just been one of those days, you know?"

"Been there," Drake said with an empathetic smile.

Walker just frowned. "Moving on," he said loudly, and ushered the pilots to their next new acquaintances. "These two are our project director and project manager," he said, as they came upon Scott and Crash.

"I guess we'll be flying the mother ship for that little UFO up in the hangar," said Murph. "I can't wait to see how she flies."

"Well," responded Scott, "if we've done our job right, you won't see her at all."

"Roger that, but he will," said Drake, thrusting an upraised elbow in Victor's direction. "Victor's our chase guy; he'll be following your bird visually using Night Vision Goggles. How long before we can get her up and flying?"

"We have a couple more days of tests planned," said Crash. "This is the first time that Dreamcatcher and the modified B-2 have been together in the same hangar, so we have to ensure that the release and recovery systems will work together as planned. Speaking of that, Scott and I were just tweaking the ground test schedule. You'll be needed quite a bit because you'll be managing the B-2's electronics."

"We're at your disposal," said Murph. "So, since Victor's going to be flying in formation with your little toy, who's going to be riding with us in the mother-ship?"

"That would be me," replied Scott, "and LORA is no toy, she's a highly sophisticated piece of remote weaponry that will be integral in the new Global War on Terror."

"Sorry about that, no offense intended."

"That's okay. You were probably just lashing out at LORA due to a subconscious fear that pilots are slowly being replaced by remote technology, making your profession irrelevant."

The pilots stared blankly at Scott. "No offense intended there either," said Crash, punching the engineer in the ribs.

"On that note," broke in Colonel Walker, "I'll show you gentlemen to your rooms."

"I can see that this is going to fun," muttered Drake, as they walked down the hallway.

"Don't worry about Dr. Stone, Captain," Walker said. "He's not so bad once you get to know him. It's just that he doesn't relate well."

"To pilots?" Drake asked.

"No, to human beings."

Chapter 27

"Okay, that's another good one, people," Scott's voice crackled in Drake's headset. "It will take a few minutes to confirm the data, but if everything is still good, we can set up for the final capture test. Let's take fifteen minutes." Down below, Dreamcatcher rested beneath the bomb bay on a foam-covered jack assembly. The team had just successfully tested the release system, "dropping" the drone so that its weight transferred from the rack in the B-2 to the jack. The tests were going well, but they'd been at it for hours and the pilots were growing weary of sitting in the cockpit and monitoring the systems.

Drake looked across the cockpit at Murph, "Do you want to go first, or should I?" Restroom breaks weren't simple for the aircrew; someone had to stay with the airplane and continue to monitor the electrical systems, even though the engines weren't running. It just wasn't worth it to take chances with a two billion dollar asset.

"You go ahead," said Murph, "but hurry back. If I miss this break my bladder won't be able to take it."

"Roger that, I'll be right back." Drake climbed down the ladder and headed for the restroom that was off to one side of the hangar. It was a one-size-fits-all affair, no fancy men's or women's accessories, just a rusty sink and a commode.

As Drake held his nose and closed the door behind him, the lift came rising out of the bunker with a single passenger. Crash looked up from his data printouts and found he had trouble uttering a greeting.

Scott noticed the new arrival as well. "Uh…hello Amanda," he said with a quizzical look. "What brings you up from the Cave?"

"I'm just taking a break to stretch my legs."

"Uh-huh," Scott still looked confused. "So, did you do something different with your hair?"

"Hmm? Oh, I just used a little more spray this evening. Does it look ok?"

"It looks fine…I guess. Are you wearing lipstick?"

"Hey, it looks like you brought us some coffee," said Crash, finally gathering his wits and stepping in to save Scott from embarrassing himself.

Amanda smiled. "Oh yes, I brought this up from the galley to save you a trip during breaks."

"Just set it on the table over here." Crash walked her over to a folding table and cleared a space among all the papers and tools. He noticed that, for the first time since they'd arrived at Romeo Seven, Amanda looked at ease with her surroundings. "It looks like you're getting over your claustrophobia," he said quietly.

Amanda laid her burden on the table. "I guess so. I hadn't really thought about it today. I can take some coffee up to the crew if you'd like."

"That'd be good. Drake's in the head over there, but you could take some up to Murph."

"Oh…uh…I'll just wait for Drake. He can take some up to Murph when he gets back."

"Suit yourself."

Presently Drake returned from the restroom and noticed Amanda standing next to the small huddle of engineers. She looked different than she had at their last meeting. He remembered thinking that she had a pretty face, but today she looked stunning. The blond hair that fell around her face like straw before was now styled with a gentle wave, falling to her shoulders with a little curl at the end. She'd replaced the drab brown outfit of the previous night with a mauve skirt and lavender top that left her arms bare to the shoulders.

Drake unconsciously smoothed out his flight suit and straightened his hair. Then he walked over to the propulsion engineer with an extended hand. "Good morning Amanda, it's good to see you again."

Amanda looked at her watch. "Technically, it's good evening," she said, and then cringed at her own words. "I'm sorry; I have an annoying habit of always being precise, even when it's completely unnecessary." She pointed to the table. "Look, I brought you guys some coffee."

"Thanks, that's very thoughtful of you. So what's a nice girl like you doing in a top secret underground testing facility like this?" It was Drake's turn to cringe. He immediately regretted his dumb joke, but surprisingly she didn't run away.

Drake and Amanda continued to exchange small talk and learn each other's backgrounds until Scott clapped his hands. "Okay people, the numbers confirm a successful test so we've only got one more to do. Let's get to it."

"That's my cue," said Drake as he grabbed a handful of cream and sugar packets and shoved them into his breast pocket. He slapped a couple of lids on two coffees and headed for the jet. Back in the cockpit, he sat down in his seat and looked up at Murph, holding out one of the cups of coffee. "I'm back," he said, "I brought you some coffee."

"Gee, thanks; like I can possibly add that to a bladder that's already overfilled. What happened to 'I'll be right back'?"

"Oh, right, sorry about that. I got to talking with Amanda and forgot all about you." Chagrined, Drake grasped for a positive note. "The next test should only take twenty minutes; I'm sure you'll be alright."

"Yeah, right," said Murph, eyeing an empty water bottle on the floor behind Drake's seat.

"Don't even think about it," said the engineer in the back of the jet.

After something closer to thirty minutes Scott finally voiced the words they'd all been dying to hear. "Alright, I'm going to call it good. That's a wrap people. Let's break it all down and call it a night."

Murph looked at Drake with a slightly pained expression. "Since you carelessly put me through this ordeal, do you think you can handle the shutdown checklist by yourself?"

"I think I can manage. Go ahead and get out of here."

Without another word, Murph climbed out of his seat and scrambled down the ladder. Drake and the engineer looked at each other silently for a moment and then burst out laughing.

Drake methodically stepped through each item in his checklist until the B-2's avionics were completely dark. Then he grabbed his equipment and climbed down the ladder to join Scott and the others for a post-test meeting. Murph joined them a few seconds later, looking much more comfortable. Drake stepped up beside him and nudged him. Having gained Murph's attention he frowned and nodded downward. Murph took the cue and looked downward, reaching for his zipper, but he found it exactly where it was supposed to be.

Scott noticed Murph's unusual movements. "Are you alright Major Murphy?"

"Uh…yeah…just fine." Murph looked back at Drake, but his crewmate had picked up a chart and was pretending to study it. "Very funny," he whispered.

"Made ya look," Drake whispered back.

"I'm confused, what grade are we in?"

"Ahem…as I was saying," continued Scott, "this last test confirms the proper functioning of the catch and release mechanism. We're finally ready for flight testing.

Chapter 28

Victor and Murph arrived at the conference room to find several engineers busily setting up the pre-test briefing. The two pilots were dressed in their flight gear, complete with survival vests and holstered nine millimeter Berettas. They took their seats at the table as Drake entered the room.

"Where've you been?" asked Victor.

Murph sniffed the air and raised an eyebrow. "You smell like a chick," he said.

"It's just deodorant," Drake replied defensively, "and I don't smell like a chick." He sat down across the table from Victor, who stared at him with a look of intense curiosity.

"What?" Drake asked with a hint of frustration.

Victor grinned from ear to ear. "You smell *purdy*," he said with a heavy drawl.

"Shut up."

"Victor's right, you smell like you just bathed in jasmine and roses. You're trying to impress Miss Dasvidania aren't you?"

"It's Navistrova, and no I'm not."

Presently the room filled. Colonel Walker entered last, just before the time hack, carrying his standard cup of black coffee. Crash stood and gave an overview of the evening's activities and then Scott briefed the details. They would test Dreamcatcher in four major phases, including ground operations, airborne deployment, basic signals interception, and recovery. Murph would command the mission while Drake monitored the autopilot, watching the B-2 fly around in circles while the engineers stepped through their test points. Victor had the most difficult and dangerous job. He would fly in formation with the reconnaissance drone and record it's every motion on camera, making notes on a miniature clipboard strapped to his leg.

At the conclusion of the briefing, Walker released everyone to their workstations. The engineers went directly to their places, preparing for an immediate start to the ground operations phase. Victor followed Murph, Drake, and Scott to the lift up to the B-2's hangar.

Colonel Walker joined the group in the hallway. "Look boys," he said, "I realize that you consider tonight's mission to be a cake walk, but don't forget that you're carrying a craft that's never been flight tested. Don't let your guard down for an instant up there."

"Don't worry, sir," said Murph, "we'll stay on top of it."

Walker and Victor stopped at the base of the lift and watched it rise toward the surface. "You'd better," the Colonel called after them. When the lift was gone Walker turned to leave, but he stopped and sniffed the air. "Why do I smell roses?" he asked.

Victor just shrugged.

An hour later, Victor stepped off the other elevator into a dimly lit hangar. The only illumination came from a single overhead fixture that gently bathed two sleek, dark T-38s in the cottony glow of a soft halogen light. The only sound was the dull echo of his footsteps as he strode across the smooth concrete floor. He'd arrived at the hangar early. He'd always done that, particularly with a tail number he'd never flown before. It made the working day a little longer, but he liked to have a little time to get to know an aircraft before taking it up for the first time. Every jet had its idiosyncrasies, things that made it unique even among aircraft of the same type. This was especially true for T-38s, since they'd had forty years to develop their character.

Victor admired the classic lines of the aircraft before him. Like other T-38s their coke bottle fuselages and short swept wings gave them a powerful yet genteel appearance, but these were unlike any Talons he'd ever flown. They were painted dark gray, not with a glossy finish like their sister jets at Whiteman, but with a matte finish – the kind that disappears into the night. Inside they had the latest in cockpit displays, with ten-inch multifunction screens instead of the traditional round dials with rotating needles that Victor was used to.

Suddenly the hangar filled with light and Victor turned, raising a hand to his eyes.

"Hey! Who the…" came a gruff voice from the blur. "Oh, it's you. You're early kid. What was your name again?"

Victor blinked as the intruder came into focus. "Michael Baron, but people call me Victor. And you're Eddie, right? You're the Triple Seven Chase Squadron's lead maintenance technician."

"That's right," said Edward Patch with a smile. He stood a full six inches shorter than Victor with tousled white hair topping a wrinkled and rugged face. He wiped a blackened hand on dark blue coveralls that looked like they held an extra two pounds of grease and offered it for Victor to shake. "I see yer trying to get a little alone time with Millie and Elaine," he said.

"You could say that." Victor tried to place Eddie's accent, but he couldn't quite figure it. He spoke with a hint of drawl that must have come from either northern or western Texas.

"Ya know why we always name aircraft after women, don't ya?" Eddie asked with a sly grin, elbowing Victor in the ribs.

"I always thought it was because they were sexy and beautiful," Victor replied, cautiously awaiting the punch line.

"Nope. Any man who's ever owned a plane knows we name 'em after the fairer sex because, just like a woman, a plane'll steal your heart just to break it and drive ya to the poor house at the same time."

Victor laughed. "I guess you named these two after ex-wives."

Eddie looked at him quizzically. "What? Nah, I've been married to the same gal going on forty-eight years now. Nope, I named these two beauties after my daughters."

"Oh…right," said Victor. He decided to change the subject. "So, are they all ready to go?"

"Not entirely," Eddie walked over to one of the aircraft and patted its sloped nose fairing, "Elaine here is due for an engine overhaul, she's grounded until it's complete. Looks like you're takin' Millie to the dance."

Victor looked at his date for the evening and decided that Millie must have been either the eldest or the favorite daughter. Her namesake carried the tail number 777, making it the flagship of the little, two-aircraft squadron. "I couldn't have asked for a better looking date," he said to Eddie. "I'm supposed to be wheels-up at midnight, so we'd better get moving. I'll build my nest in the cockpit if you'll pull the gear pins and the engine covers. Once that's complete it won't take me but fifteen minutes to get the engines going and finish the preflight."

"You're the boss."

Victor didn't believe that for an instant, but he took the statement in stride and climbed up the crew ladder. A few minutes later, with his equipment in place and a few vital systems checked, he climbed back down again to walk around Millie one last time. As he moved down the left side of the jet, he let his fingers lightly track along her smooth surface, noting the remarkably even feel of the paint job. Most of the old '38s that he'd flown had dimpled and pitted surfaces, even after coming back from a fresh repaint, but the skin of this jet was like silk. When he reached the twin after-burner cans in the rear of the aircraft, he noticed that they looked different from the aircraft he was used to flying. "What's up with the cans?" he asked.

Eddie was busy making a final notation in Millie's maintenance logbook and he didn't bother to look up from his work. "Didn't they tell ya? These jets are C-model prototypes."

"Yeah, that's why they've got the glass cockpit and the GPS upgrade."

"It wasn't just an avionics upgrade. They've got modified nozzles that give you better takeoff thrust and faster engine spool-up. They were supposed to get modified intakes too, but the Triple Seven's commander rejected them."

"How come?"

"The new intakes can't handle the transition across the mach barrier, the wave will compressor stall the engines – cause 'em to flame out. I guess he's too proud to give up that supersonic title, even if it means giving up some low speed engine performance. Just watch it when you light the burners. These engines have a little more kick than yer used to."

"Thanks for the tip. Who is the Triple Seven's commander anyway?"

"Can't tell ya."

"That figures."

Chapter 29

"Mother-ship, Talon One is in position," Victor reported over the secure radio.

"Mother copies. Break, break…all players check in," said Murph.

"Talon's up."

"Hazard's up," said Scott, seated at the monitoring station in the B-2.

"Lighthouse is up," Colonel Walker finished the check-in from the ground station. "Make me proud gentlemen."

Victor had settled into a chase position just behind the B-2. He didn't want to move too far away from it; even with Night Vision Goggles, the black jet was difficult to see.

"Okay Talon," said Murph, "let's get started. Go to Observation One. Hazard, you're cleared to begin the deployment sequence."

"Roger," Scott replied mechanically.

"Talon is moving to Observation One," said Victor. He fell back to a position aft of the B-2 at its high center and then dropped below, staying well clear of the wingtip vortices. Then he pushed his jet in close, finding the sweet spot just behind and below the bomber's tail, where he could watch Dreamcatcher fall from the weapons bay.

Scott began the sequence. "Release in ten…nine…eight…"

Victor steeled himself for the turbulence that the open bomb bay doors would cause. He tensed his arms and prepared to fight the controls to keep his jet in the same position. When the doors swung open, it was just as he anticipated, but Millie handled the rough air admirably and he soon became used to the control adjustments. An infrared spotlight attached to one of the doors illuminated the bomb bay for Victor's NVGs. Compared to all the other structures in the bay, Dreamcatcher was an apparition. Where the rest of the compartment reflected the infrared light brilliantly, Dreamcatcher's high tech surface hardly reflected it at all.

"…three…two…one…release," Scott finished.

Dreamcatcher dropped quickly past Victor and he nosed the T-38 down to keep pace. He never saw the drone's low-emission engine light off, but he recognized when it leveled out of the descent. "Baby is away clean," he reported.

"Roger, systems communication is ninety five percent," replied Scott, noting that the direct data-link between the B-2 and Dreamcatcher was running well above the minimum requirement.

Murph pushed the test along. "Alright everybody, it's time to get down to business. Talon, get in tight and monitor Baby's performance while Hazard calls out the maneuvers."

"WILCO," replied Victor. He brought the T-38 into close formation, settling in with less than three feet separating his wingtip from the drone. "Talon's in position, ready."

"Copy Talon. The first test will be altitude changes and maintenance. Check your altitude at one seven thousand even," ordered Scott.

"Affirmative, Hazard, seventeen on the nose."

"Roger, Baby is climbing to two zero thousand, check rate."

Victor glanced at his vertical speed indicator. "We're climbing at one thousand feet per minute."

Dreamcatcher performed flawlessly through several flight control tests and soon the team moved on to testing the drone's sensor suite, monitoring cell phone transmissions and radio communications from Romeo Seven. When they came to the infrared test, Murph had a special task for Victor. "Talon, this is Mother. I want you to 'box the wash' fifty feet behind Baby."

Victor understood the unusual command. Boxing the wash was a maneuver that he had used at the Air Force Academy when flying sail planes. The purpose was to move around the prop-wash of a tow plane while still attached to the tether. It involved flying in a rectangular pattern behind the tow plane, above, below, and to the sides of its flight path. "Roger, give me a second." Victor pulled his throttles back and set up fifty feet behind and above the drone. "Alright, I'm in position."

"Go ahead Talon."

As Victor flew his pattern behind Dreamcatcher, Scott narrated what he saw on the infrared monitor. "Okay, I see a clear picture of Talon, with hot spots near the engines. I can even see faint hot spots on the leading edges of the wing where the airflow is creating friction. The aft sensors are good. Let's set up the next one."

"Alright Talon, that was easy," said Murph. "Try this next one on for size. I want you to show me the same pattern, but this time set up fifty feet in front of Baby."

Victor was caught off guard. They hadn't talked about this part in the pre-flight briefing. "I'm sorry Mother, could you repeat your last."

"You heard me, box the wash forward of Baby. What's wrong, can't handle the job?"

Victor would not back down from a challenge. "Negative Mother, no problem. I just wanted to make sure I heard you right." He sighed and pushed his throttles up, driving ahead of Dreamcatcher and giving the little craft a wide birth. "Well this should be interesting," he muttered under his breath. Victor would have to fly the entire maneuver looking over his shoulder, which was even more uncomfortable when wearing NVGs. To make matters worse, he would lose sight of the drone when he crossed above it, because Millie's wings and fuselage would block his view. He could only pray that Dreamcatcher wouldn't pick that moment to go haywire and run into him.

"Mother, this is Hazard. It looks like Talon is moving into position for a start below Baby. The picture looks good here as well." Then Scott's voice took on a puzzled tone. "Wait…Wait a second Mother. Something's wrong. He's crossing over the top now, but I'm getting canopy and cockpit returns; I shouldn't be seeing this stuff. I should be seeing the bottom of his jet…"

Victor strained as he looked down through the top of his canopy at the drone. He felt the blood rushing to his head and knew that he couldn't continue to fly upside down much longer.

"That doesn't look right," said Scott. "We're going to have to run it again."

Victor relaxed his body as he righted his aircraft and returned to a position behind Dreamcatcher. "Not to worry Hazard; Baby's eyes are just fine. I felt it necessary to fly the top portion of the pattern inverted so that I could keep Baby in sight throughout the maneuver."

"Show off," Drake transmitted.

"All players, all players, this is Lighthouse," Walker broke in. "That's enough fun for today. Let's move on to the final profile and call it a night before Talon runs out of gas."

"Copy Lighthouse," Murph responded. "OK folks, let's get moving. Talon, set up back at Observation One. Hazard, prepare to bring Baby in. Both of you report when you're ready."

"Talon, WILCO"

"Hazard, WILCO"

Victor eased his aircraft back to a position just aft of the bomber. "This should be pretty cool," he said to himself. Then he keyed his transmitter, "Talon's ready."

"Hazard's ready."

"Mother copies. Begin sequence."

Victor looked down at the small drone. It was flying a few thousand feet below him and a few hundred feet in front of the bomber. Suddenly it accelerated and climbed until it was almost level with him, and then it slowly eased backwards.

"Standby   doors,"   Scott   warned.   "Doors   in three...two...one...now."

The doors cracked open just as Dreamcatcher passed beneath the nose of the bomber. Victor adjusted for the turbulence and watched as the little craft steadied itself just below the bomb bay. On the rack above, the catches snapped open, preparing to capture the drone. Then Dreamcatcher inched upward, its laser range finders searching for the edges of the bay. At first its slow climb was as steady as a rock. Then something changed.

As it passed the bottom of the doors, Dreamcatcher began to slowly pitch and bank. The movements were not gross, but the drone was certainly not steady enough to make the recovery. The hairs on the back of Victor's neck stood up. "Something's wrong," he said.

"What do you mean, Talon?" asked Murph.

"It's hard to explain," replied Victor. "She just doesn't look steady anymore."

"Talon is right," interrupted Scott. "It appears that Baby is having trouble keeping up with the changes in the airflow around her. She won't commit to the recovery."

"Are you telling me that you can't dock the drone?"

"Exactly!"

While Scott and Murph argued, Victor watched as Dreamcatcher began to pitch and roll with increasing violence. He became impatient with the others' radio chatter. "Break, break...This is Talon. Baby is bouncing all over the place and it's getting worse! If we don't do something soon she's going to hit the side of the bay!"

Scott agreed. "Hazard concurs. Baby's reactions are compounding the problem, they're increasing exponentially. We have to abort now!"

"Everyone listen up!" Walker broke in. "I don't care what you have to do; you bring that drone back in one piece!"

"Mother copies. Talon, is Baby high enough that we can close the doors?" Murph asked.

"I think so. You're going to do some damage, but they'll close."

"Alright, here's what were going to do. Talon, back up in case we throw off some debris. Hazard, I'm going to manually close the doors. As soon as Talon calls it, I want you to cut Baby's engine. Is that clear to everyone?"

Just then there was an audible bang in the bomber as Dreamcatcher clipped the side of the bomb bay. A piece of black structure flew towards Victor. He shoved his nose down and banked right to avoid the projectile, but the maneuver wasn't enough. He winced as he heard it glance off of Millie's vertical stabilizer. Instinctively he pressed the "mark" button on his GPS keypad, capturing the coordinates, airspeed, altitude, and heading where the piece was lost. Someone would have to recover that little chunk later. "What a mess," he thought. "If that thing crashes, it's gonna be Roswell all over again." He keyed his transmitter and practically shouted into the radio. "Talon's ready! Hurry up; it's getting ugly down here!"

"Hazard's ready when you are," Scott responded.

"Okay doors are closing."

Victor watched as the doors obscured the drone. They moved quickly, but not quickly enough and he could guess that Dreamcatcher was becoming even more unstable in the confined space. "Cut the engine!" he shouted.

The impact was so loud that Victor could hear it in the cockpit of his T-38, an incredible bang followed by a series of dull thuds that reverberated through the air below the bay.

Murph's voice followed quickly over the radio, his tenor was raised, his words rapid and mechanical. "Mother has multiple master cautions on hydraulic systems three and four. It looks like the impact took out a hydraulic line in the weapons bay. Talon, it looks like we're going to have some brake problems. You'd better land first while we clean this up. Don't mess up. If you block that runway we've got nowhere to go."

"Talon copies. I'm off; I'll see you guys on the ground."

Victor returned to Romeo Seven and cringed as Millie bounced down the old runway; he wondered how the crippled bomber would handle the rough surface. As he climbed out of the cockpit in the second hangar, Eddie walked up to meet him. "I heard the test didn't go so well. Is the other crew gonna make it?" the maintenance technician asked.

"I can't say," answered Victor, "It sounds like the drone took out the hydraulic lines for their ground steering and brakes. The landing could be ugly." He climbed back up the ladder, grabbed his NVGs, and walked outside. Looking skyward he could see a trail of vapor forming in the bomber's wake as the B-2 began dumping fuel. In the illumination of the goggles, the combination of the bomber and its trail looked like a sparkling green dragon weaving a serpentine path across the starry sky. "They're dumping gas to reduce their landing weight," Victor told Eddie. "That's not a good sign."

Victor watched the bomber with the NVGs until it touched down. The landing looked good; Murph had it right on the runway's centerline, but then the B-2 veered left. He waited for Murph to correct towards the center but the big jet just kept inching closer to the edge, and they weren't slowing down. "Something's wrong," he said to Eddie. "They've definitely lost steering and maybe their brakes too. If they hit the dirt at the edge of the runway, the gear could collapse. They could be killed."

"There's nothing we can do but hope they get it under control," said Eddie.

Victor stared at the bomber for a moment longer and then ripped off the goggles and shoved them into Eddie's chest. "Maybe there is something we can do." He ran over to Millie, grabbed both sets of chocks out from under her tires, and began a full sprint to intercept the B-2.

"What're you doing?" Eddie shouted after him.

"I don't know, but I've got to do something!" Victor shouted back.

In the bomber's cockpit Drake tensed as the runway grew rapidly shorter. "We're still too fast," he said, "forty knots and holding, you've got to get more pressure out of those brakes."

"I can't," answered Murph. "One of the left wheels is dragging. I've got pressure on the right pedal, but I can't straighten her out. If I put full pressure on both sets of brakes she'll turn even further left. I can't steer and I can't slow her down. Prepare to cut the engines; I think we're going off the side."

"Scott, brace for a crash!" Drake shouted over his shoulder. As he looked forward again, a shadow beyond the windscreen caught his eye. "Is that Victor?" he asked, pointing out the left side of the plane.

Victor sprinted toward the B-2, hoping that he could intercept the aircraft before it passed him. The Stealth was already dangerously close to the edge. If the left gear went into the dirt, she would snap left or even cartwheel, with deadly consequences for the crew. He could think of only one thing to do to help his friends. Even though it was a long shot, he had to try.

The bomber was coming on fast and Victor demanded every ounce of speed that he could get from his legs. He carried both sets of chocks by their tether ropes. The heavy rubber blocks beat mercilessly against his shins and knees but he ignored the pain and focused on the bomber. "You've only got one shot at this, Victor," he thought. "You'd better make it count." At the edge of the runway, just in front of the B-2, he altered his direction to aim between the nose gear and the main tires. Finally, calling on his last reserves of energy, he lunged, slinging the chocks in front of the right main tires before tucking into a roll as he hit the pavement. The left gear passed behind him, missing his body by just inches, and he rolled behind the right tires as the bomber barreled past.

Murph felt the change in inertia immediately and the B-2 started to veer away from the runway's edge, back towards the centerline. "The drag on the tires evened out!" he shouted. "I think we're dragging something with the right gear!"

"Oh no," said Drake. "It's Victor! He's thrown himself under the tires."

"Worry about that later! Get on the brakes with me!"

Drake joined Murph on the brake pedals and both men let loose a tribal "Aaaaahh!" as if it might somehow prevent them from crashing into the dirt beyond the edge. The bomber continued to veer right, passing the centerline again, but it slowed. Finally, just as the runway's edge passed under the tip of its nose, the big jet inched to a stop.

Chapter 30

"Alright, spill it!" Walker fumed, storming into the conference room with a cup of coffee in each hand.

Crash felt the need to shrink into his chair. He'd never been involved in an accident of this magnitude. He looked at Scott for help but the engineer had taken a sudden, deep interest in his notes. It was obvious whose head would be first on the chopping block.

"Well?"

"Sir, we're going to need some time to figure this out," Crash said cautiously. "It's going to take a while for us to look over the data and figure out exactly what went wrong. Dr. Stone and I will…"

"Don't give me that engineer run around crap!" the Colonel cut him off. He looked at the contractors and scowled. "We wouldn't have to pay you guys so much if you couldn't look at a situation and figure out what was going on. Now tell me what happened out there!"

Crash looked to Scott, who was still hiding in his notes. He kicked the engineer's shin.

Scott jerked up from his notes, shooting a vicious glance at Crash. "Ahem…Uh, with a cursory look at the events on sortie one," he began academically, "it appears that we did not adequately anticipate the dynamic environment created by the air flow in the B-2's weapons bay, a problem compounded by LORA's own engine exhaust. Unfortunately her flight control reactions, even at the lightning calculation speeds of the onboard computers, were just that – reactions. Each change in the air flowing over the drone dictated new flight control movements, but by the time the movements happened there was a new problem to react to. LORA's deviations from the recovery point became exponentially larger until she finally glanced off the side of the bay."

"Fortunately Victor had the presence of mind to mark the location where we lost the chunk of the drone," Crash added. "Without his quick thinking the recovery team would have had a devil of a time finding it."

Walker looked around as if he'd lost something, like his wallet or his keys. "Where is Junior, anyway?"

"I suppose he's in the infirmary sir, he got a bit scratched up saving our necks," said Murph.

"Right. Remind me to give him kudos for that one. Getting back to the task at hand...Stone, I didn't understand a word you just said. Warren, rephrase it for me."

Crash tried to break the problem down to a more basic level. "The problem, sir, is that Dreamcatcher's recovery positioning system can't keep up with the changes around her. In a normal flow of air, a reactionary system is sufficient, but in the very turbulent environment of the bomb bay it's not. In order to remain steady enough for capture, Dreamcatcher would have to go beyond reactions and learn to anticipate the currents and flows around her."

"So what you're telling me is we have an unsolvable problem?"

"Not at all sir; while the air flow in the bay will be slightly different each time, there will always be a pattern. If we had a flight control computer with the programming to learn the pattern in the first few seconds, it could conceivably anticipate each cycle and make a successful recovery."

"Great, how long will it take you to reprogram Dreamcatcher?"

"It's not that simple, sir," cautioned Crash, cringing at the reaction he knew was coming.

"You're ticking me off, Warren. Don't offer solutions if you can't make them happen."

"I'm sorry sir; I'll try to explain more succinctly," answered Crash. He wasn't sure if he used the word "succinctly" because it was the right word to use or because his subconscious just wanted to watch the Colonel get angrier. "To make Dreamcatcher do what I've described would require more than just new programming. It would require several more laser range finders and a host of tactile sensors that could literally feel the air around her. Dreamcatcher's current computers can't take that kind of input."

"Don't we have a flight control computer that can handle the data feed you're talking about?"

Scott answered this time, "We do, sir: the human brain and neural system."

"Don't push me, Stone."

Crash and Scott exchanged a look of helpless resignation as Crash prepared to drop the hammer. "What we're saying, sir, is that a human pilot flies as much by feel as by instrumentation. It's commonly known as 'flying by the seat of your pants.' A human pilot inside Dreamcatcher could conceivably adapt to the dynamic environment of the bomb bay quickly enough for a successful capture. A live pilot's ability to feel the air would compensate for the lack of sensors and computing power."

Walker downed one of his cups of coffee and stared at the floor. Crash thought he could see an explosion building, but when the Colonel lifted his head, he just looked tired. "Can we modify her to accept a pilot?" he asked.

Crash and Scott both nodded. "Yes sir, I believe we can," Scott offered.

"How long?"

"Four months."

Walker's building tension boiled to the surface. "That's not good enough, gentlemen! We need it in half that time."

"Sir, I..."

"*Sir* nothing. Everyone between me and the President wants a result from this process and they want it yesterday. Four months is unacceptable. You'll get it back here and ready for flight test in two months or I'll make sure you're both manning the research station in Antarctica for the rest of your careers!"

"Yes sir," Crash gave in, shuddering as he envisioned himself crouched on the frozen tundra of Antarctica, pinning transponders to the flightless wings of penguins. There was only one thing left to bring up. "We'll need to decide who's going to fly it, sir."

"Don't you worry about that, Major, I know just the guy," said Walker, and he downed the other coffee.

Chapter 31

Victor sat alone in the small cafeteria at Romeo Seven, holding a rag to a cut on his forehead and nursing a cappuccino. He sullenly picked at a bowl of stale popcorn from a half-empty machine in the corner of the room. He knew the coffee would artificially keep him awake much too far into his sleep period, but he didn't expect that he could sleep much anyway.

The others were well into their meeting. Victor didn't attend, having very little to contribute. His job was complete for the evening, so he'd gone to the infirmary to patch up his wounds and then returned to the cafeteria to drown his sorrows in caffeine. He reflected on the failed mission, with its smooth progress abruptly collapsing into a series of compounding emergencies. He wondered if there would still be a place for him in the Cerberus operation or if he would have to go and hide somewhere, twiddling his thumbs and nursing his wounds until his fake attendance at Squadron Officer School was complete.

"Mind if I join you?"

Victor was startled by the voice behind him. He stood and turned, trying not to spill his coffee. An unfamiliar but smiling face greeted him. "Uh…not at all," he managed to respond.

The intruder wore lieutenant colonel's rank on the shoulders of his flight suit and the triangular patch of the Triple Seven Chase on his arm. "I'm Jason Boske," he said, offering a hand to shake, "but you can call me Merlin."

Victor reached out to take the hand and started to introduce himself. "Mike Baron, but everyone calls me…"

"Victor, I know," Merlin cut him off. "I make it a point to know a little about the folks who work for me, even if we've never met. Welcome to the Triple Seven Chase, I'm your commander." He took the seat across from Victor's at the table. "I hear your first mission for us was a trial by fire."

Victor was not surprised by the revelation; he'd suspected Merlin's identity as soon as he saw the patch. He sat down across from the lieutenant colonel and tossed another piece of stale popcorn into his mouth. "Trial by fire might be an understatement, sir," he said between chews. "Eddie was pretty upset with me for getting Millie all scratched up."

"He'll survive. The scratch to her paint job won't cost nearly as much to fix as the damage done to Dreamcatcher and the B-2."

"I guess you're right, but I keep feeling like none of it should have happened, like I could have done something more to prevent Dreamcatcher from tearing up the B-2's weapons bay."

"Number one: I was sitting in the control room with Lighthouse during the whole thing, and I thought you did everything you could. Number two: don't flatter yourself. Don't take on more responsibility than you can actually bear in any given situation. The damage done today was predestined by an oversight in the engineering process, and nothing you could have done was going to prevent it. Believe it or not, this is a normal part of the development process, particularly on the covert side of things. Anyway, you did your job right, not to mention your nearly suicidal effort to save the B-2 from catastrophe. You did the Triple Seven proud, kid. Heck, you even remembered to hit the mark button when that chunk got knocked off the drone. Thanks to that quick thinking the search team has already recovered the piece."

"You're kidding."

"Nope, we're pretty efficient out here. Tonight's problems are water under the bridge; let's talk about something else." Merlin pulled the patch off of his shoulder and laid it on the table. "The Colonel tells me you want to know what all of this means."

For the first time since Dreamcatcher hit the bay Victor smiled. "Yes sir, I surely do."

"As well you should; as any young officer should want to know the history of his unit," Merlin said pedagogically. "Very well then, in 1972, before you were born if I remember your file correctly, the powers that be decided to create a covert chase squadron, separate from the test squadrons around the Air Force. As a result, the Seventh Chase Squadron was born, with four pilots and two shiny new T-38 aircraft."

Victor raised an eyebrow.

"I see you noticed that I said 'the Seventh Chase' instead of the 'Triple Seven,'" said Merlin. "Keep that in mind for later. As I was saying, four pilots, under the command of Michael 'Rat' Shaw, were based at Holloman under various cover assignments. They flew the standard T-38 practice maneuvers and stole test and development practices from the overt test squadrons. Have you ever seen the movie *Top Gun* where Tom Cruise flies inverted directly over the top of a MiG?" When Merlin said "MiG," he held up his hands and made quotation signs with his fingers.

"Yeah, there's not a pilot in America that doesn't know that scene."

"True. Well, I don't know where the Hollywood guys got the idea, but Rat and his band of misfits invented that maneuver long before Tom Cruise was playing beach volleyball and showering with other guys. You see, they discovered that when you're trying to follow a bomb through its parabolic flight path, the easiest method is to approach it from above while inverted. They even practiced this feat on each other, with one T-38 pretending to be the bomb." As he spoke, Merlin demonstrated the maneuver with the "flying hands" that most pilots use when they tell a story. "It wasn't long before their first real test mission and Rat thought that his boys were more than ready. He sent Frank Eubanks up to fly chase on a reconnaissance drone; it was a lot like Dreamcatcher but without all of the space age technology. At one point in the test, Frank had to cross from the left side to the right side of the drone. He couldn't pass underneath because of a radiation hazard that we can't discuss. He should have gone behind, but he went over the top instead. Just as the drone passed under his wings and into his blind spot, it went out of control and the dumb thing made an abrupt pitch up, right into Frank's T-38. There was no attempt to eject and no further communications from him. Both Frank and the drone went down in flames in the desert. The resulting cover-up was a pain in the proverbial neck, but the Seventh pressed on."

"You still haven't explained how you added two more sevens."

"Patience, kid. Man, you Generation-X people have no attention span." Merlin took another sip of coffee and then savored it for a while before continuing, as if to emphasize his point. "Anyway, they buried what was left of Frank and carried on. The next test involved a laser-guided bomb. Rat was in no mood to have two successive failures, so he flew the test himself. They were testing a long range loft, where the delivery jet pitches up and literally lobs the bomb in an arc towards the target. Once again things were going smoothly for the first few minutes of the test. Rat followed the delivery jet until it lofted the bomb and then he chased the bomb through its profile. Just as they'd practiced, he entered an inverted dive above the weapon. This time there was no malfunction. The bomb was following its normal guidance sequence and Rat simply got too close; he failed to remember that laser-guided bombs tend to make large corrections."

"I've heard about that," offered Victor. "It's called 'bang-bang guidance.'"

"Yeah, well it went bang alright. The weapon made a pitch correction and slammed into his canopy. That wouldn't have brought him down with today's bombs, but back then we made 'em with more volatile stuff. Even though the fuse wasn't armed, the bomb exploded when it hit Rat's jet. This time there was nothing left to bury." He pointed at the ribbons on the patch that he'd laid on the table. "That's why the patch bears these names, written in blood red; they're a memoriam to Sideshow Eubanks and Rat Shaw."

Merlin stared quietly down at the patch for a few moments, as if paying his respects to the dead. Then he slowly lifted his head and continued. "After the second accident, heads began to roll. With two fatal mishaps in as many tests; the squadron was a dismal failure. Everything was shut down. Then, in 1984, a Major by the name of Bob Windsor stumbled across the records of the Seventh Chase. He was faced with a classified project that would require chase aircraft and had nowhere to conduct his tests. It was Windsor that pushed for a revival of Biggs North One with a dedicated chase squadron, and he annoyed his superiors until they finally gave in. Under Windsor the squadron took on an entirely new format. Instead of pilots taking this as a regular assignment, it was treated as an additional duty; something you do once in a blue moon. Only the maintenance technicians were permanently assigned, and there were only two of those. As for the pilots, there have only been six of us at any given time. Each of us has another flying job and only returns to Romeo Seven as the need arises and the clearances allow. Windsor also decided that the new squadron needed a new name; according to him, the old one was bad luck. He adapted the history of failure to pave the way for success. Counting the two previous accidents, this was the third iteration of the Seventh, so he settled on the Triple Seven Chase with 'Third Time Lucky' as its motto. So there you have it kid, the whole story. How'd I do?"

"It was a bit rough for story time at the local library, but not bad," Victor quipped. "Don't quit your day job."

"Thanks, I'll take that under advisement."

The two pilots looked up from their conversation as Colonel Walker strode into the room holding two crumpled coffee cups. They both slid back their chairs and stood up out of respect for the ranking officer.

"Victor," Walker said in a commanding voice.

"Yes sir?"

"I'm told you handled your first chase mission quite well."

"Not as well as I'd hoped."

"Well, it was good enough to earn you a promotion for the next phase of this mission."

"I'm sorry, sir; did you say a promotion?"

"That's right. I'd initially planned for you to ride in the engineer's seat as a linguist during the operational phase, but it seems a new position has opened up."

"Where's that, sir?"

"In the cockpit of the new Dreamcatcher."

Chapter 32

Oso sat at his desk trying to finalize the paperwork from Sidearm's checkride. He rubbed his temples and replayed the flight in his mind. The kid had come a long way since their last flight together, but he'd still made a critical error. Oso could have ended the checkride right then; he could have flunked the kid and sent him back to the drawing board, but he had the leeway to offer Sidearm a second chance and he'd used it. The young pilot didn't waste the opportunity. He'd flown the rest of the ride well enough to graduate from the program. Despite Sidearm's early mistake, Oso allowed him to pass. He knew that Torch would not question his handling of the flight, but part of him still wondered if passing the kid had been the right thing to do. He didn't have time to dwell on it. Tank walked into the office, interrupting his thoughts.

"Hey, did you hear about the meeting this afternoon?" asked the big pilot.

"What meeting?"

"Some mandatory thing about personal finance over at the Lobos' at three o'clock," Tank said with a hint of skepticism. "The Group Commander canceled all of the afternoon's flying so every instructor can attend."

Oso checked his watch, "That's less than ten minutes from now."

"No kidding. Put your pen down and get ready to learn how to manage your cash," said Tank, rubbing his hands together with mock enthusiasm.

Oso and Tank walked into the main briefing room at the Lobos, the other A-10 training squadron in Tucson. The room was already packed with thirty other instructors and Oso guessed that the combined volume of experience in the room was well over fifty thousand flight hours. He and Tank took a seat at the back of the room and prepared to be bored to tears.

"Room! Tench Hut!" The surprised pilots snapped to attention as the Operations Group Commander entered the room and walked down the center aisle.

"Take your seats gentlemen," said the colonel, smiling at their bewildered expressions. "I guess I'm the last person you expected to see at a briefing from the Finance Office. I apologize for the subterfuge, but we couldn't publish the real reason for this meeting. Lights!"

Someone doused the lights and flipped on a projector. The colonel pushed a button on his remote and a picture of Iraq flashed up on the screen. The briefing's true purpose began to register among the pilots and a murmur swept through the room.

"I think this is going to be a lot more interesting than we thought," whispered Tank.

"Things are heating up in Iraq," said the colonel, "and it doesn't look like POTUS is gonna take it anymore. CENTCOM has tasked the Bulldogs to join New Orleans in Kuwait and set up for a potential conflict. When Boise arrives, they'll take over the in-country flying, but New Orleans isn't going home. They'll quietly reposition to King Khalid Air Base in Saudi Arabia. In this way we hope to keep the true size of the force under wraps." The colonel flipped to the next slide. It was a list of tail numbers, three from the Lobos and three from the Dragons.

Oso could feel the intensity in the room building. They all knew what was coming.

"Boys, I'll get right to the point. CENTCOM is worried that the current theater assets won't be able to cover a full-scale conflict in Iraq. They're asking for our help. We've already committed these six tail numbers to plus-up the force in Kuwait, but that's only half the equation. The brass tasked us to provide eighteen pilots to support our jets."

Another ripple of excited chatter passed through the crowd. "Ahem," the colonel cleared his throat. "I know that many of you came here because this assignment was supposed to afford you more time at home, but we are warriors first and the call to battle has been raised. For better or worse, I have two weeks to put together a detachment and get them over to the desert. I've already pulled six pilots from the Operations Support Squadron. Gentlemen, I'm looking for twelve more volunteers."

There was no pregnant pause. There was no awkward silence waiting for the first hand to go up. There was no hesitation at all. Thirty-two pilots raised their hands in unison.

Chapter 33

The Dreamcatcher team would receive no awards. They would get no medals. In fact they would get no recognition at all, save a few pats on the back. Nonetheless, what they had achieved was unbelievable. One of the propulsion twins even claimed that it had to be some sort of record, though no one could pin down a precedent for comparison. The group had returned to Wright Patterson with grim determination after the failure at Romeo Seven. No one slept more than five hours at a time for the first two weeks; they couldn't even if they'd wanted to. The goal before them loomed too large and the pieces of the solution fit together too easily, one after the other. In four weeks not only had they re-engineered Dreamcatcher, they'd re-manufactured her. Like a phoenix from the ashes, their new craft rose almost of its own accord.

Crash experienced Déjà Vu as he led the group across the same hangar to the same temporary enclosure. "Once again, sir, may I present Dreamcatcher," he said unceremoniously.

Walker eyed the new product cautiously, walking around its perimeter and slowly bobbing up and down as he examined it from above and below. "Pretty much looks the same as before," he said.

"That's the idea," Crash replied. "She's bigger, though. We had to increase the central height by more than a foot. Consequently we had to lengthen and widen it by a few inches as well."

"It's hardly noticeable. Where's the hatch?"

"You mean the PEP?" asked Crash.

"The what?"

"The PEP, sir, it stands for Pilot Entry Point."

"You can give it whatever fancy acronym you want, it's still the hatch."

"Good point." Crash smiled despite the rebuke; annoying the Colonel had become a sort of hobby.

"Just pop it open, I want to see inside."

Scott stepped up to the laptop and punched a few keys. There was a sharp hiss and a vapor rose from underneath the small craft as a piece of the lower fuselage dropped down.

Walker stuck his crew-cut head into the hole.

"As you can see, it's a tight fit," said Crash, "even more for you, sir, since it was designed for someone whose shoulders aren't as broad."

"Don't hit on me Warren; just tell me what I'm looking at."

"Yes sir. The pilot will lay prone. The PEP...I mean, the *hatch*, is approximately where his thighs will be. In front you'll see a pad that supports his chest, with molded forearm rests on either side. At the end of the forearm rests are the controls; throttles on the left and control stick on the right. Additionally there is a data entry panel, what amounts to a compact keyboard and trackball, just to the left of the throttles in the slope of the interior wall."

Walker squeezed himself deeper into the tiny cockpit. "How does the pilot see to fly?"

"Installing windshields presented numerous technical issues, so we simply chose not to," answered Scott. "Instead, you have veiwscreens that are connected to Dreamcatcher's various cameras and sensors. If you look to the forward screen you'll see me waving at you."

"There's something wrong. You're showing in black and white."

"No sir, nothing's wrong. What you see is a grayscale, infrared enhanced image." Scott turned to one of the engineers, "Cut the lights, Bob." Outside the cockpit, the hangar went dark. "You'll notice we cut the lights, but the image you see has hardly changed. The beauty of this enhanced image is that it doesn't matter whether the outside is dark or light; the computer optimizes the view for the pilot. Lights, please." The hangar lights flickered back on. "The full screen gives a one hundred and twenty degree view to the pilot, or it can be sectioned to give three different images from any side of the aircraft. Terry, bring up infrared right on screen three."

"I can see the infrared on the right section of the screen," said

Walker.

"Yes sir. You are actually looking at the input from a sensor pointing directly out the right side of the aircraft. You should see a full spectrum heat image of Major Warren, who is waving at you."

Walker let out a gruff chuckle. "Judging from that red glow in your armpits, you're probably going to need a shower soon, Warren."

"Thanks for the head's up, sir."

"Wait, there's something wrong. I lost the picture," said Walker.

"No you didn't," Scott replied, "I switched your input to the radar sensors." He turned to Amanda. "Miss Navistrova, please hand me that radar transmitter over there."

Amanda quickly responded with the transmitter and Scott held it in front of the aircraft. "I'm holding a small radar transmitter that we use for testing. Watch what happens on the screen when I turn it on."

"I see a blue blob. The shape keeps changing, with spikes and bubbles popping out on all sides."

"Yes, sir," Scott replied. "That's what you should see."

There was a long, quiet pause. Scott stood in front of the aircraft, playing with the transmitter, oblivious to the awkward silence.

"It's very pretty, Stone," Walker said with impatience. "Now what does it mean?"

"Oh, right…What you're looking at is the image translated from a radio frequency energy sensor, or RF sensor. It displays radio wave energy across the spectrum. The color is determined by the frequency; it's tuned so that an active cell phone will appear red. What you see is an interpretation of the numerical data the engineer would see at the bomber's control station; we've just translated the information into something that's…um…pilot friendly."

A series of muted grunts and grumbles emanated from the cockpit as Walker struggled onto his side. "What're these straps near my legs for?" he asked.

"Those are the pilot stimulation straps."

"Sound's kinky."

"Excellent joke, sir," Scott replied flatly. "The pilot may have to maintain the prone position for up to thirty hours. That means there's a serious potential for blood clots in his lower extremities. After the pilot is in position, a technician will attach those straps to his upper and lower legs. The pilot, then, will have full control of the system via a toggle on one side of the data entry panel. When he places the toggle to ON, each strap will release a small electric charge in sequence. After the first sequence is completed it will repeat once every half an hour."

"You're going to shock the guy? You're joking, right?"

"No sir, it's a very good method for causing the muscles to contract to keep the blood flowing. I promise the system will work as advertised."

"Save your promises. I'm fairly certain you promised me you could recover the last version of this jet in flight, and look what happened."

Scott looked dumbfounded and Crash could see that he was searching for something to say in response. Just as the engineer opened his mouth to speak, Crash grabbed his shoulder and shook his head.

"Ok, shock therapy aside," continued Walker, still stuffed inside the cockpit, "how do you see the mission playing out for the pilot?"

"The intent, sir," answered Scott, "is that he will fly the bulk of the mission with the enhanced IR display on the central section of his screen, with the RF display and a communications display on the other sections," Scott explained. "He'll be able to isolate cell phone and radio signals in the target area and then roll a cursor over the center of the source to listen in."

"It's literally point and click," added Crash. "Once Victor isolates the source he's looking for, he can capture the coordinates and data-burst them to the bomber for the attack. Aside from that, the only other major change is the recovery system. It's a one for one exchange of the hardware, so we'll make the change-out when we return to the testing facility."

Walker sensed that his engineers were glossing over something. "Give me more detail on the recovery system," he pushed.

Crash took a deep breath and spoke slowly, treading lightly. "Dreamcatcher is bigger now, sir. Consequently, we had to shorten-up the recovery arm to make the whole thing fit in the bomb bay. That means we had to give up some of the shock absorption that was built into the original system."

"Great, we took a target zone that a computer couldn't hit and we made it even smaller for the human pilot. For your sake, I hope our boy is up to the task."

"We need to get him into the simulator so he can practice, sir," said Crash.

"I know that, Major, but right now I need him focused on other things. At the moment, flying is the last thing on his mind."

Chapter 34

Oso stood in front of the door of Torch's office. He hadn't been told why he was summoned, but he knew it must have something to do with the upcoming deployment. He took a deep breath and knocked.

"Come in."

"You wanted to see me sir?"

"Yeah, I see you volunteered for the Kuwait deployment along with everyone else."

"Yes sir."

"Since we have so many volunteers, we decided to award the slots based on performance on the strafing and bombing range. Shockingly, it appears from the numbers that you're the best shooter I've got. It looks like you're the number one pick."

"Thank you, sir," Oso said warily.

"Don't thank me yet. You may be good on the range, but I'm not sure you're ready to be back in the game. The fact that you can hit a practice target doesn't give me a warm fuzzy feeling that you won't freeze up and do something stupid like you did in Clean Hunter, although the balance with which you handled Sidearm's checkride shows promise."

Torch cocked his head to one side and frowned. "Here's what we're going to do. I'm going to look you in the eye and ask you if you're ready to go to combat, if you're ready to put members of your formation in harms way. I'm going to ask you if you can translate your flying skills into a combat victory, even if it means loosing another young pilot under your command. You're going to look back at me and either say 'yes' or 'no.' It really doesn't matter which of those you choose; I'll get my answer from your eyes."

The commander stood and leaned across his desk, locking eyes with Oso, "Well Oso, what's it gonna be? Are you ready for combat?"

he asked.

"Yes sir." Oso was surprised at the confidence and finality of his own response.

Torch continued to stare into Oso's eyes for a moment longer and then sat back in his chair. He placed his forearms on the desk and looked into the dark polished wood as if seeking its wisdom. Finally, he looked up again. "You leave in a week. Don't make me regret this."

Chapter 35

Victor stood with his duffle bags on the flight line at Maxwell Air Force Base, in Alabama. He shifted his weight impatiently and tried to look as inconspicuous as possible, despite the sweat circles forming at the armpits of his blue uniform. It was almost five o'clock in the afternoon and the Alabama heat was just reaching its peak. He'd been told to show up exactly at five, but he was desperate to get out of there and did not want to risk missing the flight due to a disparity between his watch and the pilot's.

Walker had sent Victor to Alabama to hone his Arabic skills, particularly in the Iraqi dialect. He'd spent nearly five weeks in isolation, living in the neglected "overflow dorms" of Squadron Officer School, a pair of buildings that hadn't been used since Congress started shrinking the military in the late nineties. "My room didn't even have a TV," he thought. "What are we, the US Army?" He'd been allowed no human contact, save for his language coach, who refused to speak anything but Iraqi Arabic; for all he knew, the man didn't speak English at all. The only other voice he'd heard was Katy's during the weekly phone calls that Walker allowed him. If anything, they served to solidify the illusion that he was attending SOS.

As he waited for the C-21 Learjet that would rescue him from this purgatory, Victor thought back to the dark hours of the morning more than a month before, when Walker had walked him to the plane at Romeo Seven. "Walk in like you own the place and nobody will question your presence," the Colonel had said, "but talk to no one. Don't go to the gym and for goodness sake don't go to the base theater. I mean it; no human interactions at all unless you're buying groceries. This is Covert Ops 101. You have to be seen as little as possible and never noticed, part of the background. You have to exist in their world without being part of it."

"And how does this relate to Cerberus?" Victor asked.

"You're the stone that kills two birds," Walker replied, "that's why you were singled out for this assignment. Your experience and proficiency in the T-38 and NVGs met the requirements for our little chase squadron, and the Arabic language note in your personnel file made you the right guy at the right time."

"And all this time I thought you guys had recognized my superior skills as a covert operative," Victor said, his disappointment not entirely feigned.

"It doesn't work that way, kid. Uncle Sam doesn't single out renegade supermen to do his dirty work like he does in the movies. It's all a numbers game. Your data matched certain search criteria, and here you are. The trouble is, now we have to reach beyond the original assignment."

"Honestly sir, I'm not really sure what the original assignment was," Victor interrupted.

"I was getting to that. Nobody ever taught you how to just shut up and listen, did they."

Victor shrugged.

"Anyway, like I said, you were originally brought on board to kill two birds. You were supposed to fly chase during the test phase and then sit in the engineer's position during the operation. You were always slated to go to Alabama to bone up on your Arabic skills. Your job in the actual mission was, and still is, to listen to cell phone calls and radio signals that will help us zero in on the target's position. The only difference now is that you'll be listening from inside Dreamcatcher while you fly her."

The beautiful sight of a Learjet pulling up in front of him brought Victor back to the present. The entry stairs lowered and a no-nonsense face poked out. "You Baron?"

Victor thrust his ID at the interrogator. "Yep, that'd be me," he answered.

"Great, get in. Let's go."

Chapter 36

Oso dragged his three large duffle bags up to a barracks tent in Ahmed Al Jaber Airbase's Tent City. As the top pick for the deployment, he'd had the honor of flying one of the Hogs over from Arizona. He'd just finished the last leg of the three day journey, followed by hours of mind-numbing in-processing briefings. He was exhausted. With a final effort he pushed back the tent flap and peered into the dim interior. A few domed aluminum fixtures hung from wires strung along the roof. Their weak bulbs barely illuminated the two lines of cots set up on the wooden pallet floor. At the back of the tent he spied Tank sitting alone on a cot; the big pilot was poking a stick at something inside a footlocker. When he looked up and saw Oso, he let the lid fall closed, looking like a kid that had been caught with his hand in the cookie jar.

"Hey there," said Tank, "you look just about as happy as I was when I got here." Tank had arrived a day before on a C-17 Globemaster with the main thrust of the deployment.

Oso stepped up to the empty cot next to Tank's, dropping his bags like huge sacks of potatoes. He glared at his friend. "I'd like to go to sleep now."

"No can do, buddy, we gotta be at the squadron in less than half an hour. Time to get cleaned up."

"Are you serious?"

"As a heart attack. The DETCO wants to get set up and ready to go before sun-up," Tank said, referring to the Detachment Commander. "Things are getting mighty hot around here; no pun intended. Iraq will barely give the United Nations the time of day and the President has made some pretty strong statements. The DETCO wants us to be ready for any contingency."

Oso shrugged his shoulders in resignation. "Well, I guess I asked to be here, so I'd better man-up. I hope I get to take a nap before the war kicks off, though. Do I at least have time to unpack?"

"Yeah, sure. Ops is only a short walk from here." Tank made a show of holding his nose. "Besides," he said in a nasally voice, "you should at least change your flight suit, that one's rank."

"Ha, ha."

"Look," Tank pointed to the footlocker between their cots, "that one's yours; I already dusted it out for you."

"Thanks," said Oso, reaching down and opening the dark green box. Something darted across the shadows inside and he slammed the lid shut again and jumped back. "What the..."

Tank fell back on his cot laughing. "You screamed like a girl!"

"I did not," Oso defended. "What did you put in my locker?"

"That's Ned, my pet camel spider," Tank replied, still recovering from his laughter.

"Those things are poisonous you know."

"They are not. Didn't you listen to the Local Hazards Briefing?"

"No, I slept through it like everyone else; but I know for sure their bites can cause a really painful infection."

"Don't be such a wuss; I'm careful with him."

Oso cautiously opened the lid of the footlocker once more. As his eyes adjusted to the shadows, one of the desert's ugliest creatures slowly materialized. With its highly arched legs, it was the size of a softball and nearly as white. The long abdomen curved upward to a point in the rear and the head was well defined – round, with two large groups of eyes and three curved horns protruding from the front. The arachnid reared up, raising its front two legs and letting out a low hiss. Instinctively Oso backed away. "Can't those things jump? What's keeping it in there?"

Tank smiled at his own ingenuity. "I've got him tied to a leash that's secured to a nail in the bottom of the locker...look."

Oso looked back in the box. He saw that Tank had taken what appeared to be the twine used to tie off sandbags and lassoed the creature between the first and second pairs of legs. The other end the twine was tied to a nail that stood like a post in the floor of the locker. The creature gave up on its aggressive posture and began inspecting the corners of the box.

"I think I've taken some of the fight out of him," said Tank.

The spider looked up at Oso helplessly, as if to say, "Get me out of here."

"He's got nothing to eat," said Oso, not believing that he was beginning to worry about the welfare of a camel spider. "You should probably let him go."

"Not on your life, bucko," Tank looked incredulous. "If I do that, he'll come back and bite me out of vengeance. No, I think Ned's smarter than the average bug. It's either keep him or squish him; so for now I'll hang on to him."

"Fine, keep him," Oso relented, noting that the discussion had gone too far into the surreal and ridiculous. "Just get him out of my locker, please."

Tank grabbed a small cardboard box that once held a six-pack of bottled water and scooped up the spider. Oso could swear that the spider gave him a look that said, "Thanks for nothing," just before disappearing into the box.

"That's okay. Ned knows when he's not wanted," Tank said, feigning dejection, but then he looked at his watch. "Crap! We'd better get a move on. No time to unpack, buddy, just grab another flight suit and throw on plenty of deodorant."

Oso and Tank walked across the sandy expanse of Tent City and into the squadron facility, where the other pilots were busily setting up computers and connecting network hubs. The prefabricated building was small, barely larger than a doublewide trailer home, and Oso wondered if its beige interior was someone's deliberate choice, or if it was just the cheapest color offered by the contractor. There was a chest-high counter that served as the operations desk and twelve cubicles formed by shoulder-high partitions.

"You're over there," said Tank, indicating the back-left cubicle to

Oso, and then took the space across the aisle. They shuffled papers into stacks and placed binders on shelves until someone near the front of the structure loudly interrupted them.

"Room, Tench Hut!"

Heads popped out of the cubicles like prairie dogs as each man stood to attention. Oso looked to the front of the room and his eyes widened in surprise.

"What's the matter, Oso? Didn't anyone tell you I was coming?" Torch asked. "You know I couldn't let you come out here without adult supervision." Everyone chuckled. Oso laughed with them, but he wondered if they understood how much more there was to the statement than a simple joke.

"They put me on the C-17 as a last minute change," Torch said, crossing the room and shaking Oso's hand. "Lieutenant Colonel Keys turned up with the measles; I guess he never had them as a kid. I'll be your Detachment Commander for the duration."

"Great," said Oso dryly.

"Okay, all of you listen up," Torch said, raising his voice and returning to the front of the room. "There's no time for the traditional settling-in. We've got to be up and running tonight." The pilots exchanged questioning glances. "Don't get your hopes up, this is just a precaution. There's no war, at least not yet. Besides, our primary purpose here is search and rescue. The Bulldogs are taking the front position as Close Air Support."

Oso gave Tank an "aw shucks" look. He knew that the Iraqi air defenses were in poor shape, and there was slim to no chance that an Allied aircraft would get shot down. Even if a war kicked off, they'd spend it sitting alert and eating popcorn. Tank shot a look back at him with just a hint of a gleam in his eye.

"Watch it Tank," Torch admonished, "I saw that, and I know exactly what you're thinking. Hoping one of the Bulldogs gets shot down just so you get to play in the war is kind of sick, don't you think?"

"Yes sir." Tank looked at the floor and Oso tried to keep a straight face.

"Bring it in," Torch ordered, beckoning the pilots closer to him. They all huddled close to the commander in the center of the room. "Between you and me and this really cheap carpet," he said in a low voice, "I think the Nighthawks are going to take a potshot at Saddam himself as soon as the opportunity presents itself. If something goes wrong, we have to be ready to go in and pull out a survivor. This thing could literally kick off at any moment, so no one's getting any rest until this detachment is at full alert status, got me?"

The pilots responded in unison with a sharp "Yes sir."

"Alright then, let's get to it."

Chapter 37

Victor stepped off of the C-21 at Wright Patterson Air Force Base and walked over to the hangar. He knew that simply knocking on the crew door was futile; the interior acoustics would mute the small sound into a feeble tap. Instead, he reared back with his boot and kicked the door three times. Presently, it cracked. Someone in the shadows took stock of the intruder.

After a moment's pause, Crash swung the door wide and vigorously pumped Victor's hand. "Good to see you again Victor, how've you been?"

"Busy."

"Me, too; but I can't wait to show you your new ride!"

"I can't wait to see it," Victor replied, beginning to share Crash's enthusiasm; he hadn't expected to get to see the new craft so soon. "Can I take it for a spin?"

"Not quite yet, but you can do the next best thing," Crash said cryptically.

Scott was waiting inside the enclosure with a couple of other team members. "Hello again Michael," he said. "Welcome back to the team. How was class?"

"Long and painful, but I've never been more confident in my skills."

"That's good," Scott replied, "because the Colonel seems to think you may get the chance to use them sooner than we expected."

Crash and Scott took Victor through a similar demonstration to the one they'd given Walker. They spent a little more time going over the operation of the systems, but they found Victor to be a quick study.

Inside Dreamcatcher, Victor found a Velcro seam in the vinyl padding. He peeled back a corner just to get a look at the structure and was surprised to see lines of orange and silver twine snaking back and forth along the surface. "Hey guys," he called from the belly of the jet, "what's this rope-like stuff inlaid on the interior structure?"

"Oh that," said Scott lightly. "That's explosive-incendiary cord."

"It's *what?*"

"It was part of the original design. If for some reason the drone was lost in hostile territory and had to be remotely destroyed, that cord would violently reduce the craft to a lot of dust and a few unrecognizable chunks. With some of the alloys in the structure, my guess is that it would actually be a dazzling display."

"Phenomenal," said Victor with an edge to his voice.

"We designed the system to be activated by a covered toggle at the engineer's station in the bomber."

"Let me guess, the cover is red."

"Never touch the big red button," Crash said with a laugh.

Victor crawled out of the jet and squatted beneath the hatch. He was holding one of the electric leg straps. "Explain this to me one more time," he said warily, eyeing the metal nodes that were distributed along the fabric.

"I'm telling you," replied Crash, "you'll thank us in the end. You could be lying in there for more than a day. You don't want to get blood clots in your legs, do you?"

"No, I guess not, but the idea of shocking myself while confined in a tiny cockpit where no one can get to me makes me edgy to say the least." Victor stood up and walked over to Crash. "You're sure the straps won't leave burn marks on my legs, right?"

Crash cast a slightly worried look at Scott, who responded with an almost imperceptible shake of his head. "Uh...no," Crash answered. "Your Nomex flight suit will protect you from burns."

"Just don't wear any cotton, nylon, or rayon socks...or long underwear," Scott added.

"What?"

"Just as a precaution; those fabrics are more likely to ignite."

"*Ignite?*" Victor tried to say the word in his mind without making it sound menacing, but he couldn't. "So let's break the whole thing down, shall we?" he said aloud. "I'm going to be riding in a coffin sized vehicle laced with *explosive-incendiary cord* while wearing electric straps that may or may not *ignite* my clothing."

"It sounds kind of extreme when you put it that way," said Crash.

"Alright," said Victor, shaking his head, "let's get away from that topic. What about my helmet and mask, it doesn't look like there's enough room in there for them."

"Good observation," Scott replied. "You're quite correct; there isn't enough headspace in there for your helmet. Instead, we've melded a thinly padded alloy headpiece with a noise-canceling headset. He walked over to the table and lifted the gray headpiece. It looked like no helmet Victor had ever seen; in fact, it looked more like a hardened skull cap with two foam ear-cups jutting out from the sides. Scott handed his creation to Victor. "Try it on," he said, smiling.

Victor ducked his head and pulled on his new helmet. It fit snugly, but comfortably, extending from the nape of his neck to the hairline at the top of his forehead.

"The strap stretches across your forehead, rather than under your chin," said Crash, showing Victor how to snap it in place. "This way it will be more comfortable than a traditional helmet, since you have to wear it for so long."

"How did you get it to fit the contour of my head so well?"

"If you remember, you left your regular helmet with us at Romeo Seven," Scott replied. "We brought it back here and used the molded interior to shape the padding inside this one."

Victor noticed a tube hanging from the right side of the helmet. The attachment on the end looked a lot like a miniature SCUBA regulator. "What's this?" he asked.

"That tube hooks into your harness, which has a small emergency oxygen bottle."

"It reminds me of my SCUBA gear."

"It's very similar, actually," Scott responded. "Should you have to eject, or should Dreamcatcher depressurize, simply put the mouthpiece in and bite down once to initiate the flow of oxygen."

"Excellent work, Q," Victor said as he removed the helmet.

"I'll take that as a compliment, but I hope I don't look as old as he does," Scott replied.

"Certainly not, but I do feel a bit Bond-ish with all of this secrecy and technology."

"Don't let it go to your head, Double-oh Seven," Crash said with a smile. "Now, follow me, and bring the helmet with you. I've got something else I think you'll really like."

Scott and Crash led Victor to a blue Ford sedan in front of the hangar. From there they drove to a small building on the other side of the flight line. As they exited the car, Victor thought he could hear a low hum from behind the nearest wall of the structure.

"You're gonna love this," Crash said, punching a few keys on the door's cipher lock.

The trio entered the building and the hum became a definite low-pitched buzz. Victor glanced through an open door to his left and saw rows of aluminum shelving, holding what looked like hundreds of active computer hard drives. "I've seen a room like this before," he said, "at the simulator facility for the Stealth Bomber."

"Very good," said Scott.

"You guys made a simulator?"

"Only the best for our baby's pilot," said Crash, motioning him through another door.

Victor opened the door and immediately felt like the cartoon character that opens a broom closet only to fall out of a skyscraper. What lay before him was so inconsistent with the exterior of the building that he almost lost his balance. He stepped cautiously through onto a yellow metal platform and gripped the railing in front of him. Beneath his feet, a room the size of a hangar opened up, extending at least fifty feet below him and another fifty feet in front, under the flight line. Stairs wound back and forth down to another yellow platform that was still a good twenty feet above the floor. From there, a drawbridge led to a hydraulic simulator. The whole contraption looked like a small abstract pyramid topped with a windowless cube. It had four tubular legs that extended to big cylindrical actuators bolted to the concrete floor. Victor had seen similar machines at Whiteman. When the simulator was piloted, the drawbridge would rise and the cube would stand on the hydraulic legs. Then each leg would move independently, giving the occupants the seat-of-the-pants feeling they would get from actual flight.

"In this short time, you completely rebuilt Dreamcatcher *and* you built a simulator to match?" Victor asked incredulously.

"We're just that good," said Crash, but Scott frowned at him. "Okay, not really. This is one of Wright Patterson's adaptable simulators; we can remodel and reprogram it for almost any test aircraft in a very short amount of time."

"Great, I can't wait to try her out," said Victor, "but right now I could use some food and some sleep. Where am I staying, anyway?"

Crash gave Victor a confused look. "What're you talking about?" he asked.

"You know, lodging, hotel, B and B," said Victor sarcastically. He held up his hands in a bad imitation of sign language, "*Where...am...I...slee...ping?*"

Crash smiled congenially. "Apparently you haven't heard."

The sarcastic curl at the ends of Victor's lips fell away. "Haven't heard what?"

"You aren't sleeping here. We're moving the operation back to the test site. The C-130 leaves in six hours. You have from now until then to familiarize yourself with the operation of this aircraft and practice in the simulator." Crash took a three-ring binder from Scott and slapped it into Victor's chest. "Better get started, kid."

Chapter 38

Victor gazed up and down the old runway at Romeo Seven. "And...we're back."

"Second time's a charm," Crash added.

Victor turned to face the analyst, peering at him quizzically in the dark. "I think the phrase is 'third time's a charm.'"

"I was trying to be optimistic."

The noise of the hangar doors sliding open interrupted their conversation. Everyone dutifully moved their gear into the darkness until finally, after the doors slid closed, the lights came on. The sudden illumination revealed Walker, standing there with Murph and Drake.

"I should have known you'd already be here, sir," Crash said.

"It's all part of my..."

"Personal mystique, we know," Crash finished for him.

"Don't rob me of my catch phrases, Warren, it angers me."

"Sorry."

Drake stepped toward the group. Victor reciprocated by stepping forward and offering a hand to shake, but the B-2 pilot ignored him and walked straight up to Amanda. "It's good to see you again, Miss Navistrova," he said with a charming smile.

"I assume you brought us a bomber to modify?" Amanda did not smile. She was all business.

Drake was stunned. "Actually, uh, it never left the other hangar," he answered. "We couldn't take it back to Whiteman with the bomb bay looking the way it does – it would prompt too many questions."

"One of the hydraulic reservoirs was gouged and the doors and hinges took a few hard hits," Murph added. "Our misfortune also inadvertently identified a problem with the emergency brake lines in the left gear. The repairs are complete, though, she's ready for Dreamcatcher."

The conversation faded and the group moved their gear toward the elevator. One load after another they lowered their luggage and equipment into the bowels of Romeo Seven, and soon they stood clustered around the big screen in the control center.

"I guess that's it for tonight's business," said Drake. "Who's up for dessert and coffee in the galley?"

"I'm going to bed," Amanda responded icily.

"I've got some light reading to do," answered Victor, holding up the binder that Scott and Crash had given him.

"I think everyone's pretty tired," Crash offered.

"Good," Walker stepped in. "In that case, everyone hit the sack. Since the jet's ready for the bomb bay modification, I want to get cracking. We'll meet in the conference room at thirteen hundred. That gives you nine hours for food, hygiene, and rack time."

Murph looked at Victor, "Sleep fast kid."

"No kidding."

The next evening Victor sat on the couch in the barracks common room and stared uncomprehendingly at the thickly worded pages of his binder. "My brain is full," he muttered. He felt wholly unprepared for the night ahead. In just a couple of hours he would strap into what he considered to be a death trap, and then have to fly it with near perfect precision on his first try.

Victor shook his head at the thought of his simulator experience. On his first recovery attempt he'd smacked into one of the bomb bay doors before getting anywhere near the sweet spot. On his second try he'd nailed a perfect recovery, but soon found out that it was merely dumb luck. The next five attempts were a montage of carnage as he slammed into every possible portion of the weapons bay until Scott finally begged him to take a break, because he just couldn't watch any longer.

During the break, the engineer was uncharacteristically sympathetic. He told Victor that the generic nature of the flight control logic in the adaptable simulator made it less responsive to operator input. Victor wasn't quite certain what he'd said, but took it as encouragement and returned to the grind. To both of their surprise, he docked successfully during five out of the next six attempts. The two kept at it until Crash finally returned and told them it was time to board the C-130. Victor couldn't remember how many attempts he'd made, but he knew his success rate couldn't have been better than fifty percent. He'd tried to explain this to Walker, but his warning seemed to go completely over the Colonel's head. "Sounds good, kid. You'll do fine," he'd said.

The door to the barracks opened, stirring Victor from his thoughts. Drake walked in, appearing to be lost in thoughts of his own. Victor closed his binder loudly.

"Oh, sorry, I didn't know you were in here," said the B-2 pilot, sitting down heavily in an oversized chair. "Doing some last minute cramming, are we?"

"Yeah, but it's not doing any good. In fact, I think I may have injured my brain. It has a slow leak."

"I know the feeling. Don't worry about it, you'll do fine. Besides, it's the new Dreamcatcher's first flight; so if you crash and burn, they'll probably blame it on the machinery."

"Thanks for the encouraging words."

"Speaking of crashing and burning…" Drake began.

"I'd prefer we didn't."

"Uh huh, but seriously, what does that thing have in the way of an ejection system?"

"Oh that." Victor perked up. "That's one of the most entertaining parts of my new job. You see, for me to get from trapped in Dreamcatcher, tumbling out of control, to gently descending under a parachute, requires four consecutive miracles."

"What miracles are those?"

"According to Scott, it's all based on timing. Once I pull the ejection lever, a series of ballistic charges will split the fuselage like a clamshell, causing both halves to fall away and leaving me in the center with the parachute pack. A quarter of a second later, a spring in the pack will eject the drogue chute, pulling me away from the aircraft pieces. At two seconds into the ejection, my chute should open and I should be able to watch the rest of Dreamcatcher fall away to a safe distance. At four seconds into the sequence, explosives in the fuselage halves will detonate, shattering them into a hundred burning pieces and destroying the evidence."

"That doesn't sound too complicated," Drake interjected.

"Just wait," Victor held up a hand. "You see, the ballistic charges that split the clamshell will explode rapidly from the back to the front of Dreamcatcher, thus forcing the pieces away in a V-shape. This assumes I'm heading nose down toward the Earth. The trouble is, if I'm out of control, who knows what part of me will be pointed at the ground when I pull the lever. The first miracle has to put me in the correct position at the time of the ejection, keeping me from being tangled up in the wreckage. Additionally, the aircraft is so compact that the ballistic charges had to be placed within inches of the explosive-incendiary cord. The second miracle will occur when the charge splits the fuselage without setting off the cord; otherwise, I'll be cremated."

"I see; that is a bit depressing."

"I'm not through yet. The parachute pack and the electric leg straps are all attached to the upper shell that, if you recall, is going to violently explode a few seconds after the ejection. These items are supposed to tear away from the shell during the detonation of the ballistic charges, but how many times have you used a product that was supposed to tear away with a certain pressure and never did?"

"I see," said Drake, getting the hang of Victor's game. "That's the third miracle; everything that's attached to you has to separate from the upper shell."

"Exactly, and if they don't, I'll be held fast to the shell when the explosive-incendiary cord goes off. Finally, assuming all of that goes well, my chute will open. The problem is that the pack's position in the fuselage is close to my upper thighs and – if you remember miracle one – I'm going to be facing head down at the time of the ejection. Between separation and the deployment of the drogue chute, the pack will be floating freely along with more than four feet of exposed strap on each side. If the wrong part of me gets tangled with one of those chute straps, the force of the opening will tear me in half."

"You paint a pretty picture."

"Thanks, I've always thought of myself as an optimist."

"Well, at least you've led a long and full life," offered Drake.

"No I haven't, I'm only twenty-seven. I'm just getting started."

"Sorry, I've never been good at encouragement. I'd better get out of here before I drive you into doing something crazy, like going on a suicide mission." Drake cocked his head and smiled. "Whoops, too late." With that, he turned and walked out of the barracks.

Chapter 39

Drake walked over to the cafeteria to get a last cup of coffee before the mission. When he reached the galley, he stopped short. There, sitting with her back to the doorway, was Amanda. He hesitated; she'd been as cold as ice ever since they'd returned to Romeo Seven. He'd thought they kind of hit it off during the first test, like there might be some chemistry there, but now it was the opposite. She wasn't just coldly professional; she was downright rude. He couldn't take it anymore. He had to know what was going on, and he had to know right now. He took a deep breath and marched into the kitchen. "Hi Amanda, what's up?"

Amanda turned. She looked uncomfortable, even a little pale. When she saw Drake her face darkened. "Oh, it's you."

"Are you all right? You look a little ill," he said.

"I'm just having a little trouble with the underground thing," she answered. "I thought I was over it, but something seems to have triggered it again. You know what? It's none of your business. I don't want to talk to you anymore. Go away."

"Alright, that's it. What's going on with you? What have I done to deserve this?"

Amanda stood up and put her hands on her hips. "Oh, like you don't know."

Drake put his hands on his own hips and fired back. "No, I don't know, so you're just going to have to explain."

Amanda glared at him. "I know everything," she said with finality.

Drake shrugged, frustration showing plainly on his face. "I'm still lost," he said.

Amanda's shoulders slumped in exasperation. "Fine," she said, "I'll play your game and explain it all. I know all about who you really are. I read your file."

"You did *what*?"

"Walker keeps a dossier on all of us. I...I wanted to know more about you." She looked embarrassed for a moment, but then she became angry. "You started it. You were flirting pretty heavily with me during the last test."

"Look sister, if that's what you call heavy flirting, maybe you should..."

"Shut up," Amanda cut him off. "I thought we might have had something special, but I hate getting into anything without all of the facts. I can't help it; I guess it's the engineer in me. Anyway, I read your file and I know what you're hiding. I know you're married."

Drake took a step back and pushed his palms straight out. "Whoa there, Nancy Drew; I don't know what file you read, but I'm not married."

"Yes you are. It's all in your file. I can't believe you waltz around pretending to be single, preying upon unsuspecting women. Did you think you were going to get me into bed?"

"Well, I...uh..." Drake stammered.

Amanda was on a roll. "I even know your kid's names," she continued, stepping forward and poking Drake in the chest with a delicate index finger. "They're Nikki and Ben. You're busted, pal." She stopped and folded her arms, as if she'd just made the closing arguments in a murder case.

The red flush of anger that had been building in Drake's face subsided. He collapsed like a rag doll into the nearest chair. "I get it now," he said quietly.

"I'm sure you do," Amanda said triumphantly, standing over him with her arms still folded. "Well, what do you have to say for yourself?"

Drake gave no account. He posed a question instead. "When you stole the dossiers from Walker's desk, did you happen to drop them on the floor?"

Amanda's iron exterior cracked. "How could you...I mean, what are you talking about?"

"I noticed before that you get a little clumsy when you're nervous. Let me ask again, did you drop the folders?"

Amanda took a step back and turned away. "Fine, you got me. Yeah, I might have knocked one or two of them off the desk, so what?"

"Do you think perhaps you might have mixed up a paper or two when you picked them up?"

The iron curtain was now completely shattered. "Oh no."

"Oh yes," Drake smiled, knowing he'd just been given the best upper hand he'd ever had in a romantic relationship. "Nikki and Ben are great kids. I love them dearly," he paused to watch the crimson embarrassment fill Amanda's cheeks, "but they're not mine. Those are Murph's kids." He stood up, now towering over her small frame, the master of his situation.

Amanda fell into his arms, her head buried in his chest. "I must have combined the first page of your file with the second page of Murph's. I'm such an idiot," she sobbed.

Drake gently stroked her hair, enjoying the scent of her perfume. He would play this hand to the hilt. "You're not an idiot," he said sweetly. "It could have happened to anybody. I'm just relieved you're not mad at me anymore."

"Mad? How could I be mad? I just put you through the wringer over my own clumsy mistake. You're the one who should be mad."

"It was an honest mistake," he said, bending down and kissing her gently on the top of her head. "We should just start over and forget it ever happened."

Amanda looked up, their noses practically touching. She dropped her hands to his waist. "Really," she sniffed, "clean slate?"

Drake was moving in for the kill. "Clean slate," he said with finality, letting his lips part as they drew closer to hers.

"Merigold!"

Drake jerked his head up at the sound of his name. The sudden movement of his square chin caught Amanda in the nose and she staggered back with a yelp.

Walker stood in the doorway of the galley, holding a cup of coffee and looking utterly confused. "What the…What're you two…" He shook it off. "Never mind. Merigold, you need to get to the conference room, STAT. The final briefing's in five minutes." With that, he turned and disappeared down the hallway, shaking his head and muttering to himself.

Drake turned back to Amanda, only to see her cautiously checking her nose for breaks, her eyes bleary from the attack. His advantage was gone. "I'm so sorry," he said, trying to recover the moment. "He surprised me and I…I'm so sorry," he repeated. It was no use, the moment was lost. "I have to get going," he said, and turned to leave.

Satisfied that her nose would remain small and straight, Amanda flicked the remaining tears from her face, walked forward with purpose, and grabbed the retreating pilot by the wrist. She spun him around, caught the back of his neck with both hands and, pulling his head down to her level, planted a long hard kiss on his lips. When finished, she pulled her lips back, held his head in her hands and said, "Do well tonight, I'll be here when you get back." Then she spun the bewildered pilot back around and gave him a hard slap on the rear, sending him out the door.

On his way out, Drake looked back and gave her a confused smile. He couldn't help but wonder if he'd just been sexually harassed.

Chapter 40

When Victor arrived at the hangar, it was buzzing with activity. His usual ritual of a quiet moment with the aircraft was out of the question. In fact, there'd been someone with Dreamcatcher around the clock since they'd arrived; Scott's team was not going to leave this one to chance.

Victor noticed a friendly face standing underneath Dreamcatcher and walked over to say hello. "I hardly recognized you in your flight suit," he said.

Crash was beaming in his new togs, but when he responded to Victor's comment, his expression changed from a smile to a very serious look. "Keep it down," he said, "the fact that I'm wearing this is still a matter of no small bitterness around here. If you'll recall, you were the one originally fragged to sit in the hot seat on the bomber. Finding your replacement was a real mess." He dropped his voice to a whisper, "The egg heads thought that a real engineer should sit at the 'engineer's station' but none of them have any of the training needed to participate in a mission across enemy lines. You know, in case of a shoot down."

Victor nodded his head in understanding. "Right," he whispered slowly, "So you're the guy by default because you've had evasion and survival training."

"Exactly," Crash said, raising his voice to a normal level and beaming again.

"How's she looking?" asked Victor, looking up at the open hatch on Dreamcatcher's belly.

"She's ready and raring to go. I think you'll find the ride enjoyable."

"Thanks, but the ride isn't what I'm worried about; it's the recovery. If I can't dock this puppy, I'll have to bail out and we're back to square one. Plus, I'm pretty sure that the ejection will kill me.

Even if it doesn't, Walker will...just before he fires me."

"You seem a bit stressed," Crash said.

"Just a tad. On top of the recovery, there's something else that's bugging me."

"Yeah, what's that?"

"I was nosing around the bomber's cockpit last night and I noticed that there's still a big red button marked 'Remote Detonation.' Is there something you'd like to tell me?"

Crash patted Victor on the shoulder. "It's all part of life in the covert ops fast lane, buddy. We can't allow the technology to fall outside of our control. If we lose communications and have reason to suspect you're incapacitated, we'll have to take drastic measures to protect the secrets."

Victor was taken aback by the matter-of-fact explanation. "That's a little cold. I think you've been locked up with Dr. Stone too long."

"Maybe you're right. Unfortunately, that doesn't change the facts."

"So if I get into trouble, and we loose comms for too long..."

"Boom," Crash finished, in a voice that was way too chipper. "But don't worry. It's not going to come to such an extreme."

"I hope you're right."

"I know I am. It's getting close to mission time. Let's get you saddled up."

Victor climbed into Dreamcatcher with the help of a step ladder.

"By the way, nice survival vest. You look like something out of a 'B' movie," said Crash, referring to the nine millimeter that was strapped to Victor's back just below the left shoulder.

"That was Scott's idea. He had the life support technicians move it from its usual place on the front of the vest because of my prone position in the cockpit. This way I won't be lying on top of a live Beretta for the entire mission."

"He's right, that does sound dangerous," Crash replied, "and a little uncomfortable too."

They continued the arduous process of getting Victor "installed" into Dreamcatcher, as Scott liked to call it, as if he was just another piece of hardware. As Crash strapped the last of the electrodes to his legs, Victor wondered if his cotton socks were far enough from them to prevent the ignition he'd been warned about.

"You're all set," said Crash, patting him on the calf. "Don't forget to try out the electric strap system. I think you'll be *shocked* by how well it works."

"That's not even close to funny," Victor said with a grimace. "If there's any turbulence out there, just make sure to keep those accident prone hands away from the red covered switch."

"No worries," Crash replied as he closed the hatch, "besides, I haven't had a klutzy moment in weeks."

A moment later a loud clatter and a muffled yelp assaulted Victor's ears from just below the closed hatch. "What was that?" he shouted at the darkness.

"Uh...Nothing," Crash shouted back. "I was just moving the step ladder."

Two hours later the B-2 flew high above Romeo Seven and Walker's voice boomed over the secure frequency, "Mission players this is Lighthouse, everyone check in."

"Mother's up and ready," Murph replied.

"Hazard's ready," Crash chimed in, with obvious excitement in his voice. "Baby is ready as well," he added.

Victor monitored the frequency on one of Dreamcatcher's receptors. Its onboard systems were loaded with the codes necessary to unscramble the exchange, but the closed bomb bay doors were blocking some of the transmission. His reception was spotty at best. Worse, it was just radio wave interception, not a two-way link. He couldn't transmit to the rest of the team; he could only talk directly to Crash over their dedicated connection. He hadn't caught Walker's entire transmission, but he'd heard Crash and he cringed when he realized that "Baby" referred to him. "I've got to get a new callsign before the actual mission," he complained. "I can't fly around being called Baby all the time."

"Sure you can," Crash responded. "I read a self-help book that said, 'if you don't want to become a victim of your circumstance, you have to own it.' If you'd like, I can make you a patch with a picture of Dreamcatcher superimposed over a bottle and pacifier when we get back."

"Thanks but no thanks, and I don't want to know about your self-help books."

"If you're not too busy chatting back there," said Murph, "we have a test to begin."

"We're ready when you are," said Crash. "Victor, go ahead and run your 'pre-launch' checklist."

"You mean the one that tells me to sit here and not touch anything?" replied Victor, looking at the digital checklist on his viewscreen. Under the heading PRE-LAUNCH it said NO PILOT ACTION REQUIRED.

"That's the one. I'll take care of everything up here. Mother, Hazard is ready for launch."

Murph needed no further prompting. "Drop him, Hazard."

"Deployment countdown is running. Ten…nine…eight…"

Victor heard the rush of air as the bomb bay doors swung open. Dreamcatcher would plummet a thousand feet below the bomber before she leveled herself out. A message on his screen warned him of the impending drop and his muscles tightened in anticipation.

DEPLOYMENT SEQUENCE INITIATED…

"Three…two…one…launch," Crash finished his countdown.

Victor felt his own weight vanish as the aircraft dropped in freefall from the B-2. It was a surreal feeling, floating in the middle of his cocoon while a series of messages flashed on the screen in front of him.

DEPLOYMENT SUCCESSFUL

AUTO IGNITION…

IGNITION SUCCESSFUL
AUTO LEVEL ENGAGED...

He felt gravity take hold again as Dreamcatcher brought herself to level flight.

AUTO LEVEL COMPLETE
AWAITING COMMAND...

Victor cautiously took hold of the flight controls and released the autopilot. He felt the aircraft give in to his command and slowly banked back and forth in a series of small S-turns. She felt a little ungainly, but she was manageable.

"Hazard, this is Lighthouse, what's Baby's status?"

Victor selected his voice channel with Crash. "Tell the old man that she flies like a pig but she's better than the simulator."

"Lighthouse, Baby says it flies better than the simulator."

"Chicken," said Victor.

"Hey, I'm saving you from the wrath of the geeks. There are at least ten people down there that will spit in your coffee if you call their baby a pig."

"Let's move on to set one," said Murph. "Have Baby initiate a shallow left turn."

The test flowed smoothly through increasingly complex flight maneuvers and Victor was awed by the technology at his command. The screens in front of him filled his entire vision. He felt as though he were in a hang glider, with nothing separating his body from the terrain below. The enhanced black and white image of the desert underneath him was incredibly sharp, broken only by small digital flight instruments near the bottom of the screen. He could make out every detail of the Romeo Seven facility, even though it was several miles away and thousands of feet below him.

When Crash was satisfied that the little aircraft was performing as it should, he asked Victor to engage the autopilot so that he could remotely program a set of maneuvers. "I have another test for you to knock out while Baby's flying on autopilot," he said finally.

"You mean you want me to shock myself," Victor said with contempt.

"Once again, you're such a wuss," answered Crash. "Trust me, its not that extreme. Just arm the system and get it over with."

"Whatever you say, boss." Victor reached for the toggle labeled PSS and flipped it to ON. Below the toggle, yellow lights on a black rectangle warned PSS ENGAGED. Victor clenched his fists and closed his eyes, preparing himself for whatever might happen, anything from a mild shock to the aircraft exploding around him. He took a deep breath and pressed the button. Instantly both of his legs jerked as every muscle tightened. He released an audible grunt at the pain; it was as if hundreds of tiny needles had pierced his legs all at the same time. Unable to see much of his legs, he sniffed the air, half expecting to smell burning cloth and flesh.

"How was it?" Crash asked.

"Are there any messages you'd like me to pass on to your family after I kill you?"

"That bad, huh?"

"Not really, I guess," Victor conceded. "There's no doubt that it stimulates blood flow, and the jet didn't explode so, all things considered, I'd have to call it a success."

"Okay Hazard, put Baby through her paces," Walker prompted.

"Alright, Victor," said Crash, "let's try out the selective viewing mode. This could be a bit disorienting, so prepare yourself."

"Got it. She's still on autopilot. I'm ready."

"Okay, when Baby makes her next turn, focus on home base," said Crash, referring to Romeo Seven. "Use your trackball like you would use the mouse on your PC at home. Simply click on the screen and drag a rubber-band over the area you want to see."

Victor used the control in his left hand to follow Crash's directions, and a little flashing cross appeared on the screen. He held down the trigger and used the trackball to drag it over Romeo Seven. A box made of dashed lines expanded behind the cross and then went solid when he released the trigger.

"Alright," Crash continued, "here's where it gets weird. Hit the Target command on your keypad. You'll notice that the image on the screen stops moving in real time with your aircraft. You're stabilizing your cameras on the target, where they will remain – no matter which direction you're pointing – until you tell them to do otherwise."

Victor experienced an awkward feeling as the aircraft continued turning in its holding pattern while the desert scene in front of him remained stationary, changing only in perspective. "You're right," he said, "that is weird, but I'm okay if I crosscheck the gauges." He focused on the instruments at the base of his screen. Even though the picture of the outside showed a level environment, the attitude indicator showed that the aircraft was in twenty degrees of bank and the compass was turning. "I'm okay," he repeated.

"Roger," answered Crash, "then lets continue. Now I want you to zoom in on the facility. You can do this by double clicking your trigger on the center of the box. Once you've done that, it should fill the forward portion of your screen."

Once again, Victor did as he was told and the result was just as Crash predicted. The screen divided into three sections. The flight instruments moved to the base of the left screen, which was otherwise black, and the right screen went blank. He now had a perfectly clear view of Romeo Seven filling the center screen as if he was hovering just a few hundred feet away. Crash had him command a traditional infrared view on the left screen and a radio frequency display on the right. The infrared display was largely uninteresting. Romeo Seven was so well insulated that it looked cold and abandoned. In contrast the RF display was alive with activity. Small flecks of red, blue, and green flashed in a random pattern against a black background. After a few moments Victor could discern a shape amidst the chaos. Rectangular shapes emerged, formed by the constantly shifting flashes, and soon he was able to relate them to the buildings at Romeo Seven. "I have three displays now," he told Crash. "The enhanced display has zoomed in and duplicated into the infrared and the RF."

"Yep, I can see everything you can see."

"Cool; then tell me what's up with all of the activity on the RF display?" Victor queried. "I thought home base was supposed to be 'emissions silent.'"

"It is. Those signals aren't coming from the facility. Baby's receptors are incredibly powerful. What you're seeing is residual RF energy bouncing off the buildings. It comes from cell phone towers, radio stations – anything that sends out a radio signal. All of that energy propagates through the atmosphere and reflects off solid surfaces. To Baby's RF suite, that's how you'd look walking down the street on any given day. Welcome to the Information Age."

"That's a sobering thought. No wonder so many people are getting brain cancer."

"That's never been conclusively proven."

"Uh huh," Victor replied skeptically.

"The residual activity on the image means that you need to turn Baby's gain down. You need to filter out the chaff. Besides, at that sensitivity, a real signal will be too obtrusive to pinpoint."

As if to illustrate Crash's point, Walker broke in over the radio. "Hazard this is Lighthouse, give me a status report." During his transmission a bright green blob filled Victor's display, covering the entire facility.

"I see what you mean," said Victor.

"Kind of annoying, isn't it?" Crash replied, and then switched to the mission frequency. "This is Hazard, we're just doing some fine tuning. Everything seems to be in order."

"Roger, let us know when to begin the transmission sequence."

"WILCO." He switched back to Victor, "Either you or I can enter a numeric gain setting between one and ten. I'll let you do it just for practice. Try a setting of four."

Victor entered the setting using his keypad and the display immediately went black.

"Lighthouse, this is Hazard. Begin your sequence." Crash prompted.

On his left display, Victor brought up a stored image of the facility and the locations where the engineers would stand when they made their transmissions. They would use two types of cell phone and three forms of radio communication in the hope that Dreamcatcher would be able to pinpoint the coordinates of each. Red and green irregular dots appeared in sequence on Victor's display. He clicked on each one using his cursor control and each time a set of latitude and longitude coordinates appeared in the bottom right corner of the display. He crosschecked them with the pre-planned coordinates. Dreamcatcher's performance was flawless.

Suddenly Victor convulsed as pain shot through his legs. When his body relaxed, he tasted blood in his mouth and felt the pain where he'd bitten his tongue. He looked down at the still illuminated PSS ENGAGED light. "Crash?" he said with slightly impeded speech, his tongue still throbbing.

"Yeah buddy?"

"I really am going to kill you after we land."

"Why? What'd I do this...," Crash stopped in mid sentence. "Oohhh, right; I forgot to tell you to shut down the PSS." He switched to an informative tone. "Yeah, it's going to activate automatically every thirty minutes until you turn it off. I think that information was on page sixty-four of your manual."

"Thanks, I think I've figured that out now; and I'll give you one guess as to where you can shove page sixty-four."

As Victor looked down to flip off the PSS toggle switch, he noted that his fuel was getting low. The tank was down to the level they had set for beginning the recovery test, something known as "joker fuel." He asked Crash to relay his status to Walker.

"Lighthouse this is Hazard, Baby is joker. I repeat...Baby needs his bottle."

"You've been waiting all night to say that, haven't you?" Victor asked with disdain.

"It had to be done," Crash replied.

"Mother, commence your recovery," Walker ordered.

"WILCO," replied Murph. "You heard the man, Hazard. Let's bring him in."

"Baby, proceed to the rendezvous point and prepare for recovery," Crash said to Victor.

"Roger, I'm on it." Victor keyed in a command to initiate the recovery sequence. As Dreamcatcher automatically turned toward the rendezvous point, he brought up the "Pre-recovery" checklist on his left screen and began to follow the prompts.

When the bomber grew large enough to fill a third of his screen, Victor disconnected the autopilot and flew it manually, just to warm up his reflexes. As he closed in, he replayed the simulator recoveries over and over in his mind. He tried to recall the actions that caused the most difficulty and those that helped him successfully dock, but in the moment he found it difficult to remember much at all.

"I hope you're not as nervous about this as I am," Crash's voice interrupted his thoughts.

"Probably more; but thanks for making it worse."

"Anytime. Hold on, Drake is yelling something at me." There was a short pause before Crash spoke again. "Drake says don't screw up."

"Awesome. You guys are real motivators. I'm in position."

"Copy that." Crash switched frequencies, "Mother, Lighthouse, this is Hazard. Baby is in position and ready for the recovery."

"Roger," replied Murph, "begin the sequence."

"Recovery sequence in three...two...one... execute."

Victor watched as the bomb bay doors swung open. Immediately he felt the turbulence they created and found that he had a hard time keeping Dreamcatcher steady. He knew that he was supposed to be moving up between the doors, but he wanted to get comfortable with the unstable air first. He held his position for a long time.

"Hazard," Murph shouted over the radio, "what's the hold up?"

Crash had also noticed the delay and was already keying his microphone to ask Victor. "Baby, say your status, is there a problem?"

"No problem," replied Victor, his voice tense, "I just needed a minute to settle down. I'm moving in now." He hit a toggle next to his throttle control and Dreamcatcher's display switched to the area above the aircraft. Now he was flying unnaturally, looking at what was directly above him on a screen that was directly in front of him. He cautiously added power and pulled back on the stick. The bomb bay drew closer, and on the enhanced black and white image Victor could distinguish every rivet in the bay.

There was a loud "chunk" as the receiving arm released from its housing and extended. The air became even more unstable. Victor resisted the urge to stare directly at the clamps on the arm; instead, he forced himself to see the entire bay, letting his eyes sense movement in any direction. He reacted to changes in the air around him with barely perceptible movements of the flight controls, his wrist anchored on the arm pad, his fingers lightly holding the stick and rapidly moving it in all directions. Then a sudden burst of turbulence bumped him upward. The arm grew unnervingly large on the screen and he almost crashed into it.

Victor dropped a few feet and struggled to settle the aircraft. As he began his climb again, a bead of sweat rolled down between his eyes. It hovered a moment on the end of his nose before finally splashing onto the panel below him. Then, almost before he expected it, he made contact. A green LATCHED message flashed on his screen. Instinctively he ripped the throttle to idle and punched a button that shut down Dreamcatcher's engine. The bomb bay doors closed beneath him. The sound of the turbulent air faded away to calm stillness. "I'm on," he said to Crash, almost disbelieving his own words.

"I know."

Chapter 41

"Whew!" Crash stepped back from the hatch and scrunched up his nose at the blast of pressurized air. "It smells like the football team's locker room in there. What's wrong with you?"

"Hey, don't blame me," Victor responded, beginning to back himself out of the cockpit. "The men in my family are hereditarily sweaty. It's a good thing we're not hairy too, or the combination would've prevented my forefathers from continuing the line. Besides, if you guys had built an environmental system for a pilot instead of a piece of hardware, maybe it wouldn't be so b..." Victor was interrupted by a great cheer as he stepped off the ladder. He quickly realized that they'd all been listening to his conversation with Crash and his face flushed with embarrassment. No one seemed to care, though, and several people walked up to shake his hand, offering thanks for putting the last piece of the puzzle in place.

Drake walked up and punched him on the shoulder. "I'd give you a hug, but Crash is right – you need a shower."

Walker came forward and offered a beer, but Victor shook his head and declined. "That's right," Walker said, "you don't drink, do you?"

"Not at all, sir."

"I knew there was a reason I didn't trust you." Walker smiled. "Next time I'll bring you a soda," he said, and placed the beer into Drake's waiting hand.

Drake held up the beer in toast, "Here's to my favorite teetotaler," and then took a big gulp under Amanda's disapproving eye.

Walker turned to face the group. "Alright people, the party's over. I want a debriefing in the conference room in thirty minutes, so get cleaned up and I'll see you there."

After two and a half hours of celebration and debriefing, Victor lay in his bunk, struggling to go to sleep. While the rest of the team laughed and smiled, Victor's mood had remained sober. He was not ready to celebrate. Despite being exalted as a hero after the flight, he felt like a charlatan. Normally he was confident in his abilities; he flew every maneuver as if it were second nature, but not this time. He hadn't told the others his concerns. He hadn't told them that he felt as if he'd barely made it, that his docking attempt had teetered on the thin line between success and total catastrophe. He hadn't told them that he was certain his chances of another successful docking were no better than fifty-fifty. There were six more nights of testing to complete; he would either succeed and be a hero, or fail and probably die in the attempt.

Amidst these thoughts, Victor fell into a troubled sleep, until a loud banging at his door brought him straight up in bed. He rubbed his eyes and looked at the clock. The glowing red numbers showed that it was just past eight in the morning – the middle of the night for Romeo Seven. It was quiet, and for a moment Victor thought perhaps he'd dreamt the sound, but then the banging started again, followed shortly by Walker's voice.

"Put your clothes on Baron, I'm coming in," said Walker, but he gave no time for Victor to comply; he flung the door open as soon as he'd finished the statement. Victor squinted at the Colonel's silhouette, dark against the bright lights of the hallway.

"What's going on?" he asked, too tired to add a "sir" to the question.

"There's been a development," Walker answered. "Our services are required in Iraq."

"But the testing isn't complete," argued Victor, "We haven't even tested the warning and caution systems in flight yet."

"It doesn't matter. We know that Dreamcatcher works. Our intelligence sources inside Iraq are predicting a high level meeting including two of our major targets, and they've narrowed it down to a fixed time and place. POTUS thinks we might not get another opportunity like this for months. There are no 'buts' about it. Pack your stuff. We're leaving."

PART THREE

EXECUTION

Chapter 42

Victor peered out of a side window of the C-17 Globemaster, hoping to catch a glimpse of their destination, but all he could see was the endless blue ocean.

"You're not going to see it out that window, kid," said Walker. "You'd better go up to the cockpit."

Taking the Colonel's advice, Victor headed for the front of the jet and stepped onto the flight deck, unnoticed by the two pilots. As he searched for the island, one of the pilots tapped the other on the shoulder and pointed at the horizon. Victor followed his gaze. A single line of green appeared through the haze, and then another line appeared right next to it. The thin space of blue between them suggested that the Forward Operating Base was seated on more of an atoll than a full island, merely a snaking line of ridges that barely broke the surface of the ocean. At the south end the two lines spread apart to form a "C" shaped lagoon. There the cobalt blue ocean slowly gave way to lighter shades until the terrain finally broke the surface in a thin, white beach lined with emerald palms. It was a beautiful sight, but Victor felt that he was more likely to find Robison Crusoe than a runway. Presently the base appeared amidst the foliage, and the pilots turned in preparation for their final approach, putting the island out of view. Victor went back to his seat, still wondering if those two had really found the right place.

"Not much to it is there?" the Colonel asked when Victor returned.

"Are you sure this thing can land on that little runway?" asked Victor.

Walker slapped him on the back and laughed. "Don't worry; it's a lot bigger than it looks from the air. Too bad you're not going to be there longer, there're some pretty big sea turtles that frequent the lagoon."

"Yeah, it's too bad. That lagoon looked like a nice dive, but I'd just as soon get this mission done and go home. I'm sure Katy is getting worried. What are they telling her, anyway? I was supposed to be home from Squadron Officer School in just a couple of days."

"The cover stories are out the window. Fortunately for us, several B-2's are being deployed here as a show of force. You, Murph, and Drake were all listed as ADVON, the advanced personnel sent to prepare for the squadron's arrival. As far as the rest of the base is concerned, you were pulled from SOS to meet that obligation. That's what Drag told Katy. Since we're making this an official deployment, tonight's B-2 arrival will come as no surprise to the local command, and the real ADVON won't be surprised to see you when they get here."

"You're telling me that Air Combat Command is deploying half a squadron of B-2's to this island just to cover our operation?"

"No, I'm telling you they're deploying half a squadron of B-2's here because we're about to go to war. If this mission is successful, we'd best be prepared to follow up with a few heavily loaded Stealths."

Victor nodded silently. He'd waited so long to be a part of this war, but now that it loomed before him, he simply longed to rush home to his beautiful wife and hold her tight. She would bury her head in his chest and cry sweet tears. He would gently run his fingers through the silky strands of her auburn hair and feel her soft breath upon his chest. She would make him promise never to leave her side again. He would gladly acquiesce. And even though they both would know the promise wasn't true, somehow it would make them feel better.

The C-17 parked in front of a pair of brand new hangars and the group filed out with their gear. Dreamcatcher, enclosed in a large, climate-controlled crate, was lifted onto a flatbed truck and driven to the back of one of the hangars.

Victor placed a crate on the tarmac and looked up just in time to see Crash stumble down the loading ramp carrying a box labeled FRAGILE, its THIS SIDE UP arrow notably pointing sideways. Victor ran over just in time to catch the other side of the box and prevent Crash from careening headlong across the pavement. "You okay?" he asked.

"Yeah, thanks," said Crash, wiping his brow, unexpectedly allowing Victor to take the full weight of the box. "Whoa, don't drop that," he said as Victor teetered backwards, "it's filled with very sensitive computer equipment."

"Thanks," grunted Victor, turning toward the hangar with his new burden.

"Nice of Uncle Sam to send us on a paid vacation to a tropical island," said Crash, cheerfully walking next to the pilot and looking around at the palm trees and blue water.

"If that's what you want to call it," Victor grunted. "I'm not sure we're going to have much time for sun and fun, but I am going to walk down to the lagoon and take a look before Murph and Drake arrive with the B-2."

"No, you won't," Walker interrupted from behind. "The command center needs to be set up and ready by the time the bomber arrives. POTUS wants us on a hair trigger in case the target's timetable is stepped up. Sorry gentlemen, no fun until the work is complete."

With the hangar doors closed, Walker pushed the group to their limit. They slaved away in earnest until a secure phone call pulled Walker away, giving them a much needed respite. The Colonel walked over to the Secure Telephone Unit that still sat on the floor in the corner of the hangar, loudly pointing out that no one had set up a table for it yet.

After a few minutes on the phone, the Colonel became agitated, and Victor could not help but eavesdrop. "You should have asked my permission, Joe," Walker growled into the receiver. "I don't need your man on the SATCOM unit; my people are perfectly capable. That's just one more body whose presence here I have to cover for." There was a long pause, and then Walker sighed. "Fine, since he's already here, he can work on the unit, but he's not cleared for the details of this op. As soon as he's done, I'm sending him back to his tent, and he'd better stay there until his flight off the island. Got it?" Walker forcefully hung up the phone and it immediately rang again. He ripped it off of the cradle and up to his ear. "Walker, here," he said angrily. "Oh, it's you…They're where?…Great, we're not even close to ready." He slammed the phone down and turned back to the group. "Get moving folks. Our jet is on final approach and this command center is no where near operational. You're all supposed to be the best at what you do. Don't disappoint me."

As Victor turned back to his work, his eyes fell on the pile of personal gear still lying in one corner of the hangar. He looked at Scott, who was sitting at one of the tables, programming a laptop. "Hey Doc, do you have any idea where we're supposed to sleep tonight?"

Scott responded without looking up from his screen. "Did you happen to notice a line of tents at the end of the runway while we were taxiing in?"

"Yeah."

"I hope you like cots."

"Great, I thought I was done with tents and cots when I left the A-10. What happened to the donuts and cable Air Force my dad told me about?"

"It died with Strategic Air Command and the Cold War," said Crash. "But consider this: be thankful we're not sleeping in foxholes on Iwo Jima."

Nine hours later, and after only a few hours of sleep, Victor awoke to the sight of Drake standing over him. "Wake up, Victor," said the B-2 pilot with a big grin, "our targets have stepped up the schedule."

Victor's sleep had been restless, plagued by dreams that played upon his fears for the upcoming mission. Most of them dealt with the hazards of the recovery rather than the dangers of flying over enemy territory. He sat up and rubbed his eyes. The tent was dim, but a thin line of bright light poured through the split in the flaps at the entrance. "What time is it?" he asked.

"Locally it's just after eleven in the morning; just enough time to get a bite to eat and a briefing. Then it's go time," said Drake.

"Did anybody bother to ask the targets if they wouldn't mind sticking to the original schedule?"

"I know; it's terribly inconsiderate of them. War has become so uncivilized. Come on, we've got less than half an hour before the briefing."

The pilots and Crash found Scott and Walker waiting in a conference room at the rear of the hangar. Four places were set at the table, with an unmarked binder for each crew member. There were apples and bagels for breakfast, along with carafes of water and coffee in the center. A screen at one end of the room announced MISSION BRIEF in yellow block lettering set against a dark blue background.

Victor glanced around the table at his crewmates. Murph looked grave but serene. Drake looked deadly serious, but he was fidgety, playing with the stem of his apple until it finally broke off. Crash was visibly excited. He was trying to maintain an air of seriousness, but his elation at being included in the combat mission was impossible to hide.

Victor reached for his glass and the pitcher of water. The two clinked together uncomfortably as he poured and he fought to steady his hands. With the glass only a quarter full he gave up the attempt, lest he embarrass himself by spilling it in front of the others. He concentrated on fighting off his nerves. He'd flown in combat before, in Operation Southern Watch, but this was different; a lot more was riding on his shoulders.

"Secure the room," Walker ordered.

Scott masked the projector and made sure the four binders were closed before taking one more look around. "All ready, sir," he reported.

"Alright, bring him in."

Scott opened the door and a man wearing desert camouflage fatigues with the rank of colonel on his lapels entered the room; he wore a cross above his left breast pocket and Victor noted with interest that he also wore a set of wings. Walker was not a religious man, but having the chaplain pray over the troops on their way to battle was tradition, and the Colonel never broke with tradition. The chaplain knew nothing of the mission or its purpose. He knew only that the men in the room would be flying in harm's way, and that was enough.

"Go ahead Chaplain Huckabay," Walker prompted.

"Let's bow our heads," the chaplain said with a gentle smile. "Father God, we come before you now as your servants. We confess our sins and ask that you take them from us and wash us clean, preparing us for battle. Take these four men, Lord, place your hands upon them and give them peace. Send your angels to guide and protect them. Grant them victory, Lord, and then bring them safely and swiftly home. Amen."

"Amen," the group responded as one.

The chaplain walked up to each of the four men and placed his hands on their shoulders saying, "God be with you." Then he turned and left the room. Victor sat down and reached for the water once again. This time he poured a full glass with steady hands.

"Welcome to your mission brief," said Walker. "Tonight we'll attempt to take out two of the three primary targets in the Cerberus program with one strike. You've all seen the Cerberus file, so this should be a review...Slide."

The first slide showed the pictures of two men, along with their dossier information, on either side of a red line down the middle of the page. On the right side Saddam Hussein smiled back with his familiar sneer. His full name, *Saddam Hussein Abd al-Majid al-Tikriti*, took up the top two lines of his section. On the left side of the page was a picture that Victor had only seen in the Cerberus file, though he knew the subject well. The figure was wearing a white and gold *kafia* head covering and sporting a thin black mustache and short beard. He did not sneer, but looked placidly to one side of the camera, as if he was unaware of the photographer. The first line of the dossier read: *Tariq Irhaab al-Tikriti*.

"Boys," said Walker, "meet Tariq Irhaab. He is your primary target. Let me repeat that. Irhaab is your primary target."

The pilots and Crash exchanged looks. Drake raised an eyebrow.

"I saw that," Walker said. "It should be no surprise to any of you that Irhaab is the primary. It also shouldn't matter; the idea is to kill them both. In any case, the analysts, and consequently the President, believe that he is a more valuable target than Hussein. Irhaab is a 47-year-old Sunni who heads the Iraqi terrorist organization known as *a'Nur*. We also know it as *al-Qaeda* in Iraq."

Walker leaned forward and placed his hands on the conference table. "The FBI believes that Irhaab had a hand in planning the attack on the World Trade Center. The CIA believes he is the mostly likely candidate to lead the resistance movement, should we topple Hussein's regime. Both agencies agree that it's time he met his maker. You'll notice that the end of his name and the end of Saddam's are the same. The name *al-Tikriti* indicates that the bearer is from Saddam's hometown of Tikrit. We've been unable to determine Irhaab's true birthplace but, true or not, taking that name gives him more legitimacy within the Baath Party and the Sunni underground. It should also interest you to know he is very intelligent. While we don't know where he's really from, we do know that Irhaab attended..."

"Oxford," Victor interrupted, finishing the statement. "At the time he claimed to be from Jeddah, Saudi Arabia. His bachelor's degree was in Engineering Mechanics, but he stayed on to get a Master's in Explosive Dynamics."

"And that didn't raise any red flags with the Brits?" asked Drake.

Walker ignored the sarcastic question and continued, "Should the targets move to separate areas of the compound, you are to focus your attack on Irhaab's location. POTUS figures that once the regime is brought down and we have ground troops in Iraq, Saddam will be easier to flush out, but taking a lesson from Bin Laden and Tora Bora, this may be our last shot at Irhaab...Slide."

A map of Iraq appeared on the screen. Walker looked directly at Victor. "Dreamcatcher's job is twofold. First: get confirmation of the targets' exact locations and pass the coordinates to Hazard for the strike. Second: get confirmation of a successful strike by taking optical and infrared pictures for the battle damage assessment. Murph and Drake, your callsign will be Haven Zero One, Crash will be Hazard, and Victor will be Wraith Zero One."

Victor breathed a quiet sigh of relief. He would not have to be "Baby" again.

"The mission will go like this: Just outside of radar range, Haven will deploy Wraith. Then the two of you will proceed inbound together." Walker pointed to an oval on the map. "Haven will take up an orbit here while Wraith continues to the target. He'll use whatever sensors are necessary to get confirmation of the targets' positions and then relay them to Hazard. Hazard will then program those coordinates into Haven's computers and Haven will proceed inbound for the strike.

"Murph, you and Drake will carry three five thousand pound GPS bombs in the left bay, opposite Dreamcatcher. Use two weapons in the strike and leave nothing to chance. They are fitted with cockpit programmable fuses, but leave them at the highest delay setting. That way they'll bury themselves deeper into the target and minimize collateral damage to the town adjacent to the compound." Walker paused to sip his coffee. "Once detonation occurs, Haven will return to an orbit on the far side of radar coverage. Wraith will remain in the target area just long enough to get some good battle damage imagery and then bug out for the recovery. Are there any questions?"

"What if we have a weapons problem and can't employ?" Drake asked. "What's the backup?"

"Good segue, Merigold," Walker answered. "You've led right into my next slide."

The image changed again, this time showing the flight information for a pair of F-117 Stealth Fighters. The callsign list at the top read "Shadow 01" and "Shadow 02." The flight lead was listed as Lt Col Boske. "These guys are on alert in Kuwait. Joe Tarpin at the CIA has built us a secure SATCOM network for this mission and the Nighthawks are included. Should you run into a problem, pass the coordinates to me and I'll relay to Shadow; they'll take off and complete the strike. Any other questions concerning the strike phase?"

The group was silent.

"If there are no more questions we'll move on to the motherhood," said Walker. He explained the administrative details of the mission. A tanker would refuel the bomber before it entered enemy territory and then orbit and wait for another refueling when the mission was complete. Walker had given the tanker crew very little information; they knew only what was needed.

Next Walker briefed the search and rescue contingency. "There are Sandies on alert in Kuwait for search and rescue," he told them. "If you go down near the target, make your way to the safe area here," he pointed to a hashed circle on the slide well south of the target. "That will give the recovery crews the best chance for pulling you out. Gentlemen, that's all I have. I'll see you on the other side."

Out in the hangar Amanda pulled Drake aside and wrapped her arms around him.

"How's your nose these days," Drake asked with a smile.

"Still a little sore, but I'll be okay." Her face changed from a smile to a look of concern. "You're coming back to me, aren't you?"

"Don't worry," Drake reassured her, "this one's a piece of cake."

Amanda gasped and released her embrace long enough to punch him in the arm.

"What was that for?"

"You big idiot, you just jinxed yourself. You can't say 'piece of cake' right before a mission. Even I know that."

Drake laughed; even Amanda's analytical mind was subject to the common superstitions of war. "Don't worry. I'll just walk under a ladder and break a few mirrors before I leave. Do you happen to have a black cat I can borrow?"

Her face softened, "Seriously, be careful. I've waited too long to find you just to lose you tonight, so you'd better come home – and with all of your pieces intact." With those last words she rose up on her tiptoes and kissed him passionately. Drake responded willingly.

"Ahem," Walker cleared his throat loudly.

"Come on," Drake exclaimed, pulling abruptly away from Amanda and wiping his lips with his sleeve. "That's twice, sir. Give a guy a break! Besides, you said, 'I'll see you on the other side.' That means you have to go sit in a command post or something. You can't say that and then just waltz around among the crew afterward…This isn't the other side."

"Shut up, Merigold."

"Yes sir."

"I came over here because Murph needs you in the cockpit. Get up there and let's get going. It's time to rock and roll…And Merigold…"

"Yes sir?"

Walker took on a sly grin. "I'll see you on the other side; and this time, I mean it."

"Now you've got it, sir." With that Drake gave Amanda a final peck on the lips and headed for the B-2's ladder.

Chapter 43

Victor struggled violently with the controls as Dreamcatcher spun toward the earth. The feeling of vertigo was overpowering, but he fought through his dizziness and shouted into his transmitter, "Hazard, this is Wraith. I've lost control and I'm going down."

"Wraith, this is Hazard, come in…"

The radio must have failed; the transmission wasn't going through. The spiral continued, but the desert floor seemed miles away. Victor tried again. "Hazard, do you copy? I'm out of control. I repeat…I'm going down."

"Wraith, this is Hazard, are you down there Victor?"

The screen went black and Victor began to panic as the crushing darkness closed in around him. "I've lost comms and I'm going down, Hazard," he yelled, continuing to fight with the stick and throttle. There was no response. "Any mission radio, this is Wraith transmitting in the blind. I am going down. My position is bullseye two six zero for twenty eight miles. Ejecting in three…two…"

"Mike wake up!" Crash shouted into the microphone.

Victor's eyes shot open at the sound of his first name. His brow was moist with sweat, his hands shaking. As he fought through the fogginess of waking and reached for his transmitter, he realized that his right hand had been resting on the ejection lever. "Uh…Hazard, did you say something?" he asked the darkness.

"Did I say something? I've been trying to raise you for the last fifteen minutes."

"Sorry," Victor yawned, "I dozed off there for a bit and my helmet got out of position."

"Don't make me do that again. You know what a stickler Walker is for radio discipline."

"Where are we anyway?"

"We're past the last refueling, almost to the launch point. Why do you think I've been trying to raise you? I need you to run your pre-launch checklist."

"Once again...you mean the one that tells me not to do anything?"

"Well it should say, 'the pilot must wake his rear-end up.' You're lucky that I can't control the shock system from up here."

"We're at the launch point. Are you guys ready or what?" Murph shouted.

"I've got him," replied Crash. Hazard and Wraith are ready."

"Good, initiate the launch on my mark...Three...two...one...mark!"

Crash punched the execute key on his console. "Ten...nine...eight..."

Suddenly Drake shouted into the intercom, "Abort! Abort the launch! One of the doors is stuck!" An animated green drawing on his display showed that the left door hung open but the right door had jammed halfway.

Crash responded without hesitation. His hand whipped to the abort key and he pressed it, but the countdown on his screen continued, "5...4..." Crash pressed the key again and still there was no response. "I can't stop it," he yelled. "It won't abort!"

"Go to manual!" shouted Murph. "Close the doors. Close 'em now!"

Drake rapidly pressed keys on his display. He tried several different combinations of commands but nothing worked. "I can't! They're jammed!"

Victor heard the rush of air as the bomb bay doors swung open, but this time something was different. There was a pulsing sound under the wind rush, a repeating pattern like the whir of an electric motor, ending each time in a metallic thud. He watched Dreamcatcher's screen follow its normal progression as if nothing was amiss, but he knew from the sound that something was wrong. Besides, Crash had stopped counting.

DEPLOYMENT SEQUENCE INITIATED...

"Wraith the door is..." Victor heard Crash say, but the words were cut off as the umbilical connection released and Dreamcatcher dropped away. For a moment Victor felt the expected weightlessness of freefall, and then Dreamcatcher slammed into the half open door. The little aircraft tilted hard to one side and pitched forward violently; Victor felt like he was trapped on a demented carnival ride. There was a horrible grinding noise followed by another deafening crash, and then silence.

Victor gripped the sides of the cockpit and tried to keep his stomach out of his throat. He could feel the aircraft tumbling through the air. Then the deployment sequence on the screen stopped; Dreamcatcher had finally decided that something was wrong.

DEPLOYMENT FAILURE
SEQUENCE ABORT
AUTO FLIGHT CONTROLS...FAIL
AUTO IGNITION...FAIL
AUTO LEVEL DISENGAGED
AWAITING COMMAND...

"Well this sucks," Victor thought, staring at the flashing cursor. He had to get Dreamcatcher under control, and to do that, he had to get the engine started. He tried canceling the launch mode. That brought everything that was automatic offline. As he fought with his systems, his subconscious noted the feeling that the aircraft was stabilizing in a dive and picking up speed. Several thoughts passed through his mind. How long before Crash decided to hit the panic button? How long could he fight this before finally having to eject to save his own skin? He was still on the outskirts of hostile territory. If he ejected now, the Sandy team might easily recover him.

Victor pushed all extraneous thoughts to the back of his mind and continued trying to start the engine. He switched the ignition to manual mode, allowing the air rushing through the intake to spin the turbine blades. Then he thrust the throttle to maximum, sending a burst of fuel to the igniters. The response was immediate. The engine spun to life and was soon at full throttle; too soon. "This isn't helping my high-speed dive," he thought. As he yanked the throttle back to idle, the electronic instruments came to life and he could see his altitude spinning down. That made sense, but something still didn't feel right. He checked the attitude display. He was seventy degrees nose down but he was inverted. Having gained the information he needed, Victor fought Dreamcatcher to an upright attitude and then began to pull gently on the stick, fearing that a stronger pull might break the jet into a million pieces. He checked his altitude; it was passing through five thousand feet and rapidly counting down. "Come on baby."

Dreamcatcher responded to his coaxing. The artificial horizon showed the nose beginning to rise and the airspeed soon stabilized as the G forces held it in check. Victor checked his altitude – twelve hundred feet. He pulled harder but it still took another four hundred feet to level out. Finally he pushed his throttle to maximum and began a fast climb. Then he realized that he was flying blind, on the instruments alone. He had no idea what kinds of structures or terrain were out there; for all he knew, he could be headed right for a mountain. With his climb under control, he pressed a key and turned on the external display. To his relief, it all looked clear.

Victor fought with his communications panel, trying desperately to establish a link with the bomber. He could see that Dreamcatcher was passing data to Crash, but he couldn't raise him on voice or even use his text channel. There were other concerns as well. For one, he was pressing forward without regard to his flight path. He called up his navigation display and found that he was roughly on course, headed toward the target. Then he thought about the damage. What if Dreamcatcher had a panel hanging open? What if she had turned into a big radar target? He'd be a sitting duck. He called up his RF display and scanned the desert in front of him for activity – there was nothing. If they'd seen him, they certainly weren't too excited about it.

★ ★ ★ ★

Murph and Drake turned the bomber to avoid penetrating an enemy radar fence while Crash tried helplessly to gain some sort of information as to Dreamcatcher's status and whereabouts. When he finally got a data feed from the little craft, it wasn't good; Dreamcatcher was heading straight for the ground in an inverted dive. He cautiously flipped up the red cover placed his hand on the remote detonation switch.

"Wraith this is Hazard, are you there?"

There was no answer.

"Wraith this is Hazard, my finger is on the big red button, buddy. I need a response."

The altitude on Crash's display rapidly counted down; he would have to destroy the aircraft before an impact made it impossible. "Come on Mike, give me a sign," he whispered. Then, as if on cue, Dreamcatcher rolled to an upright attitude and began to pull out of the dive. He took his finger away from the switch and closed the cover with a sigh of relief. The data on his screen showed the aircraft entering a climb. It had to mean that Victor was alive and in control. "Murph, he's with us," he said over the intercom. "He's got control, but I'm still unable to raise him on comms. He appears to be heading toward the target, though."

"Get him up quick and tell him to turn around," Murph responded harshly. "We can't continue and we don't know what kind of damage he sustained in the deployment. He might have a gaping hole in his jet that's setting off all sorts of alarms down there."

"Standby," said Crash, "he's bringing more systems online. Yep, he's got his RF running. It looks clear."

"It doesn't matter," Murph shot back. "This mission is toast. We've got to get him back."

"And do what?" asked Drake. "We can't recover him. The best he can do is to fly out to sea and eject."

"He's got a point there," Crash offered. "There's no way we're going to get him back into that bomb bay unless you can get your doors open, and right now I don't see that happening."

Murph calmed down. "Okay, tell me your status, Hazard," he ordered.

"Nothing yet, I'm still working on it. I've gained enough control to change his displays, but I can't talk to him."

"What about his RF scanner. Can't he select the mission frequency and listen in?"

"No dice," answered Crash. "That system is directional and has limited range. We can't get close enough without crossing the radar fence…and I don't think we want to do that with the bomb bay hanging open."

"This cake-walk is turning into a real nightmare," said Murph.

"What about Walker's contingency plan?" asked Drake. "He said that if we run into a problem, we should pass the coordinates to him via SATCOM. He can launch Shadow to complete the strike."

"This isn't the same," retorted Murph. "This is more than a simple weapons malfunction. Both aircraft are damaged. If we allow Victor to continue and attempt to get the coordinates, we could be sending him into a barrage of missiles and gunfire."

Crash stopped listening to the conversation up front and continued his attempts to gain communications with Wraith. Nothing worked. He decided to review the data feed and look for the source of the problem. What he saw there made him smile.

RF COMMAND RECVD
<STILL HERE>
RF COMMAND REJCTD
RF COMMAND RECVD
<DONT BLOW ME UP>
RF COMMAND REJCTD

"Genius," he said out loud. Victor must have remembered that he could type commands into Dreamcatcher's RF computer. The computer could only understand a limited vocabulary of numbers and preset terms. If Victor typed his own words into the prompt, it would ignore them as nonsense, but it would report the nonsense to Crash as rejected commands. It was a brilliant method of makeshift texting, but how was he supposed to respond? Victor didn't have a data feed like his. It was a one-way communications line. Then Crash had an idea. He moved the RF screen to Victor's center display and then back to the right. Then he waited a few seconds and did it again. The data feed soon lengthened and he filtered out the command lines in his mind.

<WAS THAT YOU>

<SWITCH TO CENTER>

< FOR YES>

It was working. Crash did as Victor asked. "I've got comms," he reported, "sort of."

"What do you mean, 'sort of'?" asked Murph.

"He can send me text messages and I can answer yes or no with display switches. It's cumbersome, but it works."

"Tell him to return," Murph commanded.

"I can't. I told you, he can text me, but I can only respond with blinking displays."

<CAN YOU RECOVER ME>

<DIPLAY LEFT FOR YES>

<DISPLAY RIGHT FOR NO>

Crash responded by switching the RF display to Victor's right side.

<THAT FIGURES>

"Tell me about it," said Crash, knowing that Victor couldn't hear him.

<CAN YOU DROP WEAPONS>

Crash switched the display to center and then back to the right.

<THIS SUCKS>

"You took the words right out of my mouth," Crash said.

<SYSTEMS OK>

<NO AUTOPILOT>

<I CAN CONTINUE>

<I WILL RELAY COORDS>

<THEN I WILL DITCH>

Crash leaned back in his chair and let out a long breath. This wasn't going to be well received. "Murph I've got something."

"Go ahead."

"He says he's okay and he wants to continue. He'll get the coordinates and relay them to us using the method we've established. Then he plans to ditch."

Drake looked at Murph and keyed his intercom. "You have to admit, the guy's got some guts."

Murph was not impressed. "There's a fine line between guts and stupidity. Did you get the SATCOM online?"

"It's up and running."

"Good, you have the jet. I'm going to get in touch with Walker and get his input."

Drake took responsibility for the bomber's flight path and Murph began to type SATCOM messages into his data entry panel. He got Walker's attention and explained their situation. He explained that Victor intended to continue and get the coordinates, but that he'd have to ditch in the ocean.

There was a long pause and then the SATCOM alert chimed with a return message.

TOO RISKY. GET HIM BACK

START DITCH OPS NOW

RETURN TO TANKER. DO NOT CONTINUE

Murph breathed a sigh of relief, at least someone around here was thinking clearly. "Give Victor a 'No' signal. Get him to turn around," he told Crash.

Crash got another message from Victor.

<CAN I CONTINUE>

Crash flipped Victor's display back to the center and then to the right. Then he waited.

<NOTHING HAPPENING>

<I SAY AGAIN>

<CAN I CONTINUE>

That was odd. It had been working fine before. Crash tried again.

<NO RESPONSE>

<ARE YOU THERE>

Crash slammed his fist down on the panel. What had changed? What else had failed? He scanned the data feed again but found nothing. He gave it one more try.

<NOTHING>

<TAKING YOUR SILENCE>

<AS A GO AHEAD>

Crash stared at the screens on his panel. The data stream, the displays, everything showed that his system was working. Victor should be seeing the displays move. Then a smile broke over his face as he realized what his new friend was doing. "God speed, Mike," he whispered at the screen, and then he keyed the intercom, "It looks like that's it. I can't respond to him. I think he's going to go for it in the absence of a definite negative."

Murph's chin dropped to his chest in exasperation.

"Enjoy your email," Drake offered. "I'm glad it's you and not me."

"Thanks for the support," said Murph, and he began typing into the SATCOM.

Chapter 44

Victor had never been insubordinate before, but the temptation to take advantage of his communications problem was too great. As long as Dreamcatcher remained airworthy, he wasn't ready give up on the mission. Besides, tormenting Crash by pretending not to see his display switching had become fun.

Despite the exhilaration of "going rogue," Victor wondered if he'd bitten off more than he could chew. Managing all of the sensors was difficult enough with the autopilot doing all of the flying, but without it his workload was exceeding his capabilities. His altitude, heading, and airspeed were all suffering; he was drawing a haphazard path through the sky rather than a nice straight line. "I'm glad I don't have any passengers," he thought. "They'd be puking their collective guts out from this roller coaster ride."

With considerable effort Victor finally got his sensor array set up to his liking. The enhanced optical display in the center showed the desert ahead of him, with the cursor poised and ready to select a target. On his right side he monitored the RF display, but still there was no sign that the enemy had any awareness of his presence. On the left he kept his pure infrared display ready; heat signatures from personnel and vehicles would help him identify the correct building. He programmed the RF monitor to look for radio and cell phone signals, so that he could isolate a call and listen in.

When he was comfortable with his displays and settled into a steady flight path, Victor decided to send another message to Crash. If anything it would serve to remind the analyst that he was still in control of Dreamcatcher, and to keep his finger away from that remote detonation switch.

★ ★ ★ ★

Crash turned back to his computer as the data feed lengthened again.

<STILL PRESSING FORWARD>

<70 MI FROM BRAVO>

"Hey Murph, I just got another message from our boy," Crash reported.

"What'd he say, 'Just kidding, coming home now'?" Drake asked, looking up from the massive technical manual that was sitting in his lap.

"I wish he would," said Murph. "To say that my SATCOM session with Walker was tense would be an understatement. I've never been digitally berated before; it was markedly unpleasant. I'd love to be able to report that Victor was turning back."

"No such luck," answered Crash. "He's seventy miles from his planned hold at Point Bravo. If anything's going to go down, it'll go down soon."

"How much time does he have?" asked Murph.

"By my calculation, he's got just over forty minutes before he has to turn and head for the gulf."

"Copy that." Murph turned to Drake. "What've you got for me in solving the door problem?"

Drake closed the "Dash-One" technical manual that was slowly cutting off the circulation in his legs. He looked up at Murph and shrugged. "I've got nothing," he said with resignation. "I've tried everything in the book and a few things that aren't, and nothing works. The right bay doors are jammed solid."

"That's not good enough," Murph said. "As long as Victor's still airborne, we've got to try and find a way to recover him."

"Tell you what boss, how about you let me fly for a while and you can take a stab at it?" Drake held up the heavy binder to emphasize the offer.

"Fair enough," Murph replied, his tone a bit more relaxed.

"That'll give me a chance to show you what years of experience can do."

"I hope so, man, I really do."

★ ★ ★ ★

Victor watched the target compound grow larger on his display. It was a perfect match to the photo that Scott had loaded into Dreamcatcher's data bank. "Good," he thought, "at least this part's going according to plan." He used his cursor to drag a box around the compound just like he'd practiced during the test flight. Then he zoomed in until it filled the screen. Even when he started a turn to enter his holding pattern, the target remained fixed on his display, changing only in perspective. Without a normal forward image, it became difficult to fly again. He gave up trying to operate the sensors for a while, focusing his energies on flying by referencing his small digital instruments. Once he had settled into a routine, he slowly returned to the targeting process, adding individual tasks, one by one, until he was able to fly and work the sensors at the same time. It wasn't a matter of learning how to fly all over again, but it was awkward.

On the infrared display Victor could see a few vehicles in the compound, all parked near a building on the southeast side. Three of them had red blotches in the front, indicating that the engines were still warm. Then something in the corner of the image caught his eye. A small white circle flared and then subsided to a dim red. He increased the zoom to focus on the area and found a pair of individuals standing outside the building's entrance. Both of them appeared to be carrying rifles. Then the white spot appeared again, near the mouth of one of the men. It happened two more times before Victor finally realized what he was watching. The man was smoking a cigarette; every time he drew a puff, the hot end of the stick lit up the display. Victor laughed. Apparently the cigarette made the Iraqi an easy target for any weapon with an infrared sensor. "They should add that to the Surgeon General's warnings," he muttered.

The RF display was disappointingly blank. There were a few

sparks of blue and red, but nothing big enough to isolate for audio. Victor wondered if their intelligence reports had failed them; it certainly wouldn't be the first time. Still, the warm vehicles and the guards outside indicated otherwise. Something was happening down there. The enemy was just using good comm discipline.

Nothing new happened for several minutes and Victor started to lose hope, but then a red blob exploded on his RF display. He quickly tuned the image to narrow down the signal's location and found that it was coming from the same building where the man with the cigarette was standing. With a flash of his cursor and a few keypunches he isolated the audio. He half expected the signal to be broken and difficult to understand, but it was as clear as a bell and he recognized the voice.

"*La, la!*" the voice said emphatically in Arabic. "No, no! I told you, that is not good enough. You will have the Mercedes at the location in my communiqué in four days, or you will return my money."

"*Ya sayed,*" another voice responded. "But sir, you must understand that the normal shipping channels are out of the question. The current tightening by the United Nations is causing an unavoidable delay."

"Don't give me excuses!" the first voice replied angrily. "You made a deal. I am not one of your normal customers, some wealthy simpleton with a lot of money and no brains. I know how your business works and I know that you can deliver on schedule. Let me put it to you this way, you little beggar. I will get my vehicle, on time *and* in the correct color scheme, or you will find yourself standing before Allah's judgment much earlier than you'd planned."

Victor smiled. "Hello Tariq," he said out loud. "Tsk tsk," he clicked his tongue against the roof of his mouth, "making personal calls on company time is never a good idea." He sent another text to Crash.

<GOT THEM>

<COORDS TO FOLLOW>

Chapter 45

Merlin waited for his wingman to settle into position as the formation climbed through ten thousand feet above the northern Kuwaiti desert.

"Shadow Two is established in trail," the other pilot said in a monotone.

"Shadow One copies," Merlin acknowledged. He switched his F-117 to autopilot and made another check of his systems. "I hope this goes better than last time," he thought, recalling his last mission under the Cerberus umbrella. He knew that it was a hollow hope; the fact that he was even airborne meant something had gone terribly wrong with the original plan. Cerberus had already switched to Plan B and there was no Plan C. Walker, under the callsign Lighthouse, had given him scant details. Merlin knew only that the B-2 would be unable to drop its bombs. Lighthouse had simply ordered him to get his flight in the air; whether or not a good set of target coordinates was on the way was still unknown.

Merlin thought about his newest Triple Seven Chase recruit. He didn't know exactly why, but he had faith in the kid. If Baron still had air under his wings, he'd produce some coordinates; he had to. He was worried though. If the B-2 was out of the picture, it meant that the kid was on his own, with no method of recovery. He compartmentalized the thought and shoved it to the back of his mind. He needed to focus on his part of the mission; he could save his worries for later.

"Shadow Two, this is One."

"Go for Two."

"Give me another systems check. We don't want to leave anything to chance on this one."

"WILCO. Systems are good. What's our time to the target?"

"It looks like we're a little under forty minutes out. I'm just glad its clear up here, that haze layer we flew through on takeoff was pretty ugly."

"No kidding."

★ ★ ★ ★

An unusually cool air mass had moved in from the Persian Gulf, forcing the oil burn-off to stay low and mix with the desert dust. The resulting haze had shrouded Ahmed Al Jaber Airbase in a thick darkness that no stars could penetrate. Tent City was unusually quiet, even for this time of night. The blanket of haze had muted all sound and turned a benign stillness into an eerie silence. Oso sat on his cot, waiting for his shift to begin. Then he heard a quiet voice just outside the tent. After each statement he could hear the distinctive chirp of a secure hand-held radio, called a "brick."

"Control, this is Sandy Alert Five signing off. I'll be handing my brick over to Nine momentarily."

The brick chirped and a disembodied voice crackled, "Control copies. Sleep tight."

The tent flap opened and the pilot with the brick walked over to Oso's cot. "Hey there," he said in a tired voice.

"Hey, TJ."

"Are you up already?"

"I've been awake for the last thirty minutes. My body won't let me go back to sleep once I wake up within an hour of a shift. I think it was engine noise that woke me, though. Is something going on?"

"Don't know. I heard it too. I can't be sure, but I think a couple of Stinkbugs just took off," replied TJ, using the vernacular term for the Nighthawks.

"There's nothing on the schedule," said Oso, curiosity creeping into his voice. "I'm sure of it. I checked the spreadsheet just before I went to sleep."

"Yeah, I checked it too. Whatever's going on is above our pay grade, but if it's not on the schedule, you can bet they're headed across the border. You'd better get your crew ready."

"Good advice." Oso patted his friend on the shoulder, "I'll take it from here; you get some sleep."

"Thanks, I could use some. I hope you have an uneventful night."

"Me, too," Oso replied. A dull nasal roar erupted from the cot behind him and he turned to look at Tank, who was still sound asleep. Several amusing and somewhat cruel ways to wake his friend flashed through his mind, but he opted for a simple shake instead. Tank stirred but quickly fell back into dreamland, rolling onto his side. Oso tried again. "Tank," he whispered, shaking his friend with a bit more vigor, "wake up man, we're on." There was no response. The big pilot might as well have been in a coma. "Fine," said Oso, "we'll do it the hard way." He looked down at the box containing Ned and had a wicked idea, but thought the better of it and reached for Tank's canteen instead. Holding it a foot above Tank's head, he tipped it just enough to allow few ounces of water to splash his friend's face. Again, there was no response. Oso sighed. "You brought this on yourself," he warned, and then turned the canteen completely vertical, emptying its contents onto Tank's head.

"What the…" Tank jerked to a sitting position. He put his hands to his face and wiped the water from his eyes. "Explain to me why you're laughing and why I'm all wet," he said, pulling his T-shirt away from his chest and wringing it out.

"You left me no choice," Oso defended. "Waking you up is like trying to wake the dead."

Tank shrugged. "I'll give you that, but next time, stick me with a sharp object or something. I hate being wet."

"Ask and ye shall receive," quoted Oso, holding up a sharpened wooden pencil from his footlocker. "I'll keep this on reserve."

"So what's the deal – another long, boring graveyard shift, waiting for the Bat Phone to ring?"

"I don't know. TJ thinks something's up and I'd have to agree with him. A couple of jets took off earlier – might've been Stinkbugs – and they're not on the schedule."

"It sounds like we'd better be on our toes."

"My thoughts exactly. Get dressed and then we'll grab the wingman. They just took their own handoff from Repo, so they should be up."

"Sound's like a plan, just give me a second to feed and water Ned."

"What exactly *are* you feeding your spider anyway?"

"Small insects, lizards, whatever I can find, but I think he's sick; he's not eating much."

"He's not sick dude, he's starving. He's probably used to larger fare, like feral cats or small children."

"I take offense to that, Ned would never eat cute little kitty cats."

Chapter 46

After Victor passed the coordinates to Crash, he had a decision to make. According to the original mission, he was supposed to hang around and get pictures of the aftermath, but that was based on the assumption that the B-2 would quickly move in and strike. Now he'd have to wait for the Nighthawks to enter the picture, and that might take a while. He checked his fuel gauge to see how much time he really had. What he saw made his heart jump into his throat. He was literally running on fumes.

How had he missed that? "Task saturation," he said aloud, answering his own question. He was so busy flying and operating the sensors that he'd let the fuel completely drop out of his crosscheck. He should have had plenty of fuel remaining, but the accident must have caused a leak somewhere. He scooted back from the screens and looked down at the small warning panel next to the chin pad. A dim, amber light cautioned LOW FUEL. Victor looked back up at the display. Wasn't there supposed to be a Master Caution message that popped up on the viewscreen to alert him so he could look at that warning panel? He knew there was, he'd read about it in the manual; it was just one more thing they hadn't tested. None of that mattered now. The fact remained that he was out of gas and deep in enemy territory.

Victor began a turn to the south in a bid for friendly lines, but his controls quickly became sluggish. He looked at the engine gauges and watched as the digital RPM needle wound down to windmill speed. Dreamcatcher was now a glider. A moment later he lost all control of the ailerons; his attempts to roll left or right had no effect. The elevators were still working though, and he struggled to keep the nose from entering a dive. He looked back at the display. His right turn to the south had deteriorated into a slow tilt back to the left – back towards the target.

As Victor tried to remember how long the electrics were supposed to last after the engine died, the screens went blank. "That answers that," he muttered. He was entombed in a pitch-black cocoon, flying by the seat of his pants with only half his flight controls. The last image from the center screen still burned in negative detail on his open eyes – the target compound, growing larger, and nearly centered on the display.

★ ★ ★ ★

Crash stared at his readout in disbelief. "Uh...guys," he said, "I think something's wrong. My readout has ceased."

"I don't like the sound of that," said Murph. "What do you mean, 'ceased.'"

"As in: 'the data feed aint no more.'"

"I figured that, Crash," Murph replied testily, "but I don't know what your lack of data feed indicates. You're going to have to elaborate in simple terms that pilots can understand."

Crash could hear the tension just under the surface of Murph's reply. He took a moment to choose his next words. "The problem," he said slowly, "is that I can't tell you exactly what the lost readout means. I don't have positive or negative data; I simply have no data at all. The fact that it ended means that Dreamcatcher is no longer transmitting. That indicates some sort of failure, but it could be as benign as a loose wire or as bad as..."

"As bad as what?" prompted Murph.

"...as bad as a total system failure."

Drake looked at Murph and raised his eyebrows. "Given the way our night has gone, I'll give you one guess as to which it is."

"I'm not jumping to that conclusion just yet," said Murph. "Crash, I need you to look back at the data feed you recorded and look for patterns, anything that might lead to the sort of failure that could halt Dreamcatcher's transmissions."

"Of course," Crash slapped his forehead with the base of his palm, "I should have thought of that. Give me a few minutes and I'll get back to you."

"Don't take too long, I don't have to remind you that time is of the essence here – I have two Stealth Fighters that are on their way to turn that place into a crater."

"I'll do my best." Crash stared at the figures on his readout, but the data was just a meaningless jumble of letters and numbers. He could feel the weight of the situation getting to him. As an intelligence analyst he'd been trained to work under pressure, but the urgency of his work was usually measured in hours. Now his performance was being measured in seconds, seconds that could mean the life or death of a friend. He took a deep breath and forced his mind to focus. A pattern began to emerge, and the more he absorbed it the easier it became until finally he had the answer. "How did I miss this?" he asked, unintentionally keying the intercom switch.

"Miss what?" Murph asked warily.

"The fuel numbers," answered Crash. "They don't make sense; they're dropping too rapidly. I think Dreamcatcher sprung a leak. With all that he was doing, particularly with his autopilot disabled, it was an easy thing for Victor to miss."

"Give me a conclusion Crash," Murph pressed.

"He ran out of gas. When the engine shut down, Dreamcatcher reverted to battery power and she automatically stopped transmitting in an effort to save electricity for the flight controls. He's down guys, and according to the last position the jet transmitted, he went down just south of the target."

Chapter 47

The screen on Walker's computer wavered as he slammed his fist down on the table. When it returned to normal the words from the SATCOM link still remained.

WRAITH IS DOWN

NO CONTACT WITH SURVIVOR

ESTIMATED POSITION...

COLOCATED WITH TARGET

The Colonel's shoulders sagged as he stood and prepared to deliver the bad news to his team. He looked at his table of engineers and maintenance technicians, still diligently trying to solve the problem with the weapons bay doors. "You can put your books and charts away gentlemen. Dreamcatcher is down."

"You mean he ditched in the gulf?" asked Amanda, still clinging to the last thread of optimism.

Walker didn't mince words. "No, he crashed in the target area. We're unsure of his status; there's been no contact." He turned back to the SATCOM and sent a reply to the B-2.

ALERTING SAR ASSETS

REMAIN ON STATION

MONITOR SAR FREQ UNTIL BINGO

"I put his chances for survival at better than two to one," said Scott. "Dreamcatcher had a fail safe that reserved the last bits of electrical power for the ejection."

"Thanks, Dr. Stone, but in the future keep in mind that I'd rather not know the odds, one way or the other."

"What about the Nighthawks?" asked Amanda.

"I'm going to let them continue. If Victor is still alive, he's smart enough to get away from that target. With any luck he's already running south. I have a Sandy team on alert in Kuwait that can pick him up. I'll get them suited up, but I can't launch them until Victor initiates contact. I can't risk their lives until Victor proves that he's not already dead. For the moment, he's on his own."

★ ★ ★ ★

Victor had often discussed with his T-38 students the question of when a pilot should abandon the aircraft to save his own skin. He always told them that such a critical decision was made in the briefing room, well before leaving the ground. He told them to set limits as to the minimum altitude and airspeed that they would tolerate before giving up on the taxpayers' aircraft and pulling the ejection handles. Now, falling toward the sand in the pitch-black cockpit of a high tech paperweight, he felt like a hypocrite.

Though he could no longer see the outside world, Victor knew that Dreamcatcher was pitching over, listing to the left, and picking up speed. There was no way to restart the engine without fuel; and with a dead battery, the electronic displays and flight controls would not function. Yet he continued to struggle with the stick as if there were some way to salvage the situation. In the surreal light of extreme crisis he could only laugh at himself, until instinct finally took over and he reached for the ejection handle.

Victor had heard pilots who'd ejected from disabled aircraft describe a phenomenon they called temporal distortion. Time itself slowed down and a process that only took a couple of seconds seemed to stretch into several minutes. The moment Victor's hand connected with the cold steel of the ejection handle, time slowed to a crawl and his senses snapped to a capability beyond any he'd ever experienced.

Victor watched, with more curiosity than fear, as Dreamcatcher stepped through Scott's four consecutive miracles. He could see every spark from the ballistic charges that split Dreamcatcher into two clamshell pieces. He watched the desert floor appear before him and noted intellectually that he was still heading toward the dimly lit compound. Then something seemed wrong; he knew that the pieces of his jet were supposed to fall beneath him, but the two halves were passing behind him instead. Only a quarter of a second passed between the detonation of the ballistic charge and the deployment of Victor's drogue chute, but in that short time, a hundred scenarios of what had gone wrong and what he would do to survive the impending explosion flashed through his mind. Then he felt the tug of his drogue chute and the pieces of Dreamcatcher seemed to reverse course around him and accelerate away. Finally, after what seemed an eternity of freefalling through space, his parachute opened.

Victor let out an involuntary grunt as his body rapidly decelerated from over a hundred miles an hour to a mere fifteen. It felt as if his parachute was pulling him back up into the sky. He looked down and watched the pieces of his doomed aircraft plummet toward the desert floor, and he wondered if something had caused the incendiary cord to fail. Just then, the night lit up in a spectacular eruption of fire and sparks. He'd expected a thunderous "boom" when Dreamcatcher finally self-destructed; instead, the sound was like a volley of fireworks, with several cracks and sizzles that continued for more than a second. With the last crackle of Dreamcatcher's destruction, time snapped back to its normal pace.

Victor blinked as if coming out of a dream, and then, without a conscious command, his survival training kicked in. He checked his parachute canopy for rips and tears or twisted and broken lines; it looked good. Then he reached down to his right hip and pulled the handle that would deploy his seat kit. A "hit and run" survival kit and a single-man life raft unraveled from their packing and fell far below him, dangling from a long tether. Knowing that he had little time, Victor pulled the night vision monocle out of the front pouch of his vest and took stock of his surroundings. He was still heading toward the compound, although now he was drifting slightly to the east of it. His first instinct was to steer a course further east, and put more distance between himself and the small gathering of enemy troops, but then he saw figures running out of the buildings and loading up vehicles. He could hear the sounds of men shouting and truck doors slamming; activity at the compound had increased to a mad rush. Dreamcatcher's final death throes had spooked the targets.

The ground rush came while Victor was still peering through the night vision monocle and his fall seemed to turn from a gentle descent into a genuine plummet. There was little time to react. He grabbed for the steering handles, dropping his monocle in his haste. With just a few feet to spare he steered left, into the wind, in an effort to kill some of his forward speed. The turn was agonizingly slow and he wished that the chute was one of the nimble rectangular models instead of the cumbersome round kind. In the same instant that he finished the turn, he prepared his body for impact; and in that same instant, the impact came.

When his feet met the ground Victor was disappointed to find that the surface did not give way. He'd fallen on packed soil rather than a soft dune. Instinctively he twisted so that he would not tumble directly forward and then he let his body collapse in stages, transferring the energy of the landing. His shoulders were the last to hit and immediately he felt the pull of the chute, billowing behind him like a giant flag for any would-be captors. He unhooked one riser, causing the chute to collapse, and then reeled in the silk mass until it was a heap of fabric beside him. Only then did he cautiously raise himself to a crouch to take stock of his situation.

Victor had landed in a small depression, with the terrain rising around him on all sides, providing natural cover. "Thank you, God" he whispered, looking up at the dark desert sky. Still, there was the chance that someone had seen his descent and was already on their way to capture him. He edged up one side the depression, wishing intently that he had not dropped his night vision monocle, and was surprised to find that he was only a stone's throw from the target compound. The desert rose gradually from the compound to the crest of his depression so that he had an elevated view of the enemy activity. It was dark, but he could see well enough to note that no one was concerned with hunting a downed pilot. Perhaps they thought the explosion was an errant bomb rather than a doomed airplane. Then a black Mercedes, bracketed in front and back by tan jeeps, raced out of the compound. Saddam was making his escape. Another sedan sat next to the target building, but it was still empty and Victor realized that Tariq Irhaab had not left.

A man in olive drab fatigues jumped into the front of the sedan and started the engine while other terrorists ran back and forth from the building to toss bags into the back of three pickup trucks. There was no time for a lengthy thought process, no time to make a list of pros and cons or risks and rewards. A very simple string of logic flashed through Victor's mind. The secondary target had already left the compound in the Mercedes and the primary would leave momentarily. The Nighthawks were still several minutes away, if not more. He could not allow the primary to escape while he still had a fix on his position. From that point on it was simple, "I cannot allow the primary to escape," muttered Victor. It was his only driving thought.

Victor unclipped his parachute harness and shrugged it away. He grabbed his survival kit and vaulted over the lip of the depression. He planned to run down the hill and dive for cover behind the waist high wall surrounding the compound, but in his haste, he missed his landing and tumbled down the hill instead, rolling to a crumpled heap at the base of the wall. Finding that he was uninjured, he cursed his own clumsiness and peered over the wall. He saw that he was very close to the last in the line of pickups. The truck's bed was filled with crates and covered by a tarp, but there was a gap between the rows of crates that might be just large enough.

Victor waited for a break in the activity and then leapt over the wall and ran towards the pickup, keeping his body low. He came to a stop next to the closest rear tire, thankful that the sound of the truck's engine had masked his movements. For a moment he froze, half expecting an alarm to sound and bullets to fly at him from all directions, but no one had noticed his presence. His heart pounded as if it would burst from his chest, but he forced himself to keep moving, crawling around to the back of the truck and easing into the bed between the crates.

As Victor wondered if he'd just committed suicide, an unseen hand slammed the gate of the truck closed. His view was cut to nothing but a portion of the compound wall and the darkness beyond. A few moments of agonizing stillness passed. "Let's go, gentlemen," he thought. "If you don't get a move on, the Stealth Fighters will obliterate us all."

Chapter 48

Oso, Tank, and their two wingmen sat in the chow tent, eating a late snack and discussing trivialities. At the next table a motley crew of HH-60G helicopter pilots and pararescuemen, called PJs for short, did much the same. The idea that any of them might be called upon to conduct a search and rescue mission seemed little more than a passing fancy.

Oso studied his hot dog, smothered in chili and cheese. The toppings were more a matter of aesthetics than taste. He stared at his snack and tried to imagine a nice juicy bratwurst buried under all of that chili, rather than what he knew it to be. He'd seen the boxes of raw hot dogs sitting outside the chow tents that morning, baking in the sun. They were clearly marked "Grade D Meat, Institutional Use Only"; nothing but the best for troops in the field. Just as he brought the snack to his lips, his radio squawked, causing him to spill a big glob of chili on his leg.

"ALERT NINE, ALERT NINE: SCRAMBLE, SCRAMBLE, SCRAMBLE. ALERT NINE, ALERT NINE: SCRAMBLE, SCRAMBLE, SCRAMBLE. THIS IS NOT AN EXERCISE; I REPEAT THIS IS NOT AN EXERCISE. RESPOND, OVER."

Oso dropped his hot dog onto the Styrofoam plate and scooped up the brick. "Control, this is Alert Nine, all Sandy's are with me and we're moving now." He turned to the other three, who were already on their feet. "We're on, boys."

At the next table, a similar call came to the lead helicopter pilot. All thoughts of food were left behind as the crews raced out the door towards their separate Life Support buildings.

The A-10 pilots' survival vests and harnesses were all laid out and ready by the time they burst through the Life Support door. As the four were suiting up, a red-haired and freckled sergeant walked into the room. One of the wingman looked up. "Not bad, Slick," he said.

"That's a pretty quick response for a pencil pusher."

Sergeant "Slick" McBride ignored the wingman's comment and walked straight to Oso. "There's no rush, sir," he said calmly, "we don't have a location yet. In fact we don't even know if the survivor is alive. When you're all suited up please join me at the Rock."

Oso nodded his understanding, shot a disapproving look at the obnoxious wingman, and continued to check his equipment. When all four of them were ready, they left Life Support and walked over to another temporary building. The letters RCC were painted on the side.

The Rescue Coordination Center was the central hub for Search and Rescue operations in the Iraqi theater. It was literally a glorified doublewide trailer with so many cables and hoses streaming from all sides that it was difficult to approach without tripping. Tank often joked that all of the Hogs might crash at once if someone stumbled over the wrong cable and unplugged the whole operation. Inside, there was so much clutter that the occupants could hardly walk, but the mess was an inevitable result of having so many different organizations crammed into one space. There were stations for the helicopters, the C-130s, the A-10s, F-16s, AWACS, and Intelligence, and while each contributing unit had their own facilities elsewhere, they all maintained working space at the Rock. That made it easier to coordinate the rescue effort when crunch time arrived.

By the time Oso and his group stepped through the door, the helicopter crews were already there. Oso frowned. No other groups were present. "Where is everybody?" he asked.

Slick glanced around the cluttered space and then looked back to Oso. "This is it," he said. "You'll have no Herc or AWACS support for this mission. The Vipers have been blackballed as well."

Tank mirrored Oso's incredulous look. "What? Are they out of their minds up at the CAOC?" he asked, referring to the Combined Air Operations Center.

"They might be," Slick answered dryly, "but my orders didn't come from the CAOC, they came from an outside source identifying itself as Lighthouse. I confirmed the authorization code as Level Seven. His orders carry the weight of a Joint Chief, if not the President himself."

Tank stared blankly at the enlisted man, stunned into silence. Oso, however, had not yet lost his tongue. "I don't care if the order came from the Pope. Without Wild Weasels or Command and Control, we'll be sitting ducks for their long range air defenses. If we run into any SAMs out there without the necessary support, this rescue could turn into a Greek tragedy."

Slick was unemotional in his response. "You're preaching to the choir, sir, but both our hands our tied. I can only guess that the people running this operation are trying to limit its exposure. On the not-so-bright side, the whole argument may be academic. Right now we don't even know if we have a survivor to rescue, and your orders from Lighthouse are to remain grounded until he gets confirmation of a live soul down there."

"I don't like this," said Oso, still frowning. "This whole situation is weird."

Slick smiled and shook his head. "If you think it's weird so far, then the ISOPREP is gonna blow your mind." He slapped a thin folder of papers to Oso's chest. The cover was stamped ISOPREP, for Isolated Personnel Report, the basic identification and authentication information for a downed airman. "This ISOPREP came with the caveat that it is Top Secret – Need To Know information. You and I are the only people in the room who've been granted access."

Oso took a step back from the other pilots and cracked open the folder to get a look at the man he was supposed to rescue. He couldn't believe his eyes.

★　★　★　★

Merlin lit up his FLIR targeting system and waited for the image to stabilize. He centered his screen on Lighthouse's target coordinates and was not happy with what he saw. "No activity, Two," he said, his voice filled with frustration, "and there's just a few cold vehicles. It looks like most of them have already bugged out."

"What do we do now?" Shadow Two asked.

"That depends on Lighthouse. I'll get on the SATCOM. Maintain your course for now."

"Wait a second, One," the tenor of Shadow Two's voice rose with excitement, "I've got something."

"Go ahead, what've you got."

"It looks like four vehicles moving on a road south of the compound – a sedan and three trucks. It could be our guys."

Merlin allowed himself a moment of thin hope for success. "Keep them locked up. You're cleared to maneuver as necessary to stay with them. I'll keep out of your way while I talk to Lighthouse." He typed hurriedly into the SATCOM unit.

NO ACTIVITY AT TARGET

HAVE FIX ON CONVOY MOVING SOUTH

REQUEST CLEARANCE TO STRIKE

There was a short pause and then Walker's response came through.

CAN YOU CONFIRM TARGET COMPOUND

IS CONVOY'S ORIGIN

Merlin sighed. They hadn't actually seen the vehicles depart the compound. Although he was certain that's where they came from, in a war crimes trial, he would not be able to support that claim.

NO

There was no immediate response and Merlin decided to continue preparing for the attack. He would focus on his own job and let the Colonel struggle with the laws of armed conflict. He used his FLIR to follow the road south until he saw the same set of vehicles that his wingman had found. There was nothing inherently sinister about them, no great sign that said "Terrorist Here, Drop Bombs Now," but it had to be them – otherwise their presence was an uncanny coincidence. He looked at his SATCOM, there was still no response.

What was taking Lighthouse so long to answer? "Shadow Two, this is Shadow One."

"Go ahead, One."

"I'm at your six with the vehicles in my FLIR. This will be a shooter-shooter attack. Since you're closer, you take the lead and trail vehicles, trapping the other two in between. I'll come in behind and clean up with the center two. Any questions?"

"Negative."

Merlin locked up the second vehicle. He would drop both weapons in quick succession. It would be easy to switch his crosshairs to the next vehicle once the first was destroyed, and the vehicles were so close together that the second bomb would have no problem hacking the shift in direction. His finger hovered over the pickle switch; all he needed was the word from Lighthouse. Then it came.

DO NOT STRIKE CONVOY

CONTINUE TO COMPOUND

STRIKE ORIGINAL COORDINATES

Merlin sighed again as he slowly moved his finger away from the switch. "Shadow Two, abort, abort, abort," he called into the radio.

Like Merlin, Shadow Two's finger had been hovering over the pickle button. Tension filled his body as he waited for Merlin's familiar voice to give him the execute command. He had not considered the legalistic and ethical dilemma that weighed upon the two senior officers. He simply assumed that clearance would be given – all he needed was a word. By the end of the word "Shadow," the wingman had already mashed down the button; he'd fully expected to hear "Execute" following after, instead of "Abort." His error sent a single two thousand pound weapon hurtling toward the rear vehicle in the convoy – Victor's unwary transport.

"I jumped the gun, Lead!" Shadow Two shouted into his radio. "I released a weapon! I repeat, I have one weapon away! What're your orders?"

Merlin had no time to be angry; instead, he directed the younger pilot as best he could. "Shadow Two, shift your crosshairs half a mile west of the convoy, into the open desert; do it slowly or the bomb will lose the laser and go ballistic and probably impact too close to the vehicle."

Shadow Two tried to redirect the weapon away from the target. He slowly dragged the crosshairs away, thankful that there was nothing west of the road but open desert. The two thousand pound weapon did its best to follow orders, but its tiny flight controls could not turn its bulk as far from the vehicles as the wingman hoped. With five seconds to impact, the seeker lost sight of the laser and the flight controls locked in the streamlined position. The errant weapon impacted the sand just over a thousand feet west of the convoy.

When the bomb hit, the sedan and two of the pickups had just passed behind a great berm. The elevated terrain shielded them from the bomb's effects and they received little more than a jolt and a shower of sand. However, the last truck in the convoy did not benefit from the berm's protection. The bomb exploded close enough to pepper the truck with metal fragments as the pressure wave threw it sideways. The pickup traveled laterally across the road until the resistance offered by the edge of the asphalt forced it into a snap-roll, taking it airborne. It made a single revolution in the air, throwing all of its cargo from the bed, and then touched down at the right rear fender. As its tail caught the sand, it was turned and slammed to earth facing east. Still carrying plenty of energy, the truck reared up on its right front tire as if it was going to tumble forward onto its back, but gravity and the gentle slope of the terrain finally overcame its momentum and the rear tires crashed back into the sand, leaving the pickup in an upright position. In the meantime, the other vehicles continued to speed down the road. Watching it all on his FLIR, Merlin chuckled. The terrorists' only thoughts were of self-preservation. Some American pilot was trying to kill them, and they would not help their comrades if it meant waiting around for his aim to get better.

Moving his FLIR back to the wrecked truck, Merlin could see the heat signatures from three men and he breathed a sigh of relief when he saw that all of them were stirring. Two men slowly drug themselves from the cab of the truck while another, several yards to the north, sat up from among a pile of wrecked crates beside the road.

"I don't think I killed anyone sir!" said the wingman excitedly. "Only one vehicle was affected and everyone seems to be moving!"

"Phenomenal," Merlin replied bitterly, "whether you killed anyone or not, you just flipped the ON switch for the air defense system, and we still have to strike the compound. Turn northbound and intercept the original route. Reset your remaining fuse for penetration and let's get this over with."

Merlin hoped that he was wrong about the air defenses, but soon the sky lit up with anti-aircraft artillery tracers. He tried to steady himself with the thought that none of the enemy defenses had any clue as to the Nighthawks' actual positions, but there was always the chance of a Golden BB. "Wouldn't that just cap the evening off nicely," he muttered.

They reached the compound unscathed, and with the original target back in his FLIR, Merlin placed his crosshairs on the center of the building. Once again, the compound appeared devoid of activity. Almost halfheartedly, he released both weapons and turned back to the south, looking over his shoulder as Shadow Two lobbed his remaining bomb at the same coordinates. If nothing else, the near simultaneous explosions formed an awe-inspiring display. A lucky cameraman from CNN happened to catch the fireworks while filming the anti-aircraft tracers; the footage was spectacular.

Chapter 49

Victor had just started downing a water pack from his survival kit when his whole world turned to chaos. The sound of the explosion was deafening, like standing next to a cannon as it was fired. A moment later, the echo was punctuated by the sound of metal shards embedding themselves in the truck, followed by a terrible lurch sideways and the sensation of flying through the air. He crashed to Earth amidst a barrage of wooden crates and lay there, covering his head, until no sound remained but the distant roar of the lead vehicles, still making their escape.

Victor's whole body ached. There was a sharp pain in his left leg just above the knee, his ears were ringing, and he felt nauseous. Ahead of him he could see the two men in the cab beginning to climb out of the vehicle. Keeping his eyes locked on the Iraqis, he felt for the wound in his leg. As he reached, his hand passed through some warm mush. He winced, afraid to look and wondering if that mush was the remains of some portion of his body, but when he lifted the wet hand to his face it smelled distinctly like apple juice. Only then did he look around at the contents of all of the broken crates. He was surrounded by smashed produce – apples, oranges, and bananas. "Great," he thought, "health conscious terrorists."

Victor turned his attention back to his leg. There was a piece of wood sticking out just above the knee and his flight suit was stained with blood. Preparing himself for the worst, he yanked out the shard, but he was grateful to find that the embedded portion was much thinner and smaller than the rest of the piece. It amounted to little more than an overgrown splinter that had barely gone an inch into his body. He couldn't see the wound through the small hole in his flight suit, but he knew from assessing the culprit that treatment could wait.

There was a rustle ahead of him and Victor looked up from his leg just in time to see one of the men from the truck turn his way. Their eyes locked and the man reached for the AK-47 slung over his shoulder. Victor had no thought of right or wrong. He did not ponder any ethical dilemmas. He simply reacted. His hand shot for the nine millimeter Beretta strapped to his back and in one fluid movement he drew the weapon, flipped off the safety, extended his arm, and pulled the trigger. "Three bullets, center mass," was the only thought that passed through his mind. The other Iraqi heard the shots and came around from the other side of the truck, but Victor still held his weapon ready. He brought his left hand up to the grip for support, shifted his aim, and fired three more shots.

Both of the Iraqis fell having never returned fire. Victor leapt up and ran, limping, toward the second man, who was still holding a rifle and stirring. When he reached the Iraqi, he put his foot on the weapon to prevent him from lifting it, but the move was unnecessary. The Arab stared sightlessly at the starless sky and stammered in an unintelligible rasp. Blood bubbled from his lips and formed a narrow stream down his right cheek that glistened against the setting moon. Victor examined the man's wounds and saw that he'd taken two bullets in the lungs and the third to the heart. Then he turned his attention to the other man, who'd fallen face first on top of his rifle. He cautiously used his foot to turn the Iraqi over. "Not really three to the center," he thought. Apparently, he'd failed to compensate for the heavy trigger pull required for the first shot from a Beretta. Despite aiming for the chest, he'd put the bullet high, into the man's forehead; the other two rounds were literally overkill.

Suddenly Victor felt nauseous and staggered back from the bodies. His mind finally caught up to his actions. The world spun before him and he grabbed the side of the pickup for support until the nausea overcame him and he doubled over and vomited. He stayed there for a few moments, taking shallow breaths and trying not to pass out. He'd never killed before. He didn't despise these men, he'd simply reacted in order to survive, but the impact of what had just happened shook him to the core. "Get a grip Victor," he whispered, forcing himself to breathe deeply. He didn't have time for this. Irhaab was getting away. He fought through the nausea, forced himself upright, and headed for the truck's cab.

Victor was aware that he'd experienced multiple miracles that evening. First, all four of Scott's consecutive miracles had worked perfectly in the ejection sequence. Then there was the explosion that rolled the truck; the bomb had to have come from the Nighthawks, but someone either had really bad aim or they'd seen fit to spare his life. The fact that he'd sustained only one superficial injury during the crash was incredible. He sat down in the driver's seat of the pickup, thanked God for all the miracles, and then asked for one more: he needed this truck to work.

The truck had sustained surprisingly little apparent damage. The right window had been blown inward and there were several fragments of metal lodged in the right door and side, but the front of the vehicle wasn't bad. Even the windshield looked good, with only one web-like fracture in the upper right corner. He felt for the key in the ignition. It was still there. Putting the vehicle back in Park, he closed his eyes, uttered a simple, "Please," and then turned the starter. The engine coughed and sputtered, toying with him for a few seconds, and then died. He tried again with the same result and then a third time, but the engine just wouldn't turn.

Victor's head fell to his chest in defeat. There, in the still darkness of the desert, hopelessness crept over him; the feeling that misfortune was destined to thwart his mission at every turn. Then, just as he was about to give in to the insurmountable futility of it all, a quiet voice in Victor's subconscious said, "Try again." He obediently turned the key once more. This time, the engine sprang to life.

The truck lurched back and forth for a few hundred yards, until Victor got the hang of driving it. The vehicle was bent for sure, with an alignment that would get someone killed on the *autobahn*, but it was controllable and that was all that mattered. In front of him the desert road was hardly visible under the nearly moonless sky, and driving the wrecked truck at high speed with the lights off felt suicidal, but he couldn't afford to turn on the headlights and alert the terrorists that someone was pursuing them. He couldn't afford to slow down either; instead, he pressed the crippled truck to its limits, driving on the razor's edge between crash and control. After several minutes, his efforts were rewarded with the red glow of taillights up ahead. He slowed, hoping that the combination of distance and darkness was enough to prevent his discovery.

Now that he was able to slow his pace and control the vehicle with one hand, Victor could divide his attention. He knew that Walker and the B-2 crew would have figured out that he'd gone down, but they wouldn't know whether he was alive or dead. They wouldn't launch the rescue assets into harm's way until they confirmed he was alive. For a few moments, he considered playing dead and trying to escape without help, that way he wouldn't draw any other friendlies into this mess; but something told him that he'd never make it out of Iraq on his own. He pulled the radio from his survival vest and flipped it on. Without bothering to wait for the GPS inside to get a position, he scrolled through the canned text messages, found the one he wanted, and then moved his thumb down to the "SEND" button.

★　★　★　★

The B-2 crew loitered just out of radar range, hoping for some sort of sign from Victor. They'd been there much longer than planned and Drake tapped the fuel gauges, looking at Murph with a raised eyebrow.

"I know, I know," Murph acknowledged with a furrowed brow. "We have to get moving. Still nothing on the search and rescue freq?"

"Not a peep. Maybe he's biding his time."

"Maybe he didn't get out before Dreamcatcher augered in," Crash interjected from the back of the plane.

Both pilots looked over their shoulders and shot angry looks at the intelligence analyst. "You've been hanging around Scott too long,"

Drake said venomously.

"Look, I know it's not a happy thought. He's my friend too, but one of us has to acknowledge that there's a real possibility that he's dead."

"Look Crash," said Murph, "I know this is your first rodeo, so I'm going to let that one slide. In the future, though, we don't talk like that until well after the fat lady sings, got it?"

"Got it," said Crash quietly, looking at the floor.

"Now that we've cleared that up, the fact remains that we're bingo. We're out of gas and we've got to head for the tanker now."

"What about Victor?" asked Drake.

"We'll refuel and then see if Walker will give us permission to come back. We'll be out of radio range in just a few miles, so Victor will be on his…" Three beeps from the UHF radio interrupted Murph. The system had picked up a text intercept.

Drake looked down at the radio console and a wide grin spread across his face. There were three text messages at the bottom of the screen and they all said the same thing:

WRAITH 01 SENDS: I'M ALIVE

Chapter 50

Oso closed the ISOPREP folder. He was speechless. He just looked at Slick with his mouth hanging slightly open.

"My thoughts exactly," said Slick. "Officially, we don't know anything about this guy; I don't even have an aircraft type. All I've got is his callsign, his picture, and his description. It doesn't matter; unless he's got an evil twin – that's our boy."

Tank looked confused. "Is there something you two aren't telling me?"

Oso and Slick both took on deadpan expressions. "Yes," they answered in unison.

"Well okay then."

A digital chime interrupted the awkward silence and Slick ran over to his "office," a broom closet at the end of the trailer. He bent over his computer and all conversation in the Rock stopped. In a room that was full of voices a moment before, you could now hear a pin drop. Then Slick's small freckled frame became intensely animated and he wheeled around to face the crews. "We have a survivor! Go, go, go!"

The rescue force raced from the Rock with Slick close on their heels. "I'll radio the route to you after you take off," he said to Oso.

"Roger that. We'll be airborne in less than ten minutes."

"Make it five," Slick shouted after him.

The helicopters got airborne first, but the Hogs quickly caught up and set up a lazy weaving pattern above them as they slowly moved northward. They followed the route plan that Slick gave them and soon found their holding fix at a safe, forward control point. In the low light before dawn, the desert haze caused the ground and sky to join in a watercolor blend of brown and rose hues. It was beautiful, but it was also deadly. "Watch the floor," Oso cautioned his wingmen. The featureless terrain and the muddled horizon made a perfect trap for an unwary pilot. He didn't want the rescue to end prematurely just because one of his people confused sand with sky. Oso hated waiting like this, but he couldn't move forward until the survivor checked in and made his true coordinates known.

*   *   *   *

Victor drove south for what seemed like ages until the red lights took a sharp turn to the west down a gravel road. The path wound back and forth between low hills and he closed the gap for fear that he would lose his quarry. When the other vehicles finally came to a stop, he pulled over to the side a hundred yards behind them and quietly slipped out of the truck. The crunch of his steps on the gravel road seemed to echo against the hills and Victor decided his chances of getting closer would be better off the road. He moved into the sand, hoping and praying that the area wasn't mined.

Rather than go over the hills and be silhouetted against the lightening sky, Victor shifted around and between them as he worked his way toward the enemy camp. He moved excruciatingly slow, considering every step carefully, knowing that premature discovery would mean certain death. Finally he rounded a small hill and came within a few feet of the vehicles. There were two additional uncovered jeeps parked next to the two trucks and the sedan. "Oh good," he thought, "more people who will want to kill me."

All five vehicles were parked in a semicircle in front of three camouflaged tents. No one was left outside and Victor marveled at Irhaab's confidence. He'd just had a near miss with an American bomb, and now he didn't even feel the need to post a guard outside his tent. Of course, the question remained: Which tent was his?

Victor examined his prospects. The central tent was very different from the others. It was larger and appeared to be set over a concrete form with knee-high walls to keep out the desert vermin. Then he noticed the most tell-tail sign of all. Between the central tent and its left neighbor there was a satellite dish mounted on a tall pole. A bundle of cables ran down the pole and disappeared into the central tent between the camouflage fabric and the concrete wall. If anyone in this group were permitted the luxury of TV, it would have to be Irhaab.

Victor decided against a frontal assault and continued to pick his way through the hills until he was at the back of the camp. Even here he would have to cross several yards of flat, gravel-covered space, but at least there was a gas-powered generator producing plenty of noise to cover the sound of his approach. He took a few deep breaths and then left the safety of the hills, running as low as he could manage. He ran to the dark space between the central tent and the tent to his left, choosing the side opposite from the satellite dish. Crouched low in the shadows between the tents, he strained to hear any sounds that might give him an idea of what was happening or what kind of numbers he was facing, and he was surprised by what he heard. There were two voices, a man and a woman, and they were speaking English. The topic was odd as well. It was political, something about congressional delegates; not something he expected terrorists to discuss in their spare time. Then he realized that the conversation was coming from the TV. Whoever was in the tent was watching an American news program.

Confident in the relative safety of his current location, Victor took the time to pull out his Beretta and switch the half empty clip for a fresh one, flipping off the safety before placing the weapon back in its holster. Then he moved over to one corner of the tent and found the straps that secured it to the concrete foundation. He untied them and quietly rolled up the fabric until he could see over the short concrete wall.

The interior of the tent was brightly lit, with strings of lights running from the center to each corner. Several large rugs with intricate patterns covered the concrete floor, and brightly colored pillows were stacked against the wall, overlapping to cover the ugly concrete. Aside from the rugs, the tent was furnished with a large TV, standing against the opposite wall, as well as an ornate coffee table and a low couch, upholstered in burgundy corduroy with gaudy gold trim and tassels. A single figure sat on the couch with his back to Victor, wearing a white and gold *kafia* headdress.

Keeping his gaze on Irhaab, Victor reached down to his left leg and drew his survival knife. He'd had the knife since the beginning of his A-10 days and he'd carried it into combat before, while flying over Basra in support of Operation Southern Watch. It was strong and solid, with a five-inch steel and ebony hilt and a six-inch blade that was razor sharp. The back of the blade was straight and flat except for the last two and half inches, where it narrowed with a wicked curve. Victor liked the mean look of the knife, but he'd primarily chosen it because the balance felt good in his hand. It was easily manipulated and well suited for the Japanese style of knife fighting he'd learned in his Academy days. He remembered that training now and gripped the knife at the ready position, hilt up with the straight back of the blade against his forearm. The sharp edge faced out, aligned with his knuckles. As quietly as possible, he climbed over the wall and onto the rug behind Irhaab, who was still focused on the reporters.

Victor chose his movements carefully, rolling each step onto the rug covered floor and keeping the knife low, concealed by his forearm. He wouldn't think about it until it was all over. The mission was to kill the man; whether the B-2 did it with a bomb or he did it with a knife was immaterial. He would sneak up behind the terrorist, slit his throat and then race back to the truck and get to the safe zone. It was a simple plan; and it would have worked too, if it hadn't been for the commercial.

When the network took a commercial break, the screen went black for just a moment. In that moment Victor saw his own reflection on the TV as clearly as if he was looking at a mirror. Irhaab saw it too. He swung around and leveled a pistol at the intruder. Victor resisted the urge to reach for the gun at his back and kept the knife concealed, tucked against his right forearm. He'd lost his advantage but he could not run away – the terrorist would surely gun him down before he made it to the cover of the wall. Instead, he held his ground, waiting to see what his opponent would do, waiting for an opportunity.

"Do not move, assassin," Irhaab ordered in English.

Victor remained silent, staring blankly at Irhaab with his best poker face.

The terrorist sized up his new prize and laughed. "So now they are sending children to murder me in my tent, are they?" he asked. Still unaware of the knife, he added, "And what was your plan, to sneak up behind me and blow in my ear?" As he spoke, Irhaab stepped around the couch and moved closer to the American, continuing forward until the barrel of his weapon was pressed into Victor's forehead.

Victor stalled, waiting for an opportunity that he could already see. He answered in Arabic, "I am not as young as you suppose, but I *am* here to kill you."

Irhaab responded in his native tongue, "You speak the Iraqi dialect, do you? So you *are* an assassin – trained by the CIA, I hope. Otherwise, I would feel sorely undervalued."

Victor did his best not to smile at the terrorist's imagination. He was obviously living in a fantastical world of spooks and intrigue of his own making.

"You Americans are so arrogant," Irhaab continued. "You say you are here to kill me, yet it is I who hold the gun, while yours is tucked safely in its holster. In your clumsiness, you've provided me with an opportunity to teach my soldiers a valuable lesson. I will use you as an example, to show them why God has made me their master. Even the wily quarry that slips through their net is but a simple catch for me. I don't care how old you say you are; your government will have to send more than a boy to assassinate me." His finger tightened against the pistol's trigger and Victor winced, but then Irhaab stopped. "However, since I do not want to spill your blood on my carpets, I'll have to ask you to step outside."

Victor stood his ground, pressing the limits of his own fear. He had underestimated his opponent. During his rhetoric, Irhaab had not behaved as expected. He kept his gaze fixed on Victor and his weapon steady. He was too focused. Victor needed a bigger reaction from the man before he could act; he had to find a button in the terrorist's psyche. "You can be assured that it is not my blood but yours that will stain these rugs," he said. "And even though my government provided the means, it was God himself who sent me to kill you – He demands that you stand before Him in judgment for your many crimes."

Victor's last statement elicited the desired reaction; Irhaab's response became emotional. "Fool," he spat, turning the gun sideways and digging it into Victor's forehead, "do not dare to assume what God desires. Why, just this evening God spared me from one of your American smart bombs, just as He will spare me from your feeble attempt at..."

When speaking of the bomb, Irhaab tilted his head back ever so slightly, shifting his gaze towards the sky. It was all that Victor needed. The shift in the Arab's gaze allowed him to thrust his left hand upward, unseen, wind-milling it from his chest to smash at the gun with the outside edge of his palm. At the same time, he tilted his head to the right. The impact of his hand against the weapon caused Irhaab to pull the trigger, but the combination of hitting the weapon and tilting his head took Victor out of the line of fire.

With the gun thrust aside, Irhaab's chest and neck were unprotected and Victor brought his right hand up, striking at his opponent's chin with his knuckles and cutting a deep gash in the his throat with the knife. Simultaneously, he closed the open palm of his left hand over the top of Irhaab's pistol and twisted it out of his grasp. Then, after his right hand reached the apex of its swing, he brought it back down, burying the blade in the Arab's throat at a forty-five degree angle until the hilt reached flesh and he felt the jarring impact of metal against bone. The tip of the blade had hit the terrorist's spine.

Irhaab dropped to his knees, his eyes wide with disbelief. He tried to speak but could only produce sickening gurgles as blood poured from his neck. Victor looked deep into his eyes, allowing the hardness of his expression to soften. "I don't hate you," he said in Arabic, "but the blood of too many souls cries out for yours. Tonight justice has claimed your life."

Chapter 51

"Lighthouse says the Sandies are on station and monitoring," said Murph, looking up from his SATCOM display. "There's little more that we can do except continue to the tanker, get our gas, and head home."

"Copy that," said Drake. "It'll make the long flight home a lot easier knowing that Victor is alive and about to be rescued."

"I agree," answered Murph. "Hopefully he'll be eating breakfast in Kuwait in just a couple of hours."

Crash detected more tension than relief in Murph's voice. "You don't sound convinced," he said.

Murph frowned, "We didn't get voice contact or a set of coordinates," he answered. "If Victor was at the safe zone, he would have given us a lot more than just a simple text message. Something tells me our boy isn't out of the woods yet."

★　★　★　★

Victor stared into the terrorist's eyes and watched the shock and hatred ebb away, replaced by pure emptiness. Then he looked down and noticed for the first time that Irhaab had been gripping something black in his left fist. As the last remnants of life drained from the Iraqi, his fist loosened and the black object dropped onto the floor, rolling in a lazy half circle until it settled to a stop at Victor's feet. It was a grenade. At the same moment, two more terrorists burst into the tent, alerted by Irhaab's gunshot.

More fearful of the grenade than Irhaab's minions, Victor made a break for the side of the tent where he'd entered. Ignoring the crack of pistol fire at his heels, he took two long strides and dove over the concrete wall through the loose flap of the tent. He tried to stop on the other side, but his momentum carried him under the side of the neighboring tent. He finally came to an abrupt and painful stop against the legs of an aluminum cot. The cot was occupied by another Iraqi, hurriedly dressing to investigate the shots. The man jumped to his feet in shock. Victor looked up and saw not one, but four faces staring down at him, backlit by a few low-wattage bulbs. Instead of standing to fight, he simply threw his hands over his head and flattened out his body. The Iraqis had only a fraction of a second to be confused by his actions.

The grenade exploded with such ferocity that Victor was not sure he'd escaped injury. It sent a painful shockwave through his body and he felt as though he'd been struck by a massive piece of debris, but when he checked himself for injuries, he found that he'd suffered none at all; the low concrete wall of Irhaab's tent had shielded him. The men standing over him had no such protection. The shrapnel shredded the sides of both tents and knocked all who were still standing to the ground. The two in Irhaab's tent took the blast at close range and were cut down in an instant, followed shortly by a third man who'd been just outside the entrance when the grenade went off. Two of the men in Victor's tent were fatally wounded as well, one with a single hit to the middle of his forehead and the other with multiple wounds to the midsection and neck. The other two had skated through with only superficial damage but they'd been knocked down and were dazed, uncertain of the source of the attack.

The explosion knocked out the lighting in both tents, but the first lights of dawn seeped through the shredded walls, providing just enough light for Victor to see the two that had survived. He fought through the fog in his head and the pain in his body and struggled to his feet, knowing that his life depended on being the first to overcome the grenade's effects. He picked up the bloody knife with the blade downward and leapt over the cot, making for the closest terrorist. The man saw the attack but was too slow to grab his weapon; instead he attempted to stop Victor's advance with a left hook. With a practiced move, Victor tossed the knife across to his left hand, spinning it as he did, and caught it with the blade facing up and out. He blocked the punch with his right forearm and then shoved the knife into his opponent's chest, just above and to the left of the solar plexus, directly into the heart. He gave the knife a twist, just for good measure, and then let go, leaving it protruding from the man's chest. Then he stepped in close and spun the man around to use him as a shield.

The other Iraqi had managed to grab his rifle and point it at Victor, but he hesitated, unsure of his ability to shoot past his comrade and stunned by the sight of the knife still firmly embedded in the man's chest. Supporting the dying terrorist's weight with his left arm, Victor reached with his right hand and drew his Beretta, and for just a fraction of a second the two men stared at each other through their gun sights. Then Victor fired three shots into the Arab's chest. A fusillade of bullets ejected from the stricken man's rifle and a few embedded themselves in Victor's human shield, but the rest flew wide.

When the violence of the moment ended, there was a short silence and Victor thought he might get a rest, but then he heard more voices outside and he knew that the fight was not over. He quickly surveyed the wreckage of the tent for any signs of keys. Seeing none, he yanked his knife out of the dead terrorist and held it at the ready, not bothering to wipe it clean. No one entered the tent immediately and all of the voices seemed to come from the front, so he abandoned his defensive posture and opted for a rear escape. He tossed a cot aside and rolled under the fabric at the back of the tent, springing to his feet behind the encampment.

Victor had no desire for more killing and he knew that he was still outnumbered, so he decided not to press his luck any further by mounting an assault on the remaining terrorists. He'd been surprised by his own skill in evading death so far, but he had to admit that the grenade had done much to even the odds and he couldn't count on similar help in the future. He considered making a run through the hills and back to the truck, but he didn't know how long the crippled vehicle would hold out, particularly if it came down to a chase.

Finally he decided to take a chance at commandeering one of the jeeps. A plan formed in his mind. There wasn't time to look for holes or weaknesses – all he could do was put it into action and hope for the best.

Victor drew his Beretta, faced the tents, and shouted at the top of his lungs in Arabic, "Help! Help! They're back here! Help!" Then he dashed into the hills and began to work his way toward the front and the vehicles. His ruse worked. The sound of voices and pounding feet told him that at least two men were running to give aid to a non-existent comrade. He took it on faith that there were no more threats in the parking area and ran out from the hills next to the sedan. Running along the front of the vehicles, he stabbed at the front tires with his knife, afraid to risk discovery by firing his pistol. He finished the sedan and one truck before a bullet kicked up the dirt at his feet. The jig was up. There was no more reason for silence, so he shot the front tires of the remaining truck and then hopped into the open side of the nearest jeep, dropping both of his weapons onto the floorboard beneath him.

Bullets bounced off the hood of Victor's new transport as he fired up the engine. He put it in gear and mashed down on the gas, racing out of the parking lot and sending a hail of gravel at his attackers. He kept his head down, barely able to see over the steering wheel, while bullets whizzed by and bounced off the back of the vehicle. With dawn rapidly bringing light to the desert, Victor could see well enough to find the road out of the camp. In a few quick movements he had the jeep up to third gear, and then he let the engine scream while he felt for his nine millimeter, fearing that his serpentine driving might throw the weapon from the vehicle. When he finally found his gun, he holstered it, leaving the safety off so that it would be ready when needed, and recommitted his hands to the task of driving.

The gravel road wound back and forth even more than Victor remembered and he struggled to maintain control of the vehicle. Then the ping of bullets against metal told him that his pursuers had narrowed the gap. Seconds later his windshield shattered, forcing Victor to shrink deeper into the cockpit. He managed a glance over his shoulder and saw that there were three men in fatigues pursuing him in the other jeep. The driver had no weapon and was completely focused on catching up while the other two were firing at him with assault rifles, with one man in the passenger seat and one standing in the back.

Only the twists and turns and the uneven surface of the road saved Victor from a few extra holes in his flesh, and he knew that he could not maintain the status quo much longer. When they reached the asphalt, the balance of power would turn dramatically in the Iraqi's favor; he had to end the pursuit now. He accelerated, pushing the jeep to its limits and barely keeping it on the road. The pursuing driver could not maintain the pace, whether by simple lack of skill or because he feared that he would throw the rear man out of the jeep, and the distance between them opened.

Around the next bend and with the other jeep out of sight, Victor saw the opportunity he was hoping for. He wrenched the steering wheel to the right as hard as he could and shoved both the clutch and the brake to the floor. If it hadn't been for a berm at the next curve, the jeep would have surely rolled, but the rising sand countered its momentum nicely and it skidded to a stop halfway up the embankment. He dove out of the cockpit and scrambled to the top of the hill, drawing his Beretta as he did. The other jeep careened around the corner but the occupants didn't see him. They poured their bullets into the empty jeep. Ignoring the other two, Victor took careful aim at the driver and fired off four rounds. He couldn't see whether he'd hit the man, but the jeep lurched left, throwing the rear man out the opposite side. It hit a small hill, rolled onto its right side, and skidded to a stop a few feet from Victor.

Victor looked back up the road and quickly found the man who'd been in the rear of the jeep. The terrorist had picked himself up and was running with a slight limp towards his rifle, lying only a few yards away. Victor also heard a voice shouting from the jeep but he could see no one. He opted to go for the most immediate threat and ran towards the man down the road, firing three rounds. Two of the bullets flew wide, but the last hit him in the shoulder and knocked him off balance. He fell to the ground next to the rifle. As Victor drew closer, the man grabbed the rifle and started to turn. Unwilling to risk another miss, Victor stopped and took more careful aim. This time his two rounds caught the man in his neck and head. The rifle dropped to the ground.

The sound of heavy footfalls on the gravel road warned Victor of another threat. He turned and saw another terrorist running at him, only a few steps away. The man was holding a bayonet over his head, ready to bring it slashing down at Victor. The old quip about a knife to a gunfight passed through Victor's mind as he raised his weapon to fire, but he pulled the trigger too quickly and the shot missed wide. He pulled twice more with the weapon centered, but the Beretta just answered with harmless clicks – his clip was empty.

In a flash the Iraqi was upon him, his knife swinging down from above. Victor dropped the gun and stopped the man's wrist with crossed arms, shifting his right hand to control the wrist and using his left to guide the Iraqi's arm, tucking it under his own. Then he spun, so that his back was to the man's shoulder, allowing the Iraqi's momentum to continue forward. Still controlling the arm, Victor sat backward, causing his opponent to fall. As the Iraqi hit the gravel, the knife fell from his grasp and he cried out in pain; the reversal of his own momentum had torn his shoulder from its socket.

Victor let go of his attacker and picked up the bayonet, flinging it out of reach. Despite the terrorist's painful injury, he took advantage of the momentary freedom and tackled Victor from behind, wrapping his good arm around the pilot's throat. Victor grabbed the arm with both hands and rolled forward, carrying his attacker with him. Unable to defend himself with the injured arm, the Iraqi hit the gravel again, this time taking the full impact on the side of his face. He lost his grip on Victor and rolled flat on his back. Victor leapt to his feet and stepped on the Iraqi's good wrist. Then he dropped his knee to the man's chest, letting the full weight of his one hundred and eighty pound frame propel him downward. He felt a sickening crack as a pair of his opponent's ribs broke under the force of the impact. With his left hand, he grabbed the man's throat and pushed his fingers deep into the neck so that he could squeeze the esophagus. The terrorist's eyes bulged and he let out a rasp, barely able to breath.

"Is that uncomfortable?" Victor asked in Arabic, receiving a short nod and another rasp in response. "Good," he said. "From this position it will take less force for me to crush your throat than it would to crush an empty soda can." He paused to let the implication sink in before continuing. "I'm going to let go now, but if you move – if you even twitch – you'll never breathe again. Do you understand?" There was another rasping affirmative. Victor cautiously let go of the man's throat and relaxed some of the pressure on the chest. He could see immediate relief in the terrorist's face.

"You think you've won, but you're still going to die," the man coughed.

Victor was surprised by the Iraqi's perfect English. "I'm impressed," he said, "your English is very good."

"It ought to be. I studied at Texas A and M."

Victor knew he shouldn't be surprised. There were so many enemy officers with degrees from American schools. The beginnings of a new "Aggie" joke passed through his mind, but he let it go. "I heard your shouts at the jeep. I know you were on the radio. I need to know who you were talking to before you attempted to pith me."

The Iraqi said nothing, choosing to spit at Victor instead.

"Fine, have it your way." Victor shifted his weight back to the man's chest. He saw an immediate response as the Iraqi's face twisted in pain and guessed that portions of the broken ribs were impinging on one or two vital organs.

"Enough," the Iraqi grunted. "It doesn't matter anyway."

Victor relieved the pressure and the Iraqi's face relaxed a bit.

"I radioed in your attack. A battalion of Republican Guard had already been dispatched, alerted by an explosion south of our compound. Now they know your exact position and they will descend on you like a swarm of bees. In a few hours, they'll be dragging your body through the streets of Baghdad on *Al Jazeera* for all your countrymen to see." The Iraqi smiled through his pain when he saw the shadow of fear cross Victor's face.

Victor let the revelation deter him for only a moment and then his face hardened again. "Thanks for the head's up," he said coldly.

"You and I are not so different," the Iraqi rasped, "merely soldiers on two sides of a new war."

"That uniform does not make you a soldier," Victor said.

"And yours does not make you any less a terrorist," the Iraqi responded. "I've grown tired of this conversation, just kill me and get it over with."

"That's what makes us different. Because you are a terrorist, you would have killed me without pause. Because I am an American soldier, I'm going to let you live."

"That fascination with mercy just makes your people weak," the Iraqi spat.

"Perhaps," said Victor, "but my mercy is going to leave you with a monster headache." With his last words, Victor swung his left elbow down in an arc, adding power and support by grabbing his fist with his right hand. He struck the Iraqi with such a forceful blow to the temple that the man immediately went to sleep. Victor surveyed his handiwork. "Nighty-night, Aggie," he said as struggled to his feet. "You're lucky you ran into me, and not my brother-in-law. He'd have killed you for sure, just for shaming his alma-mater's good name."

Victor returned to the Iraqis' jeep to make sure the driver was dead. The man hung limp in his seat, having somehow managed to get his seat belt on during the pursuit. "Safety first," Victor muttered.

He bent down and ripped the radio out of the jeep and then tossed it over a hill into the desert sand. Then he walked over to the other jeep and felt around the floorboard for his knife, hoping that it was still there. His search was rewarded when he retrieved the weapon from deep under the driver's seat. With no immediate danger he cleaned his blade for the first time since pulling it out of Irhaab's throat, wiping the crusted blood on the back seat of the jeep.

At the sight of the blood, Victor felt pangs of sorrow, but it was not remorse. He understood now that he'd never hated the terrorists. He'd killed Irhaab to end his acts of terror, to protect those that would have surely died by his hand in the future. The others he'd killed for survival. They had chosen the wrong master and they'd paid for it with their lives. The last terrorist he let live. Likely or not, that man still had an opportunity to choose a different path.

Victor removed a canister of water from the overturned jeep and placed it next to the unconscious Iraqi. Then he remembered his Beretta. He walked back along the road to where he'd dropped it and ejected the empty clip, placing it in his vest in exchange for the half full clip before holstering the weapon with the safety still off. A few minutes later, he turned the jeep onto the asphalt road and headed south. He didn't take the time to consult a map or get a GPS fix on his exact position. He knew two things: the safe area was somewhere to the south, and he had to put some quick distance between himself and the promised horde.

Chapter 52

"Any radio, any radio, this is Wraith One," Victor called into his emergency radio, straining to hear any semblance of a response over the whip of the wind in his ears. There was nothing. He looked down at the small green box and decided he'd better unsnap the flexible antenna that was secured to the side. The thin plastic band fluttered and bent in the wind, but it would still improve his chances. He tried the secure frequency again. "Any radio, any radio, this is Wraith One."

There was a long pause and then the radio crackled. A faint voice replied, "Wraith One, this is Sandy One, I read you loud and clear. Authenticate blue, two six."

Victor tried to remember the day's authentication tables; the wrong code could end the rescue right here. "Wraith has gold, seven one; comeback with silver, niner seven."

The voice responded immediately, "Sandy has red, one zero. I show that you're clean, Wraith."

"You too, Sandy. Good to hear your voice," Victor said with audible relief; although, with the interference of the wind, he could still barely hear the speaker.

"Wraith, what is your status and location?"

"No major injuries. I'm headed south towards the rendezvous point," Victor replied. "Standby for more."

Victor put away his radio and focused on the road. He'd head south for another few miles before leaving the asphalt. If he was lucky, the jeep would handle the desert terrain and he could head straight for the pick-up zone. He was home free.

No sooner had Victor finished the thought than he felt a flutter in the gas pedal. The engine sputtered, and he looked down at the gauges to find that the gas needle was pegged on empty. Soon the engine coughed again and then finally quit altogether. He shifted into neutral and let the jeep coast to the side of the road. There was a spare fuel canister attached to the back of the vehicle and he hopped out to get it, but when he reached the canister he saw that it had been shot full of holes in the gunfight. There was no fuel left. "I guess I'm lucky I didn't get blown up when they shot this thing," he muttered to himself, wondering if the chaplain considered situations like this when he preached about counting your blessings.

Without another thought, Victor grabbed the square jug of water that was under the jeep's rear seat and headed off the road into the desert. He found a hill that provided some cover from the road and pulled out his evasion chart and a GPS unit. "Thank goodness for GPS," thought Victor. The days of triangulating a position were long gone. The old way of finding your location on a map required high ground and significant terrain features, and both were in short supply in the flat, featureless desert. The unit locked in several satellites shortly after he switched it on. In less than two minutes, it gave him a set of coordinates that was accurate to within nine feet.

Victor charted his position on the map and let out a dismayed sigh. He was still eleven miles short of the safe zone, not a bad hike in the Missouri springtime, but in the Iraqi desert, with the Republican Guard on his tail, it may as well have been a hundred miles. There was no sense in fretting about it; all he could do was start jogging and hope for the best. His GPS could only determine a heading once it was in motion, so Victor pulled the real compass out of his vest and oriented the map to north. He determined the heading to the safe zone, folded up the map, and began to trot. After a few steps the GPS unit established a track and he put the compass away. Now it was just a matter of following the little arrow on the screen until he reached the pick-up area; unless, of course, the Iraqis found him first. He pulled out his radio and prepared to give the rescuers the bad news.

"Sandy One, this is Wraith One, over."

"Wraith, this is Sandy One, I read you loud and clear," the radio crackled back.

Victor didn't respond. The voice was much clearer than it had been earlier and the familiarity was unmistakable. That had to be Oso on the other side. He wondered for a moment if Oso recognized his voice and then remembered that he didn't have to, he would have his picture from the ISOPREP. That meant that Oso had known all along.

Victor wanted to say something to indicate his recognition, but professionalism prevented it. He'd have to wait until they were back in friendly territory to catch up with his old friend and wipe clean the grudges of the past; for the moment, there were more pressing matters to attend to.

"Wraith, do you copy?" Oso repeated.

"Uh, yeah, Wraith reads you loud and clear as well. I'm on foot, eleven miles from the safe area. Stand by to copy my coordinates."

There was a long pause. Victor could almost hear the wheels turning in Oso's mind, trying to figure out why his survivor was still so far from the safe zone, even though he'd crashed almost two hours ago.

"Sandy is ready, go ahead with your coordinates."

Victor gave Oso his latitude and longitude and then continued to jog, knowing that each second narrowed the gap between safety and capture. On the other end of the radio, Oso would be moving the rescue force forward. They didn't have the fuel to wait for him to get to the safe zone. They'd have to meet him on the run. Still, the force would have to move at the slower pace of the choppers. This deep into enemy territory, the A-10s would have to provide constant cover.

Suddenly the hair on the back of Victor's neck stood up. Something in the air made him uneasy. He slowed to a walk and allowed his senses to take in the surroundings. The sun was climbing in the eastern sky and the temperature was rising, but it wasn't the heat that caused the change. He looked around, but he could see nothing but sand from his position. He breathed deeply. The hint of dust was heavier than before. He listened. On the edge of the quiet, he thought he could just make out a low rumble. Leaving the jug of water in the sand, he ran to the top of a small dune and looked north. What he saw confirmed his worst fears. Still far away but moving closer, a cloud of dust rose from the desert highway. A single vehicle on the asphalt road would not have created such a disturbance, nor would its noise be loud enough to reach him; only a large force traveling at a good clip would cause these signs. The situation was becoming critical.

In a few seconds, Victor was headed south again, this time sprinting over the sand with the radio to his ear. "Sandy, this is Wraith, over."

"Go ahead, Wraith."

"It looks like I'm about to have company."

"How so?"

"There's a large force headed south toward my position. I'm going to make an educated guess that it's a battalion of Republican Guard."

"That's quite a guess, what led you to that conclusion?"

"I kind of had a run-in with some Iraqi forces last night and they called for back-up before I could stop them."

"They're probably on the main road. Just head west and put some distance between you and the highway, then lay low until we get to you," said Oso.

"No good," Victor replied. "I stole one of their jeeps and it ran out of gas on the road. When they find it, they'll be able to track me west until they catch up."

"You're not helping me."

"No kidding."

"Okay, keep heading south and I'll get back to you...and Wraith..."

"Yeah?"

"We're going to get you out of there."

Victor couldn't help but smile at Oso's sentimentality. "I know Sandy. Thanks...Wraith, out."

Chapter 53

Despite his last words to Victor, Oso had a bad feeling. A battalion of Republican Guard would probably have some embedded air defenses, including one or two mobile SAM units as well as some triple-A pieces. He couldn't send in the helicopters with that kind of threat looming. Instead, the A-10s would have to stop the movement of the battalion before they got to Victor. If they couldn't do that, any chance of rescue would be lost. Before doing anything else, he needed to stop the choppers from continuing toward the threat.

Oso switched frequencies. "Jolly One, This is Sandy One."

"Go ahead, Sandy," replied the Pavehawk pilot.

"Stop your forward movement and set up a holding pattern ten miles north of Point Charlie."

"What's up, Lead?" interrupted Tank.

"I'll have to get back to you with the details," Oso replied. "For now, just stay with Jolly as 'rescort' and wait for my word."

"Copy that, Sandy Three and Four will remain in the hold with Jolly," Tank summarized the order.

"Jolly One copies all. We're setting up the hold now," the lead chopper pilot added.

Oso needed to get a first-hand look at the opposition to get a better handle on the situation, but he couldn't risk alerting them to the rescue force's presence. At this point, surprise might be his only advantage, and sacrificing that would be a grave mistake. He decided to use his survivor as an offensive asset and get some intel. He looked at his map, scanning the topography around Victor's position for the right feature, and quickly found what he needed. "Wraith, this is Sandy," he began.

"Go ahead, Sandy."

"Do you have any binoculars on you?"

"Uh, yeah, Sandy One. I have a good set," Victor answered warily.

"Good. I'm going to need you to be my eyes for a while."

Oso thought back to his ROTC days and remembered his Military Arts and Sciences class. Most of the sessions had seemed better suited for treating insomnia than anything else, but he did remember one important quote. Some famous general once said that the victorious warrior took the initiative, so that contact with the enemy would occur at the time and place of his own choosing. Oso couldn't choose the time, but he did have some leeway when it came to the place. He looked at his map again and let the thought hang in his mind, concentrating on the vantage point he'd chosen for Victor.

"Wraith, this is Sandy One. I'm going to need you to move."

"I'll do my best. How much pain is this going to cost me?"

"Not too much," Oso lied. "Look to your southeast. About half a mile away there is a high ridge. It should be obvious; it's the most dominating terrain feature for several miles in all directions."

"Roger, I see it," Victor replied.

"Good, I need you to get to the top of that ridge as fast as you can. From there you'll be able to get me a good description of the force we're facing." Oso knew that what he asked was both harsh and dangerous. On another day, with another survivor, he might worry that the man would refuse, but this was Victor. Despite their troubled parting, he knew he could count on the younger pilot's guts in the face of a challenge.

Victor stopped jogging and set down the water jug. He stared at the radio while several thoughts of protest raced through his mind. Oso was moving him closer to the road rather than farther away, and he needed to save his strength and water for a potential run for his life if the rescue failed. Additionally, the sandy terrain would make progress difficult – to the point that the Republican Guard might be nearly on top of him before he finished the half-mile journey. All of these factors were solid arguments against Oso's plan, but Victor did not voice them. There could only be one chief for this mission and Oso was Sandy One. For whatever reason, Oso felt that getting him onto that hill was the way to make the rescue happen. He would not question the idea. Still, Oso's tactical decisions had cost Victor dearly on their last mission together. Could he trust him now?

Finally, Victor raised the radio to his lips, pausing for only one more second, "Roger that, Sandy One," he said. "I'm on my way."

Chapter 54

"Sandy Three, this is Sandy One," Oso called into his radio.

"Go ahead," Tank replied.

"It looks like the survivor decided that a simple rescue was too easy for us. There's a battalion of Republican Guard on the way and they know he's on the ground."

"Sounds like it's going to be a 'target-rich environment' down there," answered Tank. "That's good. I mean, we wouldn't want this to be boring, now would we?"

"My thoughts exactly; that's why we're going to take the fight to them. Do you see the ridge on your map running north to south, just north of Point Echo?"

"Tally."

"Good. For lack of a better name let's call that ridge Tango and set up a hold just to the west of it. The survivor is moving to the top of Tango to act as recon. I need you and Four to set up your pattern on the south end of Tango. I'll take Two up to the north. Leave the choppers where they are; they'll have to wait until we can eliminate this threat before moving forward. Set your altitude to one hundred feet; they've probably got some radar in that convoy and I don't want them to get wind of us too early."

"Going in low and dirty," Tank answered, "I like it."

Oso turned toward the ridge and felt the rush of speed as he dropped to one hundred feet, watching the sand fly by at three hundred knots. Tango loomed up ahead; it looked menacing, promising a tough fight before the end of the day. He hoped that his wingman was up to it. "How's it going, Two," he asked.

"Not bad for my first combat action," replied Sidearm. "I'm just glad that you're not grading me on this one."

"Cute," Oso said to his former student, "just don't make me regret sending you out into the real world." The irony of the moment was not lost on Oso. The first student that he'd given an ounce of leeway was now his wingman in a real combat environment. After his checkride, Sidearm had been sent to the Bulldogs, the active A-10 unit just down the street from the Schoolhouse. He'd completed mission qualification ahead of his peers, and because of that honor, his Weapons Officer had seen fit to send him directly into the Sandy program – something that was almost unheard of.

When he'd been assigned to lead the alert team, Oso had more than minor misgivings about taking on the young pilot as a Number Two. But the kid's record after training justified the match-up and there were no grounds to argue. Now he was leading the rookie toward a battalion of enemy troops and he knew that somewhere ahead he'd have to make a decision. At some point he would have to put Sidearm in harm's way, and both the rookie's and Victor's lives would hang in the balance. He wouldn't know if he'd be able to make that call until the time came. Right now, all he could do was move forward on faith that his demons were buried in the Arizona hills.

"Sandy Three is established at the south end of Tango," Tank reported.

"Sandy One copies. We're holding at the north end. Stand by for further instructions."

★ ★ ★ ★

Victor put the water jug to his lips and took a long draught. Then he set it back down in the sand. The heavy jug would only slow him down; besides, if Oso's plan was successful, he wouldn't need it anymore. He put the GPS and the radio back into his survival vest, took a few deep breaths, and then began his race to the hill. He'd been a long distance runner in high school and college, but he'd let his endurance skills slip since leaving the Academy almost six years before. Now he realized that all of the track meets, all of the ribbons, all of the races of his younger days were merely training for this moment. This single event held so much more in jeopardy than a strip of blue cloth.

Victor focused on the movement of his legs and arms, the posture of his body, the terrain in front of him. He channeled the power from his core into his quadriceps, driving his thighs like pistons to propel him through the sand. His eyes searched for signs of solid ground and he ran a serpentine path through the desert to capitalize on pockets of firm terrain. His throat burned but he ignored it; instead, he focused his breathing to draw as much oxygen as possible from the parched desert air. Every time he looked up to see his objective, it seemed no closer than before, as if he was going nowhere, and he wondered if his fate was already sealed. Then suddenly the desert began to rise beneath him and the last hundred yards fell behind him in an instant. He'd made it. He checked his watch – three minutes had elapsed since he left the water jug.

"I'm here," Victor transmitted between gasps. "That's a new desert-survival-half-mile record." He tore open the last of his water pouches and placed it to his dry, cracked lips. The water was warm but it felt smooth. He held it in his mouth for a few seconds before letting it slip down his throat, savoring it because he knew it was the last drink he would get for quite a while.

Victor looked to the west of his hill. The familiar sight of four A-10s orbiting in the distance gave him new hope and strength. The cavalry had arrived. He pulled out his binoculars and looked back to the northeast. He could clearly see vehicles amidst the dust; the enemy battalion was already getting too close. There were five covered troop carriers in the center of the convoy, led by a pair of tracked general-purpose vehicles driving side by side. The tracked vehicles had low profiles with sloped fronts, Soviet-built BMP-1 platforms. The BMPs could carry several types of weaponry and Victor could see that at least one of them supported a twenty-three millimeter anti-aircraft gun, a significant threat but nothing the Hogs couldn't handle. Then, between the lead vehicles and the transports, Victor saw another piece of Soviet-made equipment, one that was bad news. Its distinctive feature was a three-pack of large missiles that pilots often referred to as the "Three Fingers of Death." It was an SA-6 mobile SAM unit.

Victor frowned. The triple-A piece was something to be respected, but the SA-6 was something to be feared. Its defeat would require careful planning and flawless execution, neither of which had been applied the last time he and Oso had faced a SAM system together.

Putting his misgivings aside, Victor moved his binoculars along the column. He saw the normal support vehicles that could be expected with this type of unit, but then he saw something else that made his heart sink. Another SA-6 vehicle brought up the rear of the column, its three missiles set low on the horizon, pointed ominously in Victor's direction. He knew that the missiles were probably set that way in travel mode, but the fact that they were pointed at him still gave him the creeps. Involuntarily, he crouched lower.

"Sandy One, this is Wraith, over," Victor said into the radio.

"Go ahead, Wraith."

"The battalion appears to be less than a couple of miles from my jeep. It's packing some serious heat with at least one twenty-three millimeter and two, I repeat *two*, SA-6 mobile launchers; one at the front of the column and the other at the rear. The twenty-three millimeter piece is in the lead, just in front of the forward SAM. There may be another one right next to it."

"Sandy One copies all." Oso pictured the enemy convoy in his mind. This was going to be harder than he'd hoped. A single SA-6 was a real challenge, but two was nearly impossible. In addition, he had no time to waste; the convoy would be at Victor's jeep within minutes. Then they'd start tracking overland until they were too close for him to mount a defense. He had to do something and he had to do it fast, or Victor was all but lost.

Each A-10 carried six maverick missiles, fourteen rockets, and four cluster bombs in addition to an eleven-hundred round mix of armor piercing and incendiary bullets. The cluster bombs would be no good until the SAMs were taken care of, and for that Oso would have to use the mavericks and the guns. He used a grease pencil to mark the convoy's general position on his map and then formulated a plan. The first half of the Irish Cross attack might be ideal if there was only one SA-6, but the additional missile launcher threw a wrench in the works. His only hope was that both SAMs might behave the same in response to the Irish Cross. Then the Hogs could pull off the attack and destroy one, narrowing the odds. At least the modified attack would keep the two wingmen safely out of the missiles' range. In a pinch, it was the best he could do.

"Sandy Flight, this is Sandy One," Oso transmitted, "we are faced with a column containing at least one triple-A piece and two SA-6 vehicles."

"Okay boss, what's the plan?" asked Tank.

"We'll try the first half of an Irish Cross," Oso replied. "We have to count on both launchers behaving the same. First, let's all get on the same freq with survivor – he's going to act as our Ground Forward Air Controller. Sandy Flight, push to the rescue frequency."

Once the rest of his flight was on the same frequency with Victor, Oso continued his briefing. "Sandy Flight, standby for an Irish Cross. One and Three will be the shooters with maverick and gun. Two and Four will be cover with gun only. Focus your attack on the front of the convoy. There will be no follow up. Egress and regroup after Sandy One destroys the first SAM. Is that clear?"

The flight members replied in the affirmative. "Wraith copies all," Victor added.

"Good," said Oso. "Execute on my mark in three...two...one...mark!"

Victor watched the four Warthogs turn eastward toward his ridge, with Tank turning slightly south and Oso taking his element slightly north. Sandy Four headed straight for the convoy and Victor felt a surge of adrenaline as the A-10 crossed the ridge right above him in a knife-edge pass, so low that he instinctively ducked. He stood up in time to see the Hog pull up in a maneuver known as wifferdill, bringing the nose of the A-10 skyward and then turning it on its edge to slice back toward the sand. Sandy Four was still outside of the effective range of the missiles, but Victor could see that that the pilot had gotten the Iraqis' attention. He smiled broadly as both launchers stopped moving forward and turned their missiles westward to point at the Hog. "Oso might actually pull this off," he said to himself.

Confusion was setting in at the convoy. Forward movement stopped and the troops poured out of the vehicles in preparation for an attack. "The targets are taking the bait," Victor transmitted. Sandy Four settled back into low altitude flight and disappeared to the south. Now it was Tank's turn. The number three Hog drove in from the southwest. As he approached the road, he pulled up and rolled in toward the convoy, lobbing a hundred rounds of "combat mix" at the southern SA-6. At that distance, the armor piercing rounds had little effect, but Victor watched with satisfaction as the incendiary rounds fell short and landed on the twenty-three millimeter artillery piece with the force of thirty or forty grenades. The vehicle burst into flames and the driver leapt out, fleeing for his life.

Victor was once again encouraged to see the lead SA-6 swivel its missiles, this time southward, toward Tank's perceived threat. Then he moved his gaze to the north and his stomach turned. The trailing SAM had not taken the bait; instead it was swiveling northward, looking for another threat.

"Sandy One, *abort, abort, abort!*" Victor shouted into his radio, but it was too late. He looked on in horror as Oso's A-10 came into view, bearing down from the north. The lead SAM had been caught unaware but the second one was ready. Victor watched helplessly as a cloud of white smoke obscured the northern SA-6. A moment later, a missile emerged with a spike of yellow flame propelling it toward his friend.

"Sandy One, break right, SAM in the air," called Sidearm. The wingman had seen it too. The number two A-10 turned toward the threat, letting loose with a hundred depleted uranium rounds. He was too far away to penetrate the SAMs armor, but Victor was thankful to see that the attack scared the Iraqis enough to foil a second launch.

Oso heard both radio calls warning him of the imminent danger and he was able to turn his A-10 forty-five degrees away from the threat before the launch. Now he pressed hard on the throttle and hugged the desert floor, focusing his eyes on the approaching missile.

From its rapid approach, it was clear the missile had retained its lock, and Oso prepared for the worst. He jettisoned all of his stores, feeling a sickening thump as six mavericks, four cluster bombs, and two pods of rockets fell uselessly to the desert floor. Then, spouting a shower of metal chaff from his wings, he climbed and turned hard into the approaching missile. He strained with every muscle, squeezing every 'G' out of his body and his aircraft as the huge missile filled his windscreen. His eyes narrowed, his subconscious prepared for death, and then the missile was gone.

Oso continued to pull with all his might despite a surreal moment of peaceful quiet when there seemed to be no threat. There was no missile in his windscreen; there was nothing but the hazy horizon and the featureless desert. Then a monstrous explosion shattered the peace. Just as he'd hoped, the missile was unable to adjust to his high-G turn. The weapon had shot past him and locked onto the cloud of chaff, but Oso could not escape its wrath entirely. It exploded just past his aircraft and he felt as if every filling were jarred from his teeth as the shockwave buffeted his Hog. Several shards of hot metal penetrated the A-10's hull. Most embedded themselves harmlessly in the base of the titanium tub that surrounded the cockpit, but a few of them ripped through the hydraulic lines in his right wing.

"Sandy Flight abort and return to Tango," Oso ordered. He turned his jet back toward the ridge and watched his left hydraulic gauge plummet to zero. Acting quickly, he flipped a toggle to isolate the system and allow his other hydraulic lines to power the flight controls. Then he surveyed the rest of the damage. To his surprise, he found that he'd be able to fly almost normally. The A-10 was beautifully designed to take a beating. He could still lead the battle, but most of his weapons were gone. All that he had left was his gun.

"Sandy Flight, check in with a damage report," Oso commanded.

The other three pilots reported no damage. "Looks like you're the only cripple, Boss," Tank added.

"Watch who you're calling cripple," Oso replied. "Wraith, tell me what you see."

"The convoy has stopped," said Victor. "It looks like Three's attack took out the anti-aircraft gun as well as the vehicle next to it. They're burning out of control now and blocking the road. The two SAMs are still operational though. The trailing piece expended one missile, but I'm sure you're well aware of that."

"Yeah, I figured that out. By the way, thanks for the heads up."

"Anything I can do to help," Victor replied. "Any chance we can just bring the choppers up to your side of the ridge while the bad guys regroup?"

"Sorry, no can do. They won't take a long shot at our jets, but they'd be happy to lob a few missiles at the slower helicopters. It'd be a shame if Jolly One got shot out of the sky right after picking you up."

"Point taken. Okay then, what's the plan?"

"Give me a sec, I'm working on it."

"Sandy One, this is Two, I've got something that might help," Sidearm interrupted.

"Go ahead, Two," Oso prompted.

"When I took my shot at the northern launcher, I grabbed his coordinates."

Oso smiled. Sidearm had done something that even he hadn't thought of. He'd used a feature that linked the HUD to his navigation computer through the embedded GPS. The GPS system was still a relatively new technology for the A-10 and the older pilots were not accustomed to it, but the young pilots had been raised on it. The new system constantly calculated the set of coordinates under the gun sight, and whenever the "mark" button was pressed it recorded those coordinates to a file. Sidearm had wisely thought to mark the SAM's exact position while he was peppering it with bullets.

"Hey, that kid's good," said Victor. "Who trained him?"

"I did," Oso responded dryly.

"Nevertheless…"

"Did you two used to be married or something?" asked Tank.

"Enough guys," Oso ordered. "We can joke later at the bar. Right now, we have a serious problem. I need something to take out at least one of those SAMs before we can take this any further. Sandy Three, tell me what you know about other airborne assets."

"There's nothing else out here, Boss. We're on our own."

"Actually, Three," Victor interjected with guarded optimism, "that's not entirely true."

Chapter 55

"How'm I doing?" asked Drake.

Murph checked the fuel gauges. "The fuel's rising. You're almost there."

Drake had been attached to the tanker's boom continuously for the last twenty minutes. In another few seconds, they would reach their planned fuel load, ready to turn towards the island. Crash was in the back with his chair leaned back, having declared that, since he had nothing else to do, he might as well take a nap. The SATCOM beeped, alerting them that there was a new message, but neither pilot moved to retrieve it. Keeping the B-2 physically attached to another aircraft was a hazardous activity; it was critical that both of them remain focused on the task.

"Haven Zero One, you have reached your assigned offload, disconnect at your..." the boom operator stopped before completing his sentence.

Drake took his finger off the disconnect trigger, waiting for the boomer to finish the command.

"Stand by, Haven. I'm being told to keep you in position."

"Figures," said Drake. He continued to fly in the boom's envelope, keeping the B-2 under the tanker. After twenty minutes of tight formation flying his shoulders and arms were tense; he shrugged a few times, trying to relax his muscles without losing his position.

A few seconds later, the boom operator spoke again, "Haven, I have a radio patch from Kuwait. Sandy Three is on the line with an urgent request."

Drake dropped his mask. "I thought Sandy wasn't told about our presence," he shouted to Murph. They couldn't have a private conversation over the intercom because the boomer's headset was hardwired to the connection through the boom.

"Let's find out," Murph shouted back. He pressed the intercom key and spoke to the boom operator, "Okay, go ahead with the voice patch."

A low crackle sounded over the boom's connection. Amidst the static, Tank's voice came through muted but readable. "Haven Zero One, this is Sandy Three."

"Go ahead, Sandy Three," Murph prompted.

"We've got a bit of a situation down here. We're facing down two mobile SAMs that are escorting a battalion of Republican Guard. The whole gaggle is threatening our survivor. We've been unable to penetrate their defenses; in fact, one of our birds was damaged in the first attempt. Somehow the survivor knew that there was an armed B-2 in the air, even though you're not on anybody's list of assets. As much as I'd like a really good explanation for all of this, right now I just need to know if you can help us take out one of those SAMs."

Drake keyed the intercom, "We…" he started to say, but Murph waved him off, as if he wanted to discuss options. Drake didn't understand. "This is a no-brainer," he shouted, still keeping his eyes on the tanker. "We can't do it. With that barn door hanging open back there, we'll be sitting ducks!"

Murph said nothing.

"Haven, do you copy? Can you help us?" The A-10 driver sounded impatient.

Murph put his mask up. "Sandy Three, tell your lead that we'll be inbound in five minutes, right after we top off our tanks."

"What?" Drake shouted again. This time he looked directly at Murph in disbelief before remembering that he was still attached to the tanker. The B-2 bucked and wobbled as he struggled to bring it back to the center of the boom's envelope.

"Relax," Murph shouted, "I have a plan."

"Oh good, you have a plan. That makes me feel much better," Drake responded sarcastically.

The abrupt maneuvers under the tanker woke Crash just in time to hear Drake's last outburst. He put on his headset and keyed the intercom, "What plan? What's going on?"

"I'll have to get back to you on that, Crash," Murph responded.

"And you'll have to get back to me, too!" Drake added, putting his mask back up.

"Sandy, this is Haven," said Murph. "We're on our way and we'll take care of one of those SAMs for you. Just keep them off the survivor until we get there."

"Sandy Three copies all. Standby for the control point and target coordinates." Tank read out a series of numbers while Murph furiously wrote on his clipboard. Then Murph read back the numbers to make sure they were correct. "That's right," Tank said. "I'll see you guys in a few; Sandy Three, out." The crackle faded.

"We're going to need another ten thousand pounds," Murph told the boomer. "Have you got it?"

"We've got plenty of gas to spare," the boomer replied. "I'm starting the transfer now."

"Thanks. Give me all the pressure you can muster, we're in a hurry."

"I'm already on it," the young airman replied.

Drake continued to hold the B-2 in position under the tanker, constantly making tiny corrections with the stick and throttles as the fuel began to flow again. "You want to clue us in on the plan, fearless leader?" he asked.

Murph ignored the question. He checked the fuel gauges. "That'll do it, boomer," he said. "We'll take that disconnect now."

"The fuel transfer has stopped. You are cleared to disconnect. Delay your turn until you're well clear. Good luck, Haven."

Drake triggered the release from the boom. When its shadow moved away from the cockpit, he pulled the throttles back and gently pushed the nose down, creating space between his jet and the tanker. As they backed away, the airman who'd been flying the boom gave them a smart salute, which Murph gratefully returned. "Good work, kid," he said before finally turning his attention to Drake. "Turn us back to the original hold point," he ordered, "and put the pedal to the floor; we don't know how much time Victor has." Then he turned and checked the SATCOM message.

STATUS CHECK

"What's going on?" asked Drake, still focused on flying the aircraft.

"Walker wants to know what we're doing," Murph replied. "This is going to be tough to explain."

"No kidding," Drake said with an edge to his voice. "You have yet to explain it to me."

"All in due time, my boy," Murph responded. He bent down and began typing away on the SATCOM.

A few moments later the system chimed again and Drake glanced down to see Walker's response.

CLEARED HOT

Chapter 56

Victor slowly panned his binoculars along the enemy column. The Iraqi soldiers were containing the fire at the front of the convoy too quickly, and before long they would be able to push the burnt vehicles aside and continue their pursuit. They would move slowly for fear of another attack by the A-10s, but they would move nonetheless. The performance of their missile systems had given them confidence.

The sound of engines spooling up caught Victor's ear, and he looked south in time to see two of the Hogs come around the ridge and turn towards the enemy. His rescuers had come up with a plan to keep the Iraqis in check. "Go get 'em, Oso," he said.

Oso had recognized the need to keep the enemy troops off balance and contrived an attack to keep them pinned down until the B-2's arrival. He knew that even though white phosphorous rockets, affectionately called "Willy Petes" by the pilots, were designed to mark targets rather than destroy them, their impact could be a frightening experience for the enemy. They are incredibly loud and they fill the air with a horrid smoke that burns the eyes and throat. Oso decided to harass the Iraqis by having Sidearm loft a few rockets from just outside of their missile range.

Victor monitored the attack on his radio. "Sandy Two is turning inbound," said Sidearm.

"You're cleared hot, Two," Oso acknowledged. "I have you covered. Just try to put the rockets somewhere near the target."

"Trust me. I've gotten much better since graduation."

"I hope so."

Victor watched as the young wingman pointed his Hog directly at the convoy while Oso arced to the east, ready to roll in and support the attack with his gun. Still well outside of the SAM's range, the wingman pulled his nose skyward and launched a salvo of rockets before diving back to the safety of the desert floor. With no guidance systems to keep them heading toward a fixed point, the seven rockets slowly fanned out. They climbed steadily until their motors ran out of fuel and then turned back toward earth in a graceful parabolic arc, each heading for a different part of the convoy.

Victor turned his binoculars back to the convoy, noting grimly that the Iraqis seemed blissfully unaware of the thin silhouettes bearing down on them. Suddenly, the hatch of one of the SAMs popped open and the driver gestured wildly at the others. It was too late. The dry, desert air erupted in a cacophony of explosions. The white smoke spread like an evil fog and Iraqi troops ran in every direction, trying to escape the burning in their throats. Many crawled under the transport trucks, obviously fearful of another attack.

Victor smiled. "That ought to slow you down," he said. Then he held his radio to his lips. "Nice work, fellas. It's pandemonium over there. They probably think you just hit them with chemical weapons."

"Thanks," answered Oso. "That ought to buy us some time while we wait for your friends."

★   ★   ★   ★

Drake watched the choppy surface of the Persian Gulf through the bomber's panoramic windscreen as the water whipped by less than a hundred feet below him. The gulf took on a blue-gray hue in the early morning light and the mist and dust combined to form a thick haze. The poor visibility was a mixed blessing. It obscured his B-2 from onlookers on the shore but it also prevented him from seeing obstacles like oil rigs until the last second. Drake clenched his teeth. His forward visibility was less than a mile, and he was covering that distance every eight seconds.

Drake flew the bomber manually. He could not use the autopilot at such a low altitude because the choppy waters made the radar altimeter unreliable. The flight control computers could easily mistake their altitude by more than a hundred feet and fly them right into the gulf. Unfortunately for Drake, that meant that the radar altimeter readout on his screen was unreliable as well. He had to fly the old fashioned way, using what he liked to call "the Mark-One Eyeball" as his primary instrument. His only comfort was the moving map on the laptop computer that was mounted between the pilots' seats. A GPS signal updated their position every ten seconds on the scaled display. The system had all known obstacles plotted precisely, enabling Drake to steer well clear of towers and rigs.

"I think I've been patient long enough," Drake complained, steering the plane left to avoid another tower. "Don't you think it's time you let us in on your little plan? At least explain why I'm dodging rigs at a hundred feet."

"I'm going to have to agree with Drake," Crash added. "Before being carried helplessly along on your crazy rescue, I'd like to know how you plan for all of us to survive. That is, assuming you *are* planning for us to survive."

There was a short period of silence during which Murph did not offer an explanation. His gaze was focused outside, monitoring Drake's performance at the controls.

When he could no longer take the silence, Drake pressed for an answer. "You *are* planning for us to survive, aren't you?"

"Of course I am," Murph answered finally. "Here's the deal, fellas. We have what amounts to a gaping hole on our underside. There's no way to tell what impact that has on our stealth, but I'm guessing it's not a good thing. I'm not about to waltz in to enemy airspace with my fly down."

"Yet my navigation computer here says that's exactly what we're doing," said Crash.

"You didn't let me finish. That's what would happen if we went in at high altitude…"

"But we're practically on the surface," Drake finished, starting to see where Murph was going.

"That's right. We'll use the surface interference to mask our problem. There's nothing wrong with the top of the plane so, with any luck, we'll just disappear into the sand."

"That's all well and good for getting us there," said Drake, "but we can't drop a five thousand pound bomb from a hundred feet. We'll be obliterated."

"Obliterated doesn't sound good," Crash interjected.

"You're right. We'll have to climb up to deliver the weapon," answered Murph. "That's why you're not just along for the ride Crash, I need your help."

"I'll do whatever you want if it helps me avoid getting obliterated."

"Good. I have a math problem for you. Working back from the target coordinates, I need you to calculate a speed, climb angle, and altitude that will allow me to loft the bomb from a few miles back. If we can get the iron in the ballpark, the GPS will take care of the fine points."

"I can do that for you, but it's going to take me a few minutes."

"I hope that's all it takes, because a few minutes are all you've got."

"We're approaching the original control point," Drake interrupted. "Do you want me to set up a holding pattern?"

"No, there's no time. Blow on through and head straight for the coordinates we got from Sandy Three."

Chapter 57

Victor frowned as he peered through his binoculars. The Iraqi officers were restoring order at the convoy with frustrating efficiency. They had rounded up most of their troops and were once again working to clear the wreckage from the front of their column. Soldiers were lined up on either side of the two destroyed vehicles and were already pushing them off the road. Victor was certain that their hands were being burnt and blistered by the searing hot metal that only minutes before had been blazing out of control, but fear of their superiors had obviously overridden the soldiers' pain.

"What do you see, Wraith?" Oso's voice crackled over the radio.

"The picture's not good, Sandy One," Victor replied. "It appears they are very close to clearing the road and getting under way. Do you think you could set up another rocket attack?"

A new voice interrupted the conversation, "Did I hear you say that the target was on the move again?"

Victor felt a wave of elation at the sound of Drake's voice. "Well that's a voice I never thought I'd be so happy to hear."

"Thanks," Drake replied, "I'm glad you're not dead. Okay Sandy One, I'm ten minutes out and about to go feet dry. Go ahead and give me the skinny."

"The Iraqi convoy is still lethal, with a pair of SA-6 Surface to Air Missile systems," Oso replied. "We've taken out their Triple-A and slowed them down, but Wraith just reported that they're close to moving again. I need you to get in there and take out one of the SAMs. Once you've accomplished that we'll clean up the rest. What do you say?"

"Sounds like a plan. I'll give you a head's up when we're five minutes out."

"Copy that, I'll be waiting for you," Oso answered. "Sandy Three, I need you to take Four and go get the choppers. Escort them forward;

move them as close to our position as you can without risking a missile shot."

"I'm on it, One," Tank replied.

Just as Victor saw Sandy Three and Four turn to the south, a puff of smoke from the southern SAM vehicle caught his attention. "Sandy break west, break west, missile off the rail!" he shouted into his radio. "It's going after Sandy Three and Four."

The two A-10s turned westward as the missile reached the apex of its flight and turned toward the earth. "I think it's ballistic," Tank transmitted. "My scope is clean. It's not tracking."

Victor watched with relief as the missile continued on a southern flight path, ignoring the Hogs. He guessed that the rocket attack had pushed one of the Iraqi SAM operators to the breaking point. Their training told them not to waste a missile unless they had a clear radar lock, but tired of being a target rather than the aggressor, the Iraqi had broken protocol. He had probably launched in hopes of getting a late lock or at least detonating the missile close to one of the Hogs.

"It's a blind launch," said Victor, "I think you're okay."

All eyes remained fixed on the missile, but with nothing to guide it, the SAM simply plummeted toward the earth. At a few hundred feet above the surface and almost a mile away from Tank's formation, the missile exploded in an orange ball of smoke, fire, and sparks.

"Alright Three, you're cleared to continue south," said Oso. "When you come back with the choppers, keep them well out of range of that thing," he cautioned.

As Tank moved off again, Victor turned the events of the last few minutes over in his mind. He felt the shock of a hunter whose prey suddenly turns and charges. Since Oso's rocket attack he'd felt relatively safe, reporting the Iraqi movements with confidence. Now he felt exposed again. The SAM operator had missed, but the message was clear: "We can harass you too."

Chapter 58

Drake brought Haven One into Iraqi airspace just west of the Shatt al-Arab, the joining of the Tigris and Euphrates rivers where they empty into the Persian Gulf. The blue-gray of the gulf rushing past the windscreen changed to deep browns and lush greens as they passed over the delta.

Murph studied the moving map. "The convoy is too far to the east," he said. "In order to attack from that direction, we would have to steer very close to Iran, if not across the border."

"Not a good idea," Drake replied. "This operation is screwed up enough without involving the forces of another rogue nation. Why don't we attack from the west, from behind the hill that Sandy One called Tango. That would mask the attack and buy us a little time to climb up and loft the bomb."

"Sounds like a plan," Murph replied. "Steer west along a heading of two nine zero. Let's get away from these waterways before someone sees us."

"Gladly." Drake banked left and took the bomber along Murph's prescribed course. "You still haven't explained the endgame," he said with a frown.

"I know. Give me another minute." Murph turned in his seat to look back at Crash. "How's it coming back there?" he asked.

"I've got it," Crash answered, "I'm just checking my work. We don't want to screw this up just because I forgot to carry the three or something."

"True. Take your time."

After a moment Crash lifted his head. "Yep, I've got it," he said. He unstrapped from his seat and stepped forward to hand a piece of paper up to Murph. "That's your speed, distance, and climb angle, along with the coordinates and altitude where you want to launch. Since it's a guided weapon, I gave you a window around those numbers where the launch will still work, as long as you're pointed directly at the target. Just put it in the basket."

"Great, I can do that. Now that you're up, I've got another task for you."

"Shoot."

"On the panel behind your seat there are several rows of circuit breakers. I need you to pull one of them."

Crash walked back to his station and grabbed a flashlight, shining the beam on a wall covered in tiny black knobs. "Okay, I see them," Crash said nervously. "There are hundreds of these things. I hope you know where the one you want is, otherwise this is going to take all day."

"It should be somewhere on the left side of the third row. It's marked 'AOA Limit.'"

Drake suddenly realized Murph's intentions. "Oh crap," he exclaimed, "You can't be serious."

"Just shut up and drive," Murph answered. "Do you see it?" he asked Crash.

"Yeah! Here it is," the analyst responded. "What do I do with it?"

"Just grab it and give it a good yank."

Crash did as he was told and the little knob extended a couple of millimeters out of the panel. "Okay, it popped out, and now I can see a white ring around its base."

"Good, you've got it."

"Got what?" Crash asked, strapping back into his seat. "What did I just do?"

"You disabled the bank angle and angle of attack limiter," Drake answered with a shake of his head. "You made it so that we can fly inverted without the automatic flight controls stopping us."

"I did *what*?" Crash asked.

"The bomber's autopilot will take over if the computer senses too much bank or an impending aerodynamic stall," Murph explained in an academic tone. "If we exceed certain climb angles or bank angles, the autopilot will assume control and try to right the aircraft. You've just turned that feature off so that we can roll the plane over on its back."

"And why on earth would I want to do that?" Crash asked.

"After we launch the bomb we'll be in a very exposed position, belly up to the SAM," Murph explained. "We're going to turn our good side – the top – toward the SAM's radar in an effort to spoil any last minute shots."

"Basically we're going to do a barrel roll with a three hundred thousand pound bomber, over the top of a battalion of enemy forces and two Surface to Air Missile systems," Drake finished.

"Oh crap," Crash said, repeating Drake's earlier analysis.

"At what point do you plan on taking the aircraft and executing said acrobatic maneuver?" Drake asked.

"I don't. I need to manage the bomb's release down to the last millisecond, especially if the convoy is moving again. You'll have to fly the barrel roll for us."

"What about slice through?" Drake asked, referring to the tailless bomber's tendency to slice through the horizon like a boomerang when turned on its edge.

"If the simulator is accurate, you'll be able to prevent it with negative-G pressure on the stick. What little slice through we experience will help us get back to the safety of the surface that much faster."

"Whatever you say, Boss." Drake rolled his eyes and checked his map. "It looks like we're almost due west of the target now, I'm turning inbound."

★ ★ ★ ★

Victor lay prone on the top of Tango, hoping that the Iraqis were still unaware of his position. His face showed sour resignation. "Sandy, Haven, this is Wraith, over."

"Go for Sandy," Oso responded.

"Haven's listening," Murph added.

"I hate to be the bearer of bad news, but the convoy is on the move again." Victor watched through his binoculars as a puff of black smoke belched from the tracked SAM vehicle and it lurched forward. Men were running to armored personnel carriers that were already beginning to inch forward. The burnt BMPs lay on their sides beyond the edge of the paved road.

"Roger that, Wraith, we'll set up another rocket attack to slow them down," said Oso.

"Stand by, Sandy One," Murph cut him off. "We're only a couple of minutes out with the heavy iron. That'll be stronger medicine than the rockets."

"Sandy One, this is Three," Tank interrupted. "Jolly Flight and I are established in a hold just south of Point India."

"One copies. That's close enough. Leave them there and return to your hold at Tango."

"Sandy Flight," said Murph, "we're inbound on our final run. We're going to fly right over your little hill there, so I suggest you move your flight north or south."

"Done," Oso answered. "Sandy Three, make your hold one mile southwest of Tango; I'll take Two a mile to the northwest. Let's make some room for the big guns."

★ ★ ★ ★

Drake leveled the bomber out on his final attack heading, hugging the top of the dunes. He was barely thirty feet above the desert and picking up speed. The big flying wing shook and buffeted in the thick surface air as it whipped over the sand at nearly five hundred miles an hour. It kicked up a cloud of dust in its wake, drawing a billowing trail across the barren landscape.

Drake glanced back at Crash, who sat at his station in the back of the jet, gripping his armrests as if he was trying to squeeze blood from them. The analyst's position in the back of the aircraft amplified the affects of the turbulence and he looked green with nausea.

"You okay, Crash?" shouted Drake.

"Don't talk to me! I've got to focus on not puking right now!"

Murph looked at Drake with an expression of fierce determination. "I don't need to tell you that we only have one shot at this," he said. "Since the convoy is moving, I'll have to take a radar shot to update the coordinates."

"Line of sight will prevent that until we start our climb," Drake cautioned, "it's going to be tight."

"I know. As soon as we're over the hill I'll fire off the radar; with any luck we'll have updated coordinates just in time to loft the weapon. I'm opening the doors of the good bay now."

Drake could feel the added drag shaking the bomber as the doors opened; they were pushing the already damaged aircraft beyond its design limits. He glanced back at Crash again. "Give me an update, Crash," he ordered.

"We're getting close," Crash responded, checking his navigational computer. "Just fly straight and pray my calculations are correct. If any parameter is off by too great a margin, the bomb will miss and all of this will be a waste. If we drop it too fast or too high, the weapon will overshoot the target. If we're too slow or too low it will fall short, detonating way too close to Victor." Crash held up a hand. "Here it comes...Wait for my command...Three...two...one...now!"

Drake pulled back on the stick, willing the shaking behemoth to climb. Slowly, like it was moving through molasses, the nose tracked upward until Drake froze the angle at eight degrees above the horizon.

★ ★ ★ ★

Victor stood atop his hill and looked out to the west. He could now clearly see the approaching bomber and marveled at the awesome sight. For a moment he stood transfixed, his sense of time and danger lost. The black jet shot across the surface of the desert like a stingray across the ocean floor, dragging behind it a cloud of sand and dust. Suddenly, adrenaline roused him from his trance-like awe and his eyes went wide as it dawned on him that this incredible spectacle was heading right for him.

It wasn't the bomber that Victor feared; it was the sand that it carried behind it. The blast of sand from the bomber's wake would hit with such force that it could tear the skin from his body. Crouching and turning at the same time he dove from his perch toward the lee side of Tango, becoming fully airborne as the terrain on the eastern side dropped away. He tucked his head and twisted so that he would hit the sand in a roll. Just as he made contact, the roar and shadow of the Stealth overtook him and an explosion of sand and dust burst over the ridge, cascading down the hill like an avalanche. Victor tucked his head into his arms and tried not to breath in the choking cloud.

★   ★   ★   ★

As the bomber crested Tango, Drake saw the convoy for the first time. The Iraqis were moving faster than he'd expected.

Murph saw it too. "Our heading is bad," he shouted. "You've got to adjust!"

"I see it," Drake answered. He shoved the stick to the right, turning the bomber nearly on its edge and stressing the wings to five Gs, a level he was used to in the T-38, but not the B-2. With no G-suit to help counter the effects, blood began pooling away from his brain and his vision began to narrow. He tensed his muscles to fight off the threat of G-lock.

As soon as Drake leveled the wings, Murph fired the radar at the convoy. It took several tense seconds for the radar picture to come up.

"You're in the zone!" said Crash, staring at his computer. "Launch now!"

"Just a little longer," said Murph, "we don't have the picture yet."

"We're going to loose the window," said Drake.

"No we're not! Just give it one more second." Murph banged on the dashboard above the radar screen. "C'mon you lazy piece of junk," he shouted at the computer. Then the picture was there.

"Let's go buddy, we're out of time," said Drake.

"Almost there...Almost there," said Murph. He moved his cursor over the gray dot that represented the SAM and hammered down on the trigger, transferring the new coordinates to the GPS guided weapon. "I've got it! I'm updating the SAM coordinates now!"

★ ★ ★ ★

In the northern SAM vehicle the radar operator saw nothing but the static caused by the immense sand cloud at the surface. Unable to hear the excited shouts of the soldiers in the vehicles ahead, he ordered his driver to continue south.

"I can't," the driver responded. "The vehicles in front of us have stopped."

"Don't just sit there like an idiot. Find out what's going on." The operator stared at the interference on his screen while the driver did as he was commanded. Suddenly the younger Arab began shouting in earnest from outside the hatch, but the operator could not understand the words. "Slow down you babbling moron. I can't understand you!" he shouted.

The driver stuck his head down into SAM vehicle. His face showed sheer terror. "*Sayed, Sayed*," he screamed. "Do something! A great black beast is rising out of the desert."

Unsettled by the soldier's wild eyes, the radar operator trained his beam westward. He was mystified by what he saw on his screen – nothing. He shook his head. He continued to sweep, certain that his driver would not cower like a beggar unless he'd seen at least something coming their way. Finally his efforts were rewarded. A small blip appeared on the screen.

★ ★ ★ ★

"Missile Lock, Missile Lock," a calm feminine voice chanted into Drake's headset. "They've got us! Come on man!" he shouted at Murph.

"Missile Lock, Missile Lock," the voice persisted.

Murph mashed his finger down on the release button. "That's it!

Weapon away!" There was an audible thump and a slight shudder as the ejector pushed the five thousand pound bomb from the bay.

As soon as the Bunker Buster fell free from the bomber, Drake began an arcing roll to the right. The nose of the jet tracked up and the right wing dipped. A feeling of being trapped in the surreal overtook Drake as he rolled through the vertical and watched his own bomb miss his wingtip by inches. As the Stealth became totally inverted he pushed forward on the stick, causing the nose to track skyward and forcing the G-meter to zero. A few loose items in the cockpit floated up from the console as if the crew were astronauts in the Space Shuttle. Then, looking past the falling bomb, Drake saw a cloud of white smoke billow up from the desert road.

★   ★   ★   ★

The SAM operator had tried to wait for a better lock, but the screams of the driver were too much for him. With barely enough energy to hold the track, he launched his missile. Then, even before the roar of the rocket reached its crescendo, the blip disappeared. He couldn't believe his eyes. One moment it had been there, slowly getting stronger, and then it was just gone. With no track to guide it, the missile would go stupid. He hesitated, hanging on to the futile hope that his track would return, but the screen showed nothing. He reached for a red-guarded switch on his panel. He knew what had to be done; he had to remotely detonate the weapon before it overshot the target. He flipped up the guard and then flipped down the toggle.

★   ★   ★   ★

When Drake saw the missile, there was little he could do. He was flying a heavy bomber, not a highly maneuverable fighter. He could only delay the inevitable and hope for a miracle. He pulled back on his stick, causing the nose to track downward. All of the floating debris came crashing down as if a wizard's spell had been broken.

Murph had seen it too. "Incoming!" he shouted back to Crash.

Both pilots kept their eyes locked on the missile as it grew ever larger in the windscreen. Then, in a blur, it was past them. For a split second Drake thought that they might have escaped unharmed, but then there was a deafening explosion. The B-2 shuddered as if it had been hit with a wrecking ball and unnaturally shifted downward through the air.

Instantly, lights and alarms sprang to life all over the cockpit. The yellow Master Caution lights and red Fire Warning lights flashed in Drake's face while the warning bells deafened him. He ignored it all. He continued to fly, shoving the stick over to the left while pulling back to prevent the nose from burying itself. To his relief the B-2 responded to his command and he soon had her upright in a hard turn to the south, diving back toward the relative safety of the desert floor.

Murph handled the onslaught of warnings and cautions from the jet's alarm systems. "Engines one and two are on fire," he said in a calm, almost detached voice. "I'm shutting them down; watch the yaw."

Drake felt the aircraft begin to yaw left as Murph pulled back the throttles and shut the engines down. The condition known as "asymmetric thrust" turned the aircraft sideways and he corrected the movement with his rudder, trying to bring the flight path back to straight. In the radio background, he could hear Victor saying something, but it didn't register – he already had too much on his mind.

"The RPM is down on both, but the temperatures are still high," Murph advised. "Neither fire is going out. I've got to blow all the fire bottles to the left side."

"Cleared hot," Drake responded. As he struggled to keep the aircraft flying, the ramifications of Murph's analysis crept to the front of his mind. The automatic fire fighting system had armed all four bottles of compressed fire suppressant, but there was a problem. Normally two bottles would be committed to a single engine, one at a time, the second putting out any residual flame left by the first. But

Murph was fighting two fires at once. He had to use all four bottles on the two engines. If another engine caught fire, they would have nothing left to put it out.

A problem with the controls brought Drake's full attention back to flying. The aircraft paused for a moment before responding to each input he made with the stick. "Flight controls are sluggish," he said. "Something's wrong with the hydraulics. Even without the two you shut down, I should still have two good systems."

"Standby," said Murph, "let me check your other systems." He called up a hydraulic schematic on the screen between them. "You're right, you've lost three of your four hydraulic systems. We lost one and two because of the fires, but it looks like some shrapnel must've got the number three system as well. I'll try to isolate it and see if we can't save the fourth."

"I don't know how much longer I can keep her in the air."

"I know. Do your best to get us as far out into the gulf as you can."

"Is there anything I can do?" asked Crash.

Murph turned in his seat, lifting his visor so that he could focus on Crash through the shadows in the back of the plane. "Yeah," he said with a grave look in his eyes, "stow everything you can, pocket your classified, and get ready to eject."

Chapter 59

Victor picked himself up just in time to see the huge bomb drop from Haven's open bay. With nothing between himself and the impending explosion, he knew that he might be exposed to debris. He jumped to his feet and ran back up the hill, diving over the top and hitting the sand just past the crest of the ridge. Satisfied with the relative safety of his position, he turned on his belly and snaked his way back to the top, peering over the side through his binoculars. He couldn't believe what he saw. Just east and slightly south of the convoy, the B-2 was completely inverted. Unfortunately, the sight below the bomber denied him the luxury of marveling at that oddity. A cloud of dust surrounded the northern SAM system, and tracking upward from the cloud, a single missile accelerated toward the inverted aircraft.

"Haven, look out! Missile off the rail! Missile off the rail!" Victor shouted into the radio, but it was a futile effort; the bomber was too close to the SAM to maneuver effectively. He felt a flicker of hope as the missile missed and passed above the B-2, but he knew a clean miss was too much to hope for.

The explosions came in rapid succession. The SAM detonated first, an oblong ball of fire and black smoke, just above and to the north of the bomber. A good portion of its destructive power was carried upward by its momentum, but not all. Victor watched in horror as the bomber that carried his three friends made a strange movement downward and then immediately started trailing smoke. He was about to warn them that they were on fire when the second fireball filled the lower periphery of his vision. He quickly shrunk back from the crest of the ridge ducking his head to the sand and covering his ears. The detonation of the five thousand pound bomb shook the air around him. Even at his distance, he could feel its heat. He counted to five before crawling back up to take stock of the result.

At the top of Tango Victor stood up and looked out over the aftermath. He followed the trail of smoke and saw Haven disappearing to the south. "Good work, guys. You got 'em," he said into the radio, not knowing if they could even hear him. Then he turned his attention to the north end of the convoy and saw the cloud of smoke and debris just beginning to settle. For a moment, he couldn't find the SAM vehicle. "Could it have been completely obliterated by the bomb?" he wondered. That didn't seem likely; it would require a direct hit, which was nearly impossible under the circumstances. Then, through the settling dust, he saw a burning black hulk. The bomb had blown it well west of the road. Apparently, "close enough for government work" had applied in this situation. He panned south along the road. The damage was not limited to the SAM; two of the transports lay scattered in charred pieces along the road. There were no signs of life.

"Talk to me Wraith," Oso's voice crackled over the radio. "What do you see?"

"The northern SAM is destroyed," answered Victor. "Haven crushed it like a bug, but the Iraqi got a shot off and they took a bad hit. The last I saw, they were heading south, trailing smoke. Their bomb also took out the two vehicles closest to the target SAM. Standby for more."

Further down the road, things improved dramatically for the Iraqis. The vehicles that had continued south had fared much better. Another transport was overturned, but there were men climbing out of it, and the lead SAM appeared completely unharmed, along with a fourth transport and a pair of jeeps. Victor panned back to the overturned transport. There appeared to be several wounded now lying on the road and no one was making an effort to recover the vehicle. He decided he could report that it was out of commission too. "It looks like all you've got left is the southern SAM, a transport, and a couple of jeeps."

"Great," said Oso. "Sit tight for just a little longer. We'll take care of that SAM and you'll be home free."

Victor was just thinking that Oso might be counting chickens a little early when a flash to his right caught his attention. He panned his binoculars back south along the road and saw an Iraqi soldier, holding his own pair of binoculars up to his eyes. The other man was not searching, he wasn't panning back and forth across the horizon; instead, he was focused, his gaze fixed directly on Victor.

Victor dropped to his knees and crawled down behind the crest of the ridge. He'd just committed the cardinal sin of evasion, standing exposed on the top of a ridgeline, silhouetted against the sky. He cursed his own stupidity; because of his mistake, the enemy had found him. He crawled forward, trying to remain hidden in the sand, and peeked over the ridge at the man with the binoculars. His betrayer was now waving and shouting at the occupants of one of the jeeps. One of them produced a long metal tube with a bulbous protrusion at one end. Victor's heart sank as he recognized the unmistakable shape of a rocket propelled grenade launcher. The man from the jeep stood atop his mount and pointed the weapon in the direction he'd been given.

Victor needed no other prompting. He threw himself into a sideways roll and tumbled down the west side of the ridge. Halfway down he leapt to his feet and ran south, trying to put plenty of distance between himself and his last position. When he could no longer stand the feeling of impending dange,r he dove back into the hill, covering his head. The explosion quickly followed and a shower of sand pelted his body. He had to give them credit for aim; the RPG hit just east of the ridge-top, right in front of his former position.

Victor rolled onto his back and breathed hard, staving off a feeling of panic. If he wanted to survive he had to pull it together. He took a deep breath and thought out his next move. He needed to get a better idea of the threat.

Victor climbed back to the top of the ridge and scanned the Iraqi line. The best he could hope for was that they would continue to take potshots at the ridge with RPGs; at this range he could easily dodge their attacks as long as he saw the launches. Looking through his binoculars, he saw that they were too smart for that. Eight men were piling into the two jeeps, each team armed with at least one RPG launcher and a vehicle-mounted fifty-caliber machine gun. They turned westward and left the road, heading for his position. Victor shrank back from the ridge. His only hope was that the soft desert sand would slow their progress. He lifted the radio to his lips. "Sandy One, this is Wraith."

"Go ahead, Wraith."

"They've seen me," Victor said ashamedly. "Two jeeps armed with RPGs and fifty-cals left the road and they're headed this way."

There was a short pause. "Roger that, Wraith, don't worry; we'll get 'em."

Chapter 60

Oso had tried to fill his voice with confidence, but he knew that his words meant little. It was as if Victor had just caused the clock on a time bomb to accelerate its countdown. He had to keep those jeeps away from his survivor, but he couldn't deal with them until he dealt with the SAM. The only solution was another Irish Cross. Unfortunately, the first attack had cost him all of his weapons. That wouldn't be a big concern if he could send Tank in as lead, but he'd sent Tank south prior to the B-2's attack, putting him too far out of position. There wasn't time to move Tank's formation. The final missile had to come from Sidearm.

Tank's impatient voice came over the radio, "Sound's like Wraith is in trouble, Sandy One. What's the plan?"

Oso felt a cold sweat form on his forehead. Could he handle more young blood on his conscience? He shuddered as a chill passed through him and his breath shortened. He'd told himself he was over this. There was an insistent ringing in his ears, growing louder all the time.

"Come on, Boss," Tank pushed. "Wraith is on borrowed time."

Oso forced himself to breathe deeply. Through the ringing he heard Torch's soft but firm voice as clearly as if the commander was sitting next to him in the cockpit. "In the end, it's their choice, not yours."

The ringing abruptly stopped. Oso's breath came evenly. His hands steadied. "Sandy Flight, listen up," he commanded. "We've got to do this quick and we've got to do it right. We're going to take out the SAM first. Once that's accomplished we're going to wipe those jeeps clean off the desert floor. The attack will be an Irish Cross. My element will be the shooters with the standard maverick and gun. Sandy Two will take the missile shot. Three, your element has the cover roll; gun only. As soon as the threat is down, we'll move in on the jeeps with everything we've got. Has everyone got it?"

"Two."

"Three."

"Four."

"Good. Sandy Flight, Irish Cross on my mark in three…two…one…mark!"

*   *   *   *

Once again, Victor felt a surge of emotion and adrenaline as he watched the four Hogs break past the ridge to his north and south. Four men, three of whom he'd never met, were placing their own lives as a barrier between him and the enemy. With a mix of grim determination and intense anger, he drew his weapon, unsure of what he meant to do with it, but desperate to be a part of the attack. He flipped off the safety and held it ready, bringing the radio up as well, ready to provide more warnings of enemy blowback.

To the southeast of Tango, Sandy Four began his climb to perform a wifferdill and get the SAM operator's attention. He was safely out of the SAM's range, but the operator took the bait anyway, just as before. The SAM, which had been pointed directly west, now turned to the southwest in anticipation of an air attack, but Sandy Four simply faded back to the sand and raced away.

Directly to Victor's south, Tank entered a shallow climb. At the far edge of the SAM's range he rolled in, leveled his wings, and opened up with a barrage of fire from his GAU-8 cannon. Victor saw a series of sparks and a moment later heard a glorious crackle as the volley of thirty-millimeter rounds pelted the SAM's armor. The missiles swiveled to point at the threat but Tank was already out of range. "It's working guys, keep it up," Victor said cautiously, turning just in time to see Sidearm's A-10 roll in from the north. He turned back to the threat hoping that it would still be pointing to the south but his hope failed; the missile launcher was slowly rotating north. "He's on to you Sandy Two," Victor transmitted. "Get a move on!"

"I've got a good target," Sidearm replied with the intensity of a man that is utterly focused on his task. "I've almost got the lock."

"Wraith's right," Oso interjected, "he's tracking you. I'm rolling in to suppress."

Victor held his breath as he watched Oso bank toward the SAM and accelerate. Visions of the fiasco in France filled his mind and he feared both pilots would be lost. "You're too far away, you'll never make it," he shouted at his former flight lead. There was no response. Instead the A-10 driver entered a climb and drew a line of gun smoke across the sky, lofting a hail of bullets at the SAM. Oso had solved his distance problem by elevating his gun. As the roar of Oso's gun echoed across the sand, Victor prayed that the long range suppression tactic would be enough to save Sidearm, to save them all.

Chapter 61

Drake struggled to keep his failing bird in the air. "How's it coming over there?" he asked Murph.

"I think I'm beginning to win the battle," Murph replied. "We lost a lot of electrical components when we lost those two engines, but I recovered most of them by rerouting the circuits. I've also isolated the bleeding hydraulic systems, so you shouldn't lose any more of the flight controls. We might even make it to a runway. Work your way to a westerly heading and let's make for Kuwait."

"Great," Drake grunted as he struggled to turn the aircraft, coaxing it higher to increase their safety margin. "I'm starting a climb. I don't feel like going for a swim today."

"Me, either; I hear the water out here smells like petroleum anyway." Murph turned and looked at Crash, "Dig out the airfield info for Ali Al Salem. It looks like we're going to pay them a visit."

Crash breathed a sigh of relief, but then his expression stiffened again. "What about the danger of exposing the op?" he asked.

"We'll just have to cross that bridge when we come to it. For now your only other option is a nice swim in the oily waters of the gulf."

"No thanks. Let's stick to dry land."

After several tense minutes Drake could see the coastline approaching. He let himself relax; their chances of making a successful landing improved with every passing moment. Next to him, Murph continued to pursue the myriad of smaller malfunctions caused by the missile, but the heavy stuff was under control.

The bomber still had a functional SATCOM system and Murph sent a message to Lighthouse requesting that the Colonel clear a path for them to land at Ali Al Salem. Without that coordination they might have some friendly fire issues with the American defenses at the base. When he finished, he looked up at Drake. "Would you like me to fly for a bit and give you a break?"

"No, I've got it. You need to look over the landing info for Ali Al Salem anyway." Drake flexed the muscles in his legs, trying to drive out the pain from the constant force he had to put on the rudders. "I am sore, though," he said. "I think my right quad is going to be bigger than my left tomorrow. I'm going to walk lopsided for a month."

"Don't worry. You won't look any funnier than you already do," Murph quipped.

"I take it from the friendly banter that we're feeling confident in our survival," Crash said from the back.

"Relatively," said Drake. "Are you feeling better?"

"A little," answered Crash, handing the papers for the air base to Murph. "For a while there I thought I was going to yak all over the back of your plane here, but I choked it down. That was some nice aerobatic flying you showed us back there."

"Thanks, I'll be working the air show circuit soon. I'll call it Drake's B-2..." A loud bang and a shudder cut Drake off in mid sentence. A hideous grinding noise followed and the Stealth yawed violently to the left. Within milliseconds, the fire bell rang again and the number four engine fire warning light flashed red.

"What did you do?" Murph asked.

"Nothing!" Drake shouted, punching off the fire light to silence the alarm.

Murph brought up the engine display on his screen. "It looks like something must have come loose in number four, probably a left-over chunk of that missile. The engine's down to half thrust. It's burning and I've got no fire bottles left to fight it."

Drake's airspeed began to drop. He had to let the nose fall in order to keep control. "I'm losing altitude," he warned.

"Noted," Murph answered. "I'm going to let the engine continue to burn. Like I said, we've got nothing left to fight the fire anyway. Besides, if we shut it down you'll lose what's left of the thrust, not to mention the last hydraulic pump – and that'll kill your flight controls." He flipped through several displays until he finally dropped his hands and shook his head. "There's nothing else I can do to fix this. We've got a choice to make: We can limp toward the airfield and very likely crash well short of the runway, or we can turn out to sea and sink this top secret monstrosity in the deepest water we can find."

Drake didn't get the chance to respond. Somewhere on the right side of the airplane there was a muffled explosion and the right wing burst into flames.

"That's it. The fire's reached a fuel cell. Take her back out to sea," Murph ordered with surprising calm. "Prepare yourselves for ejection."

The B-2 streaked over the gulf, trailing thick black smoke while the distance between it and the choppy water grew ever smaller. "Okay, we're all ready," said Drake, glancing at the growing flames outside the right window.

"What do I do now?" asked Crash.

"You don't have to do anything," answered Murph. "Just before he hits the water, Drake will call for the ejection. Then I will pull the handles on either side of my seat. The system is set to automatically eject all three seats in sequence. Just sit very still."

In a futile attempt to lighten the mood, Drake added, "Keep your hands and arms inside the vehicle at all times, it's going to be a wild ride."

Chapter 62

The SAM operator was just about to launch his missile at the northern target when he saw another aircraft driving in from the northeast. He hesitated, unsure which target posed the greater threat. Then his cab erupted in a cacophony of metallic impacts and he instinctively covered his head, until a barrage of Arabic curses from the driver told him they'd both survived. He sat up. "Ridiculous American fighter jocks," he spat. That was the third time today they'd pelted his vehicle with bullets and still they could not penetrate his armor. He decided to launch against the closest target and turned back to his radar screen, but it was too late. Both targets were receding. He'd missed his chance again. Then he froze in fear as another blip appeared on his screen. Experience told him that it was too small and fast to be an aircraft.

★   ★   ★   ★

Victor watched in morbid fascination as Sidearm's maverick cut a fiery swath through the hazy sky. The missile accelerated through its entire flight path, having been fired at such close range that the rocket motor never ran out of fuel. Despite the enmity between Victor and the SAM operator, he felt an undeniable sense of dread that came from watching the lives of fellow human beings about to be violently snuffed out. At the very last moment he thought he saw the driver attempt to leap from the vehicle and part of his soul routed for the man, but he knew that it was a futile effort. The missile entered the SAM launcher like a baseball through a paper target. A millisecond later the warhead detonated, throwing burning debris in all directions. When the smoke cleared, the man who'd attempted to escape was nowhere to be seen.

A series of fifty caliber rounds kicked up the sand to Victor's right and he instinctively rolled left; he'd forgotten about the jeeps. He brought his binoculars up and saw that the Iraqis had been undeterred by the attack on the SAM; they continued to press their mission to kill him. He pushed himself back away from the crest of Tango, knowing what would surely follow. The bullets that had nearly cut his right arm off meant that the soldiers had seen him again and they would waste no time in mounting another RPG attack. Bending low, he ran south across the west side of the hill, trying to get well out of the way of the next explosive round. Just as he dove to the sand an RPG fell right on top of his previous position.

"Sandy, this is Wraith. I'm going to need a little help here!" Victor shouted into his radio.

"I'm on my way," said Oso, crossing over the convoy at a hundred feet and ignoring the small arms fire that pelted his aircraft. Out ahead he could see the jeeps, less than two miles from Victor's position and closing steadily. The smoke trail from the last RPG launch was still visible and tracer rounds spat out of the lead jeep's fifty-cal. He banged the canopy with the side of his fist, "They're too far apart!" he said out loud. The lead jeep had enough separation from the other that killing both in a single burst of thirty millimeter was out of the question. He needed help from one of the other Hogs. "Sandy Three, say posit," he transmitted, trying to determine Tank's position.

"Pulling up about a mile to your six, Boss," said Tank. "Are we gonna do something about those guys closing in on your buddy?"

"I guess we'd better," Oso replied. "I'll lead with gun, but I need your maverick on one of those jeeps."

"Consider it done," Tank answered with an almost chipper tone.

"Good. The distance between the enemy and our boy is reaching Danger Close. I'll attack from the north to keep my bullets from threatening Wraith. You come in from the same direction. We'll pull off to the east and make a turn back to the north in case we need another pass. Two and Four, I need you to stay focused on the convoy and suppress any surprise threats like a Man Portable SAM."

"Two."

"Three."

"Four."

"Which jeep is mine?" asked Tank.

"I'll take the leader if you take the trailer. How's that?"

"Sounds like a plan; lead on!"

"You still with us, Wraith?" asked Oso.

"Just barely!" Victor replied breathlessly. He felt like the battered plastic animal in a twisted game of Whack-a-Mole. The Iraqis had figured out that they could lob RPGs over the hill and were now launching random grenades in the hope of wounding their quarry with a lucky shot. So far, all of their rounds had landed long of Victor's position, but they were getting closer; it was clear that they were trying to push him back to the east side of Tango. If they forced him over the crest of the hill, he would be an easy target for the fifty-cals. "Jump in any time, guys!" he shouted as another grenade exploded just down the hill from him.

"Almost there," Oso replied. The lead jeep was forty-five degrees off his nose and inside of a mile. He pulled the A-10 above the haze and then rolled downward toward the vehicle, leveling his wings with his gun pointing twenty yards ahead of its path. He carefully depressed his trigger to the first detent, commanding the stability augmentation system to steady the aircraft so that he could refine the aim. Confident that he'd correctly calculated the lead, he firmly squeezed the trigger all the way to its limit, releasing more than a hundred and fifty rounds in a deadly blend of depleted uranium and high explosive bullets.

The Iraqis were so focused on their objective that they never saw it coming. Sand exploded all around the jeep and sparks flew off the metal as armor piercing rounds passed through it like so many knives through butter. One round found its way into the gas tank, bringing with it all of the heat of a molten uranium slug passing through steel at more than three thousand feet per second, and the jeep immediately burst into flame. The occupants made no attempt to escape. They couldn't; they'd been cut to pieces by the rest of the massive bullets well before there was time to react. "Sandy One, off hot; the lead jeep is toast!" Oso transmitted with satisfaction. He pulled off the target and began his turn to the north, looking back in time to see Tank bring the nose of his jet around to point at the second jeep. There was a long pause. Tank was taking too long to refine his aim. Something was wrong. The jeep was in perfect position and generating plenty of heat; the seeker should lock on to its signature almost immediately.

The men in the second jeep seemed undaunted by the violent death of their comrades. They ignored the carnage before them and shot past in desperate pursuit of the downed American pilot. From the back seat, one of the Iraqis fired wildly with the fifty-cal, while the man beside him positioned another RPG in the launcher and shouldered it for another shot over the ridge.

"Take the shot, Two!" Oso shouted into his radio, but Tank was already pulling away from the target. There was no maverick streaking through the air.

"Sandy Three is off dry! I had a misfire!" Tank shouted with disgust. "I think the missile's launch battery was dead. I was too close to switch weapons."

With fear in his eyes, Oso turned his gaze back toward the Iraqi jeep. They were too close to Victor; there was no time to make another pass. The soldier with the RPG raised it to his shoulder and fired.

★ ★ ★ ★

Victor ran south along the west side of Tango, only a few feet from the ridge top; so close that he had to crouch to avoid exposing his head to the tracer rounds whistling over the crest. The last grenade had been way too close, hitting behind and below him less than fifty feet away. He decided to change his tactic. He turned down the hill, barely maintaining balance and control as he tried to get on the west side of the next impact, but gravity and the unstable terrain finally got the better of him and he tumbled to the sand, coming to a rest on his back. There, looking up at the dusty sky, he saw an RPG, tracing a deadly arc across the brown haze. He sprang to his feet and ran with everything he had in the direction that would give him the greatest distance from the explosive – back up the hill. A moment later the detonation rocked his body, but the explosion wasn't close enough to knock him off his feet. Unfortunately, the second explosion was.

The Iraqi soldier had locked and loaded his weapon in record time, getting another grenade in the air before the first was even halfway through its flight path. The tactic had overcome Victor's attempts at evasion. The concussion of the grenade sent him sprawling head first over the top of Tango, with a piece of shrapnel embedded in his leg to add injury to the insult. Searing pain shot through his right thigh. He hit the sand hard but he quickly raised himself up to his knees, trying to focus through the pain, only to find that he was completely exposed to the Iraqi fifty-cal.

Staring into the face of his Arab opponent, who appeared to be refining his aim, Victor made a vain attempt to stand, but his right leg refused to support his weight and he dropped back down to his knees. The thought of raising his hands in the universal sign for surrender never crossed his mind; instead, he wondered if he could draw them close enough to put up a fight with his nine millimeter, however futile it might be. He cast a quick glance down at his leg. His flight suit was turning deep red with blood. Pragmatically, he determined that the shrapnel had probably nicked an artery, which would explain why he was losing his vision to a red blur. Through the thickening fog in his mind, the thought occurred to him that this death might be a necessary penance for slitting a man's throat only a few hours before.

Then a new sound penetrated the noise of the jeep's engine and the ringing in Victor's ears, taking Victor completely out of his current time. The desert faded away and he was back at the Air Force

Academy, face down in the red dirt of Jack's Valley, straining to pump out one more push up. The distinctive sound that had overcome the jeep's noise was there as well, only this time it was crystal clear, thumping away, the sound of long blades chopping the air into submission. He tried to look up but was stopped by the sole of a boot on the back of his head.

"Don't you dare look up, Basic," the upperclassman said. Then he raised his voice and yelled, "Basics! Tell me what that sound is!"

Cadet Michael Baron and his twenty-five classmates responded in unison, "Sir! That is the sound of freedom!" And so it was.

The Iraqi manning the fifty-cal jerked the barrel of his weapon upward to meet the new threat as Jolly One cleared the top of Tango, but he was too late. The sergeant manning the machine gun on the Pavehawk helicopter peppered the jeep with unrelenting fury. Sparks and blood flew in all directions until the vehicle finally burst into flames and rolled to a halt. The pilot skillfully brought his bird to a hover just above the crest of the ridge and a Pararescueman jumped out, trailing a rescue line as he ran down the sandy hill toward Victor.

With his last effort Victor turned to face his savior, holding on to consciousness with a failing grip and trying to focus through the red haze that filled his vision. He saw the silhouette of a man, suspended in mid air with arms open wide, and then he felt those arms surround him. They felt strong, like he'd been wrapped in iron. When he was finally lifted free of the sand, he struggled to hold on to the man but his arms failed him. "Trust me. I've got you now," said a deep voice that seemed to come from both a great distance and right next to him at the same time.

Victor let go. Logic slipped away and his thoughts would not reach completion. He was tired, sort of sleepy. He would take a little rest, just for a while, and let the strong arms and the deep voice be in charge. Consciousness slipped away into darkness.

PART FOUR

RECOVERY

Chapter 63

It wasn't until the ejection seat cleared the aircraft that Drake saw how close to the water they truly were. When the seat reached its apex, he felt as though he was suspended in time. He watched the dying bomber fly away from him, skimming just above the surface, until it finally hit with a monstrous upheaval of smoke and water. Then the seat was torn from underneath him. He began a terrifying freefall and lost his orientation until his parachute finally opened, giving him just one swing from horizontal to vertical before hitting the water with a horrendous slap. The SEAWARS parachute releases worked perfectly, activated by the saltwater to automatically separate the parachute from his harness; but there was little breeze and the chute settled directly on top of him.

Chaotic darkness enveloped Drake as he sank into the gulf in a tangle of wet cord and silky fabric. The weight of the chute held him just below the surface despite the inflated floatation collar around his neck. There was a moment of sputtering panic. Thoughts of drowning overtook him and he kicked wildly, causing the cords and silk to wrap more tightly, until his desperation finally gave way to his training. Drake let his body go limp. Then, with a single, determined motion, he kicked upward, creating a space between the tent-like cover of the wet canopy and the surface of the water. He took a deep breath and allowed himself to fall under again, taking with him a handful of silk. He felt for the nearest seam and pulled, hand over hand, until the edge came to him. When he finally pulled the fabric over his head and gasped the fresh air, it was as if he'd crossed the boundary between death and life.

Once Drake freed himself from the tangle of the parachute cord, he set about trying to board the one-man life raft attached to him by a long lanyard. Getting into the small black oval was more challenging than he'd expected and it took a few tries before he was able to propel himself over the side, praying that he wouldn't poke a hole in it with all of the metal clasps and plastic pieces dangling from his harness and survival vest. Once he was settled in the raft, he lay there, staring up at the hazy blue sky and breathing heavily.

After a moment's rest, Drake began trying to find the others, lifting his own spirits by slipping into his usual juvenile sense of humor.

"Marco!"

After the violence of the ejection, an eerie quiet had settled over the gulf. There was no sound except for the soft splash of water at the crest of the gently rolling waves.

"Marco!"

At the top of a wave, Drake saw another figure, clambering into another black, one-man life raft. His parachute floated nearby and a white strobe flashed from his shoulder. The figure looked up and recognition and relief flooded his face before he disappeared below the crest of another wave.

"Drake!" a voice shouted from beyond the swirling green. "I thought I heard your voice!"

Drake paddled his raft in the direction that he'd seen Murph and soon caught sight of his friend again, only a few yards away. "You're supposed to say 'Polo,'" he said with an impish grin.

"What on earth are you talking about?"

"You know, Marco Polo."

Murph brought his hand to his chin in mock contemplation. "Fourth...maybe fifth...nope, definitely fourth," he said.

"What are you talking about?"

"Your brain," answered Murph. "A large part of it is definitely trapped in fourth grade."

Just then another raft came into view over the rolling sea. "Marco!" Crash shouted, waving his paddle in the air.

Drake looked at Murph with an "I told you so" smirk and then turned towards Crash, waving his own paddle, "Polo!"

Murph rolled his eyes and shook his head. "We just sank a top secret, two billion dollar jet in the Persian Gulf and you two are playing pool games."

"Hey, just because you're an old..." Drake began, but Crash cut him off.

"Be quiet guys. Did you hear something?"

The three men stopped talking and listened. Crash was right. There was a low, almost imperceptible humming noise amidst the gentle wash of the waves. At first it was difficult to make out but soon it grew louder, and then louder still, until it became the deep buzz of an outboard motor.

A dark gray motorboat sped into view, bouncing across the waves, piloted by a tall, broad shouldered man wearing the tan uniform of a US Navy lieutenant; he was obviously at home at the helm of a watercraft. The pilots began shouting and waving their paddles until the Navy man turned towards them, bringing his boat to idle in the midst of the three rafts. The lieutenant stared in disbelief at the soaked but cheerful survivors for a moment and then cut the motor. "One of y'all go by the name of Murph?" he asked in a Georgian drawl.

Chapter 64

Victor tried to open his eyelids but they fought him, as if they were unwilling to let him wake up. With considerable effort, he forced them to part, but saw only haze and shadows for his efforts. He was lying down, that much was obvious, but he couldn't tell where he was. There was a periodic beep coming from somewhere in the room and he thought he could make out the silhouette of a person standing over him on the left side of the bed. "Who's there?" he tried to ask, but no words came out. He felt heavy, as if his entire body was made of lead. His hands and feet would not respond to his command. The simple act of opening his eyes and processing the scant information they provided had worn him out. After just a few moments, he gave in to exhaustion and let his eyes close again, sinking back into unconscious slumber.

Victor didn't know how long it had been, but when he opened his eyes the second time it required much less effort. The haze was still there and he lifted his right hand to rub the sleep from his eyes, pausing when he realized that his arm and hand had responded to the command. That was progress. After a while, his vision improved and he could see from the dark green fabric roof above his head that he was in a tent. He was lying on a mobile hospital bed, surrounded by light blue curtains hanging from the type of wheeled aluminum supports found in battlefield ER units. The silent figure at his bedside turned out to be an IV tower, which held a bag half filled with fluids that ran down a tube and into his left arm. To his right, there was a small folding table, with a lamp and a bottle of water.

With each passing moment, Victor found that focusing his mind became easier. He was definitely in some sort of battlefield intensive care setup. There were wires running out from under his blanket to a blue box with all sorts of lights and digital readouts, but he had no clue what it all meant – except for the pulse readout. Fifty-five beats per minute. That didn't make much sense given his current state of distress; they must've drugged him.

The thought of being drugged worried Victor. Was he sure he'd been rescued? Had the Iraqis captured him? He shook his head, trying to fight through the haze in his memory. His last moments on Tango slowly came back to him. The gunner onboard Jolly One had taken out the jeep and then the PJ had jumped out and grabbed him. He really had been rescued. "Paranoid much?" he muttered aloud as he relaxed back into the mattress, confident that he was on friendly soil.

Victor's relaxed state only lasted a moment. The memory of the rescue also brought back the memory of his injury. He'd taken a bad hit in the right leg. Worried, he slowly sat up again, propping himself up on his elbows to look at the contours made by his limbs under the hospital sheets. There appeared to be two legs. Cautiously, and with trepidation, he lifted the sheets. Much to his relief both legs looked surprisingly healthy and suddenly he was less concerned with his wounds and more concerned that he was completely naked.

Victor surveyed the damage to his legs. There was a wide bandage wrapped around his upper right thigh, but it looked clean, with no blood soaking through. On his left leg, just above the knee, was a patch dressing – just a square of gauze held down with white medical tape. He reached down and gently pressed against each bandage with two fingers, wincing against the sharp pain from his right leg, but noting with satisfaction that the wound in his left leg felt like little more than a shallow bruise.

Victor noticed a pair of white boxers and gray sweats folded neatly on a chair beside the monitor rack. With great effort, he swung his legs over the side of the bed and then pulled on the boxers and the sweatpants, leaving the sweatshirt lying on the chair. Next he examined his chest and the myriad of wires running from taped sensors to the monitor rack. He looked like a human stereo system. He turned off the monitor to prevent any loud alarms and then set about the painful task of pulling all of the tape and sensors off, thanking God that the men in his family were smooth-chested. He stood, supporting some of his weight with the rolling IV tower and padded out of the enclosure. Beyond the blue fabric he found a green tent flap and pushed it aside, squinting against the bright sunlight that assaulted his eyes.

"Well, look who's up!" a familiar voice exclaimed.

Victor turned to his left, trying to find the source of the voice. When his eyes adjusted to the light, Drake's smiling face came into focus. He was seated at a small folding table, playing cards with Murph and Crash. All three of them stood at the sight of their friend, beaming to see him up and around.

Victor let his gaze expand from the card game to the rest of the world around him. He had not stepped outside, as he'd first supposed when the light blinded him. Instead, he was standing in an aircraft shelter. Sunlight streamed down through a big hole in the roof where jagged concrete and twisted rebar curved downward toward the interior of the structure. The floor below the hole was cracked and broken as well, with pieces of its own rebar jutting out like man made stalagmites.

Victor immediately knew where he was. He was in a HAS, a Hardened Aircraft Shelter designed for two fighters, and the hole in the roof told him that he was on the abandoned side of al-Jaber Airbase. This was one of the hangars that had been taken over by the Iraqis during the invasion that preceded the last Gulf War. An American bomb, dropped to take out the jets that the Iraqis sheltered here, had made the hole in the ceiling and beat up the floor. Victor chuckled at the sight. It had been more than two years since his last tour in Kuwait and nothing had changed.

The space was bright, lit by the high desert sun streaming through the great hole in the roof as well as through the partially open hangar doors. The interior was set up for makeshift living quarters with another small tent next to Victor's, and from the cots that he could see beyond the open flap he surmised that his friends had been living there. In one corner of the hangar, next to the doors, was a refrigerator and a long table covered with bottled water and snacks; there was even a bowl of apples and oranges. The sight of the food sent a surge of hunger through his stomach. He felt like he hadn't eaten in days. "Tell me what's going on," he said, rubbing his temples to push back the fog that kept creeping up on him.

"Looks like you're still a bit toasted on that cocktail the doc cooked up for you," Drake said.

Victor ignored the statement. "I mean what're we doing on the old side of Jaber?"

"The kid picks up quick," Murph observed.

"How'd you know we were at Jaber?" asked Crash.

Victor furrowed his brow. He lifted an IV laden hand and emphatically pointed to the hole in the ceiling.

Murph answered for him, "This is the only Allied base in the theater with aircraft shelters that look like this. More than a decade after Desert Storm, they still can't be repaired because of the ongoing litigation."

"Litigation?" asked Crash.

"Yep. The Kuwaitis contracted the French to build these shelters during the mid-Eighties. The shelters were supposed to withstand the impact of a two thousand pound bomb, which was exactly what we used to penetrate them after the Iraqis took them over. Even though the shelters' failure helped us save Kuwait, the Arabs sued the French because the roofs hadn't performed to standard. While the lawsuit drags on, the Kuwaitis have to leave these in their current state. They built more shelters on the other side of the runway, leaving this side abandoned until the Frenchies pay up." He turned to Victor, "To answer your question, kid, we've been quarantined – for lack of a better term."

For the first time, Victor noticed the other occupant of the room. A young man in battle-dress stood next to the food table, the worn black stripes on his sleeve marked him as a US Army corporal. He was quietly talking on a handset attached to a SATCOM voice unit and there was a sidearm holstered on his hip. "An armed guard?" Victor asked incredulously. "Do they think we're going to try to escape or something?"

"His real job is to keep nosy people out more than to keep us in," Drake answered, "but I wouldn't try to make a break for it; I'm not sure he wouldn't shoot you."

"What day is it?"

"March twenty-third, Iraqi time," said Crash. "It's Sunday; you've been out for almost three days."

"No wonder I'm so hungry."

"I'll bet," Drake laughed. "Walker has us locked in here until he figures out what to do about the *situation*." When he said the last word, Drake held up two fingers of each hand in mock quotation marks.

"What *situation*?" asked Victor, mimicking Drake's gesture.

Drake answered with a question. "What did you see of the B-2 during the battle?"

Victor rubbed his temples, fighting to push back the fog again. He closed his eyes. After a moment, the brown haze parted and he saw Haven climbing away from the sand, their bomb bay door open to strike the Iraqi SAM. He opened his eyes and stared at his three friends. "You came back to help Sandy Flight! You took out the SAM. If you hadn't come back I'd be dead right now."

Drake nodded slowly, "And..."

Victor closed his eyes again. "And...you were hit! The last I saw you were fading off to the south, still burning." He walked over to the table and began shaking each of their hands. "You guys took a missile for me. Thank you."

"Any time," Drake said with a smile. "Well, not any time, but maybe once in a blue moon...Okay, to tell you the truth, once was really enough."

"You can buy us a latte the next time we see a Starbucks," Murph offered.

"I'll make it a Grande."

"Better make it a Venti," said Crash as the three sat down and picked up their cards again.

"But that doesn't tell me what the *situation* is," Victor made the quotation sign again.

"Like you said, we left the battle area in bad shape," Murph answered, shifting cards from one side of his hand to the other, "and from there it just got worse. We put out two engine fires, but it took all of the fire suppressant we had. To compound the loss of hydraulics on the two failed engines, the shrapnel took out the number three hydraulic system as well. Then, as if to drive the nail in the coffin, the number four engine caught fire and we finally had to eject over open water. Somehow Walker got our coordinates and had us brought here. By the time we arrived, you were already laid out in that makeshift ER over there."

A shadow fell across Victor's face. "Uh oh...Walker. Is he here, in Kuwait?"

Murph didn't answer; his eyes were drawn to the entrance. Victor perceived a change in the light of the room. Someone had darkened the doorway.

"It's *Colonel* Walker," the man at the entrance said, "and you've got a lot of explaining to do."

Chapter 65

Richard Walker stood menacingly at the hangar entrance, but before he could say another word Amanda brushed past him and into the shelter, running straight into Drake's open arms. All protocol was forgotten and she kissed him deeply before tucking her head to his chest in a long embrace.

"I thought you'd be killed," she said to Drake with a pout in her voice. "What were you thinking?"

"I was never in any real danger," he lied unconvincingly, "and I was in good hands the whole time," he added, glancing at his two crewmates with a grin.

Victor looked back at Walker with a sense of impending doom, but saw that he still hadn't walked much past the entrance. Instead of commencing his inevitable tirade, he appeared to be clearing two more individuals with the guard; their faces were obscured by the trick of light and shadow around the doors. Victor looked back at Amanda and saw that she'd released her death grip on Drake and was heading his way. Much to his surprise she wrapped him in a big hug. "I'm glad you're okay," she said, and then, surprising him further, she backed up and slapped him hard across the cheek.

"*Ow!* What was that for?" Victor asked, rubbing his cheek.

"That's for putting my Tony in danger!" Amanda glared at him.

"That's Drake, honey," Drake said quietly. "They…they call me Drake."

"Whatever you say, sweetheart," Amanda turned her head and gave him a cute little grin before returning to her glare at Victor. "I know you ignored the order to ditch. You went back in there and the rest of us had to clean up your mess."

"Excuse me ma'am, may I cut in?"

Victor looked up from Amanda's stern face to see Oso's, and he immediately realized the A-10 pilot was one of the men Walker had been clearing with the guard. "Hey Boss, looks like they finally let you off the bench, eh?" Victor attempted a joke, except the "eh" came out more as an "oof" due to the collision of Oso's fist with his abdomen. As his legs gave way and he dropped to one knee, Victor recalled how much he hated Oso's body shots; he never saw them coming. Murph and Crash stood up in unison, knocking over their chairs, and Drake took a menacing step toward Oso, but Victor held up a hand, motioning them back. "Easy guys," he grunted as he regained his feet, "it's alright. That's just how he says hello." He stepped forward and did his best imitation of Mohammed Ali throwing an uppercut before offering a hand to Oso, who shook it firmly. Victor pulled him into an embrace and clapped him on the back. "It's good to see you, man," he said. "I'm glad it was you that came to my rescue. I never had any doubt that you'd get the job done."

Oso returned the embrace in kind. "You were right all along. I had to let go of the control that I never really had. I'm just sorry it took me so long to see it."

"Well Victor," said Walker, finally walking into the hangar, followed closely by Slick, "it looks like your effect on people has two common threads. They all want to hug you, and then they want to punch your lights out. Guess what...I'm not going to hug you."

"I was afraid of that, sir," said Victor, unconsciously taking a step backward. "I'm really sorry that I crashed your plane."

"How about 'I'm sorry that I crashed your plane after ignoring orders to disengage, causing a series of events that endangered the secrecy of the operation, not to mention the lives of numerous comrades, and resulted in the loss of a two billion dollar jet in the middle of the Persian Gulf'?"

"I thought that would take too long to say."

"Shut up, Victor. I still have to find some way to explain this whole mess to the oversight committee. Shoot kid, you took a basic mission failure and turned it into a complete disaster!"

"Mission failure?" Victor was stunned. "Wait a second," he said, realization slowly washing over him. He looked at the questioning faces around the room. "You guys don't know." A big smile spread across his face.

"What's your problem, kid?" Walker asked.

"I think it's the anesthesia again," said Crash.

Victor looked at Walker, his expression turning deadly serious. "I completed the mission, sir."

"You what?" asked Walker, confusion clouding his face. Then the angry expression returned. "No, moron, you didn't. You passed the coordinates to the Nighthawks, but they were too late. We're certain that both targets escaped before the fighters were able to bomb the compound. That's what I'm trying to tell you, the mission was a total bust."

Victor was undaunted, "No sir, that's what *I'm* trying to tell *you*. It wasn't."

"I don't understand."

"After I went down, I hitched a ride on one of the vehicles that left the compound. Incidentally, it was the one that got knocked off the road by one of the Stealth Fighters' bombs. I assume you called them off. Thanks for that."

Walker just folded his arms and furrowed his brow. He was waiting for his explanation.

"Okay," continued Victor, drawing out the word. "Long story short, Hussein got away, but he was the secondary target. I followed the primary to his hideout. I met Irhaab face to face and had a conversation with him before shoving my knife through his neck and into his spine. After that, he dropped the grenade he'd been hiding and blew himself to pieces. The primary target is dead, sir. How's that for completing the mission?"

Walker merely blinked. He ignored the high fives that were taking place at the card table behind Victor and responded in a steady tone, "That will help smooth things with the oversight committee, although

I'll try to put it a bit more delicately than you did. In the future, kid, try to remember that we don't talk about the messy details. You didn't shove a knife into the man's spine; you 'neutralized' him. In any case: good job. At least now I won't have to kill you."

"Any time, sir."

"Don't get too excited," said Walker, holding up a hand. "As I said, it's good that I don't have to kill you, but I'm not happy with you. If you hadn't gone cowboy, we wouldn't be in our current situation."

"I'm still not clear as to what exactly the *situation* is," said Victor.

"Quite simply," Walker explained, "there is a two billion dollar Stealth Bomber in one hundred and fifty feet of water in the middle of the Persian Gulf."

"Can't we just blow it up?"

"Unfortunately, blowing it up in place is not a viable option, it's just too big. The resulting pieces would create a bigger mess to deal with. No, we need help." Walker looked past Victor and addressed the rest of the team. "That's really what I came by to tell you all. General Windsor has authorized me to bring in a small Navy salvage team. They're going to raise the B-2 to towing depth, drag it out to the Indian Ocean, and then scuttle it."

"So...problem solved?" asked Drake.

Walker sighed. "It's going to take about twenty more clearances than I was authorized to give and a mountain of paperwork, but yes, Merigold, problem solved. You can all go home."

Postlogue

While Victor recovered, the team remained in their makeshift home in the abandoned hangar. Oso said his goodbyes and promised to keep in touch as he and Slick returned to their unit; Operation Iraqi Freedom had motored into full swing and they were needed. Walker came and went at random, in between trips out to the middle of the gulf to monitor the salvage effort, which the Navy team conducted under the auspices of a mine clearing operation.

On the fourth day of the salvage operation, Walker's mood took a turn for the worse. He paced about the hangar, muttering under his breath and snapping at anyone who got in his way. Murph asked if something had gone wrong with the B-2 recovery, but the Colonel only growled at him, "It's covered. It's none of your concern," and stormed out of the hangar. That was the last Victor would see of him for some time.

A few days later, the weary members of the Cerberus team were all put on a transport aircraft out of the region – not to the States, but back to the atoll in the Indian Ocean. From there they each made it safely to their homes, where Murph, Crash, and Victor had some careful explaining to do. A few satphone calls from the atoll had helped alleviate their wives' concerns, but up to that point they'd been out of touch for thirteen straight days. Peggy Murphy and Carol Warren were not pleased with their husbands' long absences, but they'd been around the Air Force long enough to know that such things were unavoidable. Victor, however, had the difficult task of explaining two new scars in addition to his long disappearance. Katy, already a skeptic when it came to the trustworthiness of Victor's commanders, was a hard sell.

"I can't get a hold of you for two weeks and all you can offer me is 'Sorry dear, that's combat'?"

"I told you that it would be hard for me to call you after I was

WRAITH 337

pulled out of Alabama..."

Tears started forming in Katy's eyes. "But you didn't tell me you were going to a 'forward base' to plan a war. You told me it was some sort of exercise, and then you didn't call for a day, and then a week, and then another. I was worried sick. Then a few days ago Drag calls to say that you've been in an accident moving some equipment; that you're ok but it'll be a while before you can call. How am I supposed stay calm when the day after the war kicks off, they tell me you're too hurt to talk on the phone?"

Victor tried not to show his relief. She was upset, but at least she was buying it. She would never know how close he'd come to death, how far he traveled beyond the front lines. "I'm so sorry sweetheart. I should have hinted that the 'exercise' could take weeks. In my defense, the operation did take longer than anyone expected," he offered, resorting to a half-truth.

She fell into his arms, still sobbing quietly. "I was afraid that something had happened to you and they weren't telling me. I was afraid you weren't coming home. I kept waiting for the chaplain to knock on our door. Promise me I won't have to go through that again."

He ran his fingers through her hair and smelled her sweet perfume. "I promise, Love, I promise," he said; and even though they both knew it wasn't true, it still made them feel better.

Two weeks after his return, Victor began his B-2 training; his year of T-38 purgatory was over. He and Katy often invited Drake over for dinner, but the two pilots avoided discussions of the mission that founded their friendship. Mostly they talked of squadron gossip and Drake's long distance relationship with Amanda.

Soon Victor moved into the Tiger Weapons Office at Drake's old desk. Murph had moved on to an instructor position at the B-2's new Weapon School and Drake had taken over his command of the shop with Victor as his second. The two of them were still rearranging the desks and furniture to their liking when Drag appeared in their doorway, gently rapping on the frame with his knuckles.

"You boys mind if I come in?" he asked in his raspy, nicotine-laden voice.

"Not at all, sir," Drake replied.

"I have something to discuss with both of you."

Victor and Drake exchanged a wary look, sensing something ominous in the senior officer's tone. "Shoot," said Victor.

"What're your plans for say, the next four weeks or so?"

Victor looked at Drake, who just shrugged. "Our calendars are clear sir," he said.

"Good," Drag said with a smile, "then come with me. I have some papers for you to sign."

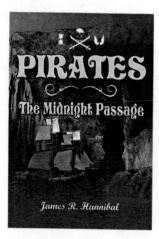

Title: *PIRATES THE MIDNIGHT PASSAGE*
- Author: James R. Hannibal
- Price: $14.95
- Publisher: TotalRecall Publications, Inc.
- Format: PAPER BACK, 6" x 9"
- Number of pages in the finished book: 322
- 13-digit ISBN: 978-1-59095-725-7
- Month and day of publication: June 14, 2010
- Distribution arrangements: Ingram, Amazon.com, Barnes and Noble, etc.
- Publicity contact information:
  Nigel Roberts, 718-473-5205
  Nigel@RobertsPubAgency.com

THE MIDNIGHT PASSAGE debuts the chronicles of Jim Thatcher and the intrepid crew of the sloop Adventure. Pirates, puzzles, and peril await the privateer crew as they seek to recover the vast treasure of Morgan's Lost Gold from the mysterious Aztec underworld of the Midnight Passage.

Betrayal! A treaty is signed, and suddenly the British privateers are named pirates by the very Crown they serve. Some embrace the new title and the bloody life that comes with it; others, like Captain Jim Thatcher, are not so eager to turn against the world they love. Exiled from Port Royal, Thatcher and the crew of the Adventure set out on a new mission. They seek to recover a vast fortune in gold and emeralds that disappeared a half-century before, hoping it will be enough to buy their pardons. But Thatcher soon learns that the Adventure is not the only ship on the hunt for the treasure. An Indiaman pursues them across the Windward Passage; it is the Havoc, captained by Thatcher's long-time nemesis, Edward Teach, the infamous Blackbeard. Fleeing the powerful pirate ship and following a questionable treasure map, the crew takes refuge at the mouth of an underground river system, the ancient Aztec underworld. They are trapped by the Havoc; there is nowhere to go but forward, but there are worse things than pirates in the Caribbean. Deadly puzzles, booby traps, and something even more sinister await the crew in the darkness of the Midnight Passage.

LaVergne, TN USA
03 August 2010
191934LV00002B/34/P